SALT

L.A. FERRO

SALT: by L.A. FERRO Published by Pine Hollow Publishing

Copyright © 2024 by L.A. FERRO

Cover by K.B. Barrett Designs

Proofreading & Editing: Chrisandra's Corrections

Published by Pine Hollow Publishing

Cataloging-in-Publication data is on file with the Library of Congress.

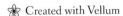 Created with Vellum

Note to Readers

For anyone who understands that hearts find love, not people, for a heart doesn't see an obstacle.
It sees its other half.

Please read responsibly.
A list of potential triggers can be found on my website.
www.authorlaferro.com

.

PROLOGUE

CAMERON

"You can't be in here. Get out!"

"What are you talking about?" I say as I stand crouched over in a tent in nothing but my soaked bikini.

"It's not appropriate for you to be half naked in a tent with me."

The fact that he noticed I'm half naked makes my heart happy. My entire body hums with excitement. Fucking finally he's noticed I'm not a child anymore. I'm twenty-one. I'm an adult. A woman—one who has zero plans of leaving this tent.

"Well, seeing as how this is my tent, I won't be leaving. I came in here to get dressed."

"Fuck..." He groans as he rolls over on my air mattress, throwing his arm over his eyes. What the hell is going on with him? I've never seen him like this. Everett Callahan is the epitome of poise, always self-assured with complete control over his expressions and whatever emotions lurk behind his molten dark eyes. But right now, he's something else.

"So, you're not here to deliver my annual roses?" I quip back.

Every year since my eighth birthday, it's always been roses.

That was the year my father moved our family from the East Coast to the middle of nowhere here in Illinois. My father threw the party together at the last minute, inviting his friends instead of mine since I didn't have any, seeing as how we'd just moved here. Most of the guests brought typical gifts for a young girl, Barbies, Easy Bake Ovens, craft supplies, but not Everett. Everett brought me roses. In his defense, he came alone. His wife Moira didn't accompany him to the party that year, and when my father mocked the gift, he shrugged and said, "I have a son, not a daughter."

Maybe it was his looks. The man turns heads everywhere he goes with his expertly tousled jet-black hair, strong jaw, and broad physique. He's an Adonis, and most would say he's as cold as one too. I couldn't tell you if it was the gift or the man who beguiled me; all I know is that from that day forward, I was smitten.

"The roses are the least of our concern right now. You can't be in here, Cameron. Leave now!" He bites out, his tone laced with something more than just annoyance.

"I told you this is my tent. I need to get dressed. Why are you in here anyway?"

He rolls from side to side. "The letter."

"The letter? What letter, Everett?" I ask as I check the floor next to the air mattress to see if perhaps this mysterious letter fell off the side. He shifts, and then I see it. Sticking out of the back of his suit pants is a white envelope with handwriting I'd know anywhere because it's not just anyone's writing. It's my dad's, and right now, Everett has a piece of him that I don't.

I quickly reach across the bed and snatch it out of his pocket before he can argue that it's not mine, even though my name is clearly scrolled across the front.

"It arrived today, but Cameron, don't read it. Not here, not now. Just get your bag and get out. Change in my car if you must..." His voice trails off before he brings his legs up and practically curls himself into a ball as much as a man his size reasonably can. Everett might be forty-six, but he doesn't look it.

SALT

He runs every morning and hits the gym in the evenings. The man
is in better shape than men half his age, but you wouldn't know it
right now. I stare at the envelope and contemplate my next move.
Whatever is in this envelope contains some of my father's last
words. While I'm curious to know what they say, its contents can't
change the past, words can't bring him back, and right now is
monumental. I'm collecting a moment with someone who is real.
Someone who holds the power to make me happy, someone who
has the potential to be my future if he'd only allow himself to get
out of his own way.

I shimmy around the mattress that takes up the entirety of my
tent and grab my duffle bag for a change of clothes. His eyes aren't
even open anyway, and the way he's currently cradling his head,
even if they were, he wouldn't see me. I don't bother trying to be
quiet about unzipping my bag in search of my summer dress. He
shouldn't be in my tent if he doesn't want to be around me. We
share a house. I don't see what the problem is. It's not like I'm
going to climb onto the mattress with him, even though it's
precisely what I'd like to do.

"Cameron," he warns in that sharp, absolute tone the rest of
the world gets from the man behind the suit. It's one I rarely get. I
wouldn't say he thaws, but for me, he bends.

I can't help the taunt that quickly falls from my lips. "They're
just boobs, Everett. Don't look if it bothers you." I untie my bikini
top, and it easily falls. "We're both adults—"

He hastily tries to sit up, making it to his elbows before he
spits out, "You're a fucking kid, Cameron. You can't be in here
with me. You live under my roof. We do not change in front of
each other, we have separate wings of the house, and we most
definitely don't sleep together. You're my best friend's little girl. I
practically raised you. You are not an adult, not in any way that
matters to me." The last word is barely uttered before he falls back
onto the air mattress breathless, his chest heaving as he struggles
to pull air into his lungs.

"Too late. It's done," I say as I pull my dress into place and slip

3

off my wet bottoms. I bite my tongue to prevent the words I want to say from spilling from my mouth. The ones I gave him were enough of a taunt to throw back. Anything more would only bolster his claims that I'm indeed not a grown woman. The average person heard a reason to leave. I heard a reason to stay. His words might have told me to get lost, but they also said he's noticed me, and more than that, I now know sharing this small space with me makes him nervous, which means I make him nervous. The older I've gotten, the more aware I've become of his imposing silences. He's always careful with his words, more comfortable saying nothing at all than words he'd regret. But what most haven't learned, I've mastered. His silence oftentimes speaks louder than his words. Plus, I'm not leaving this tent when something is clearly wrong with him. With my dry clothes on, I sit beside him and reach for his wrist. "Everett, what's going on? Are you okay?"

He snaps his arm back. "Don't touch me, Cameron. I'm fine. I'll be better once you leave."

I roll my lips and shove down the disappointment that comes from how easily he's able to dismiss me. Admittedly, I want someone I shouldn't want, someone most would say I can't have, but I've never been one to follow the rules. Nothing fun happens when you color inside the lines. So, what if he's twice my age and was my dad's best friend? Depending on who you are, that can be interpreted as one of two things: forbidden or a challenge. I'm a girl who sees the latter as true.

"Fine. Since you won't let me help you, I'll just go get someone else." I move to get off the mattress, confident that the last thing the stony-faced Everett Callahan wants is anyone to see him in this state.

It's not until my fingers graze the zipper that I question his overall disdain for the situation. I would have bet my entire trust fund that Everett would rather have me stay in this tent than allow another person to see him like this.

He mutters a few words I can't make out before saying,

"Wait, I'm sorry. Don't leave me." My heart instantly skips a beat. Those were the last words I was expecting him to say. I was ready for another round of barbed commentary as I fought to stand my ground and not leave this tent. After all, it's my birthday, and not only did the gods grant me my birthday wish and Everett Callahan actually attended my party, but they threw him in my tent, on my fucking mattress. But his words are ones I know didn't come easily, or maybe they did. Maybe in whatever fucked-up hell he's currently living, he's unable to keep his mask in place. "I just need to lay here for a minute, and then I'll leave. I'll leave as soon as the world stops spinning, and I can feel my legs."

Holy shit. Not only did Everett Callahan show up to my twenty-first birthday at Salt Lake, but he must've eaten one of the pot brownies. What the hell? I sit back down on the air mattress, and the movement immediately makes him brace like he's falling. "Cameron..." he groans my name again.

"Did you eat one of those brownies on the picnic table?" He moans a little louder, and I have my answer. I invited some guys from the baseball fields where I work during the summer, and they invited people who also invited people, and this small gathering blew up way more than I planned. There were only supposed to be ten of us, and the next thing I knew, there were almost a hundred people here. No one in my immediate circle smokes, but I'm not a stranger to weed in all of its forms. I'm in college. I've tried a lot of things, but edibles? Edibles are something I steer clear of. You can't regulate the high, and they're usually slow release, which means Everett isn't going anywhere anytime soon, and I can't say I'm mad about that. "I'm going to take your non-response as a yes."

"Please don't sit on the bed. This is already bad enough," he says, clutching my pillow before covering his head.

"I'm sure you missed it since you decided to enter a stranger's tent to begin with, but there isn't exactly any place else for me to sit, and I'm not leaving. What would happen if you threw up and choked on it because you're too fucked up to help yourself? You can't even sit up."

"I'm not going to throw up, Cameron. Just stop talking and stay on your side and don't touch me." I lie down beside him, careful not to touch him. I'm perfectly fine with taking things slow. Tonight has already answered every birthday wish I have had since I turned seventeen. I feel like I've waited a lifetime for this. Everett and I are in the same bed and that's something I've fantasized about since I started having sexual thoughts. He shifts beside me, pulling me from my reflections, and I hear him mutter into the pillow, "Just stop spinning... Please stop spinning."

His world is spinning out of control while mine is falling into place. Best birthday ever.

I don't know how long we lay there. Time felt like it had ceased to exist. Everett's state of inebriation was not ideal, but his proximity was everything. With each groan and subtle shift throughout the night, his body inched closer to mine throughout the night, and I got my fill. As his inky dark eyes, which I've sworn countless times were plucked straight from the night sky, flicked between open and closed, I studied the rigid lines of his immaculate beard and counted every freckle. There aren't many. Only two. One is tiny and rests right below his left eye. When his lids are closed the thickness of his long lashes hide it away from the world. The other is small, but if one were ever to wish herself a freckle, it would be the one that sits to the left of his impeccable cupid's bow, one I've dreamt of pressing my lips to countless times. When his body finally went still, and his labored breathing stabilized. Slowly, I removed the pillow he had pulled over his face to drown out the noise outside the tent and shield himself from me. His slip was an anomaly. Everett Callahan is refined, never caught with a hair out of place. The Callahan name is respected and revered because he made it so. But sometimes, it's our imperfections that make us perfect.

Somewhere in the middle of the night, his face faded out, and my dreams moved in. The reality of him was replaced with a fantasy, one that felt too real. It was the best dream I'd ever had because, in my dream state, his warmth enveloped me. We weren't two strangers in the night. We were lovers. He pulled me against his front. His big, warm hand rested on my stomach, and his nose nuzzled into my neck. I was his. A treasure he didn't want to let go of, or at least I thought I was, until the firm hand that caressed my skin bit into my hip and the warmth that had engulfed me was replaced with cold. It could have been the cruel end to a dream I wished would last forever, the kind we never want to end but always do that woke me, or maybe it wasn't a dream at all. As I sit in my empty tent, I'm programmed to believe that the former is true until I hear a car starting up in the distance. It wasn't a dream.

Left with the deafening silence of his absence, I should feel dejected, but I don't. Instead, I pull his pillow to my front and lie back down with a smile. Everett Callahan touched me. He touched me once, and I will see to it that he does it again. Last night, I saw something else as I stared at his chiseled face, watching him sleep. I saw a man and not the untouchable God I've made him out to be. Men are flawed, even Everett Callahan, and now that I know he's not immune to weakness, I plan to be the hellion ready to exploit it.

But first, I have a letter I need to read.

CHAPTER 1
EVERETT

ALMOST ONE YEAR LATER

"Y ou have got to be fucking kidding me right now," I say as I pull into my driveway.

When my flight landed at nine a.m., I hadn't intended to be gone all day. I assumed my meeting with Connor would be just that, a meeting to go over what he needed me to step in and handle while he was out of town. What I thought would be quick turned into a three-hour practice and another two hours discussing how things ran around the stadium daily. I did all this in my damn suit pants and long-sleeve polo, not realizing that's what my son had in store for the day. A suit is like a second skin to me, but not in ninety percent humidity, and even though I knew coming home wouldn't be quite the load off I was looking for, considering I knew my house wouldn't exactly be empty, I didn't think there'd be a rager going on either.

"Damn it," I curse as I slam the door to my car. There are security cameras all around my property. There haven't been any parties here since I left town, and she decides to throw one the day I return. I hoped she would have grown tired of these games now that she has Parker Michaelson on her arm, but I should have

9

known better, or at least I should have suspected it after the way she left the stadium today without so much as a shared glance. It's unlike Cameron not to make her presence known when I'm around. She's been doing it since she turned seventeen, or maybe that's just when I started noticing. Her world was turned upside down that year, so I gave her grace and dismissed her antics as a plea for attention from a young girl who was hurting, but that was five years ago, and now I'm afraid my dismissals have morphed into a silent acceptance. However, Cameron is not the young girl she once was. She's all woman, and over the past year, she's gone out of her way to ensure I've noticed.

Stepping through the front door, there are six sets of eyes on me, none of which I know, but it doesn't change my response. "Get the fuck out of my house before I call your parents!"

This is a small town, and the threat holds more weight than calling the cops. As I walk down the hall toward my kitchen, I hear music outside, but it will have to wait because the sight before me stops me in my tracks. Standing before me, wearing nothing but a thong swimsuit, is Cameron Salt. She's reaching for a glass on the top shelf with her back to me. I should clear my throat and announce my presence. I shouldn't be looking at long, lean legs or admiring the weight of her perfectly sculpted cheeks, and I definitely shouldn't be thinking about how good my best friend's daughter's ass felt pressed into my groin the night of her twenty-first birthday. I wasn't prepared for her living under my roof as a teenager, but back then, I had a wife. Now I don't, and she's no longer underage.

So, I say the only thing that makes sense. It's the only thing that can remedy this impossible situation. "I think it's time you move out."

"Excuse me," she says as she turns around, my words not registering until she sees who's delivering them. Her hands grip the glass she's holding tighter than I'd like as she processes what I've said. The last thing I need right now is for her to slice her hands open. "You want me to move out?" She questions slowly as the light in her bright blue eyes starts to dim into shades of gray as they always do when she's upset. Fuck. Anger I was prepared for. Sadness I was not. This is the second curveball she's sent me since I arrived home today.

Not once has she acted like the girl I left behind, and I'm starting to think it's because she wasn't a girl at all. That's the box I created for her. It's the one that made me feel comfortable with our arrangement because the alternative makes me a wolf in sheep's clothing. I loathe the way this woman has crawled under my skin. That's why I stand firm in my choice.

"You can't stay here forever, Cameron. The deal was—"

"The deal was I could stay here until I finished school. I still have half a year, Everett." Her voice subtly cracks as she says my name, and while the despair in her tone might be minor, the punch it lands on my chest is anything but. I'm half tempted to take it all back. She started college a semester late as she worked through the grief of losing her parents. Damon entrusted her care to me, but to what extent? A loud crash outside pulls my attention toward the back window.

"This is why you need to go, Cameron. You intentionally push my buttons, and I don't understand why. I'm done with your antics."

That's not the whole truth, but it's enough. Some truths are never meant to see the light. It doesn't matter that I no longer see a girl, at least not in the way I should. I used to see my best friend's daughter, the one I've given roses to on her birthday ever since she was eight, but I haven't seen that girl since the night of her seventeenth birthday when she ran away with pieces of my sanity and maybe something more.

As I approach the back door, she says, "You're kicking me out because of the party?"

"It's one of the reasons, yes. I don't have time for these childish games. I'm an adult with grown-up responsibilities, which is something you clearly don't have a clue about. You have plenty of money to get your own place. If you want to throw parties like this, you can do it at your house, not mine. I'm done."

"Done?" she questions, her cheeks now rosy as the lids of her eyes redden.

Shit. The last thing I need right now are her tears. Seeing them once almost killed me, and I never want to be the reason for them. I drop my head, unable to bear witness to even one, should it fall, and say, "We'll discuss it in the morning, Cameron. Right now, I need to take care of your mess."

Without another word, I pull open the back door only to realize that as smart as I am, I'm still a damned fool, but better a fool than a demon. None of this was Cameron at all.

CHAPTER 2
CAMERON

"Cam, what are you doing here so early today?"

"Everett's back," I say as I stand in the doorway as Mackenzie unpacks boxes in the announcer's booth at the Bulldog's new stadium. I knew she'd be in early trying to get things done before she left for Florida for the summer, and I needed to get out of the house. "Did you know he was coming home?"

Her slight pause in movements as she unpacks the box gives her away. "Not really. I mean, yes..." she draws off before returning to the shelving unit she was arranging trophies on. "Connor didn't call him until yesterday. I think he's been trying to convince himself that he could manage things back here while planning the new stadium in Jupiter. He finally came to his senses and called his father, realizing he couldn't be in two places at once—"

"What does Everett have to do with Connor not being able to be in two places at once?" I cut her off as movement down on the field catches my eye.

You've got to be kidding me. I came here to escape him, and here he is. My eyes lock onto his muscular back as he talks with Connor beside the field. Even in a suit and from this distance, his broad shoulders are imposing. I should stop staring. I shouldn't let my eyes drift down to his narrow waist or his toned ass, but I do because I'm a glutton for punishment, and I hate that he looks even better now than when he left. I hate believing that life seemingly went on unchanged for him since he took off without a word.

"I was getting to that. Everett is going to take over for Connor this summer."

That pulls my eyes away from him. "He's what?" I ask as my eyes practically bug out of my head. I mentally remind myself to check my jaw and pick it up off the floor. "How the hell will Everett swing coaching and the law firm?"

"I honestly don't know. This all transpired over the past twenty-four hours. Nothing was planned, which is why I didn't give you a heads-up that he was coming back. Connor literally called him yesterday afternoon, and even then, he knew his ask was steep. Everyone knows Everett eats, sleeps, and breathes Callahan & Associates." She pauses and tosses the now empty box into the corner with all the others that still need to be collapsed. "I'm not sure Connor was convinced he'd come. You know their relationship has been strained." Joining me at the window, she adds, "Seriously, I planned on telling you all this today. I just didn't realize Everett would book the first flight home and show up before I got the chance."

"Yeah, maybe if I'd had a heads-up, I could have made myself scarce last night and he wouldn't have walked in the door and asked me to move out."

"He what?" Her head snaps to mine. "Oh, Cam..." She throws her arms around me. "I'm so sorry. You can crash at our house if you need a place to stay. We'll be in Florida for the summer anyway."

I hold her tight and try to push down the hurt I feel from the mere thought of leaving his house. *My house.* "I might take you up on that offer until I can find my own place. I don't want to take the first thing I come across because I feel rushed."

She releases me, concern etched across her forehead. "I can't believe this. Did Everett say you needed to get out right away?"

"No, he said we'd discuss it in the morning."

Mackenzie cocks her brow and puts her hand on her hip. She knows me too well. That's the thing about best friends. If they're real, you can't hide shit from them.

"Ah, now I see why you're here so early. Cameron, you know postponing the inevitable will only make it hurt longer, right?"

I turn away from her and find a chair to flop into. I know she's right. I'm hurt, but that's only part of it. I haven't seen Everett since hers and Connor's wedding. He left in the middle of the night, and I haven't heard from him since. That was months ago. He didn't owe me a goodbye, but I live in his house. You'd think he'd give me something, a note, an email, a text. The list of acceptable communications is endless, but I still received nothing, and now he's asking me to leave.

"I'm not avoiding him per se. I haven't seen him in months. He knows my birthday is coming up, which also means the anniversary of my parent's accident is approaching, and then he sprung this on me. Does it hurt? Yes, but I'm also mad. I needed some time to collect my thoughts. We both know I'm good at making questionable choices and worrying about the consequences later. I didn't want to fuck this up. It's important to me."

She leans against the front of the desk and crosses her arms. "How did it come up? Did he say he wanted you out right away? Did he sound mad? I need more details."

Mackenzie is the only other person I would ever give details to. We got close working at the concession stand at Hayes Fields together last summer. She had secrets, and so did I. It was during that time I divulged my crush on Everett Callahan. Having a crush on a guy isn't a crime, but when there's a twenty-plus-year age gap and the man is your dead father's best friend and business partner, not to mention the same one you went to live with after your parents died in a tragic car accident, it gets a little complicated. At least for some. Not me. In my eyes, love is love. I have fawned over that man for as long as I can remember. He's been my first and only crush since I knew what the word meant, and now he's all I have, and he wants me gone. When it comes to Everett, I know I don't have a clear head. It's hard to step back, so hearing Mackenzie's thoughts will help me better understand my own.

"I was in my swimsuit searching for a glass, completely unaware he was home, and literally the first words out of his mouth were, 'I think it's time for you to move out.' I haven't seen him since your wedding, and those are his first words to me." I can't help the indignation in my tone at the end.

"Was it the white thong bikini?" she questions as though that makes a difference.

"Yes, but I'm not the only one who wears those. Everyone wears those these days. Watch when your Midwest ass goes to the beach in Florida. You're suddenly going to feel like you're wearing one of grandma's moo-moos with how covered you'll be compared to most. Evan's dumbass threw a freedom party to celebrate his divorce. Of course, I put on my swimsuit. I planned on sitting poolside and having a front-row seat to the shitshow."

"Back up," she starts to pace the space in front of the desk, "So Everett walked in, saw you in the kitchen, and immediately told you he thinks you need to move out. You realize he probably thought you were the one throwing the party, not Evan, right?"

I lay my head back and stare at the ceiling. "Yes, he insinuated as much before he stormed out of the kitchen to shut it down."

"And you didn't stand up for yourself? That's not the Cameron I know. Why didn't you tell him it wasn't your party?"

I spin in the desk chair and close my eyes. *Why didn't I defend myself?* There are a few reasons, but the first and most glaring was the suffocation I felt being in such close proximity to him. The man makes me weak in the knees, and it's only grown disgustingly truer the older I get. Even disheveled from a long day at the stadium, he was ridiculously attractive, maybe even more so because the lock of hair that fell onto his forehead as he spoke to me wasn't something the world gets to see. Nor do they get a sneak peek of his chest hair because he was so hot in the humidity he couldn't help but unclasp the top two buttons in search of relief. The world gets to see the mask. I get to see the soul behind it, and what a beautiful soul it is. Until he opened his damned mouth. Being head over heels for someone who doesn't reciprocate the feelings sucks. But I can't let it go. I've tried. Even if he never loves me back, I'd still love him because he deserves it, because he's worth it.

"What would you have done if the person you want more than anything in the world asked you to leave?"

"Easy. I'd fight for him. I don't think Everett wants you gone. I think he's jealous and doesn't know what to do with the way you make him feel. Think about it." I sit up in my chair and give her my full attention. "The day of my wedding, you showed up on Parker's arm. You'd already been hanging out together, but that day, you let Parker put his arm around you and kiss your neck. To anyone else in attendance, you looked like an official couple. Everett couldn't take his eyes off you that day, and the next day, he was gone. Before then, you had said you felt things between the two of you were changing. Like he was finally seeing you the way you wanted him to. Didn't you say he caged you in at the sink while you rinsed vegetables one night the week before the wedding?"

"Yes, the kitchen is one of the only other rooms he ever frequents besides his office," I say quietly as her comment has one of my favorite memories flooding vividly into my mind.

Cooking is not my specialty, but I had just gotten home when I overheard Everett flippantly mentioning to one of his associates that he hadn't had a home-cooked meal in ages as I walked past the cracked door of his home office. With a bit of extra pep in my step, I hurried to the kitchen, determined to make him a meal. There weren't many ingredients in the fridge, but he had peppers and meat, the main ingredients for stuffed bell peppers. So, I pulled up a recipe and got to work.

I was browning the meat on the stove when he walked up behind me and placed a hand on either side of me as I sliced and cleaned the peppers. "What are you doing?" Every hair on my body was acutely aware of his proximity. It felt as though literal electricity was zinging between our bodies. I wouldn't have even needed to take a step to be firmly plastered against his front. I could have simply leaned back, but I didn't.

"Making dinner," was all I managed to answer. I was too nervous to say more. I didn't want to break him free from whatever haze had fallen over him and brought him into my space.

His hand lightly trailed up my arm, and he said, "Smells good." I could feel his body pull toward mine like a magnet. His heat enveloped me, and my skin pebbled with awareness. As I cleaned the seeds out of the pepper, I swear I felt his free hand gently brush against my hair as my entire body was innately cued into his every move, but something stilled his hand. The next thing I knew, he squeezed my shoulder and said, "Please don't cut yourself." And then he walked away.

"And I know for certain he was always watching you. I noticed it from the first time I met you. You tried to force his hand with your Parker scheme, and it backfired. I get the idea. You were trying to make him own his feelings. The cooking incident was just one of many tender moments the two of you started sharing last summer, but then you pushed him. Maybe if you hadn't started a fake relationship with Parker, things would have kept progressing between you and him."

I stand from the chair, unable to sit, my anxiousness winning out over the levelheadedness I was trying to maintain. "So how does that pertain to the now? I can't go back and undo what has already been done."

"I'm saying he's jealous. I think he said those words last night because he can't stand watching you with other guys. But believe it or not, jealousy is a good thing. Or, at the very least, it's an indicator of more. If he's jealous, he's thinking of you, and he's afraid because he knows he has something to lose."

"Knock, knock," Connor says, catching us off guard. I instantly hold my breath as I wait for Everett to round the corner behind him. "I think we're missing some boxes, and we need some clarification on where to take a few. While the guys could, and they don't mind the workout, I'd rather not have them lift heavy boxes more times than necessary."

Connor looks like his father, though his hair is lighter and his build is leaner. Until Mackenzie showed up last summer, the pair were the two most eligible bachelors in town. I'm not immune to Connor's good looks. It's just the charm that was always lacking for me. I felt like the unwanted sister for the longest time, and we're not even related. I was like a gnat he couldn't swat away. Don't get me wrong, he was never mean, but any inclusion always felt like an obligation and nothing more. Now that I'm best friends with his wife, our relationship has changed. What always felt like toleration has started to feel like friendship.

"Where's Everett?" Mac glances back at me, sensing I'm on pins and needles.

"I left him with Coach Teague while I came up here to get my marching orders."

"Are you still down to help me today? I'd like to finish the offices and announcer booth before we leave at the end of the week," she asks me as I sigh an anxious breath of relief.

"Let's do it. Who says I can't lift boxes while wearing heels?"

I'm down to help but I don't care to cross paths with Everett, and if I know Connor, he'll hole me up somewhere rather than make me run around the stadium in heels.

Connor's eyes drop to my feet. "You are not lifting shit wearing those. The last thing I need to deal with today is you twisting an ankle or falling. You can help unpack boxes, and at noon ..." he checks his watch before adding, "The staff uniforms are arriving."

"Really?" I clasp my hands together. "I thought they weren't due in for another week."

He shrugs. "I guess they got them done ahead of time. Can't complain about efficiency."

Another perk to being Mac's best friend is that she helped sell my pitch to Connor about letting me design the new team uniforms. Mackenzie designs spaces, and I design clothes. We were always meant to be best friends. I was desperate to get some kind of actual design gig on my resumè before graduating, and this was the perfect opportunity. It's hard to find design internships, especially ones that actually put you in any type of position to showcase your ability. I explained all that to him, but it was the part where I said I would do it for free that sold him. Connor is already bleeding money in enough areas that the cost savings of not having to hire a designer was a no-brainer. To my surprise, he actually liked all of my first-round drafts. I was fully prepared to go back to the drawing board multiple times, but my designs impressed him so much that he asked me to assist with designing the staff uniforms and logo wear for the team shop here at the stadium.

Mackenzie wraps her arms around Connor's waist and pushes up on her tippy toes for a kiss. "I didn't get my morning kiss yet."

He grabs her jean-clad ass hard, making me jealous, not of him but of the affection. Connor looks at Mac like she's his purpose, his reason for existing, and I want that.

"That's because you left before dawn to come down here. I never should have given you a key." He kisses her sweetly before smacking her ass and pulling away. "That's all you get."

"Hey..." she drones, clearly not ready for their moment to end.

But he doesn't relent. Turning on his heel, he slaps the doorframe before saying, "An eye for an eye, baby. You thought to deprive me of my morning meal. Now you get to go hungry."

"Let's go, Salt. I said you could unpack boxes, not stand there and look pretty."

I start toward the door to follow after him but not before teasing Mac, "Morning meal?"

"You have no idea, though I'm not sure why he called it his

morning meal. It's more like every meal," she says as we walk down the hall.

"Lucky bitch."

"Yeah, well, maybe we can compare notes when I return in August. What's that saying? Like father like son? Maybe the fetish is hereditary."

I don't say anything out of fear of delusion, but it's in that same vein of fear that I find my fortitude. I can't reach for what I really want if I don't lose my fear, and I want Everett, but I'll deal with that in a few hours... after I've found my words and apparently my backbone.

CHAPTER 3
EVERETT

"I don't know if I said it yesterday, but the place looks good, Con," I say, stepping into his office adjacent to the announcer's box. Crossing the office, I stand at the window overlooking the field. "I can't believe you're walking away for the summer."

"You know I'm not walking away. Mackenzie landed the biggest job of her career, and it happened to be an hour outside of Jupiter. She'll be down there till August." Connor married his wife, Mackenzie, earlier this year. To say he's obsessed would be an understatement, but I am surprised he's not making accommodations for travel. I'm sure Mackenzie offered to come home on weekends, and the flight from Illinois to Florida is short. It's not an ideal weekly commute, but it could be done. What he's built here is his passion. "Are you having second thoughts about helping me? I understand if you've changed your mind after that crash course I gave you yesterday. It's a lot—"

"No, Connor," I turn away from the window. "I haven't had a change of heart. I know how important this is to you. Plus, it's not like I can't work from here." I gesture toward his desk.

He takes a sharp breath and raises his eyebrows. "You realize you won't be able to work in here all day, right? The team practices three hours per day, four days a week."

"You share this office with your assistant coaches. Is that what you're getting at?"

"No, Dad." He pinches the bridge of his nose. "Yes, I do share this office with the assistant managers somewhat. My office is always open, and they use this space as needed to work, but Dad..." He rocks back on his heels and nods toward the field. "You realize part of filling in for me means you're the head coach for the season, right?"

Shit. When I agreed to help Connor for the summer, I gave him my answer before I even had a chance to think through what it fully entailed. Our relationship has been strained since his mother and I divorced. We've been making progress over the past year, but it has yet to return to what it once was. Hell, maybe it never will, but a father can hope. That's why I didn't hesitate. I never make snap decisions, but he's my son. There was no chance I was going to say no. However, had I thought this through, I may have made some concessions. For starters, hiring a head coach for the summer.

"Connor, you realize I haven't played baseball since high school. I'm a lawyer. I'm not a damn coach. You're going to Jupiter to secure backing for a Florida location and expand your organization. You don't want your home team, which sent three players to the major leagues last year, to be run into the ground in its debut season at the new stadium. You realize how big this is, right?"

"Dad, I've thought about all of this. I considered hiring someone for the summer, but I don't trust anyone else with this. You're my blood, and you have a vested interest in seeing that this doesn't fail..." His hand squeezes the back of his neck. "And at the end of the day, you're also the man who taught me everything I know, and I don't mean business. My love for baseball, the passion came from endless summers of playing catch with you, going to games and watching baseball on the floor of your office while you worked. You're not as out of touch as you think, you're definitely not out of shape, and you have my assistant coaches..." He runs his hand through his hair, and I see his stress. I know this isn't easy for him. If it hadn't been for Mackenzie landing that job in Florida, he probably would have waited another year or so before trying to expand. Even then, there's no way he would spend any time away from his new wife, and since Jupiter was always part of his long-term goals, he made it happen sooner rather than later. I can't fault him for his dedication and tenacity. He's pouring himself into this the same way I poured myself into starting Callahan & Associates. The anxiety written all over his features, coupled with the plea in his tone, tells me there will be no hiring of another coach, but to ensure I do things his way and not mine, he adds, "You want the old us back. I need this." His words are now a challenge as much as they are a plea.

My eyes hold his, and my answer is quick and sure. "Done."

His eyes narrow slightly on mine as though he's waiting for me to add some stipulation. I'm a lawyer through and through. There's always an argument to be had and terms to negotiate, but now I'm quiet, which I know makes him uneasy, especially when that's the last thing I've been lately. I've forced his hand enough over the past year. It's only fair he forces mine.

When I give him no words, he says, "Let's officially meet the team. I wanted to give you the lay of the land yesterday, run you through a day in my shoes, before I officially introduced you." He pauses, holding the door for me before grabbing my shoulder. "Had to make sure you were still all in."

The second we start down the steps toward the field, I spot her. Cameron Salt. She's a damn beacon with her copper-red hair shimmering in the sun. Running into her was inevitable seeing as how she lives under my roof, but I didn't expect to see her here. I told her last night we'd talk, but she was up and out of the house before I came downstairs. Kicking her out of the house is the last thing I want to do, so when she skipped out on our morning conversation to discuss the matter, I started devising a carefully constructed schedule that ensured our paths didn't cross, and now that's already gone to shit. I mentally begin ticking off the seconds it takes for her to turn around and notice I'm here. She always notices. It's as though she has a sixth sense for detecting when I'm near. However, before I can count more than two seconds, a familiar voice on the field calls out, "Mine," garnering my attention as he catches a pop fly.

You've got to be kidding me. "Parker Michaelson is on the team?"

"He technically made the team last year. The only reason he got benched and worked the concession stands instead was because he was appeasing his dickhead college coach. As much as I hate to admit it, Parker is good. It's why his coach didn't want him playing for me. His coach wanted the credit if he got scouted."

"What changed? I know he didn't drop out." His father, Kipp, wouldn't allow it, and neither would my ex-wife, who is now his stepmother.

"His coach took another job. I'm confident he'll get picked up by a feeder team this summer."

Great. I already wasn't thrilled to be coaching this summer, but Parker Michaelson being on the team adds a layer of complication I don't need, and I don't mean my ex-wife. Moira would be the lesser evil in this equation. When I left town the day after Connor's wedding, Parker and Cameron had become an item, and seeing as how she's here, it would appear that is still true. The last thing I need is another reason for our paths to cross. My first decree as head coach will be no girlfriends at the stadium during practice. Family and friends can come during games. Practices will be closed to the public. Period.

"Coach, I didn't know it was bring your parents to work week," Parker goads as he elbows one of the players next to him, who I can already tell I'm going to like because, unlike Parker, he doesn't find the comment entertaining.

I stay quiet as I slowly rake my eyes over every player, carefully assessing their form and aptitude. Baseball isn't just about hitting and fielding. You have to be able to read the game, and part of that is reading people. Parker demonstrated these abilities at one point. It's why I trusted him and his older brother, Elijah, with family secrets, even though they are not my blood. However, it's clear that the maturity I thought he possessed was selective. He disagrees with how I handle my business, but what he hasn't put together is that I don't care. I don't seek anyone's approval when I make decisions. I make them because they are right. If he wants to keep being obstinate, it will only make his season harder. His immaturity is already proving to be his weakness. He can't see past his personal feelings enough to put together that there must be a valid reason I'm here today when I haven't been home in months.

"Bulldogs, listen up. I have an announcement. We are expanding, as some of you may have heard through the rumor mill. It was always part of the plan. Having a facility in Jupiter puts us next to the big boys during spring training every year. It makes it convenient for coaches and scouts to visit our stadium and discover our talent. While I wish the timing could be better—"

"So, then it's true. You're leaving for the season," number seventeen interjects as a few players harrumph and mutter a few curses under their breath.

"As I was trying to say, the timing isn't perfect, but the deal is now, and I can't walk away, especially when it means more visibility for players in the long run. Coach Teague and Coach Denver will still be here, but my father, Everett, will be filling in as the interim head coach until I return."

The wind subtly kicks up, but the humidity today is thick, so the scents in the air stick, and one, in particular, makes my stomach knot. It's roses. Always roses. I've put more thought into her scent than I should, but her choice of fragrance steals my thoughts. I've pondered countless times why she chose it. Was it because she loved it, or did her reasoning run deeper than the scent? Roses are red, like her hair, and there's no denying she has a fiery personality to match, but there's also duality in her choice.

One I've tried to push aside because the idea that it has anything to do with the hand that gave her the rose is no place for my mind to dwell. Whatever the case may be, it worked. I can't smell a rose, let alone look at one without thinking of her, and it's that damn scent that has my eyes trailing toward the spot I saw her standing moments ago. I throw up my walls, fully expecting my eyes to collide with her crystal blue orbs, but they don't. I should be relieved to be greeted with her retreating form as she exits the stadium. It's better that she's not here, and I just said my new goal was to avoid her, but I'm a smart man. I should have known setting a goal without a plan in place to accomplish it doesn't make it a goal at all. It's merely a wish. I was so distracted by her presence that whatever words Connor continued to give the team were lost on me. It's not until he turns to me and says, "Coach, would you like to say something?"

My eyes immediately connect with Parker when I redirect my focus back to the field, expecting the news of the announcement to wipe the smugness off his face, but instead, I find a scowl. There's more than anger lurking behind his deep-set wrinkles of displeasure. It's more than worry. He knows I wouldn't come after his career. Would I work him hard? Hell yes, but this is different. It looks like worry and smells like fear, which tells me I haven't been gone long enough. I gave him time, and now it's up, but I don't have time to worry about his love life with Cameron. I have a commitment to my son to uphold and an organization to help run.

"Most of your faces look familiar, but my name is Everett Callahan, for those who don't know me. I won't bore you with some long speech I know you don't care to hear. I'm also not going to stand here and ramble off statistics or accomplishments to try and convince you that I am the best fit for this position. Those points would be moot. Instead, I will say this: my job is to support you and our staff so that the organization as a whole can be its best. Today is only the first of many unforeseen and insuperable decisions that will impact you should you continue down this path. Professional athletes are not immune to trades or

27

organizational changes. It's part of the game. I suggest learning to channel those feelings into your game. Stay hungry. I want hungry players on this team. It's that desire that motivates us and pushes us outside of our limits to keep going despite adversity. You don't have to respect me, but you will respect your teammates and this program." I take off my suit jacket, something I should have done the second I stepped out of my Mercedes. I have no plans of coming in here and strong-arming these boys into submission. This is their future on the line, not mine, and respect isn't something you can demand. It's earned. They'll either realize that and show up, or they won't. "Let's see what we're working with," I say before stealing the ball cap off Con's head and starting practice.

CHAPTER 4
CAMERON

"Hey," Parker says as he enters the team shop where I've been sorting through logo wear and uniforms.

"Hey," I toss back without so much as a glance in his direction, my focus entirely on the uniforms and gear. All these items are for employees and will be stored in a closet, but I've laid them all out to ensure that they are to spec, not just on colors but also on fit and material. The ratio of cotton to polyester is important, and I've heard stories in school about clients who ordered shipments where suppliers cut corners on blends to save money. Cotton is typically more expensive than polyester, so sometimes you'll see it marked one way online, but then you receive the order, and the blend counts are slightly off. It may seem small, but that variance can make a big difference in comfort and wear. Polyester technically holds up longer, but it also snags. I want these uniforms to be perfect. Not just for my resumé but because I want to impress Connor. While I may have designed them, Connor chose the suppliers and placed the orders, and I want to see to it that they are right.

Parker's hand finds the small of my back. "Do you need help in here? We've already unloaded the last truck and got two hours of practice in today, and I'm pretty sure this is the same place I saw you this morning." I check my Rolex—the one my father always used to wear—and see that it's almost five o'clock. "The fact that you had to look at your watch tells me you probably forgot to eat lunch. Come on, this will all be here in the morning. Let's get something to eat at Eddie's down the street."

He kisses the side of my forehead, and I can't help the way I stiffen. It's my fault I'm in this mess with Parker. I'm the one who had too much to drink and came up with the half-cocked idea to start messing around with Parker. I feel like I defiled him in a way. Parker is a genuinely good guy, and I knew he and Everett weren't on the best of terms, which made him easy prey. I wanted to get Everett's attention and make him own his feelings, just like Mac said, and I thought him seeing me with Parker might accomplish that. But it did none of those things. Instead, it backfired. Spectacularly, I might add, because now Parker and I are close. We aren't dating or even in a situationship, but we hang out. We do things that couples would do, like go out to eat, catch an occasional movie, and show up to parties together. But we're not intimate. The problem is I know if I allowed it or gave him a signal that I wanted it, we would be. He's made it more than abundantly clear he'd be down, but I don't want to cross that line. I can't. Crossing it would only end in hurt.

"Parker..." I start.

"Can we not talk about it? Just have dinner with me. It's been a long day, and we both need to eat."

I finally look at him, and I see it. Everett being home is wearing on him too. Everett is now Parker's coach. Parker's issues with Everett are worlds different than mine. His feud is more of a clash of principles, or at least I think it is. I'm still not sure I completely understand it. Everett didn't truly wrong him, and Parker has never fully divulged precisely what made him agree to our little fake dating arrangement for Connor's wedding, but if I had to guess, like me, he was trying to make Everett feel something.

We just ordered burgers and fries, and Parker has already

downed his second glass of water. He's unusually quiet, and I know why. I know he said he doesn't want to talk, but I also don't like our silence. We've been friends for years, and I don't want to fuck that up now. Hell, I'm hoping I didn't already royally mess it up.

"I know you said you don't want to talk, but I don't want to pretend."

"You were fine with pretending a few months ago," his tone is laced with a hint of irritation.

I take a drink of my beer. I wasn't expecting his comment to be so snarky, but I suppose I deserve it a little.

"You weren't exactly an innocent bystander. I get that I was the ringleader, but you were more than happy to play the puppet role."

"Things change, Cam. Maybe I don't want the puppet role anymore."

I take another long pull of my drink. This is not at all where I saw this conversation going. Would Parker be down to fuck? Yes, but there's a difference between fucking and what he's insinuating, or at least what I think he's implying. I'm not going to make the mistake of assuming.

"Okay..." I spin the bottle in my hands. "Then what role do you want?"

His eyes hold mine, and I know the girlfriend card is on the tip of his tongue, but I also know if he said it, it wouldn't be genuine. He's had months to play it if that's what he wanted. The timing of his ask is all wrong, and he knows I know it.

When I quirk a brow in a silent challenge, he says, "I played the part but didn't blindly make a deal. The deal was that I'd help you if you helped me. It's time for you to help me, Cam."

Damn it, I don't know where he's going with this, but I feel I'm not going to like it.

CHAPTER 5
EVERETT

I'm just turning the corner to grab a coffee when I see Connor walking down the breezeway with a tall woman whose dark brown hair runs halfway down her back. At first glance, I thought it was my ex-wife, but Moira has grown snootish over the years. She walks with an air of class and sophistication she wasn't born into, but rather my money provided. I don't resent her for it; I was happy to provide for her. I only notice it now because it's a striking contrast from the woman she once was. Whoever he is giving a tour to now is far too lax to be Moira Michaelson.

As they continue walking down the corridor, I return my focus to the fancy cappuccino machine and make a mental note to buy regular coffee on my way home tonight. I like my coffee black, but this place doesn't open up to the public for another two weeks, so the shipment of provisions doesn't arrive for another week. The mere thought of worrying about coffee instead of my next meeting already makes me feel lighter. When I arrived here a few days ago, I thought I'd be in an office managing the back end of the business. It's been so long since I started my own company that I forgot that in a startup, you wear all the damn hats. I'm still determining why I allowed myself to believe I would be a figurehead, ensuring direction and stability were maintained. Connor does all that while coaching a winning team, contacting scouts, setting up tournaments, and running the damn stadium.

The first thing I did after Connor officially announced I would be the head coach for the summer was send my brothers an email saying I would be taking on a silent partner role for the summer. The email couldn't have been in their inboxes for ten seconds before I was on a FaceTime call with Colton and Garrett. They both thought my email was either a prank or my way of letting them know I was terminally ill. After I explained the situation with Connor, they were both fully onboard. I've never truly taken a vacation, or even a break, for that matter. Even now, I'm here early because I can't fully step away. All week, I've been getting to the stadium earlier than necessary to check emails. I passed my cases over to Colton, and in exchange, I've taken on overseeing and mentoring some of our less senior-level lawyers. Still, the workload associated with those responsibilities is almost nil. We only hire people who are capable.

With my coffee in hand, I head out toward the field. It's something I've done every morning this week. I stare at the field, reflect, and plan, but today, it looks like that will not happen. I can see Coach Teague and Denver on the field. Because the presumption of innocence is ingrained into my DNA, I don't immediately assume they are attempting to meet behind my back. Instead, I pull out my phone and check to ensure I don't have any missed calls, texts, or emails from them or Connor alerting me to a meeting that somehow slipped through the cracks. When I see that I don't, I stop just short of stepping out of the shadows of the walkway. I have no reason to believe they are up to something, but I also wasn't aware of a meetup, and eavesdropping feels essential. Better the enemy you know than the one you don't. I don't think Denver and Teague have a reason not to like me, but that doesn't mean they aren't upset that Connor didn't ask one of them to step up for the summer. The last thing Connor or I need is someone sabotaging the opening season.

Before I get a chance to let conspiracy theories run away with my thoughts, another person jogs onto the field. The small spike of anxiety that existed vanishes when realization sets in. It's Parker. Stepping out of the shadows, I make my way to the field. As I approach, Denver notices me first but doesn't say anything. His eye holds mine for a beat, and I know without words why he isn't acknowledging my presence. He's letting me eavesdrop, which tells me this meeting wasn't planned by him or Teague but rather by Parker. *Interesting.*

"For a lot of the guys, this is their last shot. They're in their senior year of school, and if they don't make it, that's it. We don't want this season to be an afterthought just because Connor is more focused on the future than the now."

His back is to me when I say, "Have I given you a reason to believe I'm not dedicated to ensuring this team has one of their most successful seasons to date?"

Teague and Parker both turn toward me simultaneously, but it's Parker who is clearly taken back.

"Yeah, you have, actually," Parker says, widening his stance. "So far this week, the team has spent half of its practice time helping move furniture and inventory into the stadium, and what little practice time we have squeezed in has been subpar at best. We're not here to simply stay in shape. If that were the case, we'd be at the gym. It's cheaper."

I don't appreciate his smart tone or that he didn't come to me with this, which speaks volumes about where we were a year ago. I know he's unhappy with how I handled things last year, but I don't have to explain myself or my choices to him. Last summer, I asked him to step up and marry someone for protection. I wince a little at the memory. In my head, the ask isn't as egregious as it sounds. After all, I wasn't asking him to do something I hadn't done myself; at the end of the day, it was only meant to be temporary. Nothing about it was going to be authentic. It was an exchange of names, period. However, the girl who was supposed to be his met my son first. The rest was history. I can't help that Mackenzie chose Connor over him. That has to be what this is about. I've treated Parker like a son where most wouldn't. He's not my blood; he's my ex-wife's stepson and not my responsibility.

I see two more players coming in through the south gate. "And I'm assuming you're not the only one who feels this way, seeing as two of your teammates are here an hour before practice starts as well."

Denver and Teague look over their shoulders, but Parker doesn't, cementing that all this is news to them too.

"No, I'm not. Our warm-ups were tired at best, and the training reeked of rec league-level aptitude. This isn't Little League. We don't all get a damn trophy. We need someone who isn't washed-up and didn't peak in high school."

Teague coughs into his hand. "That just earned ten laps, Michaelson."

I hold up my hand. "No, that's fine. I want you guys to speak your mind. You don't think the workouts are up to snuff, and that's because they're not, but that's also why I'm the coach and not you. We technically couldn't start our season until the SEC Tournaments were officially concluded, which means that practices starting Monday will look a lot different. As for the washed-up, peaked in high school part..." I run my thumb over my lips and drop my eyes, thankful I traded in my suits for athleisure today of all days. "Since the three of you arrived early today, you can join me for my daily workout. We'll see if that gets you warmed up and if you're still vertical by the end of practice. I'll run your laps."

"You're on, Callahan," Parker says, quickly taking the bait.

I understand Teague's knee-jerk reaction. Not only am I Parker's elder, but I'm the interim head coach. There's a level of respect that comes with both of those positions, no questions asked. While I'm years beyond looking to people for validation, I'm not beyond earning respect. I won't just step in here and demand it. If I need to prove myself to these boys for them to play hard, so be it. Game on.

We've just finished practicing base drills, and I can tell Parker is running on fumes. I'm in good shape, but I'll admit I'm starting to get fatigued. We're going on our third hour of practice, and the heat is beginning to set in. I may have underestimated the depth of his dissension.

"Alright, balls in," I call out, and half the team sighs in relief before I say, "We're going to work on leads and steals. After going over footage from last year's season, I noticed that the number one area in which the team consistently fell short was bases stolen. Half of you were part of the team last year. Moretti and Warson are the exceptions. They can sit this one out."

As the team walks back to the dugout to grab a quick drink, I hear one of the guys, say quietly, "Tap out already. This is your fight, not the team's."

I don't get a chance to hear what Parker says in return because as I grab my bat to hit balls, Denver asks, "So what's your plan if he doesn't drop from exhaustion?" I don't immediately answer because, honestly, I hadn't thought that far when I challenged him. "I mean, don't get me wrong, he looks tired. If I had to bet money, he's probably got another thirty minutes, an hour max, before he gives up, knowing he's still going to have to run laps but—"

"He wasn't the only one who questioned my dedication and ability to do what they do. If this is what it takes to prove I'm not fucking around, that I care just as much as Connor, then I will. I'll do this every day until they believe it, and if they don't, so be it, but you better believe they'll be winners."

After drinking half of my bottle of Gatorade, I grab my glove and a ball and step onto the field, ready to start throwing some pitches and picking guys off when Parker jogs out of the dugout, his eyes connecting with mine for the briefest of seconds before he takes off down the foul line and starts running laps. It's not the pomposity I expected. Even in defeat, I would have guessed he'd give me lip service. Perhaps something about how I didn't truly win because he's only conceding for the team. In the end, it doesn't matter. Defeat is defeat, but I have a feeling this is just the first of many.

By the time I pull into my driveway for the evening, I'm exhausted; not just from training with men half my age but from all of it. The training, the personalities, and the sheer amount of work. If you had asked me a week ago if I'd grown complacent in my own career, I would have said no and meant it. Lawyers are constantly having to evolve. No two cases are identical, but it's more than just knowing the law. It's knowing people, reading them, predicting their next move, and knowing what makes them tick. As a lawyer, your interpersonal skills are continually adapting. Your attention to detail, organization, and time management are all constantly on. I come home for one week to run a stadium and suddenly feel like running a law firm is easier. It could be the familiarity. I have done it my whole life. Or maybe it's that I want to impress my son so I'm going extra hard. I don't want to let him down. I want to be the man he used to see. The one he looked up to, relied on, and respected.

It's the thought of being that man that has me feeling like a complete ass when I open the garage and see Cameron's car. The last thing I wanted to do was hurt anyone, let alone her, but that's precisely what I did. This time of the year is already hard enough for her, and then I had to pile onto it by blowing up on her the first night I got back into town. But in my defense, it couldn't be helped. I had so much weighing on my mind after the day I spent with Connor. That same day, I realized helping him meant stepping back from my own business in a big way.

Then there's her. I left because of her, and when I came back, it was as though I hadn't left at all. Everything I thought would disappear didn't. I needed space. I needed to get away from the thoughts that started to cloud my better judgment, the ones encouraging me to step over the line.

My best friend died and more or less left his daughter in my care. While Cameron believes her staying in Waterloo was a choice, it was anything but. However, that detail isn't known to anyone but me. Damon was one of the most brilliant men I knew. It's why we became Callahan & Associates. My brothers saw it too. Damon was a rare breed. He had a true gift. Sure, any of us can talk in circles and say things without actually saying anything at all. It's what we are trained to do, but Damon could make someone telling the truth feel like honesty was a lie. I never met a person who knew Damon and didn't love him. He was a great man, but even great men do stupid shit, like when the fucker entrusted the care of his daughter to me. It's one of the many mistakes I've learned my longtime best friend and business partner made. Outside of my brothers, he was the only person I trusted with my deepest secrets. I believed we told each other everything, but if that were true, I wouldn't have Cameron.

As I walk through the front door, the malty scents of caramel and chocolate make my mouth water. I'm not typically a fan of sweets, but I haven't eaten since breakfast, and the smell of homemade food only reminds me of my hunger. I'm glad she's home. When I pulled into the garage, I saw her car, but that didn't guarantee she would be inside. The smell of dessert tells me she's not only home but relaxed. The woman isn't a chef by any means. She only started cooking within the past year, but baking is something I've seen her do a few times over the years since she's lived in this house.

Around the time she first came to live with us, I heard noises coming from downstairs in the middle of the night. Naturally, I went down to investigate and found her baking cookies while Connor sat at the island seemingly eating them at one a.m. It was then that I overheard her tell him that baking helped let go of the bad because it required her to focus. She explained how baking is a precise thing. The slightest miscalculation can ruin a recipe. From where I stood in the shadows, I could see him shoving cookies into the towel drawer on his side of the island. Her mother, Amelia, wasn't the homemaker type. Instead, she spent her time at spas, shopping, and attending lunches with her socialite friends. To this day, I'm not sure what Damon saw in that woman, especially after the things I learned following their deaths.

"Ouch..." I hear Cameron hiss out as a pan simultaneously clangs against the marble countertop, pulling me from my thoughts.

My feet carry me to the kitchen faster than I can blink. "What happened?" I demand before assessing the scene for myself.

Her eyes quickly find mine, but they don't linger the way they usually do, which bothers me more than it should.

"Don't worry about it. I'm fine. Give me five minutes, and I'll be out of your kitchen," she grumbles.

Damn it. We're still at this. I haven't seen her in days. After I told her I thought it was time she moved out, she did a hell of a good job of staying out of my sight. The only way I knew she'd been coming and going was by checking the security cameras. She's done an excellent job of ensuring she's not around when I am, which tells me two things. Cameron Salt doesn't just know me a little, she knows me a lot; she knows my subtleties and nuances. Living under the same roof, we were bound to cross paths, but not to the extent we had been prior to me leaving town. Cameron wasn't conveniently in my space. She was intentionally in it. Another revelation that I shouldn't like.

Her back is to me when I step up from behind and gently grab her arm to assess the burn myself. Her skin instantly pebbles, and her breath audibly catches. A long second that feels like a short eternity stretches between us before she says, "I said I was fine."

She attempts to pull away, but I don't let her. "We need to talk," I say, keeping my voice unaffected even though I'm anything but inside. I pin her between myself and the sink, flip on the water, and dampen a hand towel. "I shouldn't have acted the way I did. I came home and assumed the party was yours."

"Since when do you care if I have parties?" she asks, her tone quieter and less contentious.

Good fucking question. Do I like the kids throwing parties here? Not exactly, but I allowed it for many years. It's better here than where I couldn't watch them. One bonfire out in the fields when I was seventeen changed the entire trajectory of my life. I didn't want to see history repeat itself with Connor or anyone's kids, for that matter. But that's not what this is now. I wasn't mad about the party per se. Rather, I was upset about what parties entail and how she was dressed. Even though I know the root of my discontent, it doesn't mean I care to own it or accept what it says about me. Monsters can live inside of us, but it doesn't mean we must let them out to play. I've done well enough taming my beast. I've made it this far. What's another couple of months?

I place the cool, damp towel on her arm. "If you want to stay until the end of your senior year, that's fine..."

"Everett—"

"Let me finish," I cut her off before she can distract me from finishing the thought that just came to mind. I know what's triggering my deplorable thoughts. Which means I know how to end this madness. I take a step back and immediately miss her warmth. "If you stay, there are going to be some rules."

"Rules," she repeats as she slowly turns to face me.

"Yes, rules. The first one being no more parties."

I watch as she adjusts the towel on her arm. "Again, what do you suddenly have against parties?"

"You're living under my roof, which makes you my responsibility."

"Your responsibility?" she questions bemused. "You were just about to kick me out."

Her ice-blue eyes connect with mine and do things to my stomach. Why does responsibility suddenly somehow feel like a claim that isn't mine to take? Either way, I made a promise to my best friend that I'd watch over his daughter, that I'd keep her safe. It's not her fault I gave her father my word or that I'm now a divorced man who notices things he shouldn't. I'm angry with myself enough for the both of us that I have impure thoughts of her at all and even more indignant that I haven't been able to find the strength to push them out.

I step around the island, putting more distance between us. "Look, I don't need to explain myself to you. But this summer, I have a lot on my plate between working at the stadium and the firm. I don't need to come home to my house filled with strangers. You, of all people, should know how important helping Connor is to me."

"Okay," she starts, but I cut her off once more because I want to get everything out and be done with this madness.

"I want you home by midnight every night. No exceptions."

"Everett, what am I, seventeen? You can't be serious."

I place my hands on the island and dare to meet her eyes again. "Dead serious. I don't need to lose sleep wondering where you are or who you're with, and I don't need the noise that comes with those late-night entries, which leads me to my next rule. No boys in the house." She removes the damp towel I placed on her arm, and I drop my gaze and grip the ledge hard, fighting my desire to go over there and put it back on.

"This is absurd. Why can't I have guy friends over?"

"Easy. I don't know what's happening under my roof when I'm not here or while you're off in another room. I don't need you pregnant and unmarried on my watch."

"First of all, I'm not a virgin. If it's my virtue you're trying to protect, it's a little too late. Second, this is total bullshit."

"Watch your mouth, Cameron."

"Oh, now I can't curse either."

"Not when you're speaking to me."

"Fine." She slaps her hands on the counter, leaning in, her light pink crop top highlighting her braless, erect nipples. "I'll speak in terms I know you'll understand. Your rules are a double standard because of my gender. Connor was never subjected to these same rules when he was living here."

"You're not wrong, but it has nothing to do with your gender. When I had Connor under my roof, I had a wife helping me raise him. I clearly no longer have that."

The way her eyebrow quirks up tells me my rules may not be

the answer I'd hoped they'd be, but I don't dare backtrack now. I said what I said. It doesn't have to be fair. My house, my rules. Picking up the dish towel she threw down, she turns around and grabs the cake pan from the counter behind her only to set it down on the island and slide it toward me. "Cake?"

"Sure..." I say pensively.

"Here, let me get you a fork." I watch as she grabs a fork and walks around the island, setting it down next to the pan.

"You're not having any?"

"Oh, I baked the cake. I can't eat it too." Then, grabbing the water bottle she was drinking, she sets it down on the other side of the pan. "In case you choke on your misogyny."

Turning on her heel, she exits the kitchen. "Cameron," I call out after her though I know it's useless. She's not going to come back, and I have yet another interaction I could have handled better to add to my ever-growing list. The woman manages to steal all my rational thoughts when I'm in her vicinity. Fucking hell. She could just move out. However, I know she won't. I just made this a game for her.

CHAPTER 6
CAMERON

"How is it possible I have nothing to wear!" I screech as I storm out of my walk-in closet and head toward my bed, shooting Mac a text.

> Cameron: You said it's just the family, right?

I blow out a breath and hope she's by her phone. Dinner is at 4 pm which means I'm supposed to be there in fifteen minutes.

> Mac: Yes, Connor is grilling.

> Cameron: What are you wearing?

> Mac: Wear the black halter top with that black and white printed skirt with the slit up the slide. He likes that one on you.

> Cameron: This is why you are my best friend. Tell me this was all a cruel joke, and you're not really leaving for the summer.

> Mac: Get dressed and get your ass over here!

I just finished pulling on the skirt Mac said I should wear when there's a light knock on my door.

"It's open."

The door opens slightly. "Are you decent?"

"Yes, Everett. Since when have I ever invited you in while I was naked?" I say with a little added cheekiness, given where things ended last night.

It's seldom that any words affect Everett. He's a lawyer. The man wears a constant look of indifference no matter the situation, but the slight clench in his jaw when he puts his hands in his pockets tells me that mine have, and that's new.

He ignores my impudence. "I was just seeing if you were ready to go."

"You came by to see if I'm ready to go?" I question, trying to understand why he'd stop by my room to ask me at all.

"Yes, I'm leaving for Connor's and..." He rolls his lips and drops his eyes. "You know what, never mind. I'm not even sure why I asked. You're probably going out after dinner."

I haven't ridden in a car with Everett since I was seventeen. Sure, we live in the same house, and we attend the same family functions, but we don't ride together like father and daughter or anything else for that matter. It's why my brain is stumbling now. The lack of sleep I got last night because I stayed up replaying every touch and dissecting every word in the kitchen, trying to piece together where we stand, could very well be getting the best of me now. I know I'm operating on less than sufficient neurons, but I'm pretty sure I'm reading between the lines just fine.

He turns, his hand on the knob when I say, "Were you about to offer me a ride? Because if so, I'll take it."

His head turns slightly toward the sound of my voice, but he doesn't give me his eyes. "Be down in five," he says before exiting my room.

I don't care how out of sorts this man has me. There's no way in hell I'm turning down alone time with Everett Callahan, and a car ride to Connor's guarantees I'll have it twice.

"What's it like having a best friend who can read minds? I freaking called it. Greedy and jealous. You realize when the dam breaks, you're in for it. I hope you've been dusting off the cobwebs with toys, at least."

"Oh my god," I can't help but laugh.

She knows I haven't had sex in over a year. I've been irrationally committed to Everett since the night we shared in my tent on my twenty-first birthday. In my mind, the second his hand trailed up my thigh and he pulled me into him, I was his. It doesn't matter that he left the second his conscious thoughts alerted him to what he had done. I feel it in the depths of my soul. In those few fleeting seconds, he knew who I was, and I was exactly what he wanted, what he craved.

"I also think you are reading into the silence on the ride over way too much. This is new territory for both of you. He wants you all to himself. Period. Since we've been over here talking, which has been at least forty-five minutes, he's glanced in this direction at least three times, and we know it's not because he's looking at me. I'm just going to say it because it needs to be said. If you want to have an adult relationship with that man..." Her eyes flick back up to the house where the guys are outside grilling before adding, "Because that's what Everett is, he's a man. He's not a boy; he's not a guy in his twenties who's flip-flopping between partying and commitment. He knows what he likes and what he wants. If you want to take him on, you need to put on your big girl panties and sack up. You rode here in silence. Don't do the same on the way home. Use that pretty little mouth and start asking questions. Tell him what you want. Show him you're not a little girl anymore."

I down the rest of my mojito on that note. "He hasn't exactly given me the chance. Night one, he accused me of throwing the party, and then last night, things started out nice but..." I trail off remembering the last time we shared a tender moment in that same spot.

When he approached me at the sink for a moment, it felt like we were back in the kitchen last Christmas. It's childish and maybe it only serves to show my age—something I can't change—but I couldn't sleep, and I remembered I hadn't made Christmas cookies for the next morning. I realized there were no kids to wake up and Santa wouldn't be coming, but it makes me happy. My dad used to make them with me every year. We'd make the cookies, decorate them, and then pick out the best ones to set out. It's a tradition that hasn't left me. I was washing the mixing bowls while waiting for the cookies to come out when Everett came down and startled me. He asked if the dishwasher had broken, and when I gave him an unamused sidelong glare, he crossed the invisible line again. The one I know exists for both of us. It doesn't matter that I want to break it down. Not only is all of this new territory for both of us, but it's still taboo and forbidden. Everett isn't just an older man. I'm not naïve. I've always known what a relationship between us would look like to the outside world. How it would be perceived, the rumors that would start; but in my eyes, none of it mattered. It didn't matter as long as, in the end, he was mine.

The time of night and the eve of the day quickly registered, and he realized what I was doing and why. His hand found my upper back, and he apologized. That same hand dropped lower when I gave him no words, and he shut off the water. My face turned toward his, and he said, "Tell me how I can make it right." His thumb slowly stroked over my back. The move was innocent enough, meant to comfort, not incite, but that's exactly what it did when the subtle brush of his thumb caught the hem of my nightshirt and his finger grazed my bare skin. The air seized in my lungs, and my skin instantly pebbled. As he stared at me, his eyes never leaving mine, I saw the heaviness there. The weight of the chemistry that had been building between us since my twenty-first birthday was undeniable, but that night, I saw more. What we shared had been years in the making.

"Cameron, I understand how his words put you on the

defense, but I think—" Loud music and a truck pulling down the gravel drive have her words falling short.

"What is Parker doing here?"

"What do you think he's doing here? He is technically Connor's stepbrother now. Wait, did something happen between you guys? You sound upset."

"Come on," I nod toward the house. "I need a refill."

She holds up the bottle of wine she brought when we walked down here for girl time. "I have enough for two more glasses. Spill."

I hand her my glass and bend down to unstrap my heels before pulling up the hem of my skirt and taking a seat on the dock to dip my feet in the water.

"I used him, and now he wants to use me."

"Use you how?" she says as she empties the bottle of wine between our glasses.

"That is indeed the question," I say before looking down and noticing a fly had flown into my glass. "Damn. Come on. I need a new glass," I say as I reluctantly pull my feet out of the water. "This fly is obviously a sign that it's time to pay my dues."

⁓

"Hey," Parker says as I load my plate with food.

"Hey," I echo his greeting, attempting to keep things short in hopes that he doesn't want to pull any shit tonight. I swear it's like I can feel Everett's eyes on me, and he's not even in the room. I hate feeling guilty talking to Parker.

"Come sit with me?" he asks, nodding toward the Adirondack chairs circled around the firepit instead of the patio table.

"Sure." The moment we walk out the back door, I feel eyes on me, and not just Everett's. I'm sure Mackenzie is staring as well. We do look somewhat suspect going off to eat by ourselves instead of joining everyone else at the table. I want to ask what his deal is and why we can't just join everyone else, but the question would be pointless, so instead, I ask another burning question: "Where is Moira tonight?"

His brow furrows, and a slight scowl takes over his face at the mere mention of his stepmother's name. Another reason I couldn't just say no when Parker called in his ask. We have too much in common. Moira Michaelson, formerly Moira Callahan, leaves a bitter taste in his mouth too. The fact that Parker and his father, Kipp, are here speaks volumes about the type of man that Everett is. Kipp was one of Everett's closest friends in high school, and they're still friends even after his wife cheated on him, divorced him, and then went on to marry the man she had coveted since high school.

"I don't know. She hasn't been around much lately." I can hear the indignance in his tone. "I don't care to talk about her," he adds before taking a big bite from his burger.

I push the potato salad around my plate. I am hungry. I should eat. The carbs will help sober me up. I've had one too many drinks since we got here, and I need a clear head, even if it's the last thing I currently want. All the anxiety of the past week has been eating away at my sanity.

"Okay, so what do you want to talk about then?"

He shrugs. "Nothing. I just wanted you to sit with me." His eyes lock onto mine, and he says without words this is one of the moments where he's pulling his card. I don't say anything more as I lean back into my seat and take a bite of my food. Sitting I can do.

After finishing my food or what I could stomach considering the roller coaster of mixed emotions I was feeling, I excuse myself to the restroom. Splashing water on my face, I try to get a grip. I'm buzzed, not drunk; I ate enough to keep my head on when all I really want to do is let go. The problem is, letting go is the last thing I can do. If there's any chance of rekindling the spark I know is there between me and Everett, I can't get drunk and act a fool. Doing so would only hurt my chances of proving to him that I'm not a little girl anymore. I'm a grown-ass woman capable of having an adult relationship.

I turn the cold water on and splash my arms in an attempt to find my center and a semblance of clarity. It's easy to see what we want to see when we're crushing on someone. It's normal to overanalyze and obsess over every minute detail... "Completely normal," I finish the thought out loud as I grip the granite sink base and look at myself in the mirror. "Stop being a coward. Everett's back. You've prepared for this moment for months." I pull out my fire engine red lipstick and reapply it with a pop, giving myself a little needed pep in my step.

Exiting the bathroom, I'm just reaching the end of the hallway when I catch a glimpse of Everett heading toward the front door. Is he leaving? Not a day has gone by since he left town that I haven't plotted all the words I'd give him when he got home, and not only have I said nothing, but I've also basically made myself invisible. After he told me to move out, I stayed away, ensuring our paths didn't cross, too scared to watch the future I'd been dreaming up in my heart be ripped away. I've watched enough dreams die to last a lifetime.

Picking up my pace, I hurry toward the front door so I don't miss him before he gets into his car and takes off, leaving me behind again. He's rounding the car when I step out onto the wraparound porch. "You're just going to leave?" I call out after him.

Those molten black eyes flick up to mine, and my heart skips a beat. It's not an uncommon occurrence when it comes to him. It's a reoccurring episode that can't be helped when I know I have his attention.

"It looks like you have a ride," he says dismissively as he drops my gaze and reaches for the door handle.

"I came here with you," I rush out, my voice slightly cracking with the jitters coursing through my veins. I'm not this girl. I'm a confident woman. I mean, for god's sake, I strut around the house in thong bikinis. I know exactly what I'm doing every time I do it. I want him to look. I want him to feel something for me. But teasing a man and growing a pair of balls to go after him currently feel like two very different things.

Pulling open the door, he rests his hand on top of the car. "That didn't mean we would be leaving together," he says.

I take a step down the front stairs. "So you were just going to leave without asking me if I was ready to go?"

His polo is fitted so expertly across his well-defined chest that I can see the measured breath he pulls into his lungs from here before saying, "I ate my dinner. I spoke with my son. You didn't look like you were ready to go, and I am." He pauses, rasps his knuckles on the roof, and adds, "You're a smart girl. I'm sure you didn't come out here for a reminder of the rules, so if—"

I cut him off as I make my way down the remaining steps. "Do you want me to leave with Parker?"

His face is impassive, giving nothing away. His eyes stay locked on mine as I slowly approach the car. "It's probably better that you do."

My heart rate kicks up a notch as a mix of trepidation and anger slowly rises. Was that a passive flirt?

"What does that even mean? God, you're infuriating," I say, my tone holding back zero restraint. The time to be bold and take risks is now. Change doesn't happen staying inside our comfort zones.

He raises a brow and crosses his arms. "What is it that you want me to say, Cameron?"

I roll my eyes and shake my head before meeting his gaze again. "I want you to say no, Cameron. I don't want you to leave with Parker. I want you to get your pretty little ass in the car and leave with me the way I thought you would."

His face stays impassive, and for a moment, I believe I've read everything wrong and all I am is an inconvenience. The burden left to his care once my father died, but just as my insecurity is about to snuff out all of my false bravado, there's a tick in his jaw. It's so small, had I blinked, I would have missed it; part of me still questions if it was ever really there at all. But then he says, "Get in the car, Cameron."

Without another word, he gets in, and I follow as my heart threatens to explode. His lips said, "Get in the car," but my mind heard, "I don't want you leaving with Parker."

I took a risk. I earned my reward. There's no way I'm not getting in that car.

Of course, I get in, and once again, we're drenched in silence just as we were on the drive over to Connor's. It doesn't help that, sitting in his car, I'm surrounded by the deep, warm, woodsy notes of his scent. He's always smelled so earthy to me, like the salt from the sea and the musk of the woods. It's comforting, and right now, it's too allaying. I can't stay in the confines of my comfort.

"Why did you leave?" I risk looking at him instead of at the nothingness that exists outside of my window.

"Excuse me?" he questions, somewhat confoundedly.

"After Con's wedding, you left. Out of nowhere, without a word, you just left."

His brow slightly creases as he keeps his focus out on the road. "I've been in Boston. That's hardly leaving, Cameron."

I pause, taking a second to consider my next words because they can't be taken back once they're out.

"You know what I mean, Everett." It's subtle, but an accusation all the same, and no one likes to be called out. Now the question is, will he own it? He's quiet, but the way his left hand grips the steering wheel more firmly is an answer, even if he chooses not to use his words. That grip tells me two things. I do affect him, and my heart flutters from the small victory, but it also tells me whatever words he chooses will be more of the same, a web of truth tangled in spin. As the silence stretches, my hurt morphs. It's no longer about where he and I stand. It's deeper than that. He left. "You left, Everett. You left me all alone in an empty house."

I don't say any more. I can't. If I do, I might break. He knows what I'm saying. I have no family. I have an aunt I barely know and a brother who may as well be a stranger. I haven't seen him since I watched my parents' caskets get lowered into the ground. I just don't care. I stopped caring about the people who don't lose sleep over me a long time ago. I had to so that I could stop dwelling on the things I couldn't change. It's the only way I could give myself a shot at shaping my future into what I wanted. So here I am, an orphan of sorts, and he just leaves.

His eyes briefly flick to mine, only to return to the road just as quick when he sees the sadness. "Sometimes an empty house is better than living with the depravity that existed when it was full."

I'm sick of the mind games. I know it's intentional. It's his way of giving me truths, saying all the things he wants to say, things that take weight off his chest but leave me hanging by a thread until he gives me another morsel. His words just now are a truth. The question is who is he referencing. Is he referring to the memories of a failed marriage that haunt the halls, or is it the thoughts of doing wicked things with me that torment him? This is where I would usually give up, telling myself he's not ready but finding contentment with the small gain. In this case, the car ride, but I can't bite my tongue. Not when he's been gone for months, and whatever words and stolen touches I'd normally have saved up in a love jar are depleted, used up, and left void as his absence spoke louder than any small advance.

"Does that mean you left because of me?"

I know he feels my eyes pinned to the side of his face. I know I'm making him anxious, and if history has taught me anything, it's that he doesn't like to be pushed, but that's also why I was careful with my wording. My question was innocent enough. I can spin it to mean something else if I find myself in a situation I need to backpedal out of. However, I don't know that I would because the buzz of electricity I feel now is too intoxicating. Pushing his buttons this way, playing his game and using his own words against him is much more satisfying than taunting him by hanging all over another man ever was.

"Why I left does not matter."

"It does matter if it's because of me, Everett I—"

"Whatever you were going to say, don't." His tone is sharp. "Wherever your thoughts are leading you, stop. There's no point in pursuing them. It will never happen, Cameron."

Well, that answered one question. I was right. The depravity that haunts him is me.

"Why do you journal?"

He does a double take my way before turning his attention back to the road. I love knowing I'm now fucking with him the way he so easily messes with my head. He was so sure he knew what I was getting at when he delivered those stern words, and now he's wondering if he didn't just give up something I wasn't asking for at all.

Letting out an exasperated breath, he says, "There are many reasons, but mainly to let things go. It's a form of therapy."

Hook, line, and sinker. He not only took the bait but walked right into my next line. "Maybe I'm something you need to get out of your system."

CHAPTER 7
EVERETT

I'm a workaholic. I know this. It's why I got to the stadium hours ago. My inbox has over thirty flagged emails, and my type A personality is threatening to give me a panic attack. I don't think I've ever in my entire adult life had more than one email flagged for more than a few hours because I get shit done. You can't build your empire on the things you're going to do. It's the things you've done that solidify your reputation. I've been here since five a.m. I have a perfectly good home office I could have worked in for the past twenty-four hours, yet no work was done. All I managed to do was cancel the two engagements I had planned on the East Coast and flag these damn emails for follow-up.

I slam my laptop shut and walk over to the wall of windows overlooking the baseball field. I know why I can't focus. I thought leaving the house would help, but leaving has done nothing but make me more anxious. It's my own damn fault. When we drove home from dinner at Connor's, I didn't say anything back. I always have the last word, but I didn't. I said nothing when having the last word mattered most. Instead of closing a door, I opened it. I opened it, knowing I'd never step through. Why? Because the view is everything. Some would call it masochism, taunting myself with dreams I'll never reach for, but I see it as the penance I deserve for the deviant, perverted thoughts that haunt me. I didn't say anything back for two reasons, the biggest being I was done hurting her. I've already apologized to her more times than I have any other person in my life. I don't have regrets, therefore, apologies aren't necessary, but every move I make with her anymore feels like a misstep. Probably because it is. The second reason is just another amoral strike against me because it's purely selfish. I didn't fucking say anything because I liked knowing she still wanted me. I like knowing she thinks about me the same way I think about her.

"Damn it." My cock starts to thicken, and I immediately shove my hand into my hair. I can't sleep, and I can't work, and I already know I can't fuck her out of my system. I tried that when I was in Boston. No one managed to hold my attention. Grabbing the duffle bag I packed with extra clothes, I change into my running attire. Exercising always brings clarity, and if it doesn't, at the very least, it will lead to exhaustion and maybe sleep.

Running three miles around the perimeter of the stadium did the trick. I responded to ten of the thirty emails demanding my attention via voice-to-text. When I finished my laps, the team started showing up for morning practice, and to my surprise, Parker stayed in his lane. He kept whatever snide comments he may have had to himself. I can't be sure where all his anger is coming from. I thought it had to do with Cameron, but after dinner at Connor's this past weekend, I don't think that's it. If he wanted to be more than just friends or, worse yet, friends with benefits, he would have been different with her. While he hoarded her attention, no doubt intentionally, he wasn't intimate with her. At least not in the way he was at the wedding the last time I saw the two of them together. Then there's the fact that, at the end of the night, it was my car she left in. Again, another fucking detail that shouldn't matter. It shouldn't make me feel any type of way. If anything, I should be championing a union between them.

Either way, Parker's gone, the team's gone, and I got through a full practice with no issues. The stress I had for the past twenty-four hours has abated, and now I know the first task I need to tackle the second I get upstairs to my office: a cozy fucking couch. If being at the stadium is what it takes to put her out of my mind, I will live here for the summer until Connor reclaims his position.

No sooner than I toss my empty Gatorade bottle into the trash can in the concourse, I catch a glimpse of long red hair and an ass I'd know anywhere entering the team shop. And just like that, the resolve I had moments ago slips away. Connor and Mackenzie left for Florida, so I know she's not visiting Mackenzie, and the team is gone. The only people here are the concessions manager, the cleaning crew, and me. She has no reason to be here.

I pick up my stride as I make my way down the corridor until I reach the shop window, and I peek around the corner where the brick wall meets the glass, not wanting to give away my presence. But apparently, every plan I set is destined to go to shit because the second my eyes connect with her form, I'm storming into the shop.

"What the hell are you doing?"

She instantly grabs the shelf to steady herself as my question startles her.

"Everett, Jesus. You scared the crap out of me." She rolls her eyes and climbs another step. "What does it look like I'm doing? I'm stocking shelves."

"You're not about to stand on that box to reach the top shelf. Get down. I'll do it."

She laughs. "Is that why you stormed in here like I was robbing the place? You thought I was using this box for another six inches of height?" Reaching down, she flips open the top. "It's a box of hats, Ev. It wouldn't have held my weight. I set them here for easy access so I could put them away quicker," she says as if her intent was obvious.

"Why are you here, Cameron? It's the summer before you graduate. If you're serious about pursuing a degree in fashion, you should be looking for internships that align with your career goals." I meet her by the stool and steal the box of hats. "I can put all of this away, or better yet, the new shop attendant can put it away when they start training later this week. Go home. I'll let Connor know he doesn't need you to run errands for him this summer."

Her cheeks heat, and her blue eyes start to turn gray. "I won't be going anywhere, Everett. I work here."

"You most certainly do not. You don't need to work, but I'll talk to Holden if you insist on a summer hobby. I'm sure he'll let you work at Hayes Fields until school starts again. Go home. I've got this."

She steps off the stool and puts her hand on her hip, her attitude affecting me in ways it shouldn't. "I'll say it again, Everett, because apparently, you're determined to see and hear what you want instead of what's real. I work here, and I won't be leaving." She snatches the box of hats from my hands and adds, "As for getting a job that aligns with my degree, I got one. I designed this box of hats, along with every other team logo item in the shop, thank you very much. If you don't want me here because suddenly being around me is unbearable, then you can leave. You have no reason to come into this shop."

She turns on her heel and stomps off toward the cashier counter. "Cameron—"

"Don't apologize. I'm done with all of them, Everett. Don't worry about the letter. I release you from whatever vow, oath, or pact you had with my father. I'm no longer your burden. As for being in your space, I'll leave, but I'm not quitting my job here. So you'll have to suffer through the summer knowing I'm down here."

"Cam—" I try again.

"Leave, Everett." Her back is still to me when her hands slam against the counter. "It's what you're good at, and we have nothing more to discuss."

I bite my tongue and resist the urge to walk up behind her, as I've done more times than I should. I can't help myself. I've always noticed Cameron Salt. However, I'm not sure that is saying much. Everyone notices her. It's impossible not to. Just like the sun, she never stops shining. She loves to talk; she'll talk to anyone about anything, regardless of status. Cameron doesn't see those things even though she's always had it. She has a sense of humor and doesn't hold bitterness or resentment even when warranted. The woman is confident, and she goes after exactly what she wants. It's because I see all those things that I don't correct her. I want to tell her how very wrong she is, but I don't. What she's proposing is for the best. I need to let her go. Boston wasn't the answer. It didn't rid me of her in the way I'd hoped, and maybe that's because I knew she wasn't really gone. She was still in my life, still in my home, and therefore still in my head.

Unlike the last time we parted, I don't let her have the last word. Before I exit the shop, I stop and say, "Saying sorry isn't always an admission of guilt. Sometimes it's said just because the person cares."

I don't look back before I walk out. There's no point. I keep inserting my foot in my mouth when it comes to Cameron, which is something I never do. I wasn't going to apologize like she assumed. Tactfully backpedal? Yes. She wasn't wrong when she said I've already apologized too many times. Plus, I wasn't truly sorry. Nothing I said was untrue. It was my delivery that could have been better. Every interaction I have with her could be better. She's right. I shouldn't need to go into the team shop. However, her presence will be a nuisance. It's not unbearably horrible. In fact, it's the opposite, unbearably intoxicating. Knowing she's in the same vicinity as me and staying away will require strength I'm learning I no longer possess. I take the stairs two at a time, determined to get to my office and the bottle of gin that Connor left in a gift basket. I'm sure the basket was

Mackenzie's idea, but the fact Connor allowed it means something. It's progress.

The tension that's riddled my body since I returned home barely gets a chance to ebb from the thought of all this madness when I open the door to my office and find long dark hair, slicked back and pulled into a high ponytail, with not a strand out of place. My ex-wife is standing at the window overlooking the field.

"Moira, what are you doing here?"

Moira has always been a beautiful woman, but somewhere along the line, that natural light, her inner beauty dimmed. For years, I tried to be everything she wanted. Her basic needs were always met. Every dream she had, I gave it to her. The problem was I wasn't the one she wanted to dream with. I knew our marriage wasn't conventional. We were forced together at a young age under duress. At the time, marrying her was the only way I could protect her. We were friends before our nuptials were the only answer, and I thought our friendship would grow into more with time. For a while, it seemed to, but as time passed, our love did not grow. I guess for that to happen, it would have needed to be there to begin with.

"Is that any way to greet me, Everett? What has got into you?"

I pinch the bridge of my nose and drop my head. Well, that's something. At least I know my crass responses aren't just reserved for Cameron. Apparently, they extend to Moira as well.

"It's been a long day." I head toward the desk and sit before reaching into the drawer where I stored the bottle of gin. "To what do I owe the pleasure?" I ask, gritting back the sarcasm as I search for a glass.

"I went to your office today when I heard you were home, but when I got there, Sheila said not only were you not in, but she didn't expect to see you all summer. When I walked down the hall to speak with your brother, he said I could find you here."

I find a sleeve of paper cups; not ideal for drinking gin, but they'll get the job done. Pulling a cup off the top, I raise it. "Would you like a drink?"

"No, I can't have carbs on my diet," She waves her hand dismissively.

"Gin doesn't have any carbs," I let my eyes rake down her body, one I know has zero flaws apart from her c-section scar from birthing our son, but even that doesn't count. That scar was an anchor for me in our marriage. Every time I saw it, I was reminded of the gift she gave me. I told myself she didn't have to love me. She gave me a son who did. Nothing about her figure has changed. I don't bother telling her she doesn't need to diet. She knows she doesn't, and the compliments I gave her only ended with her asking for a divorce. "You said you went to my office. You found me. What is it that you need?"

"Why do you assume I need something?"

I throw back the two fingers of gin I poured myself in one go. This is it. This must be the karma I earned myself speaking out of turn to Cameron all week.

"You don't?"

"I saw Cameron working in the team shop downstairs."

"So you came here to discuss Cameron?" I pour myself another drink.

She firmly presses her lips together, letting me know my responses are wearing on her, but her unannounced presence is doing the same for me.

"I'm making conversation, Everett. I care about Cameron, I practically raised her," she adds as she runs her fingers along the credenza opposite my desk.

"She came to live with us at seventeen. That hardly counts as raising her."

"You know what I mean, Everett." She stops in her tracks, her eyes finding mine before she adds, "We've known her since she was born."

If her eyes didn't say it, the accusation in her tone does. I'm trained to read between the lines. Cameron is still under my roof. Her father wasn't just my best friend. Damon was my business partner, and he died with a small fortune of his own, which Cameron inherited at twenty-one. She turned twenty-one a year ago. There isn't a good reason for her to still live with me. She doesn't need my money, nor does she need to live in my house, yet she's still there, and whether Moira is commenting on it indirectly or not, that means people notice. Knowing my name is circling the rumor mill is perturbing, but it's part of the territory living in a small town.

"Cameron is no longer your concern. Damon was my best friend, and you and I are no longer married." I don't bother addressing her insinuation.

"That's hardly fair—"

"Why are you here, Moira?" Cameron is the last person I care to discuss with my ex-wife. She can speculate all she wants. I don't owe her anything.

"I went to your office to discuss the fundraiser this fall—"

"You could have called or sent an email to—"

"If you'd let me finish." She leans against the credenza. "Garrett said you wouldn't be in all summer because you'd be here. We were married for over twenty years, Everett. You don't take time off work. I was worried. The man I know eats, sleeps, and breathes Callahan & Associates. I assumed you're dying or going through some type of mid-life crisis, so I wanted to drop by in person."

I take a long drink of gin. I hate that those are her first assumptions, just like they were for my brothers. I was around for my family. Do I have a work ethic? Yes, but there's nothing wrong with that. It gave her a damn good life.

When I don't immediately answer, her hand flies to her heart. "Oh my god. Are you sick?"

"What? No, I'm not sick, Moira." I'm in better shape than half of the guys on the team and almost twice their age. Before she can make any more fucked-up inferences, I say, "I'm coaching Con's team for the summer."

Her eyebrows rise in surprise, probably more so at the fact that

I'm actually doing it and not because I can't. "How did I not know this?"

"It's new and you've been out of town. Connor called me last Sunday and said he needed a favor. Of course I agreed." I don't bother telling her I agreed before understanding the full extent of his ask.

My patience is running thin, especially after her baseless accusation; passive or not, she knows what she was insinuating, and out of all the fucking people to believe a rumor or even give it breath... let's just say I'd expect more from her after everything we've been through.

"You know I tried, Everett. I never wanted to come between the two of you."

She did try, but Connor didn't handle our divorce well at all. The second he found out about it, I became enemy number one. Learning Moira's truth—our truth—helped, but the damage had already been done. I know what it's like to look up to someone and believe they hung the moon only to feel betrayed later. It fucking sucks. I hate that I made him feel that way by keeping our separation private. Moira asked me not to share it, and I respected her wishes. Had I known it would hurt our son as much as it has, I would have never agreed.

I've sacrificed a lot for the woman standing before me, and since our divorce, we've kept up appearances, maintained the charity, and still had family dinners at least once a month, until this year. She's the mother of my son. I'll always respect her, but her apology just now, if you could even call it that considering the word sorry wasn't spoken, felt empty. That, coupled with her accusatory tone since she arrived unannounced, has me changing my own.

"Moira, please get to whatever business it is that you want to discuss. I have work that I need to tend to."

"There he is," she says as if she knows me so well. I hate the condescension I hear. The mockery. It makes me look back on our marriage through a different lens. Was she always this patronizing, and that's why I busied myself? When I look at my brother Garrett's marriage, it's the definition of happy. The man can't wait to go home to his wife. Sure, I've always had a strong work ethic, but maybe I would have prioritized my time differently if I had the right woman on my arm. "I want to move the fundraiser to August," she says, reclaiming my focus.

"What? Why would we move it back to August? November makes more sense. August is back-to-school month. Donors' pockets are thin, coming off the heels of summer vacation spending without throwing in tuition costs. Plus, holding it in November gives people something to do indoors when the chance of cold, shitty weather is greater."

She pushes off the credenza and waves her hand. "Yes, I've thought of all that, but I don't think it will be the issue you believe it to be. Most of our donors have deep pockets. The details you brought up would be a moot point for them." Reaching into her Hermes bag, she pulls out her phone and scrolls. "Seventy-five percent of the funds we raise yearly come from the same thirty donors, all of whom we know are well-off and loyal to the cause."

"Yes, but it's the twenty-five percent who come and give what they can, sacrificing their last twenty-dollar bill for the name of the cause to which the event brings the most hope."

I throw back the last of the gin in my cup as I watch her process my words. Moira is smart. By the way her chest deflates, I can tell she was hoping I'd silently oblige like always. My words are most likely a reiteration of her thoughts, which I can tell is causing her some level of distress. I can't say that doesn't make me a little happy after her implied insinuations.

I expected her to give me a reason for the new date, but when her spine straightens and her eyes flash back up to mine, she says, "August fifth is the date the MacBeth fundraiser will be held this year." She puts her phone away and heads toward the door. Bracing herself on the frame, she turns back to me, words clearly on her tongue, but she says nothing and instead walks out.

Good riddance.

CHAPTER 8
CAMERON

"Thanks again for letting me stay here. How's Florida?"

"Hot, but the house we are renting for the summer is on the water, and the owners are even letting us use the boat. You need to come down and spend a weekend with us. We can lay out by the pool while Connor plays cabana boy."

"Hey, I thought the two of you were going to be so busy you didn't have time for anything else. Why is Everett here if Connor is running around down there wearing aprons and playing drink bitch?" I ask as I throw my suitcase on the bed in her guest bedroom.

"Cam, you know he's busy, but on the weekends, he's going to try to be home with me. He has other goals while we're down here, if you know what I mean."

I know exactly what she's referring to. Connor didn't want to fly home on weekends to work in Waterloo because he didn't want to miss an opportunity to put a baby in her. They've been trying since their wedding, which hasn't been too long. Mackenzie is fine with it not happening right away. Granted, I'm sure there is some level of disappointment that affects her every month when her period shows up and she doesn't get to give Connor the news he's hoping for.

"If you were trying to sell me on coming down for a weekend, you probably should have left that last part out. The last thing I want to hear is the two of you fucking while I'm in the other room becoming a born-again virgin."

"Fine, we'll schedule it for two months from now and have both you and Everett down. The two of you should be sleeping together by then, and we only have one spare bedroom."

I fall backward onto the bed. "You think coming to your place was a good idea?"

"I do—"

"Make sure Cameron uses the alarm system while she is at the house. I want it armed at all times." I hear Connor in the background.

"Did you hear that?" She asks.

"Yes, I heard. Why is he so worried about the alarm? Do you guys have something crazy valuable in the house I should be aware of?"

"As a matter of fact, we do... you."

"Haha, very funny. Well, right now, I'd be open to a home invasion with a masked man having his way with me. Forced entry —the whole nine yards. My brain won't have time to shut it down the way I have every other offer that's come around in the past year," I say as I roll over on the bed and inspect my new room for the foreseeable future. It's not the royal-blue four walls I've become accustomed to at Everett's. Mackenzie is great with interior design, but this room has yet to be touched since she moved in. It's plain and screams designed by Moira Callahan. Apparently, I'm destined to be reminded of that woman everywhere I stay. Connor grew up in this house. It was Moira and Everett's home before they gifted it to Connor for his eighteenth birthday. I bet Mackenzie hasn't decorated this room yet because she has plans to turn it into the nursery. "You swear you haven't told Connor about my crush on his father?"

"I promise, but..."

"But? You can't leave me hanging on a 'but,' not when it comes to this."

"Sorry, I had to go into the bathroom so Connor wouldn't overhear our change in subject. What I was going to say is I think he suspects something."

I sit straight up on the bed. "What did he say? I need the conversation verbatim." Connor's lack of approval could end things between me and Everett before they start.

"When I told him you wanted to stay at our place for the summer until you could find a place of your own, his exact words were, 'I guess that means she's not fucking my dad.'"

"And what did you say?" I ask as I bite my nails, a terrible habit I haven't had since I was a teenager.

"Well, initially, I didn't say anything. The comment put me in an awkward spot. It caught me off guard, and I couldn't tell if he was fishing, joking, or legitimately believed that was what had been going on. So I went with, 'Why would you say that?' and his response was, 'Cameron has been obsessed with my dad for years. He's single, and she's no longer jailbait.'"

"That's it?" Out of all the comments he could have made, that's tame. "How was his tone? Lighthearted, annoyed, relieved, indifferent..." I hear a toilet flush. "Did you really just pee with me on the phone?"

"As if you haven't been in the bathroom with me at the bar while I peed. I needed to pee, and I had to make my reasoning for coming here authentic."

I hear the faucet turn on and grow impatient. "Well..."

"I was getting there, sheesh. It was obviously said with a great deal of sarcasm, but it's also clearly something that's been on his mind, which means he's had time to sit with the idea. I don't think he loves it. Cam, I know you've already considered how a relationship between the two of you will look to those who have been in your life forever. It will be shocking, but I know my husband, and I think if he sees that his father is happy, he would be accepting of whatever that looks like."

There's a knock on the door... "Mackenzie, we're going to be late for our reservation."

"I gotta go. Text me if you need anything," Mac says right before she cuts the call.

I toss my phone across the bed. Mackenzie's opinions on my relationship fuel my hope that all of this will turn out as I've always wanted. Not only is she my best friend, but she's new to town. She and Connor were married a week after meeting each other. Mac has a unique outsider perspective on top of having a family connection. Connor is her other half. If she doesn't think he'll stand in the way, the only person who can is Everett, and I can feel him breaking.

I knew exactly what I was doing this afternoon when I said I'd move out. I said I wouldn't force his hand. That ended badly the last time; he literally booked a red-eye to Boston the same day. Hindsight is a bitch. It was a low blow that showed my age, but I wanted him to feel something. I wanted him to admit his feelings are more. I'm confident that's what this is now, or at a minimum, I'm sure that's where his short fuse is coming from. He didn't stop feeling things for me, and now he's stuck with me, not only at home but at work too. If I had to bet money on it, that's part of why he entered the team store like a bull in a china shop. His conflicted thoughts about what he should feel versus what he does feel got the best of him.

Absence makes the heart grow fonder, or at least that's what the old adage says. Sure, he's technically been gone for a few months, so if this axiom is true, our reunion shouldn't have been so toxic. However, we weren't lovers, there was no romantic relationship between us, or at least an acknowledged one, but there were entanglements, and it's those damn knots that we're struggling to untie now. I am off-limits to him. I understand that. In his mind, all that exists are reasons he and I can't be together. Which is why I'm leaving. I must show him the reasons I should be in his space are greater.

The creaky-ass screen door downstairs pulls me out of my

thoughts, and I'm immediately out of my bed. While I'd love to hope that whoever is at my new front door is Everett, I'm positive he hasn't missed me enough to show up yet.

"Who the fuck is here? No one knows I'm here yet," I grumble as I head downstairs.

I make a mental note to text Mackenzie about getting the security system's app on my phone to check the cameras instead of answering the door miles outside of town while I'm alone in a big, empty house. The only reason I'm not freaked out now is because I actually locked the front door when I came in since I had no plans of leaving for the night. When I reach the Romeo balcony that looks over the foyer, I spot a white BMW in the driveway through the transom window and immediately know who my visitor is.

"What the hell are you doing here, Evan?" I say as I open the front door.

"Hannah kicked me out."

"Wait, you threw a divorce party. How is she just now kicking you out? Hasn't that already happened?"

His left arm finds the door frame, and he leans in. "I need a place to stay."

"Then go to Everett's."

I start to close the door when he sticks out his foot. "That was my first stop, but apparently, I can no longer stay there."

I pull the door open a smidge more. "Wait, Everett wouldn't let you stay at the house?"

Evan is on my list of least favorite people. I don't feel bad that his wife cheated on him with his best friend or that she kicked him out. Hannah is Connor's high school sweetheart who cheated on Connor with Evan. The fact that he would entertain fucking Connor's girlfriend while Moira and Everett extended their home to him speaks volumes about his character, but to then believe Hannah wouldn't cheat on him too... that's just plain ignorance. Whatever the case may be, foolishness or self-importance, I'm willing to overlook those things just to hear why Everett has suddenly rescinded his hospitality.

"He pulled in behind me when I was grabbing my duffle bag out of the trunk and said, 'This isn't a hotel. You need to find somewhere else to stay.' It was obvious something, or someone, had already pissed him off..." he trails off, rubbing the back of his neck.

"Well, he's right. That crap you pulled hosting a freedom party while he was out of town was shitty, and you're almost thirty years old. You're too old to be acting like that and mooching off him. You're not poor. You have a good job, which means you can afford a hotel."

I start to close the door again when he says, "She cleared out my checking account. It's why I didn't push Everett. I need his help figuring out what my rights are, and I didn't want to further piss him off."

"One night, Evan, that's all you get. In case you forgot, this isn't my house either." My eyes hold his; it's on the tip of my tongue to add "and Connor wouldn't want you staying here either" but I don't. He knows that, and while I don't care for Evan, he's obviously having a bad day, and I'm not trying to be an asshole. So I throw the door open and add, "You can have the couch."

There are other guest rooms, but I don't need him to feel comfortable. He's the exact type who will take advantage of your kindness and bleed you dry, leaving you bitter and making you question if you were ever kind to start.

"Thanks," he says. I hear the front door close behind us, and I head to the kitchen. If Evan is staying here tonight, I will need a stiff drink.

"How did you know I was here anyway?"

"I'm still on the family location sharing," he says, following behind me. "I was going to see if you'd sneak me into the basement or pool house, and then I saw that you were here, and I knew Connor had already left for Florida. Why are you here? Did Everett give you the same speech?"

I pull open the freezer in search of the Watermelon Whiskey I know Mac keeps in there. We always have it on hand for shots. Uncorking the frosty bottle, I forgo searching for a glass and instead take a long pull straight from the source. The sweet and salty notes immediately hit my tongue, instantly settling my nerves and promising to alleviate the anxiety threatening to settle in.

"Something like that," I say with my back to him. I hear him pull up a stool to join me, but I don't acknowledge it. The last thing I need is for Evan to think we're friends or, worse, suspect anything is going on between me and Everett. "It's been a long day. I'm going to my room."

Bottle in hand, I exit the room. Evan's drama is the last thing I need to get involved in.

❧

"Is it casual Friday?" Parker asks as he enters the shop.

"Oh, you got jokes today. It's a stadium, Parker. I think I'm allowed to wear jeans."

"You can. I'm not arguing that fact one bit. However, Cameron Salt doesn't wear jeans."

Parker is right. I like to dress up, wear makeup, and look nice. It makes me feel good. Unfortunately, today is not one of those days. I couldn't sleep to save my life last night. I was so convinced I heard someone lurking around outside. I was alone living at Everett's while he was away in Boston, but I was never scared. It's probably because a big part of me knows how seriously he takes security. He may have gone radio silent and left town, but I knew the security system was always on. I knew he was watching. While Connor has a security system, I know he's not on the other end checking it with the same zeal. As soon as it was light outside, I threw my covers off and pulled out the first things I encountered in the drawers I filled with some of my clothes. Which means I am dressed down, wearing faded light-blue boyfriend jeans and a cropped white top. I didn't even grab my makeup bag before I hurried out of the house and into my car. Luckily, I at least had lip gloss and a tube of mascara in my purse.

"Did you come here for a specific reason other than to comment on my wardrobe?"

When I climb down the ladder from storing the extra inventory on the shelves above the hanging T-shirts, he's by my side.

"Cam, seriously, are you okay? You look tired."

"Ugh..." I draw out as I grab the scissors sitting on a display shelf to break down the box I just emptied. "Fine, if you insist on making this a thing. Yes, I'm tired, hungry, and overall annoyed."

He takes the box out of my hands. "Hungry and tired, I can fix, and maybe after we take care of that, you won't be annoyed." He tosses the broken-down box onto the pile in the middle of the store before adding, "Come on, I just saw the snack truck leaving, which means concessions just got food. Let's go raid it."

"Park, I'm not going out there with you. If you want to do me a solid, you can bring me some snacks."

His blue Bulldog jersey clings to his muscular chest as he turns to me, his expression bemused. "Why not? Are you still mad at me?"

We haven't really talked since the dinner we had at Connor's house before he and Mac left for Florida, and even then, there wasn't much talking. Parker knows about my crush on Everett; therefore, using him at the wedding was different. He was fully aware of what I was doing and why. The favor he asked of me is not the same. He won't tell me why he asked it, and I refuse to let him use me to hurt Everett. Walking out of this room with Parker increases my chances of Everett catching us together and drawing conclusions.

"Is that even a question?"

His blue gaze drops to the ground. "Did I kiss you?"

"What?" I question, unsure where he's going.

"At dinner with Everett watching, did I kiss you?"

"No," I answer meekly.

"Did I touch you?"

"No, you didn't touch me."

His thumb runs along his bottom lip. "So tell me why you're mad at me."

"Do you plan on doing any of those things?" His eyes return to mine, narrowing as he rolls his lips. I shrug before adding, "You know, as part of whatever revenge plan you have against Everett."

He subtly shakes his head. "Not when I know it would hurt you." Long seconds of silence stretch between us before he nods toward the door. "Want to get that snack now?"

"Yeah, I could go for a bag of blue Doritos right now."

Parker is rummaging through boxes and checking the branding to find me a bag of Doritos as I slide onto the counter and watch. Missing breakfast is catching up with me. I feel like I could curl up right here, using a box of Snickers for a pillow, and sleep peacefully until tomorrow.

"You know we probably shouldn't be stealing food. We're going to throw off the inventory counts, and you know how much that sucks."

"The concessions manager doesn't start until tomorrow, which means inventory hasn't been done yet..." He pushes another box aside and says, "Boom, blue Doritos. One bag or two? You look like you could use two."

"Okay, you've already passively told me I look like shit enough times for one day. Message received loud and clear. We can move on now."

A bag of chips lands in my lap. "I did no such thing." Then, pulling open the door on the beverage cooler, he asks, "Alani, Prime, or Iced Coffee? Nothing else is cold yet."

"Alani, please."

He slides an Alani in front of me, and I sit up and pop the tab. "So you're not going to tell me why you're so tired?"

I take a few big sips of the energy drink, still unsure if I care to share my new sleeping arrangements. "Are you going to tell me what beef you have with Everett?" I pull open the bag of Doritos as he hops up on the counter across from me with his bag of chips, drink, and power bar.

"It's nothing you need to worry about, Cam." He shrugs as he pops a chip in his mouth.

I want to pry not only because I want to know about everything that involves Everett, but also because I can tell whatever it is between them is affecting Parker, and he's my friend. I care about him. I'm convinced if he would just tell me, we could work this all out and move on. He wouldn't be perturbed, and I wouldn't be stuck in the middle, but I leave it, because while I may not have the answers, he told me he wouldn't use me to hurt Everett, knowing that it would, in turn, hurt me.

"I've been staying at Connor's all week, and last night, I would have bet my entire trust fund that someone was outside the house. I didn't sleep a wink."

"What the hell, Cam? Why are you staying at Connor's, and why didn't you call me? I would have come over."

I pop another chip in my mouth and speak around the salty morsel as it silences my hunger pains. "He has a security system. If there was someone truly out there, it would have gone off."

He jumps off the counter and runs his hands through his hair. "Cam, it could have been someone casing the place. Looking for a blind spot or way to get in. Does Connor's house have a safe room? What would you do if the alarm actually went off?"

"Okay, way to make me feel good about going home tonight. You are so not helping."

Stopping before me, he drops his hands from his head to his hips. "I'm coming over tonight. You shouldn't be alone in a house on the outskirts of town."

I'm just about to respond when Everett's voice, echoing down the tunnel beside the concession stand, steals my focus. Whatever words I hoped to eavesdrop on are lost as soon as he and a tall woman with dark brown hair enter the concourse. Their voices instantly drop to inaudible decibels.

"Who is that?" I nod toward their retreating backs.

Parker follows my line of sight. "You really have holed yourself up in that shop, haven't you? That's Lauren. She's the new Event Coordinator." I watch Everett open the door for her as they exit the stadium. Fucking great, I'm over here losing sleep, and he's already getting chummy with the new girl in town. I don't need to see her face to know she's new. A woman like her, especially in a small town, doesn't go unnoticed.

"What aren't you telling me? Why did you move out?"

"I don't have the energy for this conversation, Parker. I'm so tired. I just want to go home and sleep for, like, ten days," I pout as my already sour mood worsens.

The last thing I expected to happen when I left was to be replaced. Though I shouldn't be surprised, he clearly has a type. Tall, big breasts, long, dark brown hair; oh yeah, and someone born in the same decade.

"Fine, I'll follow you home. I'm sure Connor has something I can throw on." He looks down at his practice gear. "I need a shower."

"Park, it's fine. I'm a big girl. It was probably just raccoons, and my overactive imagination got the best of me. You know what... It could have been Evan. He stayed over Monday night after his ex-wife kicked him out and Everett refused to let him stay at his place." The Evan theory is a stretch. I only let him stay one night, and he shocked the hell out of me the next day when I came home and he was gone. I was convinced he'd still be on the couch, begging for just one more night. "Let's not forget, this is Waterloo. Nothing exciting or crazy ever happens here."

He tosses his unopened bag of Doritos back into the box. "I don't like it, Cam, and I'm surprised Everett let it happen. One more night. If you come in here tomorrow looking like shit again, I'm coming over." A text comes through on his phone, and his lips pinch. "I've got to take care of something, but if you can't sleep, or if you hear anything, call me."

~

The sound of something crashing outside stirs me awake. I lay stiff as a board, unsure if it was real or just a figment of my imagination. The second I got home, I double-checked everything, ensuring all the doors and windows were locked, re-armed the alarm, and took a hot bath before falling asleep in the middle of the bed with nothing but a towel. My body was jello, and I was too damn exhausted to move. I'm now currently internally cursing my lack of motivation. I slowly turn my head toward the window. I fell asleep in the master bedroom because that's where the big clawfoot soaker tub with my name written all over it was. I hate first-floor bedrooms. It doesn't matter if there are blackout curtains or window blinds, I always feel like there's an eyeball on the other side, finding the smallest crack to peer through and watch.

Mackenzie has full floor-to-ceiling sheer curtains, the kind that filters light, and because it's dark outside, all I see is the dim glow of moonlight. Thank fuck. If I saw a damn shadow, I'd probably have a heart attack. I lay still for seconds longer, waiting, not wanting to alert any potential serial killers lurking outside to my awakened state. Once I'm convinced that, yet again, my mind is playing tricks on me, I slowly sit up in bed and rewrap the towel around my body before searching for my phone to check the time. That's when I hear the distinct sound of a floorboard creak, and my heart starts beating in overdrive. That was a weighted creak. Connor and Mackenzie's house has a wraparound deck, and I am all too familiar with the sounds those old, weathered deck boards make. If that were an animal, the noise would have been higher pitched, shorter, and likely followed by little feet scampering.

My palms start sweating as I frantically run my hands over the bed in search of my phone only to remember I put it on the dresser right outside the master closet and bathroom door. Fuck, fuck, fuck. Now I have to risk making noise. My toes have just barely grazed the cool wood floors when the floodlight outside the window goes off. Any care I had about being discovered goes out the window as I sprint toward the dresser, grab my phone, and quickly sidestep into the master closet, gently closing the door behind me. My fingers can't unlock my screen quick enough. Parker's number is saved to my favorites and the list of people I keep close is small, so my thumb quickly connects with his name.

When the phone starts ringing, I hold it tight between my shoulder and ear as I pull one of Connor's shirts off the rack. I know I joked I was excited about being abducted by a masked man a few nights ago, but now that the reality of actually being taken is here, it's not as appealing.

"Come on, Parker. Pick up..." I quietly whine. When it goes to voicemail, I quickly pull on the shirt before shining the light around the closet. I've been in Mac's closet before, but not in the dark. I head toward the back, where I know she has dresses hanging, and tuck myself between them, weighing my next call. I don't want to call Everett. I'm determined not to be an obligation. His best friend's daughter, who he has to rescue in the middle of the night because she doesn't have any other family.

I scroll down to Elijah's name. He and I aren't close by any means, but he's Parker's brother. We see each other at family functions, and we worked the fields together. It's not an ideal choice, but neither is being chopped up into tiny pieces.

"Hello."

"Elij... wait, Parker, is that you? Why are you answering Elijah's phone? You know what? Don't answer that. I need you. I think someone is outside the house for real this time. Something woke me up, and then I heard a distinct floorboard creak, and the floodlight went off—" A call coming through steals my words. Everett is calling me. I quickly hit decline. How fast can you get here?"

"Cam, you need to answer that call."

"What? How did you know I was getting a call?"

"Don't worry about it," I can hear the annoyance in his tone.

"I'm so fucking sorry, Cam. I won't get to you in time. Answer that call."

"Parker, you said you'd come. Please, please, please, I'll let you hold my hand. Please come so it doesn't have to be him."

"It was him the second that floodlight went off, Cameron. He's already en route. Answer the call..." I hear Elijah say something in the background, and then Parker says, "I have to go."

There's no room to argue because he cuts the call.

The sound of glass breaking has me curling into a ball and pulling one of Mac's dresses off the hanger to throw over myself, hopeful whoever is breaking and entering will see a pile of clothes and not my pathetic ass. My phone vibrates in my hand, and I see Everett calling me again.

"Everett," I answer, trying hard to force calmness into my voice when all I feel is sheer terror.

"Cameron, where are you?" he demands, his voice strained with annoyance.

"You know where I'm at, Everett," I answer, determined not to be the damsel in distress that I am. Plus, he knows where I am. What the hell kind of question is that? It's that hint of annoyance that has me finding my spine. I'm half tempted to run out of the closet and take my chances with my would-be assailant.

"Cameron..." I hear a smidgeon of regret in his tone. It's been the standard between us lately. He loses his cool and then backtracks. "This isn't the time for playing games. Where are you in the house? Don't mess with me on this."

"I'm in the closet in the master bedroom."

"Good. Go to the door. To the right of it, behind the belt rack, is a keypad. I need you to enter 1010."

I can't see in here. I was too scared to turn on the light, afraid doing so would give up my hiding spot. The sound of heavy footsteps walking down the hallway on the other side of the wall has my body locked in fear. I couldn't move if I wanted to. Fucking pathetic. I want to tell him I can't, but I also don't want him to see my fear. So instead, I say nothing.

77

"Cameron, answer me. What's happening?"

"I'm waiting to see what the guy looks like before I lock the door," I answer sarcastically because, apparently, satirical utterances are my coping mechanism.

"Shit," I hear him mutter. "Don't move. Don't fucking move. Stay where you are."

I hear the click of the doorknob as the door to the master opens, and I click off the phone before whispering, "I love you." He may not hear it, but at least I said it before I met my end. The closet was the worst place to hide. If someone is here to steal, this is probably one of the first places they'd check for valuables: jewelry, safe boxes, and expensive purses. It doesn't matter that Mackenzie isn't into any of those things. They don't know that. Damn it, Cameron, all you had to do was crawl to the door and key in a code. The antique handle on the closet door subtly tinkles with what is undoubtedly the weight of a hand gripping the smoothed bronze lever. As I take my right hand and start to trace the sign of the cross over my heart. I hear the sound of sirens in the distance. The knob releases with a resounding clack as whoever is on the other side abandons their mission as the sirens grow closer.

As the telltale signs of a window opening ring out, so does the sound of the front door slamming open, followed by heavy footsteps running down the hall. It has to be Everett. I strain my ears, unmoving, convinced all of this could be a figment of my imagination. It's possible I'm still dreaming because shit like this doesn't happen here, but then the door opens, and the light flicks on. My eyes take a second to adapt to the bright intrusion, but as I reflectively blink away the dilation, my eyes connect with Everett's, and I pray this isn't a dream because I don't see annoyance or anger, which are probably warranted from the fact that I hung up the phone. Instead, I see relief and not just the reassuring kind. I see the heart-tending kind, the type that says I almost lost someone who means something to me.

But it's gone almost as quickly as it came when he says, "Let's go. You're moving back in with me. It's not up for debate. I won't accept no for an answer." He runs his hand through his dark hair, the muscle in his bicep stretching the cuff of his polo as he pulls at the long length on top. His eyes assess my pitiful position, arms wrapped around my bare legs with Mackenzie's black satin dress draped over my shoulders. The last thing I want is his pity. I didn't want him to come tonight. Damn it, I didn't dial his number.

"How did you get to me so fast?" His mouth is closed but I don't miss how his tongue runs over his teeth as he drops his head and rubs his hand over his jaw. I'm not in the mood to argue, but I want to know. He's determined to push me away, yet here he is, riding in on his horse to rescue me. "How, Everett?" I grind out, my tone a little more cross than I intended, but fuck it. I have a million emotions coursing through my body right now, and he's more than a bit deserving of my wrath, given how we've parted the past few times.

Raising his eyes to mine, he says, "You leaving me doesn't release me of you. The chains that bind my mind don't break because you say it should be so. We both know I don't dismiss my commitments, nor am I one to run. Running doesn't rid me of the obligation..." He trails off, his eyes narrowing slightly, a tell that says he's choosing his following words carefully. "The only peace to be found comes from honoring my commitments. We both know I watch you. I'm always watching you, Cameron. You coming here didn't change that."

Our eyes stay locked as I memorize his words. Words I know I will spend countless hours lying in bed thinking about later, when I'm not so rattled and he isn't towering over me stealing what limited oxygen is left in the room.

Heavy boots thud against the wood floor before a police officer breaks the silence. "Sir, is Ms. Salt in there?"

Everett holds up his hand to stop the man from entering further and seeing me in my disgraceful state of undress. "She's unharmed. We'll be out in a minute." I drop my eyes to the floor as the scene before me sinks in. I may not have been physically harmed, but my pride has definitely taken a hit. He turns to exit the closet, but not before adding. "Don't bother packing. We're leaving now. I'll send someone to collect your things tomorrow."

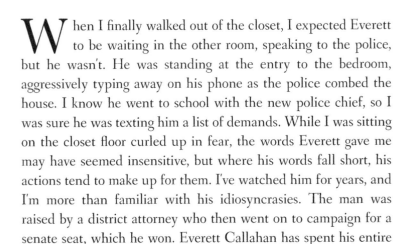

When I finally walked out of the closet, I expected Everett to be waiting in the other room, speaking to the police, but he wasn't. He was standing at the entry to the bedroom, aggressively typing away on his phone as the police combed the house. I know he went to school with the new police chief, so I was sure he was texting him a list of demands. While I was sitting on the closet floor curled up in fear, the words Everett gave me may have seemed insensitive, but where his words fall short, his actions tend to make up for them. I've watched him for years, and I'm more than familiar with his idiosyncrasies. The man was raised by a district attorney who then went on to campaign for a senate seat, which he won. Everett Callahan has spent his entire life serving, conforming, and being what people need him to be, and he's done it without complaint. It's the words he doesn't say that speak the loudest.

Seeing me, seeing that I was unharmed, wasn't enough. There was no way he was going to leave the room. Doing so meant taking his eyes off me. Standing there on his phone, I knew he was fiercely multitasking, hiring a new security company, texting the police chief and his brothers, and using every weapon in his arsenal to find the person who dared to break into his son's house. But duty aside, I saw what most wouldn't. The simple act of him standing beside the door told me he was taking something for himself. He may have used the word obligation in reference to me, a word I despise hearing from him. I want him to want to be around me for no other reason than that there's no place he'd rather be. However, obligation wasn't the only word he used. He also used the word peace. There might be a raging storm inside of him, and I might be the cause, but at the eye of every storm, there is also peace. I bring him peace.

It was that thought that I held onto as we drove home in silence once again. Everett kept his eyes forward, pinned to the road, his right hand on the wheel while his left hand occasionally ran over his bottom lip. I could tell he had words he wanted to give me, but he didn't. His choosing to say nothing felt better than any ire he may have spewed. Choosing to stay silent meant he cared. He didn't want his words to hurt me. Even though I can be a stubborn smartass, it doesn't mean I'm completely unaffected by shit. It means I'm strong and not easily swayed. I've always been boldly independent, even before my parents' accident. Losing them only made that more true, but it doesn't mean I'm not human. It doesn't mean I don't feel. I stayed just as quiet as Everett, maybe even more so because I don't think I moved an inch.

The events of the night shook me, and that's why I can't sleep now. The nap I had before the break-in doesn't help, but even knowing Everett is in the same house as me isn't settling my nerves. Throwing off the blankets, I head downstairs in search of comfort food. Popcorn and a chick flick might do the trick. Before I reach the kitchen, the light from Everett's office catches my eye. He's awake too. I contemplate walking down the hall to apologize, but I don't.

I've just finished popping my bowl of popcorn and pouring a glass of bourbon on the rocks with a brown sugar and sea salt rim. I'm not a huge fan of drinking by myself, but the alcohol serves two purposes at midnight: calming my nerves and helping me get some sleep before the morning. The second my ass hits the couch, and I look around the dimly lit space, I know settling down isn't going to be easy. I'm going to overanalyze every shadow and every creak. Standing, I decide to push aside my pride and walk to his office, but when I do, he's there, in the kitchen, with his back to me, staring blankly into the fridge.

I'm silent as my eyes linger on his dressed-down appearance. It's new. My entire life, he's been a suit-and-tie guy, immaculate— not a wrinkle to be seen or a single hair out of place. But since he's been home and helping out with the baseball team, his style has adapted. He's traded his tailored suits for Bermuda shorts and athletic polo shirts. It doesn't matter what he wears, he looks good in everything. But tonight's attire might be my all-time favorite: gray sweatpants and an all-white tee that stretches across his toned back in all the right places.

Turning with a bottle of sparkling water, his eyes collide with mine, and I suddenly feel naked. Sure, I've run around this house and flaunted my ass and tits in string bikinis for more summers than I can count, but something about the intensity in his stare now has me feeling vulnerable. I don't know what I see because I've never seen it, but I also can't look away. I can't find any words even though that's exactly what I was about to give him... words.

"Can't sleep?"

"No," I answer as I pull my satin robe around my camisole and sleep short set, a move that doesn't go unnoticed by him. We both had an intense night, and I know while his exterior says cool and collected, inside, like me, he's anything but. If I had it my way, he'd be storming across the room right now, sweeping me up in his arms and taking me to bed where we could work out our stress.

"I—" we both say simultaneously.

"Go ahead." I insist that he speaks first.

"No, that's not how it works. What were you about to say?"

"Before you came in here, I was about to ask if you wouldn't mind working in here tonight." I shrug and fidget with the lace of my satin robe. "I don't really want to be alone right now. I promise I won't bother you. I've already made popcorn and a drink, and I was—"

He holds up his hand. "I'll grab my laptop. I think it's time we discuss that letter."

CHAPTER 9
EVERETT

I didn't say yes because she asked me to sit with her. I said yes because there was nowhere fucking else I wanted to be. The second we got home, I had every notification set on my phone to alert me of any and all movement, both inside and out. Usually, I only have the outside notifications turned on, but tonight, I wasn't taking any chances. Whoever broke into Connor's house knew exactly where the cameras were located. They'd clearly been casing the place, and at this point, it's unclear if they had done so with the knowledge he was out of town, or if whoever entered the house did so knowing Cameron was inside because she was the target and not things. It's that last thought that has me breaking my silence. I've held my tongue long enough, but it's time to compare notes. Damon Salt had secrets, ones he tried to protect his daughter from, and just because he died doesn't mean they died too. We both received letters from him after his death.

"Cameron," I say her name to grab her attention, ensuring I have it before saying anything more. She's on her second glass of bourbon and her eyes have been glued to whatever fluffy romance movie she's been watching for the past hour. I don't know how channels like this stay in business. The love they propagate isn't real, yet they make millions selling false realities year after year.

Her eyes find mine, and my stomach tightens. The truth is I've spent the past three hours we've been home staring at my computer, unable to work because of the hell I've been living in at the thought of her getting hurt or, worse, losing her. "I think it's time we talked about the night of your twenty-first birthday." Her eyebrows raise slightly, and I instantly realize the error in my wording. I clear my throat, closing my laptop, "Let me clarify. I'm referring to the letter I left you. The one from your father."

"Oh," she says, eyeing her now empty glass. "If you want to talk about Dad, I need a refill." Pushing the soft throw blanket off, she rises, putting her long, toned legs on display, legs I shouldn't be looking at, let alone thinking about, but I am all the same. So when she asks, "Would you like a refill?"

My answer is easy. "Yes, make mine a double, please."

From where I'm positioned on the couch, my back is toward the kitchen, which is a good thing. As much as I don't want to take my eyes off her, I need to. I need to get a grip on myself. She might be an acceptable age, but what about everything else? Duty, honor, respect, loyalty to my best fucking friend. He might be six feet underground, but that doesn't change the fact that he entrusted me with his most prized possession.

She's back in what feels like seconds with our drinks, not spending nearly enough time making them for me to clear my mind of the reckless thoughts I can't seem to escape. When she hands me my drink, her perky satin-covered breasts are practically spilling out of her camisole, causing me to cross my legs. The last thing I need is for her to know she affects me. She's been teasing me for years, and it's getting harder and harder to ignore. Collecting her discarded blanket, she takes a seat, but it's no longer on the couch opposite me. No, now she's sitting on the far side of the same one I'm on. The move is innocent enough—she even covers her bare legs—but it's the proximity in general that's becoming unbearable. It should calm my nerves, seeing her, smelling her, having her close, but instead, the combination feeds my insanity.

"What exactly do you want to talk about? I know the envelope was sealed when you gave it to me, but I assumed it wasn't in its original packaging."

She knows me well. That damn envelope was the bane of my existence when it showed up the day she turned twenty-one. I contemplated opening it and repackaging it just as she's assuming now. After all, she didn't know the letter existed, and neither did I until it arrived. However, I ultimately decided against it. I had already received my own letter from Damon the week following his death. Aside from a father writing his daughter well wishes for a milestone life event, I didn't believe there was anything in hers of importance. But with the events that have happened recently and her twenty-second birthday coming up, I'm not convinced her letter was only regrets, hearts, and words of affirmation.

I could ask her to tell me what the letter said, but I'm not sure she'd give it to me verbatim, and I don't want to ask her something and inadvertently share information she's not yet privy to, but I've suspected for some time that, maybe even before the accident, she's known Kelce isn't her brother full or otherwise. Leaning into that will help me gauge my next question.

"Did Damon mention Kelce in his letter to you?"

Her chest visibly inflates before she takes a long drink of bourbon. That reaction tells me she knows something.

"I know he's only my half brother," she answers flatly. "But you already knew that." She raises a brow, daring me to tell her she's wrong. "So how about you stop dancing around what you really want to ask me and get on with it?"

Fucking hell. Now I'm the one taking a drink to keep my hands to myself when all I really want to do is punish her for her smart mouth.

"Fine," I finally say with a renewed vehemence as the fresh cognac heats my veins. "Kelce isn't your father's son. Which means he's not part of your father's will—"

"That's not true. He was left money in a trust fund, same as me. You were there when the lawyers read the will."

"You're not wrong that he was left money in a trust fund. However, the difference between yours and his is that his is revocable. Yours is not."

"Revocable?" she questions. "You mean like he has to meet certain criteria to keep his inheritance. I've heard of trust fund babies who lose their right to their inheritance because they went against the terms of their fund."

She's done her homework. I'm not sure why I expected anything less. Cameron Salt has always been intelligent. Her mind has always been a weakness of mine. Looks are one thing, but add a brain to that package... You'd be surprised how hard of a combo that is to find.

"Yes, that's one way a trust can be revocable. The other is that the grantor put an expiration date on it." I'm confident the only reason Kelce was ever on it to begin with, was most likely because Amelia had been present when the trust was set up, meaning there was no way Damon could cut him out completely. So he snuck verbiage into the document that ensured his assets would go to his blood and his blood alone.

"Okay..." She brings her legs up, resting her glass atop her knees. "When is his part of the trust set to expire?"

I take another drink. It's unusual for me to have conversations where I'm not certain of the outcome. However, tonight changed things. I may not be certain that Kelce was behind tonight's break-in, but I need her to take the break-in seriously. She needs to understand there is a potential threat to her and that tonight may not have been a robbery gone wrong.

"His trust dissolves the day you turn twenty-two."

It's another reason I wasn't in a hurry to push Cameron out all these years. In the letter I received upon Damon's death, I learned the truth about Kelce, and he also told me about the trust and how Kelce's last disbursement would be the year Cameron turned twenty-one. That was when her trust reached full maturity. She gained access to funds at eighteen, but assets such as property and her shares in Callahan & Associates were delayed until twenty-one. Cameron got everything, and I've been waiting for the fallout, for the day Kelce would come knocking when his paycheck didn't show up in his bank account like it has for the past four years.

Her eyes widen before she says, "Wait, do you think Kelce would come after me for money? Is that what you're getting at right now? Do you think it was him tonight?"

This is why I wanted to avoid leading the conversation in this direction. I don't have answers yet. "It's a possibility. One that has yet to be ruled out." I don't bother telling her how great the probability is, considering we don't know where he is, but she doesn't need to know that. I have no plans of letting her out of my sight anytime soon.

"I know Kelce and I were never really close. He was eight years old when I was born, but he wasn't mean either. Plus, like me, he's been getting money since the accident. I don't believe he would be behind this just for money."

I take a drink of my cognac. "You'd be surprised how people who have always had money never prepare for the day they won't."

"Everett, you wanted to talk, so stop talking in circles. If you know that Kelce blew through his trust fund already, then just say that. I'm not twelve. I won't get upset, and I'm old enough to comprehend and deduce probable outcomes."

My eyes hold hers for a beat. I know she's more than capable of understanding. I know that if I told her Kelce was broke, she'd be fine. That's not the part I'm concerned about. The part that's currently eating away at my sanity is where he is and what he knows. I don't want her finding out truths from an estranged sibling with a chip on his shoulder. Cameron has thick skin; she learned from a young age not to sweat the small stuff, especially the things we can't control. But I also know that behind her tough exterior is a tender heart. She feels things deeply, and if anyone is going to share truths about the past, it will be me. Just not yet. I don't have all the details, and she deserves every last one.

"Kelce is broke."

I don't elaborate any more than that. Of course I've been keeping tabs on him. The second I found out about the accident, I was watching him, but it was a week later, when I received Damon's letter, that I started watching for entirely different reasons. Kelce is his mother's son. Cameron and Kelce's trust funds were set up to pay lump sums to them at the start of each calendar year. He would blow through his within five months, year after year. Last year was his last payout, and when he didn't get one this year, I expected a visit or a call, but so far, nothing—aside from the fact that, at the moment, he's currently MIA.

She trills her lips and runs her fingers through her long auburn hair. "Maybe I can loan—"

"No," I cut her off, my tone firm, leaving zero room for argument. "Do you have more than enough money to help him? Yes, but that doesn't mean you should. Sometimes, the best way to help someone is by giving them nothing at all." She's quiet as she thinks over my words. It's in our DNA to help our family and those we care about. We want to make things better. I'm all too familiar with sacrificing to help others, and I refuse to let Cameron walk the same path I chose. I know she agrees, but I change the subject before she can give it any more thought. "Besides Kelce, what else did your father's note mention?"

"I don't want to talk about my father's note anymore tonight," she says with the tiniest amount of annoyance as she turns away from me and faces the TV. I watch as she sets her glass on the side table and picks up the remote, readying herself to finish the movie and ending our conversation, which doesn't work for me.

"Cameron, this is important. I need to know if your father—"

"You already know what my father had to say. You knew about Kelce, so I'm sure you know the rest too."

"I need to hear the words, Cameron." I try to maintain my calm. I can't be sure where her petulance is suddenly coming from. Obviously, talking about her father isn't easy, but this seems like more.

"I don't know why you insist on making me your jailor. It's like you want more reasons to hate me."

"What the hell are you talking about? I don't hate you."

"Could have fooled me..." she mumbles under her breath before reclaiming her bourbon.

My jaw clenches hard. I loathe that I've given her any reason to believe that I don't care deeply, but if she thinks I hate her, that might be for the better. I take another drink to curb my need to say things I can't take back and instead say, "What did he say?"

She shakes her head before dropping it and staring into her glass. "He said he was sorry that he couldn't be the man I believed him to be: good, decent, the man who hung the moon and all the stars in the sky. He talked about how he wished he could say he was a good person who made a bad choice because he knew that's how I would justify his skeletons." So far, she's not saying anything I didn't expect, aside from the part where he didn't believe himself to be a good person. I would have reasoned that comment the same way Cameron would. Good people fuck up daily. That's life, but his use of the word skeletons gives me trepidation. She pulls in a stuttered breath before adding, "And he said to trust you. You might be stony and all business, but you have the heart he never had. He said you'll keep me safe." When I don't say anything because my mind is still stuck on the fact that he entrusted the care of his daughter to me as if that were a great idea, her eyes find mine. "Are we done now?"

I divert my gaze and nod before finishing my cognac in one go. Those words sound like trouble. They make it sound like she's mine. I don't say anything; I can't. Anything that came out would be lies, and out of all the people in my life, she's the one person who can read all of them. The one person who has always seen me and the one person I can't have. I pick up my laptop and flip open the screen to pick up where I left off, mindlessly staring into oblivion.

CHAPTER 10

CAMERON

When I wake, it's still dark, and I can't be certain I'm not dreaming because there is no way this is reality. I put down three glasses of bourbon before finally passing out in front of the TV. It's why I can't really be sure that I'm actually wrapped in Everett's arms, cradled like I'm something precious, but the warmth from his front pressed against my back, and his hand resting atop the one I have curled into my chest tells me it's very real. I am indeed awake. I just woke to a reality I've finally dreamed into existence, one I never want to leave, but I have to. The need to pee is killing me. Damn it. Maybe I can slip out unnoticed, return to this spot, and consciously relish this monumental moment.

I've only moved an inch when he says, "Don't," his hand gently tightening around mine.

My heart instantly starts galloping. Everett Callahan is holding me tighter and asking me not to move. Fucking bladder. "I need to use the restroom..." I wiggle ever so intentionally to press my ass further into his groin. "I'll come right back."

I hear him pull in a long, deep, steady breath, my move no doubt affecting him. "You don't understand. You can't come back to this moment."

"But I'm here now. Why not?"

His thumb gently glides over the back of my hand. "Because this can't happen. When you get up, that's it, Cameron. Do you understand?"

I want to scream. I want to cry and say no, I don't fucking understand, but I choke it down because, while I'm upset, this is more than we've ever shared. I said I wouldn't push him, but I've dreamt of this moment for too long, and I refuse to just let it slip away, especially when he's acknowledging its existence.

"It's only me and you here, Everett. Whatever we want to happen can happen." I press into him again and attempt to move my arms so that I can touch him back.

"Cameron..." his voice is strained as his arms tighten around me more, holding me still before his nose nuzzles into my hair. My entire body sizzles, and I'm certain I'm on the verge of spontaneous combustion. Then he releases me. "Go."

The weight of his rejection hurts, and the loss of his hold is felt immediately, but it was never going to be this moment anyway. I know that as I sit up. I don't look back; I can't. Chances are he wouldn't look me in the eye anyway, not now and not when I ask, "You said we can't happen. Does that mean you don't want it to?"

"Answering that question solves nothing because it changes nothing. Go to bed, Cameron."

That's where he's wrong. If you don't ask a question, the answer will always be no. I asked the question... he didn't say no.

"You cook breakfast now?" Everett asks, startling me as I return the egg carton to the refrigerator. I turn around and find him drenched in sweat, wearing running shorts and a muscle tank. My mouth goes dry, and my head swims with the memories of how his hard chest felt pressed against my back in the middle of the night. He finishes his water and gives me a look that says he knows exactly where my head has gone. "Cam—"

"I need to eat, and last I checked, you don't have a live-in chef." I cut him off before he can make excuses or apologize for what happened. I don't want him to downplay a memory I'll never forget. I pick up the spatula and return to the scrambled eggs I was whipping up. "Plus, it keeps my mind busy." It's no secret I bake when I'm upset, but I've been experimenting and teaching myself to cook. Scrambled eggs aren't complicated. You just have to cook them slowly and add a little salt and pepper to taste. "There's plenty if you'd like to join me."

"Do I have time to shower, or are they ready now?"

His comment catches me by surprise. I offered to be nice, not because I thought he'd join me. He rarely eats a meal in the kitchen. The main reason Sunday dinners became a thing was because Everett would make time to sit and eat a meal with the family. I think that's why they stuck even after Connor moved out. It was guaranteed time spent with his father.

"Yeah, you have time," I answer with my back to him for fear that eye contact might pop whatever bubble we're in. After what happened last night, I assumed he'd keep his distance. He does it when he steps over boundaries he's insisted on setting. The fact that he isn't now says something, the task now is figuring out what.

~

"Tell me about the shop."

"What exactly do you want to know?" I ask as I pour my orange juice.

"Everything. What you designed, your plans for more, all of it. I'm certain you've been writing down ideas in your journal to throw at Connor the next time you get him on the phone."

"I designed almost everything. I changed the shade of blue from sapphire to cobalt, updated the lines on the logo so that they are double stitched and thicker, making them stand out more on the apparel, and I designed all the fan gear. The hats, hoodies, tee shirts, that's all me," I say proudly. I never saw myself designing sportswear when I decided I wanted to pursue a career in fashion, but because I'm doing it for Connor's team, a small part of me feels like I'm doing it for Everett too.

"And this will help your resumè? I know it's experience, but is it the right kind?"

"Does it bother you that much that I'm working there?"

He shakes his head. "That's not where I was going. I'm just trying to understand. Fashion is not my wheelhouse, but I don't need a degree in it to understand the importance of internships. I could pull strings and get you internships with fashion houses on the East Coast."

My stomach twists as my mind hears something else. He wants to get me internships on the East Coast because he wants me gone.

"You said the end of the school year, right?" He furrows his brow. "I get to live here through the end of the year?"

He pinches the bridge of his nose. "Cameron, stop trying to twist my words."

"But—"

"Don't try to tell me otherwise. I'm not trying to make you leave. I'm simply trying to understand your goals. I have yet to truly ask you what they are. This is me asking. This is me trying to help."

He's not wrong. I'm choosing to hear the negative, to hear him pushing me away instead of pulling me close because that's all he's ever done. I've never been anything more to him, and the idea that maybe that's changing doesn't feel real.

"Does designing baseball uniforms and team gear get me anywhere with fashion houses? Doubtful. But we all have to start somewhere, and what I'm doing for the Bulldogs... designing a brand is a lot more than most of my peers who are fetching coffees and pushing pencils."

His eyes are on me when I look up, and I can tell he's thinking. "Why do you have to work for a fashion house?"

"I'm not sure I'm following," I say before I take a bite of my eggs.

"Why can't you start your own business? Take Mackenzie, for example. She didn't finish school. She started her interior design business by becoming an influencer and posting before and after pictures of gigs she was getting. Now, almost two years later, she's landed one of the biggest jobs of her career. The private villas she's designing for Montage Resorts will put her on the map. It's going to open every door she could ever want."

I stare out the back window as I think about his words. I never considered doing it on my own. I always assumed I was going into a career where I needed to put in my time and earn my stripes like everyone else trying to become a designer. Plus, Mackenzie didn't just post a couple before and after pictures.

"What are you thinking?"

"That Connor built Mackenzie a house and let her design it from top to bottom, and she vlogged about it daily." While they live in Everett's old house, Connor built her mother and brother a home on their property so she could have her family close.

"Okay, so start vlogging your experience at the field. Uniforms arrive this week. Do some live unboxings or—"

I can't help but chuckle, and he raises a brow at my burst of emotion. "I'm surprised you know what a live unboxing is, that's all."

"I'm a lawyer. I'm very familiar with social media. Almost every case that comes across my desk deals with it in some form. Every post and comment someone shares online can be used as court evidence. I've done my fair share of scrolling."

"That makes sense. I'll have to think about it. I haven't considered doing something on my own. I'm not sure if showing the baseball stuff would be on brand, and if I go boutique, I need to find models—"

"You don't need models. If you do this, you are the brand. You're the model, your designs. Trust me, people will buy them."

His eyes drop to his plate the second he feels his words cross a line, but I don't want to lose the momentum I feel is being gained. So I change the subject. "You don't like the eggs?"

His eyes float back to mine. "I didn't say that."

"You didn't have to. You're pushing them around the plate."

He rolls his lips and taps his fork. "They were ready before I got in the shower, weren't they?"

"No... they were almost ready." It's the truth, they weren't completely done. I take another bite and slide him the ketchup bottle. "If you dip them in ketchup, you don't know they're a little dry." He looks slightly mortified by my suggestion. I point my fork at him. "Don't tell me you've never dipped your eggs in ketchup."

He gets up from his seat and crosses the room. Opening the fridge, he pulls out a jar of picante. "I'm not eight. I prefer my tomato sauce spicy."

I scoff, "Adults eat ketchup on eggs all the time. It's practically un-American not to."

He pours the picante over his eggs, ignoring my comment. Right before I'm about to defend my stance and get up and shove a ketchup-covered egg in his mouth, he says, "I could teach you how to cook."

I nearly choke on my dry eggs and reach for my glass of orange juice as he takes a bite of his eggs, now doused in salsa.

"Sorry," I hit my chest. "Went down the wrong pipe."

"No it didn't. Don't patronize me. If you don't want me to teach you, all you have to say is no thank you."

"It's not that. Everett, I've lived in this house for almost five years. I've never seen you cook."

His brow slightly furrows, and I can tell I struck a nerve, though I'm unsure why.

"You've seen me grill plenty of times. In fact, you witnessed that before Connor left for Florida."

"Grilling and cooking are not the same."

"I would disagree. Grilling and stovetop cooking both accomplish the same thing. They heat the food. One is just done over an open flame."

He has a point. I'm not against him teaching me how to cook. Cooking with him equals spending more time with him, and that's something I crave. So I stop teasing him and move on to my next undisputable point. "Okay, fine. Let's say you do cook. When exactly do you expect to have time to teach me?" Cooking abilities aside, we both know time is something he has never had.

Wiping his mouth, he lays his napkin down on the plate, and his deep ebony eyes, framed with thick dark lashes that women would kill for, find mine. "I'll make time."

CHAPTER II
EVERETT

I've been poolside alone for almost three hours, which is something I didn't expect. I came out here because I couldn't stand being inside. It didn't matter where I went in the house; if I didn't see her, I smelled her, and when I wasn't smelling her, I could hear her, and fuck if all three weren't a lethal combination. Coming outside offered me a small reprieve. As it turns out, I don't like her here, but I hate her gone. When she decided to stay at Connor's, it practically killed me.

Before she left, I thought her absence would be the answer, but it was only wishful thinking on my part. I was gone for months. If time and distance didn't manage to cure my sick heart from wanting what it can't have then, I'm not sure why I thought her living a few miles away would. But that's what we do when we're infected. We frantically try to search for a cure to heal us of our affliction. The problem is, I know there is no cure. She is poison in my veins... but fuck if it isn't everything. Life is hard, we are all cursed, and nothing worth having ever comes easy unless it has a hefty price tag, one that usually costs you a pound of flesh and your soul. But I'm starting to understand why people make deals with the devil. A pound of flesh and an empty soul seem like a fair trade to feel alive.

The back door opening draws my eyes to her, and I'm half surprised she's not prancing out here in one of her thong bikinis to taunt me. After we ate breakfast together yesterday, I worked in my office and she went to her room, where she has been ever since, only leaving to grab snacks.

Marching up to my lounger, she sits on the end and says, "I'm hungry."

"Is there a reason you bypassed the kitchen to come out here and share that with me?"

She rolls her eyes, and my finger involuntarily twitches on the keyboard of my laptop.

"Um, yeah, it's almost dinner time, and yesterday you said you would teach me how to cook. Why not now?"

The wind picks up, and I instantly smell roses. The smell I've been running from all day. My mouth ran away with my good sense yesterday when I offered to teach her how to cook. The last thing I need to do is offer to share more space and time with her when I know she's my kryptonite.

"I have a few more emails I need to send out. Tomorrow is a big day at the stadium. All the managers will be on-site to start training crew members. If you're really hungry, maybe order us some takeout."

"I can wait," she says with a shrug before standing and unsnapping the buttons that run down the center of her denim dress, unveiling her white thong bikini. "I could use a little vitamin D after being in the house all weekend." Then, walking around to the other side of my lounger, she flips open the top on the storage table next to me, pulls out a bottle of sunscreen, and sits down on my chair before asking. "Can you put some of this on my shoulders? I don't want to burn before I get a base tan."

"Cameron, I am not rubbing lotion on you."

"Why not?" she says, pulling her hair over to one side and exposing her bare shoulders to me.

Answering that question is an admission I don't want to give. She already holds enough power without knowing how deeply she affects me. Considering her request is a misstep and poor judgment on my part, but taking the bottle out of her hand is definitely a bad decision. Closing my laptop, I set it on the table beside me before wordlessly flipping open the cap. When my palms meet her shoulders, I hear her pull in a sharp intake of breath.

"Sorry, I didn't think it was cold."

When she shakes her head, I know the words she doesn't say: "It's not the sunscreen." I can see the goosebumps running down her arms. It's eighty degrees outside. She's not cold. I couldn't tell you the last time I applied sunscreen. Hell, I'm not sure I ever have, at least not to another person. I overestimated the amount I would need. My hands effortlessly glide over her soft skin, quickly coating her shoulders. The last thing I want to do is pull away when my hands feel like they were made for touching her. I take liberties and allow my hands to drift further down her spine. After all, I'm nothing if not thorough. Her shoulders aren't the only part of her that could burn. When I reach the string that wraps around her back, I dip my fingers beneath and run them along its length. There's a slight tremble in my hand as I find the strength to abandon the string when all I really want to do is pull it. However, the farther I let my hands drift down her back, the more pulling that string might have been the better option.

My eyes can't help but follow the descent of my hands, and the lower they drop, the more I see of her. The ass she dares to tease me with every chance she gets is on display, looking like a fucking Christmas present with the white string running between her thick cheeks. My cock twitches, now completely hard, as my hands dig into her hips, and she hisses, a sound that should trigger my release, but my hands don't move. If anything, they squeeze harder. Her head turns, and those crystal blue eyes connect with mine, and what feels like a lifetime of unspoken desires are shared. I want nothing more than to pull her into my lap and feel her. I want to touch her in a way I shouldn't, and what's worse, the look in her eyes tells me she wants the exact same thing.

Those pouty pink lips part, and my name is unexpectedly said in unison. "Everett."

Our eyes snap toward the intruding voice as I pull my hands away quickly, searching for my laptop to cover the shameful issue I now have. Fucking hell, I knew I shouldn't have disarmed the alarm for the cleaning lady. As Colton crosses the yard to join us, I ask, "Do you mind giving us some privacy?"

Cameron's back is to me when she nods her agreement. I pull my sunglasses back down over my eyes as she reaches for her discarded dress, but even the tint can't hide the flush on her cheeks. I might be hard, but I guarantee her pussy is wet. A pussy I have no business wanting but it makes my cock grow harder all the same, and when she stands, putting her peach of an ass inches away from my face, I bite down on the inside of my cheek. Christ.

"Did you get my text?" Colton asks, walking up to my lounge chair with his hands on his hips.

Cameron's exit buys me a few seconds when she says, "Hi, Cole," in greeting, allowing me to quickly bring my laptop to life and pull up my messages. If he texted me, it must have been in the last few minutes while my hands were wrapped up in her.

"Salt." He pulls her in for a quick hug. "Are you still seeing Michaelson, or have you already found your next victim?"

"Haha, hilarious Cole. You're one to talk, Mr. Stag—or—die. Maybe I'm destined to be an eternal bachelor like you." She swats his chest before taking her leave.

He crosses his arms and purses his lips. He knows she's right. The man is in his thirties and has never been seen with the same girl more than twice. Like me, he's a workaholic, but deep down, I know there's more to his single status than he lets on. We are too alike for there not to be, both driven by honor and pride, both loyal to a fault. I may not have always made the choices I wanted, but at least they gave me a son. Out of all my regrets, things I wish I would have done differently, he has never been one of them.

Colton's eyes flash to mine as his thumb dusts his bottom lip. "Are you fucking, Salt?"

"I'm not even going to dignify that with a response," I say as I clench my jaw in annoyance. I shouldn't have fucking touched her. If I hadn't touched her, I wouldn't be receiving his plaint now.

He takes a seat on the lounge next to mine. "Are we going to act like I didn't just witness you rubbing sunscreen all over her back? We both know that's not innocent, Everett. Not to mention the swimsuit she's wearing may as well be underwear."

"Why are you here, Colton? Did you find Kelce?"

"Maybe," he answers, unconcerned, like his visit is just another day when we both know it's not. Colton lives in Boston. He doesn't just casually drop by, and the last message I sent him was, "Find Kelce." Tongue in cheek, he says, "Your avoidance reeks of guilt."

"I would disagree. I've known Cameron her entire life, and I refuse to give legs to a rumor like that. In jest or not, that type of gossip is toxic and only serves to disrespect a member of this family."

"Dear brother, Cameron Salt is not our family—that is," He rubs his jaw, "Unless you are planning to make it so." I'm out of my chair before my mind can think better of it, and if he wasn't certain before, I know he is now. Standing toe to toe, he says, "You just gave yourself away. Quick to anger and extremely anxious."

"We're not fucking," I grit out as I try to calm the rage boiling inside of me. I don't want anyone to think differently of her because of me, and it's already happening. She doesn't deserve that dark cloud.

"Fine. You're not fucking..." He licks his bottom lip. "But you want to." I drop my head and put my hands on my hips to rein in my anger. I don't care to come to blows over this with my brother. What's fucked up is I shouldn't care this much. This entire altercation shouldn't even be happening. "Look, Everett, I didn't come here to judge where you get your dick wet. You're both adults. If Salt were walking around my house looking like that, I'd be doing more than rubbing sunscreen on her back."

Those words do nothing to calm my nerves. The thought of

him touching her only makes everything worse because, if he were to touch her, it would be better than me. Colton is fifteen years younger than me. He was a surprise to everyone after our parents thought they were done having kids. He and Cameron could make sense. And age aside, she's not his best friend's daughter or the kid who moved into his house at seventeen.

"Fucking drop it, Cole. What did you find out?"

He holds up his hands. "Consider it dropped, but in all seriousness, if you were sleeping with her, you might already have the answer to that question. Your girl knows exactly where her brother is—"

"She's not my girl, and he's not her brother," I interrupt.

"Yeah, yeah," he waves his hand. "Cameron's been keeping tabs on him, the same as you. The only difference is that when she found out he was broke, she took a visit to see him."

"When?" I ask, taken aback by his claim. I always keep tabs on her so I would know if she left.

"While you were in Boston. She took a quick day trip to visit him in Maine."

"He's in Maine?" I look toward the house just in time to catch one of the basement sheers move. She knew. The entire conversation, she knew and she lied to me.

"He's been living there for about six months, working as a crab fisherman, and that's why we couldn't find him. He was on a boat."

"You're telling me Kelce, spawn of Amelia Balian, is working a laborer's job as a fisherman?"

"Yep, he's been living with his bio dad's brother. Even though it's not Kelce, I wouldn't let her leave. We know Damon had skeletons. This could all be an ill-timed break-in, or it could be something else. I have a few theories. I was going to head over to Connor's now and see if I can't scratch one off my list."

"I want your theories, but first, I need to see a girl about a lie. Don't leave town before we talk."

~

"You lied to me. Why would you lie to me?" I demand, closing the back door harder than intended.

"I didn't lie to you. You heard what you wanted to hear," she answers from behind the bar as she pours a glass of vodka and seltzer water with lime.

"I asked you what your father said in his letter, and I specifically asked you about Kelce."

"You're right. You asked me what the letter said, and I told you. You didn't ask me what I did with that information after I read the letter. Because you still think of me as a child, you treat me with kid gloves. If you continue to think of me like an orphaned teen, you'll come up short every time. It happened, it hurt, but it isn't who I am."

I stalk over to the bar, half tempted to smack her ass for lying to me, only to think better of it once I'm right in front of her. She'd like it too much, and doing so would only hurt me. I have to stop taking liberties. Every time I do, the line between right and wrong moves, and I find myself drowning in my regrets, torn between what I have and what I want.

Instead, I take her drink. "If you want me to see you as an adult, stop acting like a child." I take a heady sip before adding, "You should have told me about Kelce. Your safety is paramount."

She snatches her glass back, drawing my attention to her mouth as she takes a long, slow drink. "I didn't think I needed to tell you things you already knew." Sliding the glass toward me, she crosses her arms. "My father was a good man. Whether he died believing it to be true or not, doesn't change that. Besides, Kelce was never the person anyone needed to fear. That person sank to the bottom of the Mississippi with him."

I slam my eyes closed as I try to push out the memories of the night I lost my best friend. I don't need any reminders to pull me away from the now. That night and all the what-ifs surrounding it have haunted my every dream since that fateful accident.

"What does that mean, Cameron?"

"It's no secret my parents had a loveless marriage, and I think

Kelce was one of the reasons for it. When I went to Maine to visit him, I never met with him. Don't get me wrong, I planned on it, but when I pulled up to the fishery, I found him working, and something stilled my hand. I didn't get out of the car. Instead, I sat and watched, and as I did, I reflected on our life together. I went there with a lot of assumptions. They were easy enough to make over the years, the sense of entitlement he seemed to wear like a badge of honor, the money he'd blow through, his arrogance. He painted a picture that would easily lead you to believe him to be a suspect in the break-in, but as I sat there with my own pain, I realized something. I was judging his. Who am I to judge pain I haven't experienced?"

"You both lost parents in the accident. You have the same pain."

She pulls in a frustrated breath like I should know what she's getting at. I think I do, but assuming things with her is off the table. "When I tracked Kelce down to Maine and the address he was staying at, I Googled the homeowner. It was a name I'd never heard of. I knew it wasn't any family of mine, but it was obvious Kelce was family. The genetics on that side are strong. The guy he was living with could have been a dead ringer for his father, and that's when it hit me. Kelce knew. I can't be sure when he found out, but he knew Damon wasn't his father, and I think he acted out because of it." Picking up the drink, she shoved at me, she downs the glass. "Everyone knows there was no love lost between our parents. Kelce and I weren't immune to that fact just because we grew up witnessing it. I think Kelce figured out the truth somewhere along the line and resented both of them for it."

Standing here listening to the amount of thought she's clearly put into this, my anger wanes, but my curiosity doesn't. "You put all that together just by watching him? Damon left nothing in his letter that would lean into those conclusions?"

Her eyes narrow on mine. "Are my thoughts really that farfetched? I thought you, out of all people, would relate to living a lie, being what other people wanted you to be instead of who you want to be. Who you are." I rub the space between my eyes. She sees so much of me. I wish she would see that I keep things close to my heart to protect hers. "Just forget it, Everett. I'm done talking. When you are ready to have a real conversation, you know, one where you exchange ideas, thoughts, and feelings without shrewdness... you know where to find me."

She quickly turns on her heel to leave, and my hand hurriedly grasps the loop on the back of her denim dress. "That is precisely what I am trying to do." I spin her around, and her mouth pops open in shock. "You want real? Fine. Your father's death hasn't been easy on me either, Cameron. But I've never wanted you to feel an ounce of hurt. If you believe protecting your heart makes me the enemy, so be it. With his death, I was left with more questions than answers. I don't know everything, which is why I asked the questions I did last night..." I release her and drop my hands to my hips. Do I know more than I'm letting on? Yes, but I wasn't lying when I said I don't know everything and I don't want to speak on theories. Does that make me a liar? Some might see it that way. Secrets and lies are both deceptions, but as a lawyer, I know there is a gray area. Not every detail is necessary for accuracy. Like her, I also keep things close to my chest. Everyone does. Some are just bigger than others. I need to know what she does, so I try again, and I'm softer this time. "It's why I'm asking now."

Pulling in a sorrowful breath, she says, "I just gave you my truth. That's all I know. Kelce doesn't want money. He never did. I believe he hates it and everything it represents. With their death, he was free of it. He was free of being Mom's pawn, another reason for Dad to stay when he didn't want to. Maybe when you're done walking through the hurt of my father's death alone, maybe I can love the lonely out of you and numb the pain. Maybe if you let me in instead of saving me, we can save each other."

Her words hit deep. I'm not used to someone looking after me and caring about how the choices I make don't come lightly; they wear on me too. It's why, this time when she drops her gaze as I once again give her no words, I let her go. I learned a lot tonight. She gave me an angle I hadn't considered because she's right about sharing our pain; our grief is visceral, and in choosing to hold onto mine, I've managed to tie one hand behind my back. Rather than letting her in and allowing her to think through the riddles he dropped at my feet with his last breaths, I suffer alone. She wants to save me, but I'm not meant to be saved. My job is to keep her safe.

CHAPTER 12

CAMERON

My alarm goes off Monday morning, and the last thing I want to do is go to work. It doesn't matter that Everett is there too. This past weekend, I had him all to myself, and even if we didn't part on the best of terms yesterday, I'm not ready to let go of having him uninterrupted. We didn't discuss our moment on the couch, but we shared one beside the pool until Colton showed up and ruined it. Though I'm unsure, I can place the blame squarely on him. Had I shown my cards about Kelce the night before, Everett may have called Colton off whatever wild goose chase he sent him on to defend my safety. I'm not trying to be irresponsible or inconsiderate of other people's time, but secrets are lies too. You can't say they are ill-timed truths because it doesn't change the fact that you kept them. Everett letting me have the last word and walk away yesterday tells me he's still keeping them. Part of me thinks he holds onto his secrets because they are the only things that give him a purpose to still be in my life. The secrets give him a reason to check in on me and watch. They fulfill whatever oath he gave my dad by existing. If you strip them away, what's left?

The answer is simple: me. I want that to be enough.

I kept that in mind as I got ready this morning. He's starting to notice me, whether he's willing to admit it or not. Even when his words are tainted with ire, he sees me. It's then that I think he sees me the most, and he hates it. But I know that not all hate is rooted in venom. Most of the time, hate comes from fear. I need him to grow through the hate so he can come out on the other side. That's why today I put a little more thought into my outfit. I put effort into my outfits every day, but I've been more lax in my choices since I've been at the stadium. Don't get me wrong, my hair and makeup have been on point. Well, apart from last week, when I came in looking and feeling like a pile of shit. I might be borderline certifiable because even though we still don't know who broke into Connor's house, nor do we have a solid motive, I'm low-key happy that I did, indeed, have a stalker because it gave my appearance a pass. Before that, I'd been wearing cute, refined athleisure, but today, I'm going with slim-fit, high-waisted white pants paired with a cobalt blue body suit. The outfit fits me like a glove. Everett may have been able to ignore me last week, but this past weekend, I held his eyes, and I'm going to make sure I keep it that way.

I'm just coming down the stairs when I remember I don't have my keys. Everett had my car picked up from Connor's over the weekend and he never handed them to me. Turning toward his office, I only manage to take two steps before he startles the shit out of me. "Ready to go?"

My hand flies over my heart as I peer up the open staircase and find him standing at the top, looking the complete opposite of me. Where I'm dressed for a day at the office, he's looking like a snack dressed for a day at the gym with his athleisure clinging to his toned chest and stretching around his biceps.

"I was just going to ask you for my keys."

He starts down the steps. "That won't be necessary. You'll be riding with me for the foreseeable future." A small part of me wants to argue and tell him that I am an independent woman and don't need a babysitter. However, a bigger part of me wants to ride with him everywhere. Not to mention, mad or not, this keeps me right where I want to be—next to him. When he gets to the bottom, he picks up the duffle bag by the door and says, "Want to stop at The Bean Hive?"

I'm unsure where this lightheartedness is coming from. Yesterday, I gave him honesty, but that's a hard pill for him to swallow when he's not ready to face his own. Those truths tend to shut him down. He retreats instead of facing them. I was prepared to put in the work to bring him back to me, but I don't dwell on it. Instead, I tuck it away and play into whatever this is.

"Are you trying to sweeten me up in hopes I won't notice the hostage situation developing around here?" I teasingly toss back as I make my way out the front door.

"You're hardly being held captive." He closes the door as we walk the stone path out to the driveway.

"Okay then. Can I have my keys to go to the store after work? I need to pick up a few things."

He tosses his duffle bag in the trunk. "Text me a list. I believe you owe me one anyway. I'll have Camila pick up whatever you need this afternoon..." He pauses before opening his door and our eyes lock. "As for the rest, let me make myself clear. I said you'd be riding with me for the foreseeable future. That means where you go, I go. Are we clear?"

And there it is. There's the denigration I was expecting.

"Crystal." I smile sweetly. "Freedom is overrated."

"I am so fucking sorry, Cam," Parker says, standing at the cashier counter in the team shop with a counter full of my favorite foods.

I slowly walk over to the counter. After everything that happened once Everett showed up at Connor's last Friday, I hadn't put much more thought into Parker letting me down. Now that he's here and the danger is behind me, I can't help but be a little agitated.

"What happened? Why didn't you answer your phone, but you answered Elijah's?"

He drops his head. "It's a long story, and I'm already going to have to run extra laps for being here instead of out there on the field."

"You didn't even text or call."

His eyes rise to meet mine. "Because I knew you were with him."

"How did you know Everett was on his way that night?" I ask as I set my coffee down and take inventory of all the snacks he picked up, including a slice of carrot cake from my favorite bakery on the other side of town.

He rounds the counter and nods toward the food. "Save me some snacks, and I'll stop by after practice. We can talk then."

He turns to leave, but before he makes it out the door, I say, "I would have answered Park." He gives me a half smile, one that doesn't meet his big blue eyes, before he exits, and it wounds me. I hate that he believes our friendship doesn't mean something to me if I have Everett. We got close. I know he has feelings for me. I have feelings for him too; they're just not romantic ones. I know the same is true for him, but I think whatever is going on between him and Everett is affecting everything in his orbit, and that includes me.

I'm just flipping open the box of donuts to see the selection he picked out, which should include white frosted long johns and cinnamon fritters, when the door opens again.

"You think I was going to eat all the donuts before practice was over?"

"Um, no..." a female voice trails off as I turn around, licking my fingers clean of the powdered sugar from the decadent morsel that will now have to wait.

"Hi, can I help you?" I ask the pretty blonde with a long braid pulled over her shoulder wearing a pair of overalls and converse.

"Are you Cameron?" she shoves her hands into her pockets as

she walks further into the store, taking a slow look at all of the inventory.

"I am."

"Everett sent me down here to train with you."

Interesting. We just spent thirty minutes in the car together, and he didn't mention this girl at all. Two people working the team shop makes sense. If I have to call off or I get sick, she can fill in, but I can't help but be a little sour about it. One, this place feels like my baby, and two, he didn't freaking tell me. Why didn't he bring it up? It's not hard. "Oh hey, by the way, I have a new girl training with you today. Her name is..."

"What's your name?"

"Stormy," her eyes slowly drag down my body, unimpressed with what she sees. "I'm not expected to dress like you for this position, am I?"

I ignore her tone and the obvious distaste in her expression. We don't have the same style. It's only offensive if I let it be.

"No, there are staff shirts that can be worn with jeans, black leggings, or an athletic skirt."

She purses her lips and nods, her eyes casually flitting over my mountain of snacks before she starts running her hands along the racks of clothes, making me anxious.

"Would you like a donut?"

She joins me at the counter. "I'm glad you offered because stealing one behind your back might have been awkward."

I laugh and take the one I already pawed at before pushing the box toward her. "Have at it. There's more here than I could ever eat."

Stormy takes a big bite out of her long john before talking around her food and asking. "So, which one of those dumb jocks out there has his strap twisted up for you?"

I practically snort fritter out my nose. "None of them. I'm friends with the pitcher and these snacks are a peace offering for a friend fail." I hop up on the counter. "Are you new in town?"

"Is this place really so small that you would know that?"

"Unfortunately, yes. Even if you didn't get dropped in my lap, chances are I would hear about the new girl from the guys. Small town means slim pickings. Any time there's a new girl in town, those barbarians out there start dick-measuring contests and lay their claim before they ever get a name."

That makes her laugh out loud. She leans against the counter and says, "You're funny. I wasn't expecting that."

"Oh yeah, why is that?"

She shrugs. "You look like one of those runway ready, mean girl, preppy bitches with their head up their ass."

"Thanks..." I drag out slowly.

"Oh, that's definitely not a compliment."

"Yeah, I got that, but I'm a glass-half-full kind of girl. You said 'runway ready,' so... that's a win." She snorts. "So where are you from?"

Even though she's not looking at me, I can see her smile fade, and I know instantly it's a sore subject or, at a minimum, it's a reminder of one.

"Nowhere worth mentioning." She pops the remaining donut in her mouth. "So, do we sit around and eat pastries all day? Because, if so, I'd like to add chocolate donuts to the list."

I hop off the counter. "Come on. I can teach you how to take inventory while I input the items and their prices into the system."

"So do we get a lunch break around here or what?"

I look over at Stormy, who's just about eaten all my snacks. I don't know where she puts it, but the girl can eat. If I ate all those snacks, they'd go straight to my hips. I mean, technically I planned on eating all of them, but maybe over the span of a few days, not in one sitting. I look down at my watch and see that it's already 12:30.

"Yeah, you can take a break if you'd like. We get thirty minutes."

She gets off the floor where she's been sorting the last shipment of T-shirts by size. "You're not going to take a break?"

I shrug. "I don't have my car today."

"I'd offer you a ride somewhere, but..." She shoots me finger guns. "I don't have a car either." She throws her thumb over her shoulder and adds, "I'm going to stretch my legs. I'll be back in a half hour."

"Sounds good."

I stand from the stool and raise my arms above my head to stretch myself just as a pair walking out to the parking lot catches my eyes. It's Everett with Moira's doppelgänger again. My mood wasn't too bad, all things considered, until this moment. This is the second time I've seen him leave the premises with her. I don't care, unpopular opinion or not, colleagues of the opposite sex shouldn't go out to lunch together. Unless you're in a group, one-on-one lunches are always more. There's always an ulterior motive. I've yet to meet Lauren, so I can't say for sure who is coming on to whom. She could be a gold digger looking for her next meal ticket, or Everett has a type and she checks all the boxes. Regardless, I know there is a motive.

I grab my carrot cake out of the beverage cooler I stashed it in before Stormy could gobble it up, only to realize I have no utensils. "Seriously," I groan, staring at it as though somehow it can solve all my life problems if only I had a spoon to eat it. Fuck it. I pick it up and take a huge bite just as Parker walks in from practice.

"Woah, slow down there, tiger," he jests as he approaches the counter.

I give him an unamused smile before saying, "You forgot to bring me a spoon."

"You could have walked down to the concession area and grabbed one."

"Yeah, but I needed a bite now." Walking down to concessions would have been a great idea, but going there to grab one would have defeated the comfort I needed from that bite at that very moment. I needed to feel better now, not five minutes from now.

"Damn, girl. What happened to all the other snacks I brought you? I told you to save some for me."

I reach for my bottle of water and take a drink to rinse down the remaining cake. "I got a trainee today, and she had an appetite." I shrug. "It's the thought that counts though, Parker. I'm not mad."

He pulls a spoon out of his back pocket. "You going to share your cake?"

"Depends. Are you going to tell me why you couldn't show up to literally save my life on Friday?"

He jabs his spoon into the cake. "Yeah, well, I suppose, in a way, I was saving another," he mumbles around a mouth full of cake.

"What the hell is that supposed to mean?" I ask as I snatch the spoon out of his hand and steal my own bite.

"Elijah got trashed downtown. I had to go pick him up."

My eyes narrow on his as I stab the cake, leaving the spoon for him. "Responsible Elijah? We are talking about your brother, correct?"

"He hasn't been handling the breakup with Annie well," he says before taking one last bite and hopping up onto the counter.

"Has he forgotten he broke up with her?"

"He's aware. I don't think he regrets it. I just think it hurts. Everyone thought she was the one, but now that she's gone, I can see that she was never the one for him. Elijah carried that with him every day, torn between caring about someone and not wanting to let down friends and family who basically had their lives planned out for them from the moment they graduated from high school. That's what living in a small town is—rumors and outdated conventions."

Before I can say a word, Stormy returns. "Hey, I grabbed you a fork for that cake you have in the cooler."

"Are you planning on eating my cake too?"

I know she said she brought ME a fork, but let's be real, the girl has literally eaten all my other snacks. She's not fooling anyone with that.

"Nooo," she smarts before she looks up and finds we aren't alone. "Didn't know you had company. Should I come back?"

Parker slides off the counter and takes two long strides in her direction. "I'm Parker," he holds out his hand for her to shake.

"I'm not interested in measuring your dick."

The water I just drank literally flies out of my nose, "Shit." I laugh as I grab a roll of paper towels and try to pat dry all the papers I've been working on all morning.

"Well, I wasn't going to ask you to measure my dick."

"No? What were you going to ask me?" She turns with her hand on her hip, giving him her full attention while I make a mental note that she has no qualms about saying whatever the fuck she wants.

"I was going to ask if you knew what material my shirt was made out of."

"Read the tag," she offers, agitated by his antics.

"I can't," he pulls at his collar. "You do work in the team shop, don't you?"

"It would appear that way."

"Well, then, you should probably know about shirts. This one, for example," he pulls it away from his chest. "Feel it."

She quirks a brow but extends her hand, running her fingers over the fabric. "It's smooth, moisture-wicking. Feels good to the touch. What's it made of?"

She reaches up for his collar to check the tag, but he snatches her wrist. "It's ninety-nine percent boyfriend material."

I laugh as Stormy says, "Wow, are you really that lame?"

He shrugs. "Maybe, but I made you smile." Then, turning to me, he asks, "What time do you get off today? Connor said I could borrow his Marucci bat to see if I liked it. I was going to see if you'd swing by the house with me since you know the code."

Technically, I can leave whenever I want. We aren't open to the public yet. I'm not sure I love the idea of going back to the house, but I did leave a few things there. I could grab them. Plus, I don't care to wait around here looking pathetic while Everett's out prancing another woman around town on a lunch date.

"We can go now if you want. I just need to close the computer and grab my bag."

"Sweet. Do you want me to toss these boxes in the dumpster on the way out?"

"Yes, please," I answer, shutting my computer and tossing my cake trash in the can before grabbing my bag off the counter.

"Does that mean I get to leave too?" Stormy chimes in as I'm shutting down.

Shit. Everett sent her down here, but he never told me I was a manager or that I would even be training anyone. He's been really good at telling me to act like an adult, but what's his excuse? He's avoiding me, which is equally childish.

"I don't see why not. Unless you need the hours? I can walk you down to concessions. I'm sure they could use a hand—"

"Or you could tag along," Parker offers.

She side-eyes him. I can't tell if she's genuinely unimpressed with him or trying not to show her cards. Yes, I know what I said earlier, but Parker isn't one of those guys. He's one of the good ones. I find his cheesiness cute, and he's not bad to look at either. The guy is stacked, has stumps for legs being a catcher, deep blue eyes, and a sandy blond mop of thick waves on his head. The guy is a catch. If my heart didn't belong to someone else, I'd try to steal his.

"I'll stay."

"Parker can drive you home," I offer, hearing the dejection in her tone.

"It's fine. I'm not supposed to leave anyway."

"To live is to break the rules every now and again. Come on, it's just a ride."

CHAPTER 13

EVERETT

"Tell me again why you're here," I ask Lauren Rhodes as I sip the old-fashioned I ordered for lunch.

"You already asked me that last week when you followed me out to my car, and I explained that I didn't realize who I would be working for when I accepted the job."

I thought I was seeing a ghost when she walked past my office last week on her way out. At first glance, you'd mistake her for my ex-wife. They have strikingly similar features, which caused quite the controversy back in the day. Immediately, I was out of my chair and chasing her down the hall. That's when she explained that a headhunter got her the job, and she didn't realize who her new boss was until she was shaking his hand and taking a tour of the stadium.

"But you know now, and yet you're still here."

She swirls the cherry around in her Manhattan. "Are we not adults now? This isn't high school anymore, Everett."

"Did you get a DNA test?"

"Seriously, brown hair and brown eyes don't make us blood. Fuck, I've been gone so long I forgot what it's like to come back." She rolls her eyes and takes a drink. Moira's father was rumored to have been cheating, and Lauren's mother was the other woman.

Lauren and Moira have birthdays three months apart. Their similar features, birthdays, and rumors made them natural enemies. The rumors intensified when Moira's parents died suddenly from carbon monoxide poisoning during her freshman year of high school while she slept over at a friend's house. Following their untimely death, Moira felt even more compelled to defend their memory. Lauren's mother never commented on the situation and was never seen with any men before or after Lauren was born. You were either friends with Lauren or Moira. There wasn't a middle ground, and now my son has hired his mother's archnemesis. "And I don't need one. I know who my father is. He's alive and well, living his best life in Spain."

"Then I'll ask again, why are you back?"

"Is this about Moira? Because as I hear it, the two of you aren't even hitched anymore, so what is this? Do you dislike me that much because of an ancient rumor?"

I pull in a deep, cleansing breath and settle into the booth. She's not going to make this quick, but ghosts don't just show up for no reason, and I'm determined to find out who she's haunting.

"I don't have a problem with you, Lauren, but your presence here will undoubtedly cause havoc in my life. We both know my son has no idea the history you have with his mother, and since Moira hasn't shown up on my doorstep, I'm going to venture a guess and say she has yet to hear that you are back in town."

Had I not had my hands full with Cameron this past weekend, I may have considered giving Moira a heads-up, but since the divorce, I've been trying to keep my distance and disentangle myself from her. After spending twenty years together, it's easier said than done.

She subtly clinks the ring wrapped around her middle finger on her glass. "I'm not here to raise the dead, but I have roots here too. My business here is mine and mine alone. I don't owe you an explanation, but I'll tell you this: it has nothing to do with your family. As for the job, I'm fucking good at what I do. I can help the organization attract big names, but I think you already know that, which is why I'm still here. So the way I see it, we can keep the past in the past and work amicably, or I walk and take my event schedule with me four days before opening day."

I can't help the subtle smile that tugs at my lips. It's been a while since someone besides Cameron has dared to threaten me.

"I'm not going to fire you." It doesn't matter that Connor hired her. I know he'd trust any decision I made. "But not because of the schedule. Connor built this place without it, and we both know I have the resources to make things happen. That being said, my plate is full, and I've seen your schedule. I don't care to recreate it for the sake of letting you go on the grounds of ancient history..." My phone lights up on the table with a security alert at my front door. When I click into the app and pull up the camera, I see Cameron entering the front door, and I reach for my glass, needing the smoky caramel brew to settle my nerves. I specifically told her I would be driving her, and she left work without me. Annoyance and dread settle over me before I down my glass in one go. I'm out of the booth when my eyes meet Lauren's. "Don't cross me, Lauren. If you do, you'll wish you never crawled out of whatever rock you've been hiding under." I toss cash on the table for our order. "Let's go. I have somewhere I need to be."

The ten-minute drive back to the stadium to drop off Lauren felt like an hour. My skin grew hotter, my heart pounded faster, and what had been annoyance turned into fury as I contemplated why Cameron went against my orders. I specifically told her where she goes, I go. How could she be so careless? I wasn't worried about leaving her at the stadium. She wasn't alone there. It's training week—there are staff around every corner preparing for opening day—and I'm not concerned about her security at my house. It's her intent that has me driving like a reckless fool, breaking every speed limit. If she left work without me, there's a good chance she plans on leaving the house too, and then I can't protect her.

Pulling into the driveway, the adrenaline coursing through my veins settles a notch as I hastily exit my car, knowing she's still inside and I'm home. With my hand on the front doorknob, I breathe deep. I don't want to lose control the way I have been so easily with her lately. The second I pull open the door, I hear laughter coming from the kitchen and immediately follow the honeyed sound. It's like sunshine on a rainy day. Her laugh has always had a soothing effect on me. It's deep, genuine, and real, just like her. I can't tell you a time when her laughter didn't come from her whole heart. It's part of her appeal, one that should have me turning away instead of running headfirst. But here I am, rounding the corner into my kitchen anyway, only to find her talking to another man.

"What did she say after that?"

"She told him the only reason he thought she belonged in the kitchen was because he didn't know what to do with her in the bedroom." A man I've never seen before answers as he opens the refrigerator. My refrigerator!

"Oh my god. I can't believe they said that in front of you."

"It's what happens when people assume they know you based on your appearance. They thought I didn't speak English."

She hops off the counter and places her hand on his lower back, alerting him to her presence before reaching around to grab a coconut water. The move is innocent enough, but he has at least a foot on her, and I see what she doesn't. I see the way his back tenses and his head slightly turns toward her, assessing her intent, looking for his moment. They're so caught up in their conversation that they haven't realized I'm standing at the entrance.

Clearing my throat, I startle them both. His black eyes find mine, and I'm certain I've never met him before. I never forget a face, but something about him looks familiar. However, I leave it be. It doesn't matter because he will never step foot in this house again.

"A word, Cameron," I say, my tone firm, leaving no room for debate.

She glowers as she twists the top on her coconut water. I know that look, but it's just usually never directed at me. She has no interest in heeding my request, but right as I'm about to speak again, she does. That's when I notice her outfit—or lack thereof. She's practically naked, wearing a long flowing dress that leaves nothing to the imagination. You can see her undergarments, and every stride she takes reveals her bare thighs. When she walks past me and into the library, my eyes land on the mystery man standing in my kitchen whose gaze is fixed squarely on her ass. What was a slow, simmering fury is quickly starting to boil over.

When he catches me staring hard, my displeasure evident, he quickly turns back toward the fridge. I won't waste my words on him when she's been my sole focus for the past thirty minutes.

Entering the library, she's sitting on a wingback chair with her arms crossed when I close the French doors behind me. "Did you forget the rules?"

She rolls her eyes. "You're going to need to be a little more specific. You've been demanding a lot of things recently. I'm not sure what's a rule and what's a mandate anymore because, I can assure you, I've broken no rules."

I don't know where the attitude is coming from or why she chose to leave work without me. When I told her I didn't want her driving and refused to hand over her keys, I sensed a little agitation but not anger. She's a smart girl. I know she hasn't forgotten the rules, so the question is: what game is she playing now?

"You left work without me. I told you I didn't want you driving—"

"I didn't drive. Parker did," she answers sardonically with a smirk.

She's poking the bear, and she knows it. I know what I said. "I said you'd be riding with me for the foreseeable future, Cameron. Me, not Parker or anyone else. Me."

"You left," she comments as she looks down at her manicure, seemingly unaffected by my terseness. "And I was done with my shift." She rests her arms on either side of the chair before giving me her eyes. "I didn't want to interrupt your lunch," she says, drawing out the last word. So that's what this is about. She saw me leave with Lauren. Rising from her chair, she says, "So if we're done here—"

I step further into the room. "We're far from done here. Rules are rules, Cameron. I'm trying to keep you safe," I say, my voice peaking with indignation as I grab the back of the wingback chair opposite the one she vacated.

"Fine. I'll only ride with you... Happy?" she questions apathetically, only further adding to my irritation.

I don't appreciate the dismissiveness in her mannerisms, and I hate believing she'd rather be in the kitchen than here with me, even though it's exactly where she should be. I wouldn't say I'm a greedy man, in fact I'd defend that I'm far from it, but right now, I'm the very definition because the last thing I want is her giving an ounce of attention to someone who isn't me.

"Far from it. Leaving early wasn't the only rule you broke. I specifically said no boys in the house, and yet there is one in my kitchen. If you are determined to feel what being held against your will is like, continue to test me. I promise you won't like the outcome."

She puts her hands on her hips, and her piercing blue eyes connect with mine, making my insides coil with dread and desire. I fear her as much as I fear for her. Her safety is paramount, but as she stands before me, looking like every man's dream, I'm worried that it's me she should fear the most. I'm the monster hiding in plain sight.

Her lips quirk to one side before she smarts. "I didn't invite our guest over—you did."

"Nice try, but I've never met that man in my life, and I wouldn't invite someone into my home without checking out their background given the events of this past weekend."

She rolls her lips and drops her gaze, shaking her head before saying, "I warned you, but you refuse to listen. You continue to talk at me instead of with me, continue to see me as a teen living under your roof instead of an educated adult." She pauses, her eyes still downcast as her hands ball into fists, drawing my eye toward her body and the nudity that lies beneath the sheer fabric covering parts of her I shouldn't see. Cameron has always put a lot of care into her wardrobe. She's far from shy, and while she likes to show skin, this outfit pushes a limit I didn't know I had. Her lips pop before she gives me her full attention once more. "The man in the kitchen is Camila's son. You ordered groceries this morning. Camila got sick, and her son, Diego, delivered them for you."

It's getting harder to ignore the blind spot that's growing when it comes to her. I'm so singularly focused on the feelings she evokes that I'm losing my damned mind in other regards. Camila has worked for me for ten years. I knew she had an older son, but I'd never met him. That's not Cameron's problem. It's mine, and I refuse to let it show.

"Even better. New rule. I expect you to wear clothes around my employees. Not whatever lingerie this is," I say as I gesture toward her attire.

She runs her tongue over her teeth before pulling the drawstring on the front of the sheer dress she's wearing, revealing a baby blue swimsuit. "Relax. It's just a swimsuit," she says as she lets the material fall down her arms before tossing it on the chair behind her. "I was heading to the pool when he walked in with your order." Then, turning on her heel, she gives me her back and an eye full of her ass in yet another thong bikini. "I'll go outside. You can see him out."

I want to slap her ass so hard for testing me. She knows exactly what she's doing, and the mere thought of watching her porcelain skin redden from the sting of my hand makes my cock twitch. Fuck. She only gets two paces toward the door before I say, "Are you trying to get him fired?"

"What?" she whips around, her face full of concern.

"I said you need to wear clothes around my employees. That's not a fucking swimsuit, it's a damn thong."

Her brow furrows. "Since when have you had a problem with my swimsuits? Women wear these, Everett. Go to any swimwear website and look for yourself."

"I don't care what other women wear. I care what you wear." Her eyes widen, and I realize what I've said. Before she can react or think to tease me further, I shut it down, knowing I don't have the strength, not when my nerves are wrecked, not when she's the reason for my sleepless nights, and sure as fuck not with her standing before me practically naked, knowing exactly how soft her milky white skin feels beneath my palm. "Don't make this into more than it is. It doesn't change anything. I won't hesitate to fire Camila and send you away. When I said I'd hold you against your will, I didn't say I would be doing the holding. I have zero qualms about sending you away until I get to the bottom of who broke into Connor's house."

Her blue eyes have darkened to shades of gray, and I know I've struck a nerve. Good. I need her to take me seriously. She can be mad all she wants, as long as she's safe. When she gives me no words, I head toward the door. With my hand on the knob and my back to her, I pause before exiting. "There's a blanket in the ottoman. Use it if you plan on leaving this room."

Cameron's determined to test the water and see how far she can push me. The problem is, she doesn't know how to swim, and if I jump in to save her now, we'll both drown.

"Banks, you need to keep your weight back. That's the second curveball he's thrown at you, and you won't hit with all that weight out in front. You react after the ball leaves his hand, not before. Try again."

Banks is one of our best hitters, but for some reason, he's acting like he's never hit a curveball. I'm watching his every move, trying to determine the root cause. His stance just now was laziness. Everyone knows you lean back, not in. His head isn't in the game, and I'm trying to deduce if it's physical or mental. Sometimes, players will over-compensate and make rookie mistakes to hide injuries. Other times, outside factors are the issue. Home life, school, work, and girlfriends can easily distract a player from staying on their game. They can't connect or stay focused. And other times, it's none of those things; sometimes, it's just a bad day. I've landed on the likely cause when a blur of red steals my focus as she rushes to the bench where Parker sits. I can tell from my spot behind second base, something is wrong.

After our exchange in the library the other day, she's gone out of her way to avoid me, which is good, but I can't stand it. I hate that she's not talking to me, and I loathe the irony in that statement because the opposite used to be true. I wanted her to ignore me. If she had, maybe I wouldn't have noticed her as much. Perhaps then, I wouldn't be obsessed and walking off the field. Whatever she said to Parker had him leaving the dugout and hastily following her down the tunnel toward the concourse without so much as notifying one of the coaches. The closer I get to the team shop, the more my anger spikes. I'm pissed she ran to Parker and not me, but the second my hand hits the metal of the door, I pause. Pausing is something new for me. I did it when I found her in the kitchen with Camila's son, and I'm doing it now, but it's not in my repertoire. I don't temper for anyone, but apparently, I do for her. I pull a deep breath into my lungs, letting them inflate, and hold it for a count of three before releasing it. I'm still livid, but at least I'm not unhinged. That is, until I open the door and find Cameron pulling his shirt off.

"Please don't tell me you left the field during practice for a quick fuck," I say, somehow managing to keep my voice level while my heart practically beats out of my chest.

Cameron turns to me, her cheeks tinged pink, but I don't see anger. I see panic. "The uniforms are too small." Turning back to Parker, she attempts to pull a new shirt over his head.

125

"I think he can manage that task himself," I assert as I walk further into the shop. His head pops through the top, and I see a telling smirk. It could simply be my remarks about the quickie, but I know it's more. He knows I don't like her touching him. There's this innate sixth sense all men and women are born with. We can sense competition, and right now, he knows he's mine. He struggles to get one arm through the shirt, and I ask, "How did this happen?"

"We wanted the uniforms to be fitted. Connor didn't want them to fit loosely, so he ordered them in a size smaller than usual. But there must have been a mix-up because these aren't just one size smaller; they are two. They sent us UK sizes, not American, which makes them two sizes too small."

"I found the measuring tape," Stormy says as she exits the back room. The girl looks like she stepped out of a hippie magazine, wearing a baggy, patchwork bohemian set of overalls with her hair in French braids down either side of her head. I don't know what her full story is. I've had my hands full between taking over for Connor and trying to go silent at Callahan & Associates. However, I've known my ex since grade school and never heard this name come out of her mouth. It's not one you soon forget. I slip my phone out of my pocket and make a note to send Moira an email asking for details on the new hire she sent to my office.

Cameron wrestles with the hem of Parker's shirt as she struggles to pull it over his toned abs. Watching her fingers brush against his bare skin grates on my nerves. "Cam, I don't think it's going to fit."

"Suck in your stomach," she groans. "This isn't happening," her hands drop as she stares at Parker, who's now stuck in his shirt.

"Do you want me to get the scissors?" Stormy asks, assessing the situation from her side.

"Fine," Cameron huffs, "Take him in the back, and I'll call Connor and let him know the bad news," she says as she pulls her phone out of her pocket.

Stormy ushers Parker toward the back storage room as I

quickly approach Cameron, putting my hand over her phone before she can press the call button. "Is this your mistake or Connor's?"

"Does it matter? Either way, the team doesn't have a uniform."

There's my answer. It's his. Cameron may have designed them, but if I had to guess, Connor placed the orders. He probably tried to save money and went with a subpar supplier. I can't fault him. Every business owner bleeds money in the first few years. You live and you learn.

"He doesn't need to know."

Her stressed eyes search mine. "How do you figure? These uniforms don't fit."

"Can you make it right in time for opening day?"

Her eyes drop to the box as she bites her thumb. "I don't know... Can I pay for a new shipment? Yes, but I don't have connections with athletic wear suppliers apart from the one we used, which I will never use again."

"Where did all the logo wear from the shop come from?"

Her eyes close as her hand clenches tightly around her phone. "Why didn't I think of that?" She starts pacing and mumbling under her breath. "Parker, can you ask Coach Teague to send every player in, one at a time, for measurements?"

"Um, hello. I'm standing right here. Why wouldn't you ask that of me?"

"Because I'd rather not be sent away, and you can't stand to be around me." She walks over to the counter dismissively and grabs a clipboard. "I'll take the measurements in here and stay out of your way."

Parker walks out of the back room with Stormy on his heels as he pulls his practice jersey back on. "Go tell Coach Teague we are ending practice in twenty minutes and have all the players line up on the first baseline for new uniform measurements." He gives me a nod and heads toward the door. "Stormy, can you please run up to my office and bring down my laptop?"

"Sure," she draws out, not bothering to hide the annoyance in her tone from my menial ask.

Once she's out of earshot, I say, "This needs to stop Cameron. You need to stop pushing me."

She presses her lips together and looks away. "Have you ever stopped to think maybe I'm not pushing you? I'm merely existing." She grabs a pen off the counter and pushes it through the top of her clipboard. "I didn't ask for your help. It wasn't you I ran to just now."

My hand hits the counter. "That's the problem. You know I want it to be me."

"Do I?" she tilts her head to the side curiously, and my jaw instantly clenches. Once again, I've said more than I wanted to, and she knows it. Adding fuel to the fire, she says, "We should probably use those steaks you ordered." I can't tell if she's trying to incite a reaction out of me considering all my missteps or if this is something else. "You just said you wanted it to be you." She shrugs. "A girl needs to eat, and you said you'd teach me how to cook. How about tonight?" I can't help but close my eyes with regret at her ask. I just told her I wished she'd come to me, and here she is doing just that. I push her away only to turn around and pull her back, unable to stand the distance. It's fucked up. I shouldn't have offered to insert myself in her space more than I'm already in it. "It's fine," she says, stepping toward the door. "I'll order something in."

Unable to stomach the regret of giving her an empty promise, I say, "I didn't say no."

She turns back. "You didn't have to."

I hate that she knows my mannerisms so well. She can read me like a book in ways no one ever has. I hate that the one person who ever paid attention is the same one I can't have, and more than that, I hate that I can't truly say no. How do you say no when all you want to say is yes?

"Six o'clock. Don't be late or you'll miss the most important part. I don't measure my seasonings when putting them on the steak."

This time, she's the one with no words, which is new. Lately, she's been determined to have the last one. Or maybe it is like she said and she's not pushing me. Instead, I'm pushing her because she's everywhere I want her to be and nowhere she should be. She pulls the clipboard to her chest and gives me a nod before heading out of the shop.

My phone vibrates in my pocket. Pulling it out, I see it's from my brother Colton.

> Colton: I'm stopping by the stadium around 4 pm. I found something and before you call me immediately, no, I won't answer. I want to see what my nephew has created.

Fucking ass. I'm sure I already know what he has to say; however, I'm nothing if I'm not thorough. That's why I asked my brothers for help in the first place. We all have our areas of expertise. We get the same information, but how we process that information is different. It's good to be smart, but it's better to be wise, and a wise man knows only fools believe they know everything.

∿

"Can you spread your legs just a tad wider?"

My eyes instantly leave my screen to watch as Cameron measures the inseam on our shortstop. I don't even know what I've been looking at on my computer. I think it's some crap about a settlement for one of my clients, something I typically drop everything to comb through meticulously, but I can't find it in me to care.

"Parker," she calls. He's currently in the dugout engrossed in something on his phone. "Come on, you're my last measurement. I need to get these numbers to the supplier ASAP. Let's go."

I am still trying to understand what his deal is, whether it's about me or something else. He's been running hot and cold. At practice, he's been keeping his tongue in check, mostly because he knows his words negatively impact the team and he doesn't want to be the reason they stay late to run laps. Instead of lashing out with words, he's been giving me the cold shoulder and looks that could kill were they tangible. But even now, as I watch him put away his phone, there's a vexation in his movements, which wasn't caused by my doing.

"Coming, boss," he says as he jogs out to the field where I had the team line up.

There was no way in hell I was letting her measure the team one-on-one in the shop. After I saw how precise her measurements were with the first player, I almost lost my shit. I would have gone down to the local sporting goods store, bought pants and jerseys off the rack, and ironed letters on myself so that I didn't have to watch her hands wrap around another man's middle to measure his waist. These are baseball uniforms, for crying out loud, not suits, but I kept my mouth shut. I'm determined not to stick my foot in it more than I already have. This is important to her, which makes it important to me.

Her measurements of Parker feel like they take a small eternity, probably because I know they are close. I watched every small smile that pulled at his pretty boy mouth, a mouth that's been on hers, and I waited with bated breath to see it happen again. To watch her pick him, but she didn't. Instead, she swatted his chest and pushed him away, rolling up her measuring tape before picking up her clipboard.

"Parker!" she calls out again. "Can you grab one of these boxes and take it to the shop on your way out?" He nods, throwing his bag on his back before grabbing the box with the small jerseys.

She's just starting to walk off the field when I hastily catch up and cut her off before she can pass through the gate. "You're missing one."

"What?" her brow furrows before her eyes drop to her list,

SALT

scanning all the names. "Everyone's here," her pen traces down the sheet.

"You forgot the head coach."

Her eyebrows raise in surprise as she pulls in a stuttered breath. "I did." I watch as she adds my name to the bottom of her list. The slant in the way she writes my name is now etched on my heart. Setting the clipboard on the half-wall that divides the fields from the stands, she pulls her measuring tape from her back pocket.

"I'll start with your neck and work my way down," she says before setting my laptop on the dividing wall for me. Her ice-blue eyes briefly flash to mine before I feel her delicate fingers graze my neck as she positions the tape. It's hot as fuck out here, but her touch sends a chill down my spine all the same. I've touched her, but as I stand here, allowing her to take my measurements, I realize I've never let her touch me. "Raise your arms," she commands before the hands that chilled my body suddenly leave. I feel the tape on my back before her fingers run along the edges, skimming my sides and causing my skin to break out in goosebumps. I close my eyes in an attempt to tamp down my reactions. I'm forty-six years old. This isn't high school. She's not a conquest or a lover, and yet here she is, making me feel more with the back of her hand than either ever have. Letting the tape go slack, she drops it to my waist, and fuck me if it doesn't cause a sensory overload. My heart rate kicks up a notch, and a blistering inferno has now replaced the chill I felt seconds ago. It doesn't help that this time when she brings the tape together to collect the measurement, her fingers gently push into my lower stomach.

My entire body goes rigid. It's as if it knows it's not supposed to like her touch, but fuck if it doesn't care the second she drops to her knees and says, "Can you spread your legs wider?" I've heard her say it countless times today, each time my anxiety ratcheting up a notch as I debated whether or not players were intentionally not standing as requested to hear her say those words while on her knees.

131

Her thumb gently presses into my upper thigh, and I grind my teeth hard, willing my cock not to react with her head mere inches away from it, and when I feel her hand leave, I revel in my victory until I make the stupid mistake of looking down. Her eyes immediately latch onto mine, and I'm confident she sees my desire. What's fucked up is I'm momentarily incapacitated, too bewitched by the image before me to clear the fog that's settled over me. "I'm done," I hear her words. Words that should be a cue, and still I don't move, but neither does she. There's a slight twitch in my hand, one that's dying to reach out and caress her perfect jaw before running itself through her red locks. Her eyes soften just the slightest as her chest heavily rises. She saw it. Even if she didn't, the electricity between us is humming at deafening decibels that can't be ignored. My hand moves an inch before reality beckons, stilling my hand and reminding me of what's not mine.

"Everett, I've been looking for you," Lauren calls out as I hear her heels click across the concrete as she exits the tunnel, making her way toward us. Cameron quickly gets to her feet, straightening her blouse and pants before grabbing her clipboard. "Oh, hi. I don't think we've met. I've been meaning to make it down to the team shop, but I've been swamped. My niece has told me a lot about you. I'm Lauren."

"Your niece?" she questions, putting her hand in Lauren's outstretched one for a shake.

"Yes, I'm sorry, my niece is Stormy. I believe she works in the shop with you."

That's news to me. I pinch my lips together hard. I don't like knowing someone closely related to Lauren Rhodes has access to Cameron.

"Oh, she hadn't mentioned that she knew anyone at work," she says, releasing her hand.

"That doesn't surprise me. She's very..." she draws off as she searches for the right word, finally landing on, "Contemplative. It takes her a while to warm up to people."

Contemplative, more like calculated and conniving.

"Cameron, I'll meet you in the team shop when it's time to go." My tone comes out more terse than I'd like. It's not her. It's Lauren. She just dropped a bomb after I warned her, and I have words, but Cameron doesn't know that.

"Sure," she answers just as curtly.

Letting her walk away pissed is better than feeding into whatever we shared moments ago. Her hate destroys me as much as her devotion kills me. Both have consequences, and right now, I'm not sure which is better.

CHAPTER 14

CAMERON

"W̲hy didn't you tell me Lauren was your aunt?" I ask as I pass a shot to Stormy.

She shrugs. "I didn't know it mattered."

In the scheme of things, it doesn't. Stormy doesn't know her aunt is my newest obsession simply because she stands to steal Everett from me. I still can't believe that after all the trouble he caused me the other day when Parker drove me home, he turned around and specifically asked him to drive me home today. I was beyond livid. Not just because of the double standard but because of the reason. The last person I saw him with was Lauren. We shared a moment, there's no fucking way he didn't feel it. I know in the depth of my soul he sees and feels me, but he continues to push me away, and when he didn't come home tonight, I know it's because of her. He's probably with her now, trying to forget me because, in his eyes, we don't fit. We'll never fit.

"Thanks for staying late and keying in the last of the inventory while I rushed that uniform order."

"Not a problem. It's not like I had anything better to do. There is literally nothing to do in this Podunk town."

"That's probably why teen pregnancy is on the rise around here," I say as I toy with the rim of my cardboard coaster.

"You didn't just say that."

"I did. Today, when I was grabbing an energy drink from the concession stand, I heard that two seniors are pregnant this year. Do you want to know why? Because fucking is literally all there is to do."

Stormy rolls her eyes. "Two pregnancies is hardly a rise. You need to get out more. When was the last time you left this small town anyway?"

"How about we take this shot?" I say, raising my glass and dodging the question. "I didn't buy them for us to look at." She gives me a knowing look and lets it go. We all have things we keep close to our hearts. It doesn't mean we don't value the friendships we have just because we keep some things for ourselves.

"Hey, did you guys come here to sit on these stools all night or..." Parker chides before another one of the guys from the team walks around behind him, slapping his shoulder. His hand is still on my back, and I don't miss how Stormy's eyes latch on to it, making me wonder if something didn't go down between them after they dropped me off the other day. Parker isn't a kiss-and-tell kind of guy, and while I didn't get the vibe that Stormy was into him, I don't know her well enough to say that she's not. Either way, she's noticing his hand placement now, and that tells me something happened or she wants something to happen. Leaning in, Parker says, "Hey, I'll be right back," before squeezing my shoulder and walking off.

"Here's to forgetting the shit we came here to drink about!" I say as I hold my shot up high before downing the silver bullet.

"That's actually pretty good. I'm normally not a shot taker, but I could probably do another ten of those."

"I mean, your head would probably hate you later, but we're not here to worry about the consequences. Do you dance?" I ask as I hop off my stool.

"Do I look like I dance?"

Solid point. The girl wears overalls and chucks to work every day. I mean, it's cute; she rocks the bohemian skater look well.

Tonight is the first night she's ditched the overalls, and I have to say I was surprised to see her showing her legs. She's still wearing chucks, but she paired them with black torn-up jean shorts and a baggy white tank with a black lacey bralette that plays peekaboo with the distressed armholes.

"Would another round of shots change your mind?"

"Can I ask you a question?"

"I'll take that as a no," I quip sardonically as I reclaim my stool. "Sure, shoot."

"Are you and Parker screwing?"

"No," I answer immediately. "But we have kissed, and he has squeezed my ass on more than one occasion."

She nods. "So he wants to fuck you. Got it."

"Parker and I are just friends, that's it. If you're interested, trust me, I am not in the picture."

"So he's a bad kisser then?"

I laugh out loud before raising my hand to get the bartender's attention for another drink.

"No, he's not a bad kisser. I'm not interested in Parker that way and vice versa. The only reason we ever kissed was because he was doing me a favor. It wasn't romantic." I watch as she stirs her Long Island iced tea with a straw and try to get a read on her, but I get nothing. I can't tell if my words settled any reservations or if she was asking because she thought we were dating. I don't pry because I have my own question to ask if we're just going to be sitting here. "So, what's the story with your aunt?"

My question doesn't faze her in the least. She doesn't even look up from her glass to acknowledge that I've spoken.

I'm just about to clear my throat and ask again, thinking she didn't hear me over the bar's noise, when she says, "Why don't you just ask me what you really want to ask me?"

The bartender finally comes over. "I'll take another spicy margarita, please." He gives me a nod, and I turn back to Stormy. The entire reason I'm out tonight is because the last time I saw Everett was this afternoon when he was dismissing me to speak with Lauren, and then he missed our six o'clock dinner. The last thing I wanted to do was be home when he got there. Am I going against his orders? Hell, yes, but I'm also not the girl who will quietly obey and sit in the corner. At least without something in return. Not to mention, I don't care to be alone. I haven't been alone since the break-in, and frankly, security or not, I didn't want to be all by myself. He should know that, and right now, I don't care if my night out sets me back. I don't want to lose me just to be with him. All I want is for him to see me the way I do him, and right now, the cocktails and the noise are subpar liars. They aren't doing nearly enough to drown out the thoughts of him. Which means I need more drinks and dirt. There's a reason I texted Stormy tonight: Lauren. I'm not one to mince my words, and I can tell she's not a small-talk kind of girl, so I get on with it. "Does she have a thing for Everett?"

"The coach... I don't think so, but I know they have a history, and the only reason I know that is because she came home in a sour mood after having lunch with him and called him a cocky bastard with an ego complex."

That doesn't settle nerves the way it should. Everett's ego is as much of a turnoff as it is a pull. You hate that he gets under your skin, and before you know it, that brooding arrogance stands on its own. You're attracted to the power, and the thing about power is everybody wants it. She might hate him now, but who doesn't want a man to fuck the hate right out of them every now and again?

The bartender delivers my drink right as Parker returns with his friend Nash. Nash is one of his childhood friends who moved away in elementary school, but his family recently moved back to the area a few months ago. He doesn't play sports, and he recently dropped out of college, and for those reasons, he's been labeled the town bad boy. It doesn't hurt that he looks the part with jet-black hair, ripped jeans, and the typical leather jacket, and don't even get me started on the man jewelry. I don't know what it is about a guy that wears rings, but I find it sexy as fuck.

His dark and stormy eyes find mine, and he gives me a nod before asking, "Want to get some air?"

I have a million reasons to say yes, but only one reason to say no. "Air sounds good."

~

"Thanks for giving me a ride home," I say as I hand Nash his helmet back. Illinois doesn't require riders to wear helmets, but I've ridden before, and without one, you'll spend hours trying to comb through your hair.

He revs the engine. "I'll give you a ride anytime, Salt." I don't miss the mischievous glint in his eye or the way his tongue darts out to lick his bottom lip as he takes his helmet. When he's sure I caught his double meaning, he puts it on.

"Bye, Nash," I draw out with a smile. He revs the engine one more time before giving me a nod and taking off.

Nash is not as "bad boy" as his appearance suggests. When we got outside, we squatted on the curb, and he divulged the real reason he asked me outside. He was playing wingman for Parker. I knew Parker would be interested in Stormy, and because she didn't come outside looking for me, it's safe to say she's interested too.

I key in the code to get into the house, and it's dark. Too dark. I thought for sure Everett would get home before me. I quickly reset the alarm, hating how I suddenly find the dark unsettling. Getting home late is one thing, but not coming home altogether is another. I didn't drink nearly enough tonight to drown out my nerves, and I'm disappointed he's not here. I know he feels something for me, and after our moment this afternoon, I believed him when he said he'd be home to cook with me. I don't want to give up. Giving up has never felt like an option. How do you just walk away from something that you want with your whole heart? However, hurting sucks.

I blow out a long sigh as I drag my ass up the staircase to my room. I need water and maybe a hot bath to unwind. My nerves are shot. I know what I need. I need a release. Opening the door to my room, I immediately jump back, my heart racing from the sight of a figure sitting on my bed. But it's not all fear. I can smell him. The woodsy scent of the earth and the salt of the sea. My hand hits the switch.

"What are you doing in my room?"

He doesn't immediately give me his eyes. Instead, he focuses on the item in his hands—my phone. I intentionally left it home after I texted Parker to come pick me up. I know Everett can track me if I have it on me, and I wanted to send a message if he did come home. He wants me to fall in line and follow his rules, but all he's given me are empty words, so I left him with an empty house.

His eyes slowly drag up my bare legs before meeting mine. "You left."

"You didn't come home." I toss my clutch onto my drafting table. "And I was with Parker. I was perfectly safe so—"

"That was not Parker who dropped you off."

I move away from the door and toward my dresser. "No shit. You can be very observant when you want to be."

"Cameron, if you can't tell, I'm not in the mood for your antics."

"Well, maybe I'm not in the mood for whatever whiplash you're about to give me," I snap back. "It's been a long day, Everett. I had to put in a rush order for the uniforms and come home to an empty house with a home invasion still very fresh in my mind. You want to sit in the dark and wait for me to come home so that you can list off all the rules I broke? Fine, be my guest." I throw my hands wide before dropping them to my hips and adding, "I'd rather be a rule breaker than a two-faced liar."

My chest is now heaving while he sits on my bed, unmoving, but I know I struck a nerve. His body language is a deceiver, just like the man. He's trained in the art of hiding his emotions. He's stuffed down his feelings his entire life, being the son of a DA turned senator, but the dark smolder in his coal-black eyes gives him away right before he stands.

"What did you call me?"

"I didn't stutter. I know you heard every last word, but I'll spell it out for you since I already know what part you're stuck on. You're a two-faced liar. You decree that I can not drive and that you will be my chauffeur, yet you assign the task to Parker after chastising me for catching one with him the other day. And as for the lying part... You told me you'd be here at six o'clock. You weren't here. I won't just sit around here alone and do nothing because you say so. I have needs, too."

I was so busy ensuring I articulated every word so I'd win, my mind dismissed how close he now stands.

"Needs?" he asks as I take a step back, not out of fear or want but because if I stand a chance of winning this argument, I need air. Air that doesn't smell like him and make me weak in the knees. Everett responds to facts. Give him anything less, and you've lost his attention. I don't plan on losing his attention on the first night he's ever visited my room. "Are you fucking the biker boy?" he sneers, stepping into my backstep.

"Are you really asking me that?"

Everett has never asked me a question that intrusive, let alone with that level of vehemence.

"Yes, Cameron, I am." He takes another step into my space, forcing me to take another back, except I've run out of room. My dresser is now at my back, and he smirks. "Last I checked, you still live under my roof, which makes you my responsibility, and that guy looks like a problem waiting to happen. I don't want to see him here again."

"You can't tell me who I can and can't see, Everett."

"I can, unless being sent away sounds more appealing. If you don't like the rules—"

"So we're back at this... I didn't break any rules by getting a ride home. He didn't come into the house. You said I couldn't have guys in the house, and I didn't. I have needs, too, Everett. You can't—"

"You keep mentioning needs, but you have yet to say what they are. What kind of needs do you have, Cameron?" he asks, caging me in and sending every nerve on high alert. He's so close. He's the kind of close I've dreamt about, and the malice in his voice doesn't match the desire I see in his eyes, but I know he's toying with me. This is revenge for me leaving my phone at home. He knows the effect he has on me, and he's playing me like a violin, killing me softly with his song. But if this is where I die, you better believe it will be epic.

Placing my hands on my dresser, I lift myself up for a seat to be at eye level before crossing my arms. "We both know exactly what kind of needs I'm talking about. You seem to want to take care of everything else..." I pause before looking him square in the eyes and adding, "How about those?"

He leans in, his eyes so dark I can't be sure if I'm back in bed waking from a dream in the dead of night or staring into the abyss I've sworn I'd sell my soul to countless times for just one taste. "Is that what you want?"

My mouth is suddenly parched as I dart my tongue out to moisten my lips and find my words as my heart races. *Don't back down. Don't back down.* "I want to come. If you can't make it happen, I'll find someone who can."

His stern glare stays glued to mine in challenge, and I can't tell if he's ready to fold or raise a bet. There's a slight tick in his jaw before he says, "Show me." I'm momentarily stunned into silence as I replay his words. Did he just say show me, or are the shot and three drinks I had at the bar earlier playing tricks on my mind? "You said you need to get this out of your system. You have my attention. So show me, or this ends now. I'm done with the games, Cameron."

"Show you what?" I stutter out on bated breath as my insides clench with anticipation.

His hand runs through the stubble on his chin as he takes a

small step back. "You said you had needs. Show me how you like to be filled so we can be done with this."

"Right here? Right now?" I question coyly, and he smirks, mistaking my confirmation for trepidation, prematurely calling himself the victor. But just as he starts to turn, I draw up my legs, thankful I wore a mini skirt, and let them fall open. "I typically prefer a bed, but a dresser will do."

Those black velvet eyes latch onto mine, and they don't move as the rise and fall of his chest becomes more pronounced. He didn't think I'd do it. He didn't believe that this was what I really wanted. That I'd actually choose him. I can see the torment in his eyes. He doesn't want to want me, but it doesn't change that he does. I give him a minute to adjust to the reality of this moment. There are no more innuendos to hide behind. There's here and now, me and him, in a dark, empty house. When he doesn't move, I slowly trail my hand down my stomach so as not to pull him out of the moment. I don't want him to overthink this and turn away from me. I want him to succumb to the desire I know lurks behind his midnight glare.

When I reach the top of my panties, I slip my hand beneath the satin fabric, and he says, "Take them off." I was already wet, wholly enraptured by his presence, but those words stop me in my tracks. He's no longer just watching. He's instructing. He's telling me what he wants, and right now, that's me. I don't move fast enough, and the next thing I know, his finger barely skims my hip bone before I feel the pinch of my panties being ripped from my body as a whimper escapes my lips. I'm so turned on right now I could come from his stare alone. "Are you ready to get me out of your system so we can be done?"

"Done?"

His jaw clenches as his hands find his hips, and he drops his gaze. "Yes, Cameron. Done. Shove those fingers in your pretty little pussy. This is the only way you'll ever get filled with me in the room. You and I aren't happening."

"But you're here now..." I slide my finger down my slit and bite

SALT

my lips when I feel my pussy clench on air, begging to be filled. "Show me yours."

"I'm not the one with something to get out of my system. You have five seconds to show me how you wanted biker boy to fill you, or I'm leaving."

Liar. There's no way in hell his honor and duty would allow him to stand here unless this was exactly where he wanted to be. So I don't push. Instead, I do exactly what he asked and push two fingers inside. The euphoric shiver that runs down my spine would have my legs falling out from under me if I weren't already sitting. My eyes threaten to flutter shut and remain that way. The feel of his eyes watching my every move as he stands mere inches away from my soaked pussy, one that he has to know is wet because of him, is utterly empowering and intoxicating. I'm not the girl he took in five years ago. I'm a woman who knows exactly what she wants. HIM.

Fuck. I can't help but close my eyes on the next pump as I shove in deeper. The sound of my arousal and the way my hardened nipples rub against the satin material of my camisole winning out over my desire to hold his tempestuous gaze, but I need more. If this is my first and last time, I need more.

"We both know it's not his fingers..." I add another digit, gliding two fingers down my center. "Or even his cock that I wanted filling me. It's yours."

His nostrils flare, and I know he wants to do exactly that. I don't care who I am to him. He's an unmarried man, and I'm sitting inches away from him with my legs spread, more than willing to let him have his way with me.

"I'm not going to touch you, Cameron, but I'll walk you through it." His eyes finally drop to my center, and I clench hard around my fingers, knowing he's finally seeing me. "If it was my cock filling you, stretching you and making your legs shake, you'd need to add a third finger, sunshine."

I bite my bottom lip so damn hard I'm sure I broke the skin. Everett just called me sunshine. A nickname is meaningful. It's a manifestation, a reflection of his emotions, what he's feeling deep down, and deep down, I now know part of him sees part of me through the same lens I see him. He's never called me anything but Cameron until now. I withdraw my fingers to add a third, and as hard as I try, I know there's no masking the slight tremble in my hand when I do. I like to think I have thick skin; not much can truly get to me except him. The shadows follow me, but I've learned to live with them. It's him who I see in my dreams. It's him that I can't stay away from; somewhere along the line, I let this man run away with all of me. He might break my heart, but I learned years ago that's what they were made for. The sound of my arousal greedily sucking my fingers in, wishing it were more, has a low moan escaping my throat.

"Fuck..." he growls out low and barely audible. "Spread these legs wider the way I would if I was slamming into you, reaching depths none of the want-to-be-men you've slept with have ever been able to touch."

They're already spread, but I push back on my heels and adjust my angle, giving him exactly what he wants, and watch as he pulls his bottom lip into his mouth. "More, Everett. Don't stop talking," I pant.

"My name breathlessly panted from those lips is the sweetest fucking sin. I don't want to hear its end, but I'm not a patient man, and bitter endings are all I deserve. Let's make this one hurt the worst. I want you to shove those fingers deep, sunshine. Imagine it is my length hitting that spot deep inside of you over and over, wringing out every last drop you didn't know you could give..." He trails off his voice, gruff and pained from what he still sees as the forbidden fruit, and my head lolls against the wall. I don't want to come. I'm not ready for this to be over any more than he is. Where does this leave us when it is over? Done? I'd rather stay here than find out. But when he says, "Circle your fingers over that little bundle of nerves that I want to suck into my mouth as you scream my name," I spiral hard.

"Ev..." I cry out as my legs shake from the most powerful

orgasm I've ever had. My head lazily rolls side to side against the wall as I try to come back down. Blinking open my eyes, his molten gaze is closer than it was before I came. He's closer. His body is rigid, his arms tightly molded to his sides, and his fists are clenched so hard that his knuckles are white. "Everett, please," I softly plead.

"Don't," he grits out, his chest heaving as he tears his eyes away from mine and starts toward the door.

I watch him reject me again, steadfast in his convictions that we can't happen, but I refuse to let him go. I refuse to let him think we can't be more. "Everett..." He pauses with his hand on the doorknob, but he doesn't turn back. "It's not out of my system."

"It's only an affliction if you continue to want it... Let it go, Cameron."

The door to my room closes before I can utter another word, but it doesn't stop me from saying what's on my mind all the same. "Not all afflictions are evil." Sometimes, it's because they exist that we discover our disease. Fear is his—not mine.

CHAPTER 15
EVERETT

I didn't sleep. I couldn't sleep. I'm not even sure why I laid in bed at all. The entire night, I stared at the ceiling, condemning myself for coveting my dead best friend's daughter. He entrusted her to me, and all I've been able to do is dream unthinkable thoughts, and last night, I snapped. Once again, she deliberately disobeyed me. She left the house without her phone, a move that I know was intentional. I'm not fucking dense. Lauren showed up, and she went MIA. The conclusions were easy to draw. Cameron assumed Lauren was the reason I didn't get home on time last night. She didn't know that I walked in the door five minutes after she walked out or that she was the cause of my lateness, nor did she believe I'd sit in her room all that time and let myself feel everything I shouldn't want.

When I couldn't stand my insomnia anymore, I came downstairs to the gym where I've been for the last two hours, pushing myself until I felt like I might actually die because death feels like a fucking fate I deserve. At least in death, I could say I didn't touch her, at least not in a way that counts. I never had a daughter, but it's not hard to imagine myself in Damon's shoes. Were he alive, he'd probably already have me killed for the sunscreen. Fuck! That was the wrong image I needed in my head

SALT

right now. I slam my hand on the stop button, get off the treadmill, and head for the sauna. Maybe I'll die sweating out my demons.

Once inside the sauna, I lay down a towel and drop my shorts before lying on the bench. For the first time in days, I feel my exertion weigh heavy on my eyelids, and I close them. But no sooner than the flashes of light fade to a jet-black backdrop, visions of her fingers sinking deep into her wet pussy seize hold of my mind, and I'm once again reminded of my hardened length. I've refused to stroke it. I've fucked women to get her off my mind, but I've never allowed myself to wrap my hand around my cock to thoughts of her. I feel my heavy tip hit my stomach as it painfully twitches, begging for release. It took every ounce of strength I had left in me not to immediately drop my pants and rut into my hand the second I got back to my room last night, but I didn't. Instead I headed straight for the shower and stood under the cold water until I couldn't take it anymore.

In my mind, I know no one sin holds more weight than another, but I've tried convincing myself otherwise for the past four years. The truth is, I started seeing her differently the night she got a glimpse of the man behind the veil. No one has ever seen me, and I mean truly fucking seen me. But the night of her seventeenth birthday, she found me standing in the shadows of the greenhouse, looking on as my then-wife shared a kiss with her high school lover. Cameron knew without words it wasn't the first time I'd witnessed Moira's infidelity. She stood by my side, watching on, and said, "Duty and honor are hallowed words, they're worth fighting for, but do they not die when they protect a lie?"

At seventeen, she saw straight to my soul. The crux of what was the bane of my existence: name, honor, family. My entire life, I have put those virtues before my wants. That night, I watched my wife kiss another man, but it wasn't until Cameron came along that I felt anyone would ever see me. She didn't see the act of infidelity as the main event. She saw me and my heart, and then I saw her.

147

Fuck it. I grab my throbbing cock and squeeze hard. If I'm already sentenced to burn in hell for the sins I've already committed, what's one more? A deep guttural moan escapes my chest on the first stroke as a vision of her withdrawing her fingers to fit three inside and accommodate my length makes its way to center stage. I already know what her soft porcelain skin feels like. I'm sure her pussy feels like silk. I squeeze harder, remembering how her juices coated her fingers. My cock strained hard against the zipper of my jeans as I looked on, wishing it were my balls covered in her essence. Damn it.

I hate that holding my cock to visions of shoving it deep inside of her already feels like the best sex I've had in years, and I'm not even fucking her. My balls draw close to my body on the next stroke as I think about how close I was to unbuttoning my jeans and giving her exactly what she wanted when her eyes rolled back as she screamed my name. That nickname has always felt like a curse when I've heard it roll off her lips. Moira always called me Everett, and in high school, friends called me Callahan. But Cameron gave me that nickname years ago at a family picnic. It came so naturally, like we were close, like I fucking meant something, and maybe I do. I hate the thought of meaning anything to her but pushing her away hurts just as much. Her leaving to stay at Connor's all but killed me. I'm a selfish prick for bringing her back here, knowing I'm already on the verge of losing control when it comes to her. Fuck.

The vision of her curled up in the closet, the flash of relief, followed by annoyance, was enough to make me feral. I wanted to save her as much as I wanted to smack her ass for thinking of leaving me in the first place... and then those words. She thought she had hung up the phone, but she didn't. I heard what she said when she thought no one was listening, and it felt like parts of my soul were physically abandoning my body, leaving to find a vessel more suited to deal with a dreamer's heart. But I wanted to dream. I still want to dream even though I know it will only make all of this that much harder to walk away from. Even if it does cause me pain, I've never felt more alive, more real, more like myself than I do sitting in the torture her light inflicts on me. Her eyes slowly blinking open and finding mine, pleading with me for more, have hot ropes of cum shooting onto my stomach. I grunt out my release, pulling long and slow, not wanting to let go but needing to get past these thoughts that plague me so I can get my head right.

As my labored breathing finally slows, I catch my breath and open my eyes to my new reality: obsession. My obsession is dangerous. My obsession is her.

~

"Last night changed things, Everett. It doesn't matter if you don't want it to. It did, and you can't take it back," Cameron says from the passenger seat as I pull into the stadium's parking lot. I should have known the silence on the drive here was a small showing of goodwill I didn't deserve. I knew I'd have to answer for my misdeeds. As I laid in bed staring at the ceiling, I thought of all the things I would tell her, knowing she might go down this path regardless of what I've said. But I can't bring my mouth to say them quick enough before she adds, "Even if you could take it back... I wouldn't want you to."

I shut off the car and press my head back into the soft leather of my seat. "Cameron, it's not going to—"

A loud knocking on my window steals my words. "Do you always get in this late? I've been here for twenty minutes," Garrett chides, standing outside my window.

I hate being interrupted, but I'm grateful for the distraction right now. Whatever words I had for Cameron weren't coming easy because she's right. Whether I like it or not, last night did change things. Now, I have to figure out how to erase it so it doesn't happen again. It can't happen again. I don't bother finishing my sentence or even addressing her before I exit the car.

"What are you doing here?"

"Good morning to you too, brother," he quips just as Cameron exits her side. "Hey Cam," he greets right before she closes her door a little harder than necessary. She gives him no words as I hear her heels clicking off toward the entrance. "What happened?"

"I'm not sure what you mean."

He crosses his arms and widens his stance. "That girl has never once ignored me. She's sunshine on a cloudy day. What happened?"

I look toward the building and catch her back just before she enters the stadium. "Nothing, that's the problem."

"Don't lie to me. I'm your brother. I know when you're giving me half-truths. I've seen the way you look at her, Everett. It's not nothing."

"I didn't touch her," I answer a little harsher than intended.

He clicks his tongue. "That's what this is..." He trails off, his posture softening as he props an elbow on the roof of my car.

"What are you droning on about? You know what, never mind. Why are you here?"

"I stayed at Connor's last night with Colton. The new security company you hired stayed a little later than expected, and a quiet house was a nice change of pace. I love my kids, but lately, I've felt more like a referee than a father. I came to talk to Lauren, but I caught her on the way in and—"

"What business do you have with Lauren?" I cut him off before he can act like he didn't just drop a piece of important information. I've asked him to help me with a lead I've been tracking down since Damon's death, and if Lauren has anything to do with that lead, I want every last detail.

"You need to figure your shit out, Everett. You're so wound up you can't think straight. We briefly talked about Lauren and Stormy last night after I showed you the small clue the cameras picked up from the break-in." It's nothing that points to them. He's operating on a hunch, maybe one Colton put in his head. Since they both stayed at Connor's I'm sure they discussed multiple angles and because it's Cole, I'm not naïve enough to believe the topic of Cameron and I didn't come up. It's why

Garrett's giving his two cents now. Pushing off the car, he points toward the stadium. "That girl in there is what you want, then own it. This..." he gestures toward me, "this will make everyone see something else. You look guilty. You're not acting like the calm, collected, level-headed co-founder of the MacBeth Foundation, part owner of Callahan & Associates, and the son of a senator. If you want to tarnish your reputation, then keep doing whatever this is."

I angrily run my hand through my beard. Sleep has evaded me for countless nights. I fall asleep for short minutes at a time, if at all, and the things I've done to forget, the things I've tried to get her out of my system, don't work. I can't focus. I know he's right. She's a poison for which there is no cure.

"You don't understand. No one fucking understands."

"I'm a lawyer, Everett. I see the sides you do. She is your best friend's daughter. You've been part of her life for a long time. You're practically twice her age. You have children older than her, and she came to live with you while she was still in high school..." His eyes hold mine on that last point, and I know he's following my train of thought. "I also know another detail. The one that twists you up the most. I know why Damon was late to the gala the night of the accident, and I know you blame yourself for it."

Of course I blame myself for his accident. It was my favor that made him late, that made him take a different route. My request put him in the wrong place at the wrong time. It's yet another unforgivable reason I can't be anything Cameron needs. How could I ever ask for her heart when I'm the reason it's broken?

"It sounds like you know why nothing can ever happen, so if we're done here, I need to get to practice," I say as I pop the trunk and start toward the back to grab my bag.

"I'm done. I've said my piece, but I'll leave you with this. When you find the person you're meant to be with, none of what I've said matters because they are your reason for existing. The rest will work itself out."

He rasps his knuckles on the roof of my car. "Keep your phone on you today. I'm expecting to have more information this afternoon."

I nod as I close the trunk. There's no point in asking him what lead he's following. He won't tell me anyway. He has a habit of keeping shit close until he knows for sure he's right. Colton is the one who will spitball with you and give you a rundown of every possible outcome he thinks could exist, which is the polar opposite of Garrett.

My phone vibrates in my pocket as I reach the entrance.

> Lauren: Can I swing by your place tonight? We need to talk.

You've got to be kidding me. The last thing I need is for Lauren to stop by the house, but I also have reason to keep her close.

> Everett: 6 p.m.

I keep it short and concise, as if that somehow excuses the acceptance.

> Lauren: I'll bring dinner.

Great. I'm so fucking screwed.

"**E**verett, are you going to be good for the game this weekend?" Coach Teague asks, gripping my shoulder as I down my Gatorade.

"Yeah, why?" I ask, hearing the strain in my voice.

"You look tired, is all. You realize most coaches don't run through the exercises with their teams, right? I think you've more than shown the boys that you're dedicated to helping them grow this season. You don't have to prove anything."

In the beginning, I felt like I had something to prove. I'm old enough to be their dad, and I've sat behind a desk for almost as long as they've been alive. So yeah, I had something to prove; but even before I took over for Connor, I trained every day. It just looked different than it does now. My physical health has always been a priority. Aging sucks, but if you take care of your body, it will take care of you, and training alongside guys half my age and going harder for longer has put wind in my sails.

"I'm not trying to prove anything to them. Not anymore. They looked good out there today," I say as I stand up and grab my board.

"Yeah, I think Parker has real potential to be a standout this season when he's not in his own way."

"I'll see if he's ready to talk."

It's no secret he has an issue with me, but I know he hasn't been running his mouth about it either. This is a small town, people talk. If he was talking, there's no way in hell whatever story he's spinning wouldn't have made its way back to me by now.

"See you bright and early tomorrow. Salt said uniforms will be in, and I figured it's best to make sure they fit before the guys get sweaty."

I toss my bag over my shoulder and try to keep my tone indifferent when I'm anything but. "She gave you her number?"

"What? No, some of us take bathroom breaks. I ran into her about an hour ago when you were running triangle drills. Side note: I know the guys think they are beyond those, but it's smart. They're all great players but being great individually doesn't make you great as a team."

"Yeah, my fear with leagues like this is everyone wants to be the standout, and they sacrifice the team for their own gain because, for some of them, it's their last shot. Their last year to play," I say as we walk up the tunnel.

"I thought the same thing when I started coaching these leagues two years ago, but I haven't run into that yet. That has a lot to do with Connor. On the first day of tryouts, he goes over the mission statement and drives home why the team exists, reiterating that if the players give him their all, he'll do the same. Each year, we have a handful of kids walk after that speech, and the ones who have stayed give everything."

"Let's hope this isn't the season that changes."

An unmistakable laugh catches my attention as we enter the concourse, and I see Cameron sitting on a bench, talking to a guy with a helmet in his hands. What little pent-up stress I was able to work out during practice is now back tenfold. That has to be the biker fuck that dropped her off last night.

"I'll see you tomorrow," I say, not waiting for a response before marching across the concourse. There's no way in hell she's leaving with him.

"Everett." She does a double take when she realizes it's me. "This is Nash. Nash, this is Everett, Connor's dad."

"Nice to meet you, sir," he says, extending his hand for me to shake, which I do so begrudgingly. I don't like that he just called me sir, nor do I like being introduced as Connor's father, at least not when every fiber of my being feels like something else to her.

I shake his hand but offer zero pleasantries. "Are you ready to go?" I ask pointedly.

Her eyebrows rise, but before her lips can move, he answers for her. "Oh, I don't mind giving her a ride home." He shoots her a wink. "Cam makes a good backpack."

Cam? I don't like how seemingly close she is to this guy that he's calling her by her nickname. And backpack? Over my dead body. "Her name is Cameron, and there's no fucking way she's ever getting on the back of your bike again."

"It's fine, Everett. Mackenzie called earlier, and she told me who my late-night visitor was last week, so there's no longer a security threat—"

"Nash, was it? Do you mind giving me a second?"

"Sure," he stands. "I'll just be by concessions."

My eyes flick back to her just in time to catch her crossing her arms and raising an unimpressed brow.

"You're not riding home with him."

"And why not?"

"Because I don't like it."

"That sounds like a personal problem, Everett. I can get a ride from whomever I want."

Her eyes narrow on mine, ensuring I caught the double meaning in her words before she attempts to step around me. I catch her elbow. "The only ride you'll be taking is from me. You'll get in my car and only my car, not because I'm demanding but because we both know you want to." I see her obstinance rear its stubborn head, and I add, "And because I want you to."

Her face reluctantly softens, but she concedes. "Fine, I'll meet you outside."

The ride home is silent, similar to our ride to work this morning. I'm not complaining. I'll take her silence over her being on the back of some idiot's bike any day. We have things we should discuss, but talking about them makes them real. Talking leads to more questions and discussions about what comes next, which are all things I don't have answers to. I know what I should do and what I should say, but right now, cutting off one of my hands feels like a far better punishment than the risk that comes with giving her words, ones that would undoubtedly inflict pain.

"Who is that?"

My eyes scan the road ahead, and I see Lauren sitting on the front porch. She's early, and I'm fucked. I had the entire drive home to give Cameron a heads-up, but I didn't. To my credit, it's not because I was hiding it. I forgot. Being locked in a car with Cameron doesn't help either. She already consumes all of my thoughts—seat her an arm's length away from me, and forget about it. It's annoying as much as it is pathetic.

I've barely parked the car before she's reaching for the handle, and I'm certain I know exactly what she's assuming. "Cameron..."

My words die before they begin as she pushes open the door and starts up the stone path toward the house.

"Oh, I didn't realize we'd have company," Lauren says, rising from the porch steps with a bag of food from Vivianno's and a bottle of wine.

"Yes," I nervously clear my throat and pray Cameron doesn't make this into something it's not. "Cameron lives with me."

"Oh, well, I'll make a mental note to order more next time."

"Next time..." Cameron questions slowly as I jog up the steps to key in the alarm code and open the door.

"Lauren, the kitchen is straight back through the foyer if you want to get the food ready."

"Sure, I'll just make myself at home."

When I turn back, Cameron's on the top step, her fist clenched and her gaze at my feet. "I want my keys back, Everett."

"Cam–"

"Now, Everett. Keys!"

"It's not what you think," I try as I step toward her.

"Don't. You lied to me to get me in your car, and then you brought me home to what...? To witness your date? To put me in my place? To further emphasize that I'm just a girl with a crush?" She runs her hand through her hair and bites her lip as she shakes her head. "Give me my keys."

"They're in the garage under the upside-down stack of terracotta flowerpots."

She doesn't even spare me a glance before storming off toward the garage, and I let her go. I let her go and tell myself it's because I need answers, but deep down, I know that's a copout. I let her go because we don't match. There is no future where she and I are endgame. When I stood here and told Lauren that Cameron lived with me, she didn't see a girlfriend, a wife, or a partner. She saw a college kid living with a guardian. That's what Damon made me with his death, and that's all I'll ever be. So, I let her go.

Closing the door, I walk through the foyer and toward the kitchen. I know damn well this isn't a date, and so does Lauren, but I am curious why she's put in all the pomp and circumstance. We aren't friends, but the way she's genuinely making herself comfortable in my kitchen as she plays music on my Alexa with a poured glass of wine in hand as she searches through my cabinets, has me on high alert.

"There you are. I hope you don't mind the music. I saw the speaker and couldn't help myself. I always cook with music on." She stops her perusal and pours me a glass, only to ask once it's in front of me. "Do you drink wine? I should have asked instead of assuming, but I feel like everyone enjoys a good glass of Merlot now and again. Not to mention, it pairs nicely with the food I picked up."

She's rambling. That's a nervous tick if I ever did see one.

"Why are you here, Lauren?"

She rolls her lips and taps her nails on her glass. "We didn't start on the right foot the other day. Lunch was a dick-measuring contest if I've ever seen one, but I meant it when I said I was not here to cause trouble. However, some things have been brought to my attention that I felt I should share. I'm too old for drama, Everett."

"Well, you have a captive audience, seeing as it's just you and me, so please feel free to drop whatever baggage you brought with you on my doorstep," I say sardonically as I take a sip of my wine. I'm not a big wine drinker, but this is actually decent, and after the past twenty-four hours, I could use a drink. I may have been brash, but it can't be helped when sitting here with her is the last place I want to be.

"My niece is Evan Grave's sister—"

"That is need-to-know information. Information you should have shared last week," I say, attempting not to lose my temper. Yelling at women is something I try hard to avoid.

She holds up her hand. "This is the story she's attempting to spin."

"Well, this sounds like a problem for you. She's your niece. Fix it."

"Will you settle down and hear me out? I came here because I want to let this play out, and I need your cooperation to do so. I'm curious where Stormy is going with this."

"Why would I entertain this, Lauren? I thought I made it clear I don't want your drama, and yet you're back with a problem nonetheless," I point out as I round the counter to get something stronger than wine.

"Because of who she is and what she might know. Her stories might be fabricated, but there is some truth spun into them. The question is, how does she have those truths?" She pauses to take a sip of her wine before adding, "I would have told you last week had I known then what I do now. Everett, you have to remember I've been gone for over twenty years, and believe it or not, I didn't care to check on anyone who still lived in this backwash old town. No one here was worth my time."

Pulling down a lowball glass, I fill it with ice before uncorking my cognac. "Let's hear it, Lauren. It better be worth my time if you expect me to play along."

"The other day, when I got back from running up to the store, Stormy was sitting in the living room with a guy I'd never seen before who was sporting a Callahan & Associates duffle bag. Obviously, my interest was piqued. That's when she introduced him as Evan Graves and told me he was her brother."

I should ask if he's still at her place, but I don't. I haven't been concerned with finding him, even though I know he's the one who broke into Connor's house. I already know his motive, and it wasn't to hurt Cameron. He was trying to steal shit to pawn out of Connor's closet. On the first night Cameron left my house to stay at Connor's, Evan went straight there after I told him he couldn't stay, and she naively let him in. At the time, she wasn't sleeping in the master bedroom; instead, she was in a guest bedroom upstairs, which gave him the perfect opportunity to case the downstairs. Having gotten into the house, he noted where all the interior cameras were located to avoid them when he returned later. I'm sure he didn't know she was in that closet scared shitless when he broke in a few nights later. He probably thought she was upstairs asleep without a worry that he was downstairs pilfering through Connor and Makenzie's valuables.

I take a long pull of my drink as I go over the details she's sharing and the ones she isn't. "You're going to need to get better at lying if you expect me to believe your niece..." I draw out the title, letting it marinate before adding, "conned you into believing she has a sibling. Sage Graves was not your sister. You didn't have any siblings," I assert, topping off my glass.

"You're right. I don't. Just because I refer to Stormy as my niece doesn't make it literal. People refer to family friends as uncles and aunts all the time. I'm sure you have something similar with Cameron."

Cameron has never once called me uncle. Thank fuck for small miracles, but I understand the sentiment. I take a drink, needing the caramel-colored concoction to take the edge off. "The more I learned about Evan, the more curious I became. I assumed you and Moira had damn good reasons why you weren't helping him out now." She turns to the cabinet behind her and pulls out two plates.

"Evan isn't a bad kid. Jaded, bitter, and maybe a little resentful —yes, but he's done a lot of it to himself. Moira and I helped him after his mother conned us. Obviously, we never expected anything in return. We saw a boy born into a house of addiction and stepped up to care for him when his mother couldn't. For the most part, he was grateful, but at the end of the day, I don't care who you are. Being abandoned sucks. He was old enough to understand exactly what happened. His mother didn't die. She'd rather do drugs than have her son. It fucked with him."

"What exactly do you think you know about Sage Graves?" she asks, her expression pinched like I'm missing something big.

"Enough. Sage was a drug addict who abandoned her son and never looked back." As I watch her sip her wine, another detail suddenly hits me. "Why would Stormy choose Evan as her brother? Or maybe the better question is, why would she expect you to believe it? If she's not your niece, who is she to you?"

"Were you and Moira happily married? I mean, I was around, and I know there were rumors, but then you guys had Connor, and you were married for almost two decades. Was it all a facade or was any of it real?" she asks, setting a salad plate in front of me.

"Lauren, I don't care to discuss my marriage with you or anyone else. I'd appreciate it if we could stay on topic." I sit at one of the stools surrounding the kitchen island and watch as she dishes out the salad.

"I am on topic. The fact that you can't see that is telling." She walks around the island and grabs her plate before leaning against the opposite counter. "Moira MacBeth is Evan Graves's biological aunt, not me, which would make her Stormy's aunt as well, if they were indeed siblings." I feel my eyes narrow on hers as I try to process whether or not I believe the words coming out of her mouth. My marriage with Moira may have been loveless, but we were friends. It doesn't make sense that she would keep that information from me. "Moira's uncle, Craig, is Evan Graves's father."

My eyes feel like they jump out of my skull. "What proof do you have?"

"My mother."

"Your mother. The same one who's currently staying at Sweet Water Retirement Home?"

She raises a brow. "Are you keeping tabs on my mother?"

"No, Connor's wife had her mother there last year. Naturally, I took it upon myself to know what residents were in the facility."

"Of course you did," she says before sipping her wine. "After Stormy dropped that bomb, I decided to visit my mom. If there was any truth in her story, my mother would know. She was a records clerk at the Waterloo police station for over thirty years. What I found out was Sage Graves did get a rape kit or a version of it at the hospital after a sexual assault occurred around the same time she would have likely conceived Evan. The hospital processed everything, but when it showed up at the police station, it went missing. All the records of her claim were gone."

"If everything went missing, how does your mother know anything about it?"

"She was the one who received it from the hospital. The kit literally went missing while she was processing it. She left to use the restroom, and when she returned, it was gone."

Craig was a dirty chief of police who had his hands in everything. His corruption and blackmail went untouched for years. "Let me guess, she didn't question that it went missing because of who was named as the assailant." She shrugs a non-verbal admission. "Have you mentioned any of this to Evan?"

"No, I haven't seen him since that day in my living room. Honestly, a conversation between Moira and me is long overdue, but seeing as she hasn't been around, I decided to come to you as an olive branch, if you will. I'm currently working for your son, and I meant it when I said my business here has nothing to do with you and yours." She pauses to take a bite of her salad. I'll give it to her. Lauren's comfort and moxie are unfitting for the current situation. They remind me of Cameron. She waves her fork at me. "Are you not going to eat?"

"You'll have to excuse my lack of appetite. This story you're spinning is news to me, and I'm still not sure I believe it."

Again, she takes another bite, unfazed by my disbelief. "What do I have to gain by lying?" I don't admit I haven't figured that out yet, but there's always something. Ghosts don't come back without a reason to haunt. "If you don't believe me, you could always ask your wife."

"Ex-wife," I correct before taking another pull of my cognac. "You still haven't answered my question. You aren't Stormy's blood. So who are you to Stormy?"

I watch as she places her plate down and picks up her wine. She's stalling, which means whatever comes out next is either a lie or a version of the truth that doesn't tell the whole story.

"I met Sage through an unlikely source I don't want to discuss.

The way we met doesn't concern you. It's a part of my past." She pauses, flipping open another container. "Unbeknownst to me, Sage had a will. The woman barely had a pot to piss in, but she had a will, and apparently, she named me as a guardian for Stormy should anything ever happen to her. But the detail Stormy doesn't realize I know is that Stormy was not Sage's biological daughter. Sage adopted her."

"Are you fucking kidding me? She leaves Evan on our porch but adopts a stranger? Pass me the bottle."

Lauren slides the bottle across the counter. "I know how it looks, but you can't judge someone else's journey because it doesn't fit your script. We both know Sage wasn't the only one around here with skeletons in the closet." As I pour myself another glass, she asks, "So, are you agreeing to let this play out?"

There's more to tell. I can feel it. But I honestly can't put together why the girl would choose this lie; however, like Lauren, I'm intrigued.

"I'm not the keeper of your secrets, Lauren."

"The way I see it, I haven't given you any information you couldn't have found on your own." She places her hand on her hip. "If there were secrets in it, they weren't mine."

My eyes narrow on hers. She's not wrong. While I know damn well she's withholding information, the secrets she shared weren't hers; they were Moira's, but everyone knows a secret that isn't yours to tell is still a secret, but I let it go. I have so many questions, but first, I need to see my ex, and right now, she's the last person I want to see. I can't believe, after everything we've been through, she would keep this of all things from me—it's time to find the stranger I used to call wife.

CHAPTER 16
CAMERON

"Cameron, what's wrong? Talk to me. What happened?"

"I don't want to talk about it. I shouldn't have answered the phone," I sigh heavily. We are a texting generation. I can't believe Mac called. The sound of my phone ringing caught me off guard, and I accidentally swiped it. "I just wanted to know how fast you could design and build me a house. I don't need anything big. I think smaller would be better. A ranch-style house, but I want those stacker sliding glass doors across the entire back so I feel like I'm on Salt Lake even when I'm inside my living room." My dad left this property to me, and I've decided I want a house here. I feel close to him when I'm here. "If you're too busy, I understand. I just thought I'd offer you the job first. It would be another project under your belt and one that can be done from home. You don't have to travel and—"

"Cam, you don't have to sell me on designing a home for you. I'll do it. I'm just wondering why you're sending me this text from the lake at almost midnight."

I need to turn off my phone's share location feature. If she knows I'm here, so does Everett. I stare up at the pitch-black night sky, but there are no stars. Not tonight. It's overcast, and the only light that can be seen filters through thin clouds every now and then. It's pitch dark out here, but the howling coyotes off in the distance don't scare me. Nothing could scare me right now. I feel numb. When Everett told me he didn't like me riding with Nash, it felt like more, especially after what went down last night. He's a man of few words, and I know whatever is happening between us isn't easy. Us. Right now, that term feels naive. I'm back to feeling like a girl with a crush because the woman who got in his car was confident she was getting in with a man who was struggling to come to terms with the fact that he has feelings for his best friend's daughter. I accepted the silence because I didn't want to push. I wanted to give him space while being in his space all at the same time. Then he parked the car, and everything felt like whiplash. There I was, nothing once more. Lauren was sitting on his damn porch with a bottle of wine and dinner. It was clearly a date, and fuck if that didn't hurt. I had to get out of there. Right now, a coyote ripping out my throat feels like the lesser of two evils.

"It's quiet, and I needed space to think. You still need to answer the other part of my question. How long will it take? Can we expedite the process?"

"I mean, I can start drawing something up tomorrow and get it to you in a few days. If you like it, I can send it to the architect we used to build the spare house on our property for my mom and brother. After that, there's probably at least a month of paperwork, followed by getting a contractor and materials. Plus, there's the terrain to consider. We could have trees taken down and get the land build ready while everything else starts, but it would be at least six to eight months before you had an actual house on the property.

"Ugh, why can't shit just be easy?"

"It's not hard. You're currently impatient and clearly avoiding something. Does this have anything to do with Everett not telling you who broke in yesterday instead of today?"

"Wait," I sit straight up on the hood of my car. "Everett knew who broke in yesterday? How do you know that?"

I hear Connor mumble something in the background. I'm

probably keeping him awake. I'm sure he's trying to sleep but would rather have a lousy sleep than let her get out of bed to take a call in the other room.

"I know because he called Connor around lunchtime yesterday, so I guess that would have been mid-morning your time."

He fucking knew all day. He knew during the uniform fittings, and he knew when he sat in my room waiting for me to come home, and he still didn't say anything. The threat to my security was gone, but he didn't tell me. Instead, he fucked with my head and gave me a reason to stay.

"Hey, I got to go. I'm serious about the house though. If you could start tomorrow, I'd love you forever."

"Okay, but—"

I cut the call before she can finish. I already know what she was going to say anyway. She was going to keep digging. She'll get the details eventually. Right now, I need to figure out my next move. Everett Callahan wasn't trying to see to it that I got him out of my system. He was ensuring I was infected.

"Want to catch the game with me tomorrow?" I say as I hip-bump Stormy.

"Depends. Are you asking, or are you asking for someone else?"

Parker has to be the someone else she is referring to, but since she has yet to bring him up in casual conversation, I don't mention it. "I'm asking for me. I don't have a date, and while I could rock up solo, it would be a lot more fun if I had a plus one. Drinking with someone always beats drinking alone."

That earns me the slightest of lip curls before she says, "Well, since you mentioned drinking—"

"Hey, girls. I brought lunch," Lauren interrupts, clicking into the team shop wearing red bottoms and a white sheath dress and looking way too fucking dolled up for a job at the stadium.

God, I hate being this girl. I'm judging her the same way I know people judge me for always looking overly dressed for most occasions, but with me, I know it's because it's my thing. I'm getting a degree in fashion. With her, I feel like it's an attention grab, and she's gunning for the one man I've been trying to claim for my own.

"You didn't need to bring us lunch. We usually grab a snack from the concession stand," I say, remembering my manners.

"Oh, nonsense. I owe you for the other night. I feel terrible. I didn't know you lived with Everett."

Stormy opens the bag she set on the counter. I swear that girl is like a black hole when it comes to food. She's constantly eating, and I have no idea where it goes. Good genetics. Lucky bitch.

"They forgot to include utensils. I'll go grab some," Stormy says, not waiting for a reply before walking out.

"So what's your story anyway?" Lauren asks as she pulls out containers from Bread Co. "Are you an exchange student?"

I guess I didn't come up during their date night since she has no clue who I am. I don't mind sharing, but I also don't care to spill all my information to my competition. "I thought you and Everett are old friends?"

It's obvious she doesn't see me as the same because my question doesn't bother her in the least. "We went to high school together, but that was decades ago. I haven't been back to these parts in many years." Her eyebrows pinch slightly as though the thought holds heaviness. "Everything feels so different now but yet still the same. I'm not even sure how that's possible. I guess time changes you, but it doesn't erase things." She shrugs before leaning onto the counter. "So how about you?"

"My parents died a few years ago, and Everett was my father's best friend and business partner. After the accident, the Callahans let me stay here in Waterloo with them instead of returning to the

East Coast to live with family I didn't know." I mindlessly flip open one of the containers she brought. Talking about my family hits differently when the anniversary of their accident is coming up.

"Is your father Damon Salt?"

"Yes, did you know him?" Obviously, she knew of him since his name is coming out of her mouth, but the way she asked and subtly shifted makes me think maybe they were friends.

"I got forks!" Stormy says, strolling back in. "Hey, can I borrow the car tomorrow night?"

"That depends. What are you borrowing it for?" Lauren says speculatively.

I am still determining what Stormy's story is. I haven't asked, and she hasn't offered anything, but she's the same age as me. Most people have their own car by twenty-two. Not everyone drives a brand new Audi as I do, but a hand-me-down or, hell, even an old beater isn't far-fetched.

"Ugh..." she draws out. "How about I tell you later?"

"Okay, then I'll give you my answer later."

"Fine. Sorry to ruin your surprise." She looks at me before turning to Lauren and adding, "I wanted to pick Cam up for the game tomorrow so I could take her out after her birthday."

My eyebrows raise. "How did you know it was my birthday tomorrow?" I stopped celebrating my birthday after the accident. My twenty-first birthday was the only exception, and even that wasn't by my planning. They never felt the same, being so close to the anniversary of my parent's death.

"I ran into Parker when I was grabbing forks, and he told me," She takes a big bite of her sandwich and, with a mouth full of turkey, asks, "How old are you going to be anyway? I assumed we were about the same age."

"I'll be twenty-two tomorrow."

Lauren puts her sandwich down before she takes a bite and asks, "Were you born here?"

I finish chewing the bite I just shoved in my mouth. "My

mother's side of the family is from the East Coast, and we didn't move here until I was around eight years old."

Her eyes are on me, but her focus is not. The blankness I see there tells me she's a million miles away.

I clear my throat and turn my attention back to Stormy. I don't have a reason to dislike Lauren aside from the fact that we're after the same man, but I also don't care to get all chummy either. "You said you assumed we were the same age... give it up."

"Oh, I'm twenty-three."

Lauren barely touched her food. She has only taken one bite when she closes her box and straightens her dress. "I have a call I need to hop on. You guys will have to finish without me."

She's two steps away from the door when Stormy says, "You never said if I could borrow the car or not."

With her hand on the door frame, she turns back, her forehead pinched, her eyes still elsewhere. "Sure."

Lauren exits, and Stormy turns back to me. "She never lets me borrow the car. Maybe she's into Everett after all. Brownie points for schmoozing over his best friend's daughter."

Great. I needed to eat something, and now I've lost my appetite.

~

I got a lot of shit done today and I'm exhausted, but where going home usually makes me happy, right now, it feels like a boulder sitting on my chest. It doesn't help that I haven't crossed paths with Everett since I walked out. I still need to settle on exactly how I feel. I have things in motion. I have a plan, one that still includes him. I've loved blindly for too long, and maybe that was selfish. When I love, I chase after it with my whole heart because, to me, that's what love does; it pursues blindly, without end. But I'm also learning to guard my own heart.

I wish my travel trailer were here. I ordered it this morning and it won't arrive for two weeks. I plan to put it on my lake property so I have my own place to go, and it will be nice to be on-site and available during construction. "Two weeks," I repeat as I blow out a long breath and look up to click the unlock button on my Audi as I cross the parking lot, only for my eyes to connect with Everett's. God, how is it that even when I'm hurt and mad as hell, he still makes me weak in the knees?

When I reach the car, he doesn't move off the driver's side door. He stays still and resolute, as though it's his right to be there.

"Can we talk?"

"It would appear you're not really giving me a choice in the matter," I say as I gesture toward my door. The corner of his perfect mouth quirks up just a hint, and I think he's about to speak, but he doesn't. Instead, his eyes stay locked on mine with a stare that feels new. It makes my heart skip a beat and my palms grow sweaty. I'm not doing this again. He did this to me when he told me he didn't want me riding home with Nash. I thought we'd actually talk, but all I got was his silence. Sometimes silence can speak a hundred sentiments, but sometimes it's just silence, and I'm done with it. "Everett, I think it's a little late to talk. The time for talking has passed—"

"I told you what happened between us wasn't going to change anything," he says as the softness on his face is replaced with pinched lips and frown lines.

"We both know that's bullshit. If you didn't want anything to change, you shouldn't have done it. You knew, Everett." I hold his eyes, daring him to tell me I'm wrong.

"I know," he admits, which has me shocked. He's not giving me any lip service or trying to say something without saying anything at all. It may only be two words, but they are two big words. They are an admission.

"Tell me what that means, Everett."

"It means I'm fearless, Cameron. I've always gone through the motions in every aspect of my life, doing what needed to be done without worrying about the consequences. They never mattered. Losing never scared me, but that's not the case

169

anymore." He looks away and angrily runs his hand over his beard.

"You just said you were fearless."

Those onyx eyes return and pierce mine. "Except when it comes to you." There's a slight stutter as he pulls in his next breath, and then he says, "You scare me, Cameron. You scare me more than anything ever has, but in that fear, I've never felt more alive."

The damn organ in my chest feels like it might give out any second, it's beating so fucking fast. *Is this real life? Did he just admit to having feelings for me?* He did, but he didn't at the same time. I mean, he said I scared him. He didn't say I want you, and he led this entire conversation by saying "I told you what happened between us didn't change anything."

"Where does that leave us?"

He puts his hands in his pockets. "Have dinner with me at the house. I'll cook."

I want to say yes, but I can't, not when his ask reminds me of the dinner date I interrupted.

"Did you fuck her?"

"No," comes out fast.

"Touch her?"

He crosses his arms. "I just told you I didn't fuck her."

"That doesn't mean you didn't touch her," I quirk a brow.

"I'm telling you, I didn't fuck her or touch her."

My eyes narrow on his and I cross my arms. "Did you tell her how?"

Those dark obsidian orbs soften right before his hand comes up to my cheek, his eyes following the path of his thumb as he gently swipes it across. "No," he says before his eyes drift back to mine. "Have dinner with me."

"Okay."

≈

"**A** chicken recipe that calls for bourbon. Are you sure that goes in there?"

He pours the bottle into the skillet. "I'm sure. It's not that much, only an ounce or two tablespoons."

"Then why don't you use the tablespoons? I thought you were supposed to be teaching me."

He purses his lips before his eyes flick up to where I'm sitting on the counter next to the stove. "I laid out all the ingredients, and rather than stand beside me, you chose to sit up there." He corks the top of the bourbon. "I thought that meant you'd rather watch than get a lesson."

"So if I hop down, you'll use a tablespoon?"

There's a mischievous glint in his eye before his pouty lips pull to the side. "Something like that."

Those heavy lashes fall slowly as his eyes drift down my body before returning to the stove. There is no way in hell I'm not getting down to find out what "something like that" means. I take a sip of my wine and count to ten in my head so I'm not too damn obvious before I casually slide off the countertop.

"Teach me."

He gives me a quick glance before extending his arm out. "Come here."

I point to the small space between him and the stove. "You want me to..." I gesture between him and the stove.

"Yes, Cameron. This part is important."

"Okay," I say as I nervously take a step. Why am I suddenly nervous around him? He's always affected me, but now it feels different.

It's different because he gave me a truth. I now know I affect him too.

When I'm within his reach, his hand grips my shoulder, and he positions me right where he wants me: in front of the stove. My entire body instantly heats with awareness.

"Do you see what I'm doing with the spatula? This is one of the key steps with this recipe. You want to scrape up any bits stuck to the pan." I watch as he moves the turner around the pan. I try to pay attention, but it's hard to focus with his hand grasping my arm and my back pushed against his front. "Here, you try. This part is only roughly a minute before we reduce the heat and add the other ingredients."

When I take the spoon, I start doing exactly as he instructed. "Why wouldn't we just turn down the heat now? Then the meat and the bourbon wouldn't stick to the pan."

"You're going to want those charred little bits. They're the best part," he says as he steps away, taking the warmth with him. "Keep scraping the bottom as I add in the other ingredients." I watch as he pulls out a measuring cup. "Three-fourths cup of heavy whipping cream," he slowly pours the thick milk into the pan.

"What are we making anyway?"

"Chicken," he says, grabbing another measuring cup.

"I can see that it's chicken. I mean what is the recipe called?"

"One cup of chicken stock," he says as he pours the stock into the pan with a little more haste. "And half a cup of sun-dried tomatoes." He adds a small bag of tomatoes to the mixture, and suddenly, his hands are back on me as one arm wraps around my waist, making every hair on my body stand at attention. He pulls me flush against his front as the other hand reaches in front of me. "Now we let it simmer," he says, his mouth close to my ear but not near close enough. "Some people add the parmesan now, but I like to add it near the end." His hand covers mine on the spoon. "You don't need to scrape anymore," he guides my hand in a slower motion. "Just ensure the ingredients are well mixed, and then we let it set." I watch as he stirs the sauce in the pan, but my thoughts are only on him. His thumb has subtly slipped under the hem of my crop top and is gently stroking the skin, melting me from the inside out. I'm scared to move and breathe for fear of losing this moment. I'm getting parts of him now that I've never seen him give, and I know while we might just be cooking a meal, it's so much more than that. I feel him breathe deeply, and then he releases me, setting the spatula down before covering the pan. "Now we wait."

I pull in a long, cleansing breath to collect myself before stepping aside and reclaiming my glass of wine. I take a big drink before turning around to find him doing the same. His eyes meet mine and I know we're drinking for the same reason. Our nerves are shot. We're barely scratching the surface of what we both want: more.

"What is this, Ev? What are we doing?"

He sets down his glass and grips the countertop before breaking eye contact and turning his gaze out the window. "I don't know how to answer that."

"Can you try?"

He closes his eyes and rolls his lips before saying, "It means there is nothing else I'd rather be doing at this moment. It means I'm right where I want to be with the person I want to be with. Does that answer your question?"

It more than answered my question, it made my heart soar. But I can tell it was a lot for him to admit, and I don't want to press for too much too fast. It's clear that while we shared an intense night together, he's not in a hurry to repeat it. I've waited this long; I can wait a little longer, especially if he keeps giving me truths. But right now, I want to go back to enjoying our evening. The heavy scares him, so I try to rewind and reset and say, "Sort of," with a shrug, as if he didn't just drop a giant truth bomb. "You still haven't told me what we're making."

His eyes drop to his glass, and he grabs the bottle of wine, topping it off as he says, "The name is not important."

"Well, what if I want to make it again, and I need the recipe?"

"Then I'll help you make it."

"What if I want to make it for you?"

He pulls his bottom lip into his mouth and shakes his head. "You're not going to let this go, are you?"

"I don't understand what the big deal is," I say as I hop back onto the counter. "It's the first recipe you ever taught me how to make." I shrug. "I'm going to try and make it on my own eventually anyway."

His eyes meet mine. "Marry Me Chicken."

Those eyes already make me weak, but his words have me stumbling. "I'm sorry—"

"The recipe," he nods toward the simmering dish. "It's called 'Marry Me Chicken.'"

He reaches for his glass, but those dark orbs never leave mine as they stare into my soul and my mouth goes dry. My brain was already spinning from all the truth he's given me today, but now I'm lost in a beautiful oblivion with a million thoughts running through my head. In the end, only one matters: the man I want to spend my forever with just made me "Marry Me Chicken."

"Stormy is giving me a ride home tonight," I say after Everett passes me my coffee.

When I opened the front door this morning to leave for work, he was sitting on the top step of the stone staircase, waiting. He told me he'd like it if I'd ride with him even though I didn't have to, and of course I said yes. He probably knew he wouldn't be getting a no, but he wasn't expecting me to say I'd be hanging out with Stormy on my birthday. After last night, spending tonight with him was a sure thing, or so he thought. It would have been, but I said yes to Stormy before he ever gave me any truths, and while I want him with every ounce of my being, I know I have to play hard to get a little. Everett knows I want him, but it's good to make a man sweat a bit so he doesn't forget how good what he has is.

His lips thin as he places his cup in the center console. "What time are you coming home?"

"I don't know. I'm not really sure what our plans are, and she just mentioned having a drink."

"I don't want you getting in a car with someone who is drinking." He rubs his hand through his beard, perturbed. "You'll have your phone on you this time?" His eyes leave the road to find mine.

"Yes, I'll have my phone."

"It's just the two of you?"

He's asking a lot of questions, questions that make my belly flutter because they sound a lot like worry and jealousy—two emotions that are sure to make him face the root of their origin.

"I think so. She's new in town, and Mackenzie is in Florida. Since I never went back to living on campus after last semester, I haven't been hanging out with my SIU friends."

"Just be careful around her."

"Is there something I should know?"

"You should never be completely trusting of someone you just met. I don't know Stormy, but I do know Lauren, and she has a history in this town."

Lauren is interested in Everett. They've both admitted they have a past, and while things are changing between us, I'm unsure where he stands with her.

We pull into the parking lot at the stadium, and as he collects his wallet and cup out of the console, I ask, "Why did you let me believe Lauren was at your house for a date?"

He pauses but doesn't give me his eyes. "Letting you believe I was touching her was better than putting my hands on you."

Without another word, he exits the car. "Ouch." His words taken at surface level sting, but if I look at them through the lens of last night, they hurt a little less. He wants to touch me, but he's torn between what he wants and what he thinks he should do. Too bad for him, I'm not, and it's my birthday.

"When you asked me to be your date today, I didn't know I had competition," Stormy says as she gestures to a bouquet of red roses as I return from the bathroom. Without even seeing the tag, I know exactly who they are from—Everett. Since I turned eight, the only gifts he's ever given me are on my birthday, and it's always been a bouquet of red roses, one for every year. "Also, when you asked me if I wanted to go to the game today, I didn't consider that we had to work during the game."

"Honestly, when I asked, I hadn't thought about it myself. Last year, when I worked at Hayes Fields, I wasn't the best employee. I came and went as I pleased, but I also wasn't the sole person running the concession stands, so it was a little easier... and I don't think anyone truly expected me to actually do work."

"Think I can get away with that?" she says as she turns on the POS station.

"Considering it's just the two of us for now, that would be a hard no."

"For now? Are we getting another person in here?" She queries as she rests her elbow on the station.

"Yes," I say as I count the drawer. "I'll be cross training someone from concessions who can fill in if one of us is out. That doesn't fix our dilemma today, but we'll be able to go watch the third inning. Since the stadium just opened, the shop will most likely be busy with new visitors wanting to check out everything and purchase merch, and then, if we're up in the seventh inning, people will probably trickle in as well."

"Why the seventh inning?"

"Most pro-stadiums stop serving alcohol during the seventh inning. That's not a thing here, but I'm betting on visitors not knowing that, which means they will be out of their seats getting their last call and we will probably get foot traffic, especially if we are up. We'll get the fair-weather fans who didn't want to make a purchase before seeing the team in action."

"Huh, you're pretty smart, aren't you?"

"I'm not sure if you're making fun of me or if that's a compliment."

She shrugs. "Me either."

I can't help but laugh. I may not fully understand her, but she makes me laugh and keeps things interesting. The sound of the security gates rising at the entrances have us both turning toward the door.

"Get ready. It's about to get crazy."

"Maybe I can ask Lauren if I can get an assistant position. I didn't realize how much work I'd actually be doing when I took this one," Stormy says as she refolds a table of shirts.

It's annoying when customers hold up T-shirts to see what size they want. Even more so when they dig through the pile, hold up all the different sizes, and then choose the first one they held up. I didn't realize how irritating that would be. Luckily, we've been busy enough that I haven't had any real time to hyper-focus on it, but every spare second my eyes get between sales or fielding questions, the messy tables grate on my nerves. We have the game on in the shop and they're tied in the bottom of the third. Even with a close game, the store has been busy, which surprises me a little. But I'm happy for Connor. I am happy to play a small role in bringing his dreams to life. Every item sold in the shop is a walking billboard for the Bulldogs on the street.

"What did you do before you started working here?"

"This and that. I kind of float around and do what I feel like doing."

"And Lauren is okay with that? Don't you want to move out or buy a car?"

She folds up the last shirt and sticks her hands in the back pockets of her ripped-up overalls before rocking back on her heels. "You're making a lot of assumptions over there. What if I'm a secret billionaire?"

"Wow, now I feel like an ass." That was a lot of rude conjecture. However, her style, age, and what she told me scream freeloader. "I'm sorry. That was rude, and honestly, I'm the last person with any room to pass judgments."

"It's fine. I'm sure you get it all the time too."

"I look like I'm a freeloader?" Her eyebrows raise, and she rolls her lips, and I realize I once again inserted my foot in my mouth. "Oh my god, I am so sorry."

She holds her hand up and shakes her head. "Don't be sorry. Your words insinuated as much before you spelled it out. But no, I was going to say gold digger."

"You think I'm a gold digger?"

"Well, yeah. You drive an Audi, come in dressed up, wearing high-end brands and a full face of makeup every day to work a summer job in a team shop at a baseball stadium..." She walks over to the hat rack and straightens a row before adding, "Plus, I know where you lay your head at night."

I pull out a box from under the counter and set it down a little harder than anticipated due to its weight. When she turns toward me in question, I play it off as intentional. "You'd be wrong. You may not be a secret billionaire, but I am... well, not a billionaire, more like a millionaire."

"No shit? So you're just banging the old man? I mean, he doesn't look his age. He looks good for what, forty-five, forty-six-ish?"

"We are not banging, thank you very much," I say as I pull out the box of jerseys that didn't fit and toss her the one with Parker's name on it.

She catches it. "What's this?"

"What do you mean? It's Parker's jersey. I'm not stupid. I know you're into him."

She throws it back. "I can't wear that."

"Why not?"

For a second, I think maybe I've again managed to offend her with my unfounded assumptions, but then she says, "Because... it's more fun to watch him squirm." She comes over to the counter. "Give me one for one of the guys he doesn't like."

"So does that mean you are into Parker?" I ask as I dig through the box and pull out McKenna's jersey. Parker gets along with everyone, but he looks at Jordan as competition since he's the other starting pitcher.

"Are you sleeping with the old man?"

"No, but I want to be."

She smiles as she pulls on McKenna's jersey. "Yeah, I like Parker, and for the record, I'm not a freeloader. I like a backpacker lifestyle, a type of nomad if you will. I just purchased a tiny home, but it won't be ready for another four months. So I guess, in a way, you could say I'm freeloading until my house is ready."

I pull on a ballcap. "I guess we're besties now."

"No," she's quick to correct me. "Friends, yes. Best friends, no. In my book you have to go through some shit to earn that title."

I shoot her a mischievous smile. "Fine, let's go raise a little hell."

"What about the shop?"

"No one has been in here for about ten minutes. I'm the boss, and there's technically a self-checkout kiosk if someone really wanted to buy."

"What about theft?"

"Are you trying to delay watching your man pitch or..."

"Right, secret millionaire. You'll pay him back for whatever is stolen."

"What? No, this is a small town. People don't steal shit. Come on," I say as I pull her out of the shop. "Let's go."

CHAPTER 17
EVERETT

I didn't like it when Cameron told me this morning she was going out with Stormy for her birthday. Not just because I'm selfish and wanted her here with me but because I don't trust Lauren, and Stormy, blood or not, is an extension of her. After I had dinner with Lauren and she shared her reasoning for being back in town, I called Garrett. He still won't tell me what his hunch is, and it's driving me fucking crazy, but because I know it has something to do with her, I gave him everything. I would have told him all of it anyway. There's not much I haven't shared with my brothers since we started Callahan & Associates. For what we do, there can't be secrets. While Garrett is holding back now, I know he's doing so for a damn good reason, one that he will divulge when and if it ever makes sense. We learned a long time ago how much weight rumors are given in small towns. They are carried by our enemies and spread through ignorance, which is why I've kept everything with Cameron close to my chest. It's why I don't just tell her everything. I'm not only trying to protect her and her father's legacy. I don't want the world to destroy her before she ever gets a chance to live freely in it. It's a chance I never got, which is why I've been adamant about pushing her away. I'm the last thing she needs. Sure, the women in this town have deemed me one of the most eligible bachelors since my divorce. I'm not blind. I read body language and listen to what people don't say rather than what they do. It's my fucking job. There's no reality where I get to walk out my front door with Cameron on my arm that doesn't piss people off, that doesn't tarnish her name and run her out of town. I already know the hateful things that would be said about me, and what's fucked up is a good part of me would believe every one of them. What those people don't know is I couldn't care less about their judgment of me. They're not thinking anything I haven't already thought of myself. What I care about is her.

It always comes back to her, and that's why I've been up all night waiting for her to get home from Wild Bills. Yes, I know exactly where she's been all night. I pulled out my phone more times than I can count to check her location tonight, and then the second she came home, what did she do? She went straight to her room. I know she was aware I was awake when she got home. I left the lights on, but that was thirty minutes ago, and she hadn't come down. I'm assuming she had too much to drink and fell asleep, which is probably best. I've already been pushing too many boundaries with her. I'm giving too much away. I'm giving her false hope, and that's worse than any lie or promise I could ever break, for there is no kindness in false hope. All that false hope does is prolong an inevitable misery.

After turning all the lights off downstairs, I headed to my room for a long, hot shower. Hot showers usually help wash away my anxiety, and after them, I'm able to close my eyes for at least an hour, and an hour would be more than any amount of sleep I've had since I got home. Knowing she's safe in the other room doesn't hurt either. I've just opened the door to exit my master bath when what sounds like a bedroom door closing catches my attention. I assumed Cameron was fast asleep, recouping from however many drinks she had tonight. She's not one to typically stay up late unless she's studying, and it's summer, so I know that's not the case. That's when a little black box in the center of my bed catches my attention. I know for certain it wasn't there when I walked in. I'm so fucking anal I notice when my housekeeper dusts the bookshelves and puts the pictures back up in the wrong order. Which reminds me, I need to leave her note. A book from my shelf has been missing. I checked the shared office in the main living area thinking maybe she forgot where it went, and I came up empty. I couldn't tell you what the title of the book was or who wrote it, I just know I'm missing a blue book with intricate details on the spine. I've stared at it for years now, and knowing it's missing just adds to the growing list of things stealing my focus.

I take one last look around the room, ensuring everything else is in order and that I am indeed alone, considering I know it's Cameron who left this for me to find. I wouldn't put it past her to hide behind a curtain just so she could watch me open it. Running the towel over my wet hair one more time, I toss it onto the armchair next to the table in the bay window before taking a seat on my bed.

"What are you up to, Cameron?"

It's her birthday, and I haven't said happy birthday, but I planned on seeing her after the roses were delivered. However, I got stuck talking shop with Coach Denver before the game. This must be a not-so-subtle reminder that I haven't said the words. I make myself comfortable, stacking my pillows against my headboard before leaning back and crossing my legs at the ankle. When I pick up the box, it's light. Whatever is inside can't be too elaborate. Taking off the lid, the first thing I see is a small piece of paper folded in half.

I added another camera to the security system. Thought you might want to use it to ensure I'm following the rules.

I immediately reach for my phone. How the fuck did she add a new camera and I didn't get an alert? I take security around here seriously. I have to. It's part of protecting those I care about from my work. The last thing I need is someone coming after me out of revenge for a case they lost. Callahan & Associates plays in the big leagues. The clients we serve have big issues, deep pockets, and a lot at stake. Opening the app, I immediately see the new square: "Cam's Room." She put a fucking camera in her room.

My hand instantly clenches my phone hard as I find the strength not to tap on the damn square. The little black box slides off my leg when I throw my head back against the pillows. I know she didn't give me a box with a piece of paper inside. If that were the case, why not use an envelope? Reaching for the box, I attempt to distract myself from pressing on that damn square, except I should have known it would only get worse. When I lift the black velveteen material, there's a black remote with a silver engraved tag reading:

Touch Me

"No fucking way." I roll over on my bed and groan into the pillow, instantly hard. She just handed me the remote to a vibrator that I have no doubt is currently buried in her sweet pussy, waiting for me to turn it on and make her come. I know I shouldn't do it. Opening my app to see what she has planned will be the death of me, but as I roll onto my back, my thumb hovering over the security app, I pull the trigger. I've already watched her fingers slide into her pussy while she came all over them, screaming my name. If we are our choices and they define us, then I'm already fucked. Commanding her to touch herself while I watched was a bad decision, but I've also never felt more fucking alive. I know I said I'm giving her false hope, but it's my hope too, and false or not, isn't any hope better than none at all?

On that last note, my finger hits the square. Fuck. I bite my hand hard when I see her. She's lying in the middle of her bed, her long red hair sprawled across the pillows, wearing a blue corset with thick straps that run crisscross all the way down her stomach. Her phone dings, and she glances at it before a mischievous smile takes over her face.

"Everett, do you like my birthday outfit? It's blue, my favorite color." I'm quiet as I watch her twirl her hair. I don't know what to fucking say. I've never been rendered speechless. She looks like pure sin. I want to storm down the hall, pull her to the edge of her bed, smack her ass for teasing me, and then sink into her for hours. My cock twitches from the mere thought of her warmth wrapped around me. "It's okay if you don't want to talk. I don't need you to talk. I like knowing you're watching." She leans onto her elbows and asks, "I bought something else that's blue. Want to see it?" Again, I say nothing. She bites her plump bottom lip, the same one I've wanted to sink my teeth into for far too long, before letting her legs fall open, revealing a blue vibrator and a glistening pussy. I instantly grab my now throbbing dick. "I know you refuse to touch me, but you didn't say you wouldn't watch, and Ev, I really want you to watch me."

Her hand slowly slides down her corseted stomach, and right before she grabs the vibrator, I press the button. Her pretty lips open with a gasp that morphs into a euphoric moan. I watch on, momentarily entranced. She is so fucking beautiful. I want it to be my hand pulling those symphonies out of her, not this damn toy, but since it can't be, I'll settle for this because right now, it's everything.

Clicking on the voice feature, I say, "Reach into your drawer and get the special toy you keep wrapped in silk behind your journal."

When she focuses on the camera strategically mounted in front of her bed, it feels like her eyes are locked on mine. "You read my journal?"

"No, but if you think I haven't heard you in there pleasuring yourself, you'd be wrong."

When I heard her, she wasn't trying to get caught. Cameron has teased me many times over the years, but never with this, not until now.

"Tell me. Did you search for my toy so that you could picture me using it?"

"Yes," I answer honestly. The first time I ever caught her masturbating, I had come home early from work one afternoon, which is something I never do. I had a splitting migraine, and when I reached the top of the landing to start down the hall toward my room, her door was cracked open, and so was the door to her ensuite bath, where her delicate moans echoed off the tile as she pleasured herself. I stood and listened far longer than I should have, and when I finally walked away, knowing staying until the end would wreck me, I heard her come, and fuck me if it wasn't my name that spilled out on a breathless moan. The next day, when she went to school, I scoured her room in search of the toy she used instead of me.

Once she has the toy, I say, "Pull it out." I love the way she listens.

Pulling the strings on the silk cover, her baby blue dildo easily slips out. "What now?"

"Now I want you to wrap your lips around it like it's my cock." A small smile pulls at her lips before she kisses the tip and drags her tongue down its length, making my dick pulse in my hand. I stroke it hard as I watch. When she swirls her tongue around the top, a drop of cum leaks from my tip. "Stop teasing me and suck it," I command as I release myself so I can press the button and taunt her the way she is me.

"Mmm," rolls off her lips, and I curse under my breath as I try to prop up my phone. Once I have my phone set against a pillow, I see that her lips are now fully wrapped around the dildo as her pelvis has subtly started to rock against the vibration of the toy. Fuck, the only way this could be hotter was if I were sitting at the foot of the bed smelling her sweetness as it glistened inches away from me once more.

My hand once again finds my length, and I tug long and slow, imagining it is her warmth wrapped around me as I push inside of her and not my damn hand. I let my thumb off the remote, and she whimpers before popping the toy out of her mouth.

"I want you to put it in with the toy."

"Everett, I don't think it will fit with the toy."

"If I were in there, would you let me push inside of you?"

"You know I would."

Fuck! Why did I ask that? It only makes staying right here that much harder. "I told you I was big. Put me inside of you."

Her piercing blue eyes cut through the camera and steal my breath. My thumb releases the button as she lets the blue tip slowly drag down her body, her eyes steadily locked on the man she knows is on the other side, the man she wants to be inside her, and while I want to watch its descent, I can only stare into her eyes as the want I see there consumes me. No one has ever looked at me the way she does. Trapped in her blue abyss, it's not until her eyes flutter closed and her teeth bite into her bottom lip that I realize she now has both toys inside her. My thumb reclaims the button, and she drops from her wrist to her elbow as she props herself up with one arm.

"Turn over, sunshine." Her heavy lids stare into the camera in question. "Rest your head on the bed and put that ass you like to tease me with in the air." Fucking hell. More cum leaks from my tip once she's in position. There's a reason Cameron wears thong bikinis all fucking summer; she has a perfectly round ass, thick without being too muscular. It's the kind of butt you want to sink your teeth into, literally. When I see her hand snake up between her thighs to push the dildo back in, I press the button, and at this new angle, I can see her clench around the toy. "Are you still thinking about me?"

"Always... fuck me, Ev."

"If I were behind you, my hands would be digging into your hips as I pulled you back on my cock, thrust after thrust, ripping those intoxicating mewls from your pretty mouth." Her hips instinctively begin to rock, controlling the pace instead of her hand as she pushes back on the dildo. My own strokes follow suit, mimicking hers, as though I was indeed behind her, pleasuring her just the way she likes it.

"Everett, I'm not going to last," she moans. I let off the button on my remote, not wanting this to end, but it's her hurried pace as she rocks back on the dildo in shorter, faster thrusts that has my hand doing the same. She's chasing her release, and fuck if I don't want her to have it. "Come with me, Ev. Please..." Her hand fists in her comforter, and her cheeks tense as her orgasm takes hold. "Ev... Mmm, so good..." she draws out.

Her words send me over the edge as warm cum coats my hand. "Fuck..." I grind out as I catch my breath. There will be no getting over Cameron Salt. I'm fucking lying to myself to say otherwise. This is now the second time I've come in my hand because of her, and there's not a time in my life that I can recall having a better orgasm. How fucked is that?

"Did you come with me, Ev?" she asks softly as she tries to regulate her own breaths.

"Yeah, sunshine. I did."

She rolls over, pulling a throw blanket with her as she covers herself before saying, "Thanks for the birthday present."

Before I can respond, she presses a button on her phone, and the screen goes black. My head sinks back into the pillow, and I close my eyes. "I'm so fucked."

I t's been a week. One week of torture, one week of pure hell. I've barely seen Cameron since the night of her birthday. The next morning, when I came down for work, she was in the kitchen looking more beautiful than I'd ever seen her before. Every day I see her, I swear I see her more. I see things I didn't know I was missing. I've been staring at her for years, but somehow, I missed the scattering of freckles on her left shoulder that resemble the little dipper, the way she brushes her hair behind her ear when she's nervous, and maybe most of all, the way she always gives me her full attention when I'm talking to her. It's the last one I think I've always noticed, but I took it for granted, and now I hate it. I hate it because she hasn't looked me in the eye once, not since I told her no.

One week ago, as she stood at the refrigerator filling her tumbler with water, our eyes connected for the first time since our shared release. My feet instantly brought me to her side, where I found my hands cradling her face, her mouth inches away from mine. I saw everything I wanted reflected in her crystal blue eyes. She wanted the same things, and I wanted to pretend a little longer that I could be the man to give them to her; that I wasn't the man that would ruin her, wasn't the man that would break her heart with ugly truths and things we can't change, but I didn't. Instead, I let her go.

Her hand reached out for mine as I released her, and her bright eyes pleaded with mine as she said, "Please, Ev. I want this. I want you to touch me."

"I can't. You don't know what you're asking."

Those were the last words I gave her. We haven't talked since, and it's tearing me up. My hand rested on her doorknob almost every night as I stood outside her door and battled with myself over all the things I wanted to say, only to settle for walking away because letting her believe her own assumptions are better than the truth I have. She doesn't understand that not all stories need to be told. They don't all have happy endings. She wants to keep me but doesn't understand this is the only way she can.

"Hey, do you have a minute?" Lauren says as she pushes open the door to my office with a knock.

"Most people knock before entering, Lauren," I say without glancing up from my computer. She's the last person I care to entertain right now.

"Nice to see you too, Everett. I had to make a change to the last tournament. The coach from UA couldn't make it until Friday night. I moved the schedule around so that the Bulldogs would be the first game he sees."

Damn it. That's a good call, one that requires I at least be cordial. "I'm assuming that's not all you came up here to talk about since a schedule change can easily be communicated via email."

She walks across the room and stands beside the window. "No, it's not. What I want to talk about is personal."

I take off my blue-light glasses and spin my chair toward her. Lauren coming to me with something personal feels out of place, which is more reason to listen. "I'm listening."

"Mind sharing some of that liquid courage?" she asks as she nods to the cognac on the shelf behind me.

"Sure," I say as I spin around to grab the bottle and pour two glasses. After the glasses are poured, I turn back around. "I don't have any ice. Hope you don't mind it neat..." My words die off a little when I realize how close she's moved. While I poured the glasses, she crossed the room and found her seat on the corner of my desk. Lauren has always been attractive, and that hasn't changed with age, but she's not my type. I hand her the glass I poured and take a long drink before reclaiming my chair. "Well..." I gesture with my hand for her to start.

"Do you remember Jenny Busch's wedding?"

"Yes," I lean back in my chair. "That was over twenty years ago, but I vaguely remember."

Jenny Busch's wedding was the talk of the town. A small-town girl marrying into a dynasty. It's all anyone could talk about for months, made worse by the fact that she convinced her soon-to-be husband to have it here in Waterloo. What started out as a small wedding soon encompassed the whole town. I am trying to remember why I got invited.

"Do you remember Ramsey, Granger, and Amber?"

"I do, they were hanging out with Damon that night."

She nods and takes another sip of cognac, holding it in her mouth and letting the flavors marinate before swallowing hard. "Do you remember who Amelia was hanging out with that night?"

"I don't know. That was a long time ago," I say as I close my eyes and try to remember details from the wedding. I remember that night being one of the last nights everyone hung out before Damon moved out to the East Coast. We graduated that summer, and he was getting his master's at Cornell. I pinch the bridge of my nose, and that's when I remember seeing Amelia sitting in a corner talking to Brady Busch. Damon was pissed. Rightfully so, he did marry a gold digger, but I don't know where Lauren's going with this walk down memory lane. "What parts specifically are you trying to get me to remember?"

"I just want to know what that night looked like for you because, for me, it looked a lot different. That night changed—"

"Hey, Everett..." Cameron steps around the corner only to step back when she sees Lauren sitting on my desk. "I'm sorry. I didn't realize you had someone up here. I'll come back—"

"No," I say a little louder than intended as I rise from my chair. "Lauren was just leaving."

Cameron's eyes flick between us, and I'm sure she sees my bluff. Lauren was right in the middle of trying to tell me something, but I'm not about to let the woman I can't get off my mind walk away from me again. When I turn to Lauren, she raises her eyebrows at me, her expression now as equally offended as it is intrigued.

"Right, well, maybe I can stop by later, and we can finish our conversation." I don't correct her. Instead, I clench my jaw, intent on not showing more cards than I already have. Lauren was here to tell me something, but the way she sat on my desk and attempted to take a walk down memory lane with me suggests

SALT

maybe she has other ideas about us. While I don't care to entertain those, I don't entirely want to push her away, especially since Garrett is still sniffing around her trail. He wouldn't blindly follow a trail without good cause. Stopping in front of Cameron, she puts her hand on her hip and asks, "Hey, is Stormy picking you up for the away game on Saturday?"

"Yep," she answers as she rubs her thumb over the top of her forefinger. It's her tell. She's lying.

"Okay, well, maybe I'll tag along. I should probably go to one of the games since I work here." Her gaze flicks back to mine, and she gives me a once-over before finally taking her leave.

Once I hear her heels click down the stairs, I say, "Close the door."

"Oh, I didn't plan on staying. I just came up—"

"Close the door, Cameron."

"Fine," she fumes as she shuts the door. When she turns her gaze back on me, it's only a moment before she focuses her attention out the window.

"You lied just now. Why?"

"No, I didn't." She rolls her eyes. "Or I don't know that I did. Stormy has a way of making plans for us and letting me know at the last minute."

"You've been avoiding me," I say as I walk around my desk and lean against the front.

She crosses her arms. "Didn't realize you cared."

"We both know that's bullshit."

"Do we? You said we were trying. You asked me to have dinner with you and made 'Marry Me Chicken.' Then, on my birthday, we shared something, Everett. You may not have been inside of me that night, but we both know your words were. I know you want me, Everett, and you're scared, but I don't understand it. Help me understand it. Tell me why your answer is no when we both know you want it to be yes." Admittedly, my reasons for saying no are getting harder to hold onto, but that's only served as more of a reason to push her away rather than pull

191

her close. My softening to the idea doesn't erase its perversion. When I take too long to respond, she asks, "Is it because of my dad?"

I grip the side of my desk and drop my gaze. "Yeah, Cameron, he's a big part of it. He was my best friend, and I doubt he'd be okay with me defiling his daughter if he were still here."

"I disagree. He'd want to see the two people he loved happy."

"What if I can't make you happy?"

"What if you're my soulmate?" she takes a step toward me.

"You think I'm your soulmate?" I hold my breath as my stupid heart beats out of rhythm, waiting for her response.

Closing the space between us, her wedge nudges my boot before she says, "You tell me. How's walking away been going for you?"

My arm is pulling her against my front before my mind can argue. She stumbles on her wedges and braces herself on my chest, her hands instantly burning scars onto my soul. Her touch feels too good, and when her big blue eyes land on mine, I'm a goner. Leaning my forehead to hers, I warn, "We can't come back from this, Cameron. I can't erase something like this."

Her tongue darts out, moistening her lips. "Promise?" My free hand slides up the side of her neck before twisting into her auburn locks as my lips skim over the top of hers, and it's already the best kiss I've ever had. "Please," she pleads as her hand twists in my shirt, dissolving my willpower.

My mouth crashes to hers, and it feels like I am breathing for the first time. All the weight that's been sitting on my chest for years is lifted as her soft lips mold against mine. Everything, the anxiety, the fear, the fog, it's all gone. Replaced with only her. My tongue dips inside her sweet mouth, and we both let out soul-deep moans of rapture. I've never shared a kiss like this in my forty-six years, one where the person I'm kissing wants me just as much. Don't get me wrong, I've shared lust, but this is more than that. Lust seeks physical pleasure, and while I want that too, I want what's wrapped in this moment more. I want the emotional well-

SALT

being and the person tied to the other end of it. I want the long-lasting fulfillment that only comes from a more profound place.

Her hands slide up my chest and wrap around the base of my neck, setting off a tingling sensation that racks my body with awareness. She owns me. Every piece. The hand I had rested on her hip slowly reaches around to finally cop a feel of her perfect ass just as my cell phone rings. Fuck.

I pull back, and she moans in protest. "Don't answer it... Stay with me."

"That's Connor's ringtone," I say as I brush my thumb across her cheek, my eyes full of apology.

Her brows furrow as she steps back and drops her gaze to the floor. Damn it.

"One second," I say as I answer the phone. Connor rarely calls, so if he's calling, it must be important, but so is Cameron. "Cam—"

"It's fine, Everett. I didn't come up here to stay anyway." Tucking a strand of her red hair behind her ear, she heads toward the door, and I fucking hate it. Leaving is the last thing I want. Then, when she reaches the door, she says, "I was only stopping by to let you know I won't be home tonight. You have time."

I have time. What the hell does that mean? What does she mean she won't be home tonight?

"Cameron, wait." Her big blue eyes pierce mine before they drop to the phone in my hand, reminding me of why she's walking away to begin with. My hand tightens around the phone, and my heart wholly divides. She gives me a soft smile, and then she disappears around the corner.

She's not making me choose. I know she would never do that. So why does it feel like I have to?

CHAPTER 18
CAMERON

"Hey, have you seen my phone?" I ask Stormy as I look around my camper.

"No. Maybe you left it in your car."

I lift the throw pillows on the couch for the tenth time in the past twenty minutes before putting my hands on my hips, thoroughly peeved. Out of all the days to lose my phone, the day I kiss Everett Callahan for the first time would officially be the worst. "I already checked there."

"Where's the last place you remember having it?"

I throw myself back on the couch and trill my lips as I stare at the ceiling. That's when I remember Mackenzie sent a text while I was waiting for Stormy to pack a bag. "Shit. I left it in your room."

She holds her phone up. "We have mine if there's an emergency, or we could always go back."

"I don't want to leave now that we are here. It's an hour back... unless you've changed your mind about staying here, and that was your subtle hint."

"Nope, this kind of shit is right up my alley. I told you, I bought a tiny house. I'm jealous of this whole setup. I wish I had somewhere like this to park my place." She tosses a bag of marshmallows at me. "Ready to start up that fire?"

Once we got our cocktails poured, we came outside and found a spot next to the lake to start a fire. It's so peaceful out here, but I'll admit having someone here with me is better than sitting on top of my car in the dark. I only wish I hadn't left my phone. Honestly, it's probably better than what I did. There is something to be said about making a man miss you, not letting him have everything all at once. I'd like to say it's what I've intentionally been doing with Everett, but that wouldn't be the whole truth. The old me, the one he knew before he left, was ballsy. She was no holds barred, but dare I say, I've grown up. I hate to use that term because it suggests that the girl I was then was immature, not fully grown and capable of making life choices, such as who she wants to be with, and I don't see it that way. The way I see it, the time we spent apart these past few months was a test of sorts. It gave us both time to deal with what we were feeling. He thought I wanted Parker, and I know part of him still believes Parker would be better for me. I'm confident that's why he left, so he wasn't a factor. Everett would accept misery if it meant I was happy; what he doesn't understand is that I'd do the same. If I thought I couldn't be what he needed, I'd walk. That's why I've been careful since he came home. I'm all in. I've been all in for as long as I can remember, but seeing how feeling anything for me pains him every time we push a boundary kills me. A little space is good, or at least I hope it is. Right now, one night feels like one hundred years.

"So, if you had property, you'd plant roots? Doesn't that defeat the purpose of a tiny house?" I ask, taking a bigger drink of rum and coke. I made it stiff, hoping to relax my anxious mind.

"It does, but it doesn't mean the idea isn't nice. I don't see myself ever planting roots."

"Why is that?"

She mindlessly pokes the fire with a long stick as she stares at the flames. "Don't have anyone or anything to keep me rooted. So why stay?"

"You have Lauren. Is she not staying here? You guys have been here a little over a month now. I assumed maybe this place was starting to grow on the two of you."

My question is twofold. I do care how long Stormy stays. She's an acquired taste, but the same can be said about me, and I like her. I'd hate to have to say goodbye before we could be epic. She has a lot of Thelma and Louise potential, but I'm also selfishly wondering if that means Lauren isn't staying either.

"I don't know if Lauren has plans to stay here. She doesn't talk about it, but something happened here. Coming here wasn't easy for her, but she came, and while I know she did it for me, I'm hoping the time she spent away from here has healed her. I know time can't heal everything, but it can help." She takes a drink before asking, "What about you? Did I hear you mention to Lauren that you have family on the East Coast? Are you staying here for your crush on Everett, or do you have another reason for staying?"

I purse my lips trying to recall the conversation she's referencing. "Oh, you mean when she brought us lunch. Yeah, she was prying and asking what I was to Everett. I couldn't tell if it was because she was interested in dating him or genuinely curious. But yes, after my parents died, I found out that my brother was only my half brother. My father cut him from the will because he wasn't his blood."

"So your mom had an affair?"

I roll my lips before saying, "My father wrote a letter, which I received on my twenty-first birthday. It held apologies and cryptic confessions and said things without saying anything at all. My letter was written before he died, which means it was cautionary. No one knows how or when their time is up. I think he left some words unsaid because he was protecting my mom. He didn't want to shine a negative light on her." I take a sip of my drink and look up at the sky. "When it came to his words revolving around Kelce's paternity, he said, 'Time discovers the truth.' Those words, coupled with what I know about my parent's marriage, lead me to believe he didn't know the truth about his son until after I was born. My parents had a shotgun wedding after they found out she was pregnant. If I had to guess, my father learned that truth around the time I was born, and that's why he stayed with my mother."

I know my father; he was a planner and always careful with his words. He was a good man and would have never wanted to say anything that would lead me to believe I was the reason why he stayed in his loveless marriage. Once I notice a long stretch of silence has passed between us, I pull my gaze out of the stars, fearful I bored her to sleep with my tales. When my eyes look in her direction, I find hers zeroed in on me.

"Do you think your dad stayed faithful to your mom even after he discovered the truth?"

"You never did mention why you're here," I say, as I pull in an anxious breath and change the subject.

"Sorry, that was too personal." She rubs her hands together. "It hits close to home is all. I never knew my father, so I suppose some part of me always looks for his motive for leaving in other people's stories. I'm not the best at dealing with things that are important to me. I notoriously fuck up, but my intentions are always rooted in love. I'm rambling now, but long story short, the opinions of others easily impact our own. I wanted to scope out the people here before sharing myself. I guess I'm a little guarded, and my reason for being here is important. I didn't want to mess it up."

She pauses, and I can tell whatever she's holding isn't easy. I know what it's like to carry the weight of heavy demons, so I say, "You don't have to tell me. I didn't realize it was that serious. I'm only making con—"

"No." She shakes her head. "It's okay. Have you ever felt like part of you is missing? Something you can't quite put your finger on? When my mother passed, it made me want to find my father. I hadn't cared about finding him when she was alive. Why should I give two shits about a sperm donor? But recently, I've cared. I've cared a lot."

Her comments resonate, but not because I didn't know my

parents. Rather, I always felt like I had one parent, and the other one didn't fit. My mother and I were polar opposites. Don't get me wrong; I loved her, but that was out of respect for who she was— my mother. That love was not founded on bond or friendship. Regardless, I know what it's like to feel out of step, to feel like a part of you is missing even when you should be whole.

"I think sometimes it takes falling apart to fall back together. After I lost my parents, the grief I felt tested my faith. For a long time, I carried guilt because I wasn't in the car with them. I should have died too, and in that grief and loneliness, it's easy to also feel like something is missing because it is. The people woven into our hearts are gone, but at some point, you learn to rebuild around that loss, and slowly, piece by piece, you are whole again. Caring and seeking those truths are part of finding your pieces."

She leans back in her chair and stares up at the sky. "That was heavy." She blows out a breath. "But you're right. It's why I want to find my dad. I only ever had my mom's story. That's her truth, but what's his? Maybe they are one and the same, but I need to hear that from his mouth. Once I have that, maybe I'll discover I've been whole all along; my pieces just fit together differently now."

Her gaze returns to the fire, where she watches the flames dance across the logs, and I fall silent with her, lost to the serenity of the crackling embers. I sit back in my chair, feeling slightly lighter after our conversation. In this life, you don't run into many people that you can connect with on a deep level. At the end of the day, most of the people we call friends are acquaintances, more or less. We watch our P's and Q's, pick and choose what parts of us we want to share, and go on with our lives. Rarely do we sit and give them one hundred percent honesty about anything, let alone matters of the heart.

"So, if you're not planning on staying around, when are you leaving me?"

She tosses her poker stick into the fire. "I'm more of a fly-by-the-seat-of-my-pants girl. I'm not a planner, but I'm also not flighty. I'll stay for the summer to finish my commitments working at the stadium."

"Well, that's something to celebrate!" I shake my glass at her as I get out of my chair. "Ready for a refill?" I don't make it more than two steps before I trip over nothing and fall on my ass. "Shit, I made that drink stiffer than I thought."

She comes to my rescue with a smile on her face. "Are you okay?"

I stare up at her from my spot on the ground. "That fucking twig tripped me."

With a laugh, she extends her hand. "Come on, red, it's time for bed."

"Hey, a nickname, I think someone's starting to like me. Best friend title, here I come."

She laughs, "Let's go. You're cut off."

~

I could have sworn I left my phone in Stormy's room, but when I dropped her off this morning, it wasn't there. It wasn't anywhere in the damn house, and I know for a fact I had it when I got there because I texted her from the damn driveway, letting her know I was there before she told me to come in, and Mac texted while I was in her room. We don't have to be at the stadium today because the team has an away game, but I still woke up at the crack of dawn anxious as fuck to get home. If I had my phone, I might have had a little more chill, but the fact that I couldn't check it to see if Everett called or texted me was gnawing away at my sanity.

Driving down the tree-lined path that leads to the house, I step on the gas a little harder, only to pump the brakes as the house comes into view and I see the car parked in the driveway. Lauren *fucking* Rhodes is here. Pulling into the driveway, I try to quiet the voices in my head, filling it with doubt and going over every worst-case scenario as to why she would be here again. I flip

down my mirror and check my face. Not only did I race out of the
trailer to come home, but I also opted out of freshening up, a rare
move on my part. I was so wired I couldn't help myself. Pro tip:
buy good makeup. Good makeup wears well, and you don't wake
up not looking like the girl he fell asleep next to.

When I attempt to open the front door, it's locked. "What the
hell?" Everett has always been extra regarding security, but he's
never been in the habit of locking doors when guests are over. I
key in the code, and the door opens, but the second I step inside, I
wish I hadn't.

"Oh, you're home. Did you and Stormy have fun last night?"
Lauren says as she walks down the catwalk that stretches from the
upstairs bedrooms to the open staircase. Why the fuck is she
upstairs? "Stormy mentioned something about camping," she
continues as she walks down the stairs. My ears hear her words,
but my eyes are zeroed in on her appearance. Her hair is slightly
mussed, and she's definitely wearing second-day mascara; one eye
is darker than the other. Did she fucking sleep here? I've yet to
find any words by the time she reaches the bottom and says, "I
think you left this at my house last night." I look down and find my
phone in her hand. My damn phone, the one I haven't been able
to stop thinking about since I realized I left it behind. She
swooped on it, no doubt realizing it was mine, and used it as an
excuse to come here and see Everett rather than waiting until I
brought Stormy home today.

"Thanks," I force out, even though it's the last sentiment I feel.

"Lauren," Everett's voice echoes from the hallway upstairs
before he comes into view, and his eyes land on me.

"I'll see you later. Stormy mentioned picking Cameron up for
today's game, and I think I might tag along. I should probably
attend an away game to see the team in action and check out the
competition." His eyes don't stray from mine as Lauren
approaches the front door, but mine do. Fuck that. Right now,
there are no words that would make any of this acceptable. I'm
heading up the steps two at a time, eager to escape this hell I

stepped into, when Lauren says, "It was good seeing you, Cameron. Bye, Everett."

The door closes at the exact moment Everett throws his arm out, catching me around the waist. "Don't touch me." I push venom into my voice as I try to shove down the hurt.

"Cameron, stop. It's not what it looks like."

I swat his arm away and step back. "Oh, so you didn't have a sleepover with another woman on the same night I said I wouldn't be home?"

"Cameron, it's not what you're thinking."

"And that wasn't a no," I say as I storm past him to my room and slam the door before he can follow me. There is no scenario that excuses letting another woman stay the night. He made a rule that I couldn't have guys over, and after everything we've shared recently, it shouldn't have to be said that the same rules apply to him. I guarantee if the roles were reversed, he'd be just as pissed. Locking the door, I slide down the back and squeeze my eyes closed.

I hear the front door open and close, and my heart cracks a little more. I don't know how much more it can take before all that's left is pieces. He didn't even try to convince me otherwise. He didn't fight for me. For us. "This is why you're building your own place, Cam."

My phone chimes, and I reluctantly pick it up. I don't want to talk to anyone, but I do because I had plans with Stormy anyway, and everyone knows the best way to get over something is to drown their problems in a bottle; any bottle will do.

> Stormy: Did you find your phone?

> Stormy: I just thought of something. If you didn't, I don't have a way of getting a hold of you. I guess I'll just show up at noon if I don't hear back.

I groan... and accidentally swipe out of responding, but when I do, another message catches my eye.

> Everett (11:32 p.m.): Cameron, please answer me.

"What the hell?" I immediately click into the strand. "When did you send me this?"

> Everett (5 p.m.): Where are you going tonight?

> Everett (8:40 p.m.): Will you consider coming home tonight?

> Everett (10:02 p.m.): Lauren is here.

He tried. He texted. He wanted me to come home, and he didn't hide her from me, but right now, his effort isn't taking center stage because something else is. How are the messages I received from him last night marked as read when I didn't have my phone? It's always locked.

"What are you up to, Lauren Rhodes?"

~

"I can't believe he hasn't put Parker in yet," I say as I try to lean over the stadium railing to get a better view of the dugout. "When did you last talk to him?"

"I saw him this morning, actually; he was fine. Maybe a little perturbed, but fine."

I do a double take at Stormy before resuming my study. Parker must really be interested if he stopped by her place before heading to the stadium to get on the bus.

"If he stopped by your place before the game, I bet he was late getting to the bus. That has to be why he didn't start."

"No, he didn't stay long at all. He didn't even come inside. I don't think he was late. That was his reasoning for not coming inside."

We are tied in the eighth inning, and bases are currently loaded. McKenna is pitching, and while he's doing a good job, the other team is making him throw. I can tell from here that the weight of the game, coupled with his pitch count, is getting the better of him right now. If I can see that, why hasn't Everett? He knows the game. That's when I catch movement from the dugout in my peripheral, and I see Parker storm down to the other side. Damn it, we should have sat on the other side. If we had sat behind the other team's dugout, I would have a better view of ours. It's easy to guess what's happening, even with an obstructed view. Parker is giving Everett an earful. The next thing I know, Everett leaves the dugout and walks out to the mound.

"He's pulling, McKenna."

"You think?" Stormy says, joining me at the rail.

"The coach can only walk out to the mound once during an inning to talk to the pitcher, and I doubt with bases loaded in the eighth it's a pep talk when his other starting pitcher hasn't entered the game." As McKenna walks off the mound, Everett squeezes his shoulder, and Parker jogs out. Fans clap as McKenna returns to the bench, and I call out, "Let's go, Park. You got this." He doesn't acknowledge me. I didn't expect him to; he's in beast mode now. But Everett does. His dark eyes zero in on mine as he walks off the field, like he's known exactly where I've been standing the entire game. Before he turns away, his eyes drop briefly to my jersey, and his jaw clenches. I'm wearing Parker's jersey. I kept the original uniforms that didn't fit. When I offered his to Stormy, she passed again, so I put it on. I didn't wear it as a dig at Everett. I wore it to support Parker. Either way, he's pissed, but the way I see it, if anyone has a right to be offended right now, it's me.

"I can't believe I'm nervous right now. Who am I?" Stormy screeches.

"A girl that wants some post-win action!" I say as I bump her hip.

"Oh, we're not screwing."

"What? Why not... I mean, unless you're waiting for marriage or something. That's totally cool."

She laughs. "No, I'm not waiting for marriage. You're cute. I told you I don't plan on sticking around, and I think we both know Parker isn't exactly fuck buddy material."

I already liked Stormy. Now I might love her a little. She's protecting his heart, which means she cares, and who can't respect that? "Well, damn. I was hoping one of us was getting laid." I grab her arm as Parker winds up. "Okay, this one counts."

Stormy's hand covers mine, and I can feel her tense up. She's into this too. Being a fan is very different when you have a personal connection to the players on the team. His first pitch is a perfect strike, right over the plate. Most first throws with a new pitcher are. Few batters will swing at the first pitch, but this guy not swinging will prove to be his mistake. Parker may not be the closer, but he's every bit as good and doesn't throw the same pitch twice. The difference between the two usually comes down to stamina and the diversity of pitches in their arsenal. Closers usually can't last as long as starters and usually don't have as many quality pitches. He threw the first ball right to him. All he had to do was swing. The next pitch won't be the same.

"Strike two," the ump calls out, and the Bulldogs fans cheer.

"That was his curveball."

"What's a curveball?"

"Seriously?' My grip on the railing slightly loosens before I tighten back up. "Don't worry about it now. All that matters is we need one more out, and he has one pitch left to get it." Technically, he could throw fifteen balls at this guy, but I'm not going to get into that. I'm pushing all my good juju into this next pitch.

He releases the ball, and the stadium practically cheers in unison as it hits the catcher's glove, and I start jumping up and down.

"Did we win? Does that mean we won?"

"No," I laugh. "We still have the ninth inning, but we held them back with bases loaded."

"Is now a good time to pee? I've been holding it for the past two innings, not wanting to miss Parker."

"Yeah, he won't bat, but hurry up."

No sooner than Stormy walks away, Lauren is at my side. After I picked myself up off the floor this morning and got a quick shower, I texted Stormy that I would pick her up just so we didn't have to carpool with Lauren. Riding with her was the last thing I wanted to do, but after I sent the text, I followed it up with a never mind. Your odds of winning your battles are greater when you know your enemy. I've had worse enemies. One that greets you while double-fisting two beers isn't too bad.

"Hey, I saw you had one of these, so I thought I'd grab you another while I got one for myself," Lauren says, stepping to my side.

I guess this isn't one of those stadiums that cuts the beer off early. Most minor league stadiums aren't, and this is a smaller venue that doesn't have the same backing as the Bulldogs.

"Thanks, can't turn down a free beer."

My eyes study her mannerisms as she sidles up to the rail to stand next to me. She is very pretty, and on the ride here, she and Stormy talked about the road trip they took through the Smoky Mountains last fall. Apparently, they broke down on the side of the road and ended up walking for two miles until they found a cabin where they could bum the Wi-Fi. When they walked up, they discovered the renters were there for a bachelor party. It sounded like they had a blast, and as I listened, a big part of me was jealous. I didn't get to have those experiences. I'm not sure I would have ever had them with my mom, but I know I would have had them with my dad.

"Are all the games this intense?" Lauren asks before drinking her beer.

"At this level, yes, most games are close. Sometimes you run into a team that's playing just for fun, but most of the time, it's pretty competitive." She nods as she scans the field. "Do you follow baseball, or is this an Everett thing?"

My comment about Everett doesn't faze her in the least, which leads me to believe she was expecting it. "I'm not a stranger to the sport. I dated a few players back in my day, but I don't turn it on TV or go to games for the joy of it. As far as your Everett comment goes..." She glances at me and cocks a brow. "You think Everett would be easily duped by a fair-weather fan like me?"

"No," I answer surely, even though I know she already knew that. But I play along.

"Yeah, I didn't think so. Good thing that with age comes a few new tricks."

Before I can respond or give her comment any real thought, the sound of a ball clanging off a bat steals my focus as I watch Gunner hit a home run.

"No freaking way!" I say as I watch him round the bases. A home run in the ninth in a tied game is just what we needed. I know that run just pumped up the bench. There is no way the guys are going to lose now. I feel it in my soul.

"What did I miss?" Stormy says, stepping up to my right.

"Number nine just hit a home run," Lauren answers.

"Hey, since you and Stormy have been hanging out and Everett and I are old friends, what if we do a barbeque this weekend?"

Is she for real? She's asking me this right now. Now the real reason she bought me a beer comes out.

"If you're trying to win me over to get to Everett, you're barking up the wrong tree. It's not like he's my dad. Getting on my good side won't win you any points with him."

"Oh, come on, you couldn't call a cab!" Stormy yells from beside me, and both Lauren and I turn to her, our mouths agape. I know she says she's leaving, but I think this town is growing on her, or maybe it's just the guy on the bench because the uninterested girl who walked into the team shop with a take it or leave it attitude looks like she's starting to care. "What? He was calling those balls strikes and they were clearly low and right of the plate."

By the time I turn back to the game, stunned that she used the correct terminology after not knowing what a curve ball was, the

Bulldogs are retaking the field. Damn. We only got one run, but one is all we need to win. Now, we just need to hold them.

"Come on, Park, you got this!" I yell out as he takes the field. On the outside, I don't look the part of a super fan. Apart from today's jersey, I'm typically overdressed for a ballgame. But I've basically lived at the fields for the past five years. I started coming to games to get closer to Connor, and it didn't hurt that Everett tried to attend every game. The love of the game sneaks up on you, and before you know it, you're drinking beer because that's all they have at most fields and hollering like a trucker.

"So, Sunday?"

Jeez, she is persistent. I thought she'd drop it after my comment and Stormy's interruption, but that was wishful thinking.

"Tomorrow, Sunday?"

"Strike!" The ump yells.

"Two more, Park. Let's go!" I take a drink of my beer, which is getting warm. "I'll have to check with Everett. I know he's been busy between filling in for Connor and working at the firm."

"Foul ball."

I'm missing the end of the game with all these questions. The next pitch connects with the bat and is caught by the shortstop.

"As long as you don't have any plans tomorrow, I don't think there are any schedule conflicts. I already mentioned it to Everett last night. He said he just needed to run it by you. So here we are."

They talked about it last night! Ugh, I mentally groan and try my best not to let my annoyance show that she was at the house with him last night and I wasn't. At least he didn't commit to another dinner date.

"I'm supposed to hang out with Parker and Nash tomorrow," Stormy says.

Oh, hell no, I will not be the third wheel again. "Parker can come too. When Connor is in town, we always make Sunday barbeques a thing. Tell him to bring Nash too." If Everett is going to throw the doors open, so am I, rules be damned.

"Strike!"

The roar of the stadium drowns out any more words as the guys all rally around Parker, smacking his hat and ass before lining up to shake hands.

"Come on. Let's go down," I say as I pull Stormy behind me to get closer to the field so we can congratulate Parker on his win. The second we get to the fence, Parker runs down the field toward us. He jumps the fence in one hop, and I step out of the way so he can get to Stormy, but it's not her he was after. The next thing I know, he's spinning me in his arms.

"Did you see that?"

"Yeah, Park, you looked good out there. I'm pretty sure I heard a scout from the Arizona Arrows was here." He squeezes my ass hard before setting me on my feet and pulling my face to his and placing a closed-mouth kiss on my lips.

My hands immediately find his chest as I push him back. "Parker—" I start, only to be cut off.

"What the hell was that, Michaelson?" Everett barks, storming up behind me.

"What was what? Me winning the game and making you look good?"

"You know I didn't call you to the mound. Jenson is our closer."

Fuck. Now I get it. Parker was using me. He's using me to get to Everett. That's still really shitty of him to do to Stormy. I know she said they aren't hooking up, but I know feelings are involved either way.

"This ends now, Parker. What the hell is your problem? You've made me your enemy since I returned from Boston. The least you can do is tell me why."

"You really want to do this here?" Parker questions.

"I don't see why not. I have nothing to hide. I haven't wronged you."

"Moira is cheating on my dad."

"What?" Everett questions, his face marred with confusion. "How is that my problem?"

"Because you couldn't satisfy her, she had to look elsewhere. Now she's my problem. My dad doesn't deserve that. You know what he went through losing my mom, and now he's with your slut ex-wife—"

Everett cuts him off, grabbing him by his jersey. "Moira is many things, but a slut isn't one of them."

"If you're going to hit me, go ahead. I'd love a reason to wipe the holier-than-thou look off your face. It doesn't belong there."

The two of them are locked in a staring contest, a test of wills. I know Everett doesn't go around looking for fights, but Parker has been asking for one. The last thing either of them needs right now is to make more of a scene. Everett is currently the face of the Bulldogs as the head coach, and if the scout from Arizona is still here, this won't look good, so I step in.

"Everett, come on. Let it go. This isn't the place. You got your answer," I slide my hand up the front of Parker's shirt and attempt to look like I'm fixing the top button. "People are watching, and this isn't a good look. Let it go."

Everett slowly releases his shirt, and his hands move to his hips. "What proof do you have?"

"An address in Texas that belongs to a Chad Hailsop. She tells us she's going there to help her friend Courtney with the Uplift Women's Charity Gala, but she doesn't stay with her or at the Four Seasons she claims to have a standing reservation at. Every week, she's gone a minimum of three consecutive nights. Every time she's gone, she's with him."

Everett drops his head, and I see it. He knows something, or if he doesn't, at the minimum, he has a suspicion. They were married for over twenty years. How could he not? However, he wouldn't say anything even if he did.

"Have you mentioned your theory to your father?"

"No," he clips out.

"Don't." When Everett looks back up, his eyes flick between us before landing on mine. "Are you with him?"

"What?" I question.

"You're wearing his jersey, and when I walked over here, his mouth was on yours. So I'll ask again, are you with him?"

"No, that wasn't—"

He tosses me his keys. "Go wait in the car."

I don't hesitate. I'm already pissed at Parker for pulling that stunt as it is. He promised he wouldn't use me, and he did. When I steal a glance at Stormy, she shoves her hands in the front pockets of her jeans and walks with me.

"I'm sorry. I didn't know Parker would do that. I hope you know it didn't mean anything. He was using me to get a rise out of Everett."

"I know," she answers, her tone indifferent. I'm not sure I'd be as unfazed as she seems to be had the roles been reversed.

"Are you sure you're not upset? I consider you a friend, and I try not to hurt the people I care about."

I hear her sigh as we walk. "I learned a long time ago to let go of things I can't change. Being unbothered doesn't mean I'm oblivious. It means I'm choosing not to engage."

Fucking solid advice if I ever did hear any. Now, mirroring that enlightenment will be the task.

CHAPTER 19
EVERETT

I felt like last night would never end. I knew I had made a mistake the second I let Cameron leave my office. I officially crossed a line, a big fucking line. I touched her. I put my mouth on hers, her soft curves molded into mine, and for those few fleeting seconds, my world ceased to exist, and all that was left was her. I felt like I had met my soul on her lips, and it rendered me speechless. I could have stayed with her like that forever, or at least it felt that way until my son called. I touched her, I kissed her, I met the other half of my damn soul, and then I let her go. But to my credit, and for as pompous as it may sound, I thought when I texted her she'd come home. The girl I kissed in my office waited for that kiss for years. It's what she wanted. She begged for it. I didn't understand why she didn't come home.

Of course I tracked her phone. I could see she was at Stormy's house all night, so when Lauren showed up on my doorstep around nine thirty p.m., I was conflicted as much as I was curious. Did Cameron know Lauren left to come over to my house? After thirty minutes and one drink, I was done guessing, so I texted Cameron to let her know. I thought out of all the texts, that one would have gotten a reply if not given her an immediate reason to come home. She doesn't have to say it. I know she doesn't like

Lauren coming around, but I can't push her away. The more drinks we had, the more I learned. The last text I sent to Cameron was eleven thirty p.m., and it was at that time I checked her location again, but when I did, I got a surprise. She was home, or at least her phone was, which told me that Lauren had her phone. I wanted to demand a lot of things when I discovered that little nugget of information, but I didn't. Somehow, I managed to bite my tongue, and I'm glad I did.

The two-hour drive to the game gave me a lot of time to reflect on the conversations I had with not only with Lauren but my brother Garrett. As soon as I threw the car in park, I sent him a text.

> Everett: I know what your theory is.

And as I walked into the stadium, I sent another.

> Everett: Drinks tomorrow. My place.

Now that I'm home, visitors are the last thing I need tomorrow. Today was a nightmare from start to finish. I didn't want to leave Cameron the way I did this morning. I wanted to follow after her and demand that she hear me out, but I had to get on the road so that I was on time for the game. These games are a big deal for Connor and the organization he's built, and Lauren informed me last night that she knew of one scout that would for sure be at today's game. That's one potential placement for one of my guys.

When I turned the corner, I saw Lauren hand Cameron her phone, and as I backed out of the driveway rather than sit outside her door, I hoped when she calmed down and found the time to read my messages, she'd see that I tried. That I did, in fact, tell her about Lauren and hadn't set out to hurt her, and then the game happened. If there had ever been a day to start putting weight in synchronicity, today would have been it. As though the morning wasn't enough of a sign to stay away from Cameron Salt, the game this afternoon should have been. She's been the source of my torment since I got home, but watching Parker run to her, spin her around, and grab her ass before putting his mouth on hers only confirmed I am a glutton for punishment. I'd like to say I could walk away, that I could let her go, but that would be a lie. If it weren't, I wouldn't have stormed across the field this afternoon. Did I want to tear into Parker for his stunt on the mound? Yes, but my desire to kill him for touching what feels like mine was greater. It was she who pulled me across that field, not self-serving vengeance for him trying to pull rank over me. Which he'll more than pay for. Time and time again, it's her. It will always be her. It's been her for longer than I'll ever admit. I've noticed her because my soul always saw its other half. It just looked different before, but I'm good at pushing aside what I want. Shoving down my own desires is what I excel at. It's why I popped a sleeping pill before getting into this scalding hot shower in hopes of actually staying in my room.

We didn't talk on the drive home this afternoon, even though I had a million words. I couldn't. I was torn between yelling at her and pulling over on the side of the road and giving her every fantasy I've had since I watched her play with her pretty pussy. Neither option would have been appropriate, and I'm tired of saying and doing things with her that I fucking regret. If I touch her again, it won't be from a place of anger. She didn't attempt to speak either; I think she was emotionally drained like me. Not speaking to the only person you want to talk to is hard. Not kissing away the insanity is harder. But that's not us. We're not in a relationship. I can't kiss away madness or spend hours in the sheets correcting her bratty behavior because she's not mine. Not in the way I want her to be.

I shut off the shower and quickly dry my hair before heading to bed. The pill I took must be kicking in because my brain is muddled. Nothing makes sense right now; there is no reason to be awake. Nothing good can come from staying awake. That's the last thought I have before sedative-induced sleep takes me.

My eyes jolt open, but my body doesn't move as my ears are acutely attuned to the deafening silence cloaking my room. I'm sure I heard something. What else could have woken me from deep sleep? I know it's not my thoughts; for once they are quiet. It's then I remember why I quit taking sleeping pills years ago. They make me groggy.

As my eyes lazily open and close, my mind drifts in and out of a dream state, and I convince myself that am indeed hearing noises. Nothing is real right now. The alarm is on, and Cameron is down the hall, safely sleeping in her bed. Miraculously, reassurances of her safety start to lull me back into a slumber until the bed dips beside me. I force my heavy lids open once more. Exhaustion from my lack of sleep over the past weeks has finally caught up with me, and now I'm hallucinating, or at least I thought I was. Until heat from a warm body envelops my back and the sweet scent of roses hits my nose.

"Cam—" I attempt to say her full name, but the weight of my tongue prevents me from doing so.

It doesn't matter anyway because my question is answered when lips press against my shoulder. "Are you expecting someone else?"

My heart starts galloping. This can't be happening. Of all the nights she could have decided to come to my bed, she has chosen this one. Finding my strength, I roll over. "Cameron, you can't be in my bed," I say sternly before my eyes land on her very exposed breasts, and I slam them shut. If I thought my heart was galloping before, it's full-on fucking sprinting now.

"Closing your eyes isn't going to make me disappear. I'm done slamming doors. I'm done not saying everything I want to say because I'm too scared to cross a line. I'm done walking away, believing it could be the last time, the one that pushes us to the point of no return, because the truth is, what scares me the most is never feeling again the way I feel when I'm with you."

Her words feel like they are literally ripped from my heart. Doesn't that mean something? Doesn't that mean this can't be wrong? How often do you find someone who can read the invisible ink on your soul? I've lived twice as long as her, and I can say she's the first. If she is my sin and my sin is my death, I will gladly die for her. My arm darts out, and I pull her naked body flush against mine, catching her off guard and making her gasp. God, she feels good. My head drops to the crook of her neck, and I inhale deeply, scared to open my eyes, fearful of changing my mind.

"Cameron... I don't want to let you go. You have to know that by now, but this... things will never be the same."

"Swear it."

"What?" I pull back and search her eyes for meaning.

"Swear things will never be the same because I don't want to go back. I only want to go forward. The only future I want includes you." Her hand comes up and caresses the side of my face. "I want you like this."

My mouth crashes to hers as my entire body hums with electricity. I've never felt more complete than I do right now, pressed against her skin to skin. My tongue dives deep the way I wanted to in my office as I drape my leg over her body, pulling her impossibly closer. Her hand slips around my neck and her fingers rake through my hair at the base, making every strand on my body stand at attention. Fuck, I'm only kissing her, and it's already everything.

I release her mouth, desperate to explore every inch of her. My lips trail across her jaw as my hand slides down her back, where I grab her bare ass hard. I'm extremely turned on and borderline pissed off that I'm only just now allowing myself this. Somehow time was stolen from me because it doesn't seem fair that I had to wait this long to find her. To have her.

"Ev," she pants as she grinds herself against my hard length.

I instantly roll her onto her back and settle between her legs, pinning my cock firmly against her slick core. "Is this what you want, sunshine?" I hover above her, our eyes locked as I run my tip through her folds.

"You have no idea how bad."

I drop down to my forearms. "You're wrong. I've wanted it just as badly, for probably just as long." I press myself against her hard. When her pretty mouth pops open, I steal a kiss, dipping my tongue in softly before pulling back and biting her lip. "Too bad you'll have to wait a little longer."

"What?" ardently rolls off her lips.

"I've wanted to taste you," I say as I pepper open-mouthed kisses down her chest before cupping one of her perfect tits and sucking her nipple into my mouth.

"Mmm," she moans loudly as her hips buck against my torso. I bite and tease her nipple, admiring how hard it gets for me before releasing it and thoroughly ravishing the other. With both nipples pert, I drag my tongue down the center of her soft stomach, peering up at her beautiful face framed by her perky tits, the ones I just had in my mouth. When I reach her pubic bone, her eyes find mine, and for the first time in my life, I don't look away. I've always looked away during sex. Sex has only ever been a carnal urge, a craving that needed to be satisfied, but not now. Now it's different. I'm vulnerable; I'm trusting her with something— something deep that comes from a place I'm not familiar with— but I know I never want to leave. As I dip my head, I place a closed-mouth kiss on her lips, my eyes never straying from hers before I run my tongue straight up her center. Her legs quiver as a whimper escapes her throat. "This can't be real. It feels too good, and you've barely touched me."

I loop my arms around her thighs. "Sunshine, in the morning, there will be no mistaking where I've been." Then I pull her flush against my face, my tongue spearing her tight pussy as my eyes roll back. Fuck. Her hand fists into my hair as I dip in as far as I can, desperate to taste her and make her feel good. The way her tight walls flutter around my tongue tells me she's not going to last. She's too worked up; like me, she's wanted this for far longer than this moment. I flatten my tongue and lick her straight up her center until I reach her tight little bundle of nerves and suck hard.

"Oh god... fuck." Her fingers tighten in my hair as she grinds her pussy against my face, chasing her orgasm.

"That's it, come on my face, sunshine," I say before spearing her with my tongue once more.

"Ev," she pants right before her orgasm hits, and her legs tremble. Her juices coat my tongue, and I greedily lap them up, so fucking turned on that they exist because of me. Once I've cleaned up my mess, I crawl up her body and take her pretty mouth long and slow. She came fast, but I don't want to rush through this with her. You only have your first time once. She pulls away from my mouth, her hand finding my jaw. "I want you inside of me. Please tell me that's on the table."

The second I made the conscious decision to pull her naked body flush against mine, it was on the damn table, but I need to be sure this isn't just years of pent-up of sexual tension. "Are you sure you won't regret this in the morning?"

"Regret is for things we don't do, not the things we've done." Her hand runs through my hair as her eyes study my face. "You have been all I've ever wanted for far too long."

"This is where I should say we should probably talk about last night, this afternoon, all of it, before we—"

Her finger presses into my lips. "Not now. Sometimes words are gentle, and other times they're ugly; they have the power to change before our very eyes. They are deceivers, but this..." Her other hand drifts up my side, her delicate touch igniting a fire that heats my flesh and melts my bones. "This can't be faked."

"You're trying to kill me, aren't you?" I say as I gently kiss her lips, and my tip nudges her entrance, reminding me I'm bare. "Shit," I push up onto my hands and reach for my nightstand.

"What's wrong?"

"I need to get a condom."

Her legs wrap around my waist. "Please don't."

The last thing I need right now is an accident. "Cameron—"

"I haven't been with anyone in over a year, Everett. I have an IUD, and I'm clean. I want to feel you...unless that's not what—"

"Don't even think about finishing that sentence," I say as I settle back between her legs, my arms caging her in so she has nowhere else to look but at me. "You know I want the same thing. You've known it for years."

She thrusts her hips against me. "I don't believe you. A man that wants it just as bad as I do would already be inside of me."

I growl and rock against her clit hard before greedily taking her mouth one more time and saying, "Or maybe I'm not in a rush to make this a memory." I align my tip with her entrance, and her soft walls immediately pull me in. "My god, sunshine, you feel so good, and I'm not even all the way in." I push in a little further, and my cock twitches as a bead of pre-cum leaks from the tip. I'm not going to last. When she bites her lip, I pause. "What's wrong?"

She shakes her head. "Please don't stop."

I lay my forehead against hers. "Does it hurt?" She said she hasn't been with a man in over a year, which made me way fucking happier than it has any right too.

"Please," she pleads as her hand finds the back of my neck and she pulls my mouth onto hers. My mind momentarily struggles before I let it go and fall into her. I'm hurting her by going slow, by prolonging this moment that she's wanted for so long. I want to treasure it, and she wants to experience it. Both are beautiful. As our kiss grows hungrier with need and desire, I fully seat my cock, and we both groan loudly. I give her a second to acclimate to my size. I know she wants this, but I don't want to hurt her.

"I'm going to fuck you now, but if it hurts, you tell me to stop." She nods. "I'm going to need your words on this one, Cameron. You are too important to me."

"I'll tell you to stop."

I push up onto my elbows and widen my legs, digging my

SALT

knees in as I pull back and push in slowly, once, then twice, admiring the way she molds around me. Fucking perfect, but it's when my eyes scan down her body to watch myself disappear inside of her that I go feral. My length glistening with her juices has me pushing in hard, desperate for more, her little mewls every time I bottom out only provoking me. With every thrust, she gets wetter, and the sound of our arousal, coupled with the smell of sex, permeates my room, only elevating my desire.

"Fuck, you're wet. I think this is my new favorite sound. Tell me you'll let me hear it more than once." My words have her clenching around my cock hard.

"Every day," she answers unequivocally.

I pound into her at a piston pace, unable to control myself. She's better than anything I ever could have imagined. There is no measure. Nothing could ever compare. This, right here, right now, erases anything that came before her. She is all I see. Her porcelain skin is already turning rosy, her soft lips swollen and reddened from the passion of our kiss. "You're really good at being bad, sunshine. I'm always going to want more of this, more of you." Her nails digging into my biceps as I thrust into her feel like a challenge. I want her to leave her mark. I want her to break my skin. I need the pinch of pain and the promise of a scar tomorrow to serve as a reminder that this wasn't a dream. Somehow, I fell asleep and woke up in a reality where she was mine. I thrust in hard, admiring the bounce of her breasts before pausing to hook my arm under her knee, bringing her leg up, and changing the angle to reach new depths. She whimpers as I push back in. "Is it too much? Am I hurting you?"

Her hands trail up my arms and wrap around my neck before beckoning my mouth with their pull. "You're so deep, Ev. No one has ever had me like this."

My cock twitches, her words making me feel things a man of my vintage surely should have felt by now. We may not be each other's first, and I probably won't be her last...

Fuck, why does that thought make my chest tight? I shove it

219

down as her soft lips expertly mold with mine, and I slowly pump into her, desperate to hang onto what we have here and now because it's everything. Her words tonight have caught me off guard, every one speaking directly to my soul, especially those last ones. Her soft body beneath me, those ice blue eyes hooded with desire locked on mine, and the way I feel her pussy clenching around my length sends me barreling into my own release. I drop my forehead to hers, knowing I'm a few pumps away from making this a memory.

"If you still want me in the morning, you can have me."

"Always?" It's a question, not a confirmation, and I know exactly what she's asking me. She's asking for more than one night. She's asking for an us, but it's the longing in her eyes and the depth of her ask that sends me spiraling.

"You need to get there. Fuck, get there," I say as I slam into her, hitting my new favorite spot two more times before I feel her walls spasm around me, and I lose it. My head drops to the crook of her neck as I fade in and out and let go. She's it. This is it for me. It's her, or it's no one. I kiss her neck and pray. If it can't be this life, let it be the next.

The rhythmic rise and fall of a warm chest and a heartbeat beneath my hand stir me awake. As my eyes adjust to my dimly lit room and the sun peeks through the slats of the curtains, I'm reminded that last night wasn't a dream. For a few hours, I was hers, and she was mine, and everything that never made sense suddenly did. My world felt whole in ways it never had as I worshipped her body for hours, memorizing every peak and valley and everything in between. Even now, her warm body molded against mine as I hold her while she sleeps, is an earthly paradise I never want to leave.

I gently let my thumb brush over the soft skin of her breast as I kiss her shoulder. There's no sneaking out of this bed. I'm not sure

SALT

I would even if I could. Waking up wrapped around her is the only way I ever want to wake up. My leg is draped over hers, her body pinned flush against mine as my arm wraps up her middle. Even in my unconscious state, my heart knows what it doesn't want to lose. I let my eyes drift over her porcelain skin. My stomach knots with a mix of emotions when I see the pink marks from where I sucked and nipped her breasts countless times and the reddened patches where my beard blemished her milky white skin.

"Ev," she says groggily, as her fingertips slowly drag up my arm, leaving a trail of goosebumps in their wake. "Can we..."

"Everett." The sound of my name being called and the front door closing has us both momentarily freezing, unsure if what we heard was real. "Everett," Moira's voice grows louder as her heels click up the steps, and I dart out of bed like the damn house is on fire as Cameron pulls the covers over her head.

I've just pulled on my briefs when the knob to my door turns, and I rush to meet it as it opens. "Moira, what are you doing?" I demand, blocking her entry.

"I came to talk—"

"You don't live here anymore. You can't just walk into my house," I interrupt the second it becomes clear this isn't an absolute emergency. Her eyebrows rise as the vexation in my voice catches her off guard, and she attempts to look past me, to which I lean into view, cutting off hers. I step toward her, pulling the door to my bedroom closed as I do. "I'm going to need that key back." I hold out my hand.

"Do you have someone in there?"

"The answer to that question has nothing to do with me asking for my key back. Our son is an adult who no longer lives in this house, and you are married to another man. You have no reason to have a key to my home."

"I'm sorry. I didn't realize you had someone in your bed. I didn't see a car outside."

Shit. I don't need her drawing conclusions about who is in my

221

bed. "Did you ever drive anywhere when we were together?" I try to thwart off any further inquiries.

"You must like her if you're still in bed at noon on a Sunday."

It's noon? Fuck. I don't think I've slept in until noon since high school. Good thing our tournament started early this week. All games wrapped up yesterday, otherwise today would have been a game day I would have slept straight through. I keep my face impassive. "I'm not discussing my sex life with you." I hold out my hand. "Key," I demand once more.

She shakes her head and reaches into her pocket, handing me her ring of keys. "You put it on there. You can take it off." I quirk a brow, unsure where this sudden sentiment is coming from. This keyring is the same one I gave her the day I drove her here and handed over the keys to her dream house. Nothing I ever did was enough for her. I know now it couldn't be. I wasn't her person, but it doesn't make the sting of all those years hurt any less.

I take the key off the ring and hand it back. "You said you wanted to talk. What was so important you had to barge in unannounced?"

"Lauren Rhodes is back in town."

Seriously, this now! Of all the fucking times. To Parker's credit, Moira has been notably absent. It's why I haven't had a chance to address Lauren's claims with her. I should be the bigger person and state firmly what I know, but she just walked in my house and pulled me away from the only place I want to be. Not to mention, she fucking lied to my face for over a decade.

"Yeah," I say slowly. "This isn't news. Lauren and your niece, Stormy, both work at the stadium."

I know damn well Stormy isn't related to Moira. Lauren said as much, and I confirmed it, but it's a solid segue into the other conversation I want to have.

"Niece?" Her eyes widen. "Wait... back up." She brings her fingers to her temples. "Did I hear you right?"

"Yes, your niece, Stormy. She's been working at the stadium for weeks now."

Technically, I'm not one hundred percent piggybacking off Lauren's tale. It was Moira's name that rolled off Stormy's lips when she strolled into my office, catching me off guard. I had just finished practice when she knocked on my door and said Moira had sent her up and that I would find a job for her at the stadium for the summer. I wasn't in charge of hiring any of the staff. That was done before I stepped into Connor's role. It wasn't until Lauren asked me who hired Stormy that I realized her deception. The discovery was another detail that corroborated her story that she didn't know what Stormy was up to in her scheming. It also told me that Evan gave Stormy information about our family because Lauren wouldn't have known to tell Stormy to use those words when she saw me. Moira and I have worked together on side projects our charity work has brought to our door for years. We've discretely helped domestic violence victims find sanctuary and jobs while trying to start over. My initial thought was Stormy was another one of those individuals. I assumed I had an email in my inbox waiting to be read from Moira detailing who she was.

"Everett, this is all news to me."

"I can see that. How about we take this to my office?"

Her eyes trail down my body. "Did you forget you're still in your underwear?"

"Nope. I'm very aware. I'll swing by the laundry room on the way down."

After throwing on a pair of athletic shorts and a T-shirt, I enter my office to find Moira perusing my shelves. For the most part, the house is the same. I was never home enough after our divorce to care to change things aside from the two rooms I spend all of my time in: the master and my office.

"I didn't know you were a collector of first editions."

I close the door behind me. "I'm not. That's Damon's collection."

"Oh." She's quiet as she stares at the books. "How's Cameron? I know this time of year is never easy for her."

Damon's crash happened weeks after Cameron's seventeenth

birthday. She's never truly celebrated a birthday since. The entire month, she's typically somber. The closer we get to the anniversary, the quieter she grows, choosing to reflect in silence and be alone. However, every year, her grief changes. I wouldn't say that time has healed her pain; healing only comes when we are ready for it, but time has taught her how to cope.

"Working at the stadium has helped busy her mind, but I guess we'll see how the next few days go."

She crosses the room and sits in one of the leather armchairs. "Well, maybe you can talk her into visiting Mackenzie that week. They've grown close over the past year and getting away from this place would be good for her."

I clench my jaw, not because her idea is bad but because the last thing I want to do is send her away to grieve in someone else's arms, but I'd gladly do it if I knew it would bring her peace.

"Then we wouldn't have anyone to run the shop."

I don't make the comment to be inconsiderate of Cameron, but rather, I want to get back to the reason we are here. Lauren Rhodes and Stormy.

"Are you saying you don't trust my *niece* to run the store alone?" She rolls her eyes. "Come on, Everett. We were married for over twenty years. Do you really think I would keep a secret niece from you? I can't believe you fell for that."

I was just about to sit down, but now I need a drink. "You managed to hide a nephew from me for almost half that time."

I can't help the way my anger rises with her silence. Silence is acceptance. Evan Graves is, in fact, her nephew. She knew, and she didn't tell me.

"Everett," she says my name with a sigh. "I've never told anyone. Kipp doesn't even know. It was a secret I planned to take to my grave." With my cognac poured, I turn to her, my expression bemused. I may not have been the love of her life, the man she wanted to marry, but out of all the things I could be, the keeper of her secrets was undoubtedly one of them. Secrets are what brought us together to begin with, but I suppose I should have known better. Secretive people have secrets, little ones that grow into big lies. "Who wants to find out their father was a monster? I thought by not telling him, I was saving him a world of hurt. If Evan found out his father was a rapist, the dark cloud that already lingers over him would only get darker. In my opinion, that truth would not set him free. If anything, it would hold him captive."

Evan's truth is one thing. I can sympathize with her reasoning, but she's leaving out something else. She had a damned sister too. "And what about Sage, Evan's mother? What was the reason you didn't tell me the truth about her?"

Her eyes drop to her hands. "By the time I figured out who either of them was to me, we were going through our divorce, and I was tired," her voice breaks as she stands and heads toward the window. I'm sure finding out there was actual fire behind the smoke rumors of her father's infidelity created wasn't an easy pill to swallow. All those years ago, people believed Lauren Rhodes was her sister, born out of an affair. It turns out she wasn't, but someone else was. "I already could never repay you for all the debts I owed. You'd given up so much by the time I discovered the truth, I kept it to myself. I was done being your burden, a mess you had to clean up, a person you had to protect."

I understand that, and if she had told me, I would have taken those words to my grave. I'm sure there's more there, but I don't care to dig into it. What's done is done. We can't rewrite our history. "It's in the past," I say as I grab the baseball sitting on my desk.

She pushes a strand of hair behind her ear. "I can't believe you hired Lauren."

I quickly abandon the ball to reclaim my drink. "I didn't. Your son did. You've been out of town a lot lately." She averts her gaze. It's such an obvious tell, one I'm currently grateful for because while she's in the mood for giving up her indiscretions, I ask, "What business do you have with Chad Hailsop?"

Her hand covers her heart. "How do you know about that?"

"Parker, he thinks you are cheating on his father," I say indifferently as I take a drink. "Does Kipp know?"

She nods. "Yes, Kipp knows."

"Well, maybe you should consider talking to Parker and Elijah sooner rather than later."

"We planned on telling them at the end of the month." Her eyes find mine. "You know I hate asking you this. I've always hated asking you this... Promise you won't say anything."

My eyes intently hold hers, ensuring she feels the depth of their irony. "Have I ever said anything?" It's curt and lands its mark. "Moira, I think it's time to go. I do have a guest I need to see out, and I'd rather not have my ex-wife in the house when I do it."

Her hand tightens around her purse. "Right, I forgot about that." Reaching into her pocket, she pulls out her keys. "I'll see myself out."

For the first time in over twenty years, I watch Moira walk away and feel nothing. I don't feel the need to dig, pry, or save her. We can tell ourselves we've moved on all we want, but until we can look at them and feel nothing, it's only a wish.

CHAPTER 20

CAMERON

I've been downstairs for thirty minutes, and my nerves are getting the best of me. I pull at the high neck on my summer dress, trying to find relief that I know won't come because it's not the heat getting to me. It's him. Last night was the best night of my life. I've pinched myself twice, literally still unbelieving that any of it was real and not a dream. Not only did I find the strength to go to Everett's room. He let me stay. Waking up with him draped over me was heaven. For a few seconds, I got to bask in him and the night we shared. And then Moira happened. He darted out of bed faster than I could blink when he realized she was seconds from walking in on us. His reaction is what has me uneasy now. We didn't say much, and the things we did say felt honest, but part of me is wondering if they weren't just lust. Years of pent-up longing burst at the seams, and now the regrets we promised we wouldn't have are precisely that: regrets.

My phone pings, pulling me from my dejected thoughts.

> Stormy: We'll be there in ten. FYI, his brother tagged along.

The way she says "his brother" instead of using his name has me on edge. Stormy's name precedes her. Nothing is black and white with her. She's the kind of person you should never take at face value, but maybe she forgot Parker's brother's name.

Cameron: Elijah?

I stare at my phone, waiting for bubbles to appear, and they don't, which only makes my anxiety that much worse. I blow out a tense breath and look out the back window. It's probably hot as hell outside but it looks nice, and sitting pool side with a cocktail sounds like a remedy to my current anxious hell. With my mind made up, I head outside and shoot Stormy another text.

Cameron: Come around back. I'm at the pool.

Digging through the fridge in the swim-up bar, I hear a horn double honk, which must mean Stormy has arrived. That definitely wasn't ten minutes, but I don't care. I need company, something to take my mind off the man inside who has yet to make an appearance. A stiff drink sounded good, but I reach for a pale ale instead. They have higher alcohol content, and since I won't be rocking a bikini today, I don't care if I get bloated from drinking beer.

The back gate opens, and Stormy walks in with three guys on her heels, none of whom are Parker. I recognize Nash right away. He's hard to miss wearing a leather jacket in the fucking summer heat. The guy behind him has to be his brother. They both have the same strong jawline and jet-black hair. And finally, I see Elijah. That's strange. Why would he come but not Parker? Unless Parker is still upset about everything that went down after the game. I would have thought getting his suspicions about Moira off his chest would have lifted a weight, but I know he's close to his dad. I understand wanting to protect his heart. However, it's not fair to blame Everett for Moira's infidelity if that is indeed what this is.

"Salt, where are you, girl?" Nash calls.

I hold up my beer, drawing their eyes toward the swim-up bar.

"Cameron, you've been holding out on me. You didn't tell me you had a private lagoon in your backyard," Stormy says, making it to the bar first.

"I don't, Everett does."

"Either way, I now see why you're not in a hurry to leave," she says as her eyes rake over the grotto. "What are we drinking?"

"Whatever you want. The bar is pretty stocked now that it's summer."

She nods before inspecting the refrigerator below and scanning the selections.

"Salt," Nash says, sliding past Stormy and pulling me in for a hug. "I missed you at the bar last night."

"The bar?"

"Yeah," Stormy answers. "Everyone went out for drinks last night to celebrate the win."

"You going to introduce me to your girl or what?"

My eyebrows shoot up. His girl? Nash is great, but we're just friends. A complication is the last thing I need right now. I'm just about to correct him when Nash releases me.

"I already told you. She's not my girl." With his arm around my shoulder, he says, "She was my backpack."

"Right," his brother mocks sardonically, leaving me to believe Nash must have said a little more than he's letting on for his brother to assume we are anything other than friends. Tall, dark, and handsome, steps forward, extends a hand, and says, "I'm Emmitt."

"Cameron," I say as I take his hand. Handshakes are a gesture I love, but they seem so nineteenth century anymore. Most guys greet you with a head nod now.

"So, it's not Salt?" his head tilts to the side.

"No, it is. My name is Cameron Salt. The guys at the fields usually call me Salt. You know, the whole athlete thing where everyone calls everyone else by their last names."

"I wouldn't know. I didn't play sports. I prefer the stage," he shrugs. "I like Salt better anyway."

"Yeah, why is that?"

He smiles, and the sexiest dimple appears, not two, just one, making it all the more alluring. "Everything is better with salt."

Stormy chuckles as she pops a beer. "Real smooth, Romeo."

"Hey now... I'd offer you some love too, but I already know you can't calm a storm." On that note, we all start laughing.

I hear the back door open, and my stomach feels queasy. It has to be Everett walking out. He's the only person that was inside. Moira left almost an hour ago now. After Everett left the room, I snuck back into mine. I showered and did my business before subtly cracking my door just enough so I wouldn't miss anything downstairs. I assume they went to his office because there was no eavesdropping to be scored, and then she showed herself out.

"Can you show me to the bathroom?" Stormy asks, and I nearly fly across the pool bar to kiss her, thankful for the interruption. Nash still has his arm around my shoulder, and while it feels lighthearted, it's not a look I want Everett to see.

"Yep," I link arms with her and head toward the pool house. The last thing I want to do is walk past Everett. I know avoidance is a shit response to dealing with anxiety. However, I'm also not ready to deal with whatever regret might be written on his face. At least by avoiding him, I can hope for a little longer that last night changed things for him the way they did me. That what we have is irrevocable. It's not something that can easily be discarded; it can't be ignored because we are the beginning and end. "Where's Parker?"

"He said he had something he needed to take care of... but I'm not sure I buy that. When we went out last night, something he needed to take care of today never came up. I think he feels shitty about the spot he put you in yesterday, and Everett currently isn't his favorite person, so that doesn't help."

I know Stormy says she and Parker aren't dating or hooking up, but I feel like she knows him well for someone who is doing none of those things. Parker wears his heart on his sleeve, but it feels like they have more late-night phone calls or hangouts than she lets on.

"And what about you? I still don't see how you're not a little pissed off at either of us," I say as I pull open the door of the pool house.

"I mean, maybe if I hadn't known about the fake wedding date incident the two of you shared, I'd feel some type of way, but honestly, after getting to know both of you, I don't see anything but really good friends..." She trails off, releasing my arm and staring up at the exposed wood beam ceiling. "Damn, this is just the pool house? It's hella nice. If I were in your shoes, I'd claim this place for my own."

I don't say anything. I've never really given much thought to staying in any other part of the house, or the property, for that matter. I have a nice room, and if I want to use any other part of the house, I can. But moving out here would only put me further away from Everett.

"The bathroom is around the corner to your left."

She flops onto one of the oversized chairs. "Oh, I don't have to pee. I could tell Nash was making you uncomfortable."

I take a drink of my beer and sit on the loveseat opposite her. "Is Lauren coming? I know she mentioned coming with you yesterday at the game."

"She was right behind us. Parker was supposed to pick me up at the house. Instead, Elijah showed up in his place with Nash and Emmitt."

I feel like she's not telling me something. It sounds strange that Parker would cancel and send Elijah and his friends in his place to pick up Stormy, especially given I know he's into Stormy. Not to mention, I find it odd that Stormy would entertain the three of them without Parker. Something doesn't fit, but the last thing I need is more drama on my plate. So I keep my mouth shut.

"What are you guys doing in here? Come on." Elijah startles us, pulling open the door.

I know he's been going through some stuff after his breakup with his longtime girlfriend. Everyone thought they would get married, but then he broke her heart. He's probably down for anything to keep his mind off her, and that is something I can relate to right now.

"We're coming," I say, vacating the chair. "Did you want to grab a swimsuit? It's hot out today, and I'm not sure overalls are exactly poolside attire."

"Maybe not a swimsuit. They're not really my thing but shorts I can do."

We've barely made it two steps outside the pool house when Nash swoops me up and throws me over his shoulder. At the same time, I see Elijah surprise Stormy from behind.

"Nash, put me down," I say, still trying to hold my beer until he starts running, and I toss it to pound on his back. "Nash, I'm serious."

"Cry me a river, backpack. It's time to get wet." My protests are silenced a second later as we're plunged into the pool's deep end. I hold my breath as the refreshing embrace of the cold water envelops me. Being thrown into the pool was the last thing I wanted, but as I sink to the bottom, the chill invigorates me. It's just the right amount of crazy I needed to find my voice instead of trying to hide behind my fear. A hand wraps around my wrist and pulls me up to the surface right before two hands circle around my waist, and Nash is there. "Don't tell me you can't swim because then I'm going to feel like an ass."

I wipe the water out of my eyes, grateful I wore waterproof mascara today. "I can swim. Sitting at the bottom of the pool was an act of goodwill."

His pouty lips purse, and his eyes narrow. "Goodwill?"

"Yeah." I push his arms off my waist before quickly placing my hands on top of his head and adding, "Now you're going down." Once he's under, I push off his shoulders with my feet and get a head start toward the shallow section.

"Hey, get back here." I feel him right on my heels. He's one stroke away from being able to grab my ankle. That's when I see Elijah pulling Stormy to the pool's edge, and I'm caught. When Nash realizes I'm not fighting to get away, his gaze follows the direction of mine.

"I should probably make sure she's okay." He nods and pulls me with him into the shallow water in one swoop so we can walk out. His hand slips down my back as we walk out of the pool. At the same time, my eyes find Everett sitting in an Adirondack chair in front of me. While his sunglasses hide his eyes, his clenched jaw tells me he doesn't like what he just witnessed. Good. Neither did I, but he's not doing anything about it either, and doesn't that say something? I drop his gaze like I never met it all and walk to the towel box. When I flip open the lid, Nash reaches around me, pulls out a towel, and drapes it over my shoulders before grabbing one for himself. No sooner than I turn around to take one to Stormy, she's at my side, pulling one out for herself. "Come on, let's get some dry clothes."

~

Stormy was fine; she could swim. However, she didn't give many more details than that because, let's be real, it's Stormy. From what I gathered from the few things she did share, Elijah's move caused some sort of PTSD moment for her. She was embarrassed by her reaction. Once, I got her some dry clothes, and she had a minute to collect herself. I tried to reassure her that she had nothing to be ashamed of, but sometimes, the weight of our self-consciousness can't be avoided.

While she dressed in the bathroom, I selected a high-necked romper and pulled my hair into a tight bun. I was going to check my makeup, but since Stormy is in my ensuite, I forgo waiting. I don't want her to feel rushed, and my makeup isn't an emergency. I left my purse downstairs last night, and it has my to-go makeup case inside. I take one last look around my room, making sure I'm not forgetting anything, only to pull open the door and forget how to breathe. Everett's standing there, his hand positioned to knock, his expression worn.

We stand there for long seconds, drinking each other in, the events of last night flicking through my mind like a highlight reel featuring the best moments of my life.

His brow pinches as he drops his hand. "Hi," is all that comes out.

"Hi," I roll my lips and try to bring my mind to focus on the here and now.

"Are you okay?"

"I got wet. We both know I can swim. I'm fine," I answer, blinking away the fog.

"I'm surprised you didn't opt to put a swimsuit on."

I step outside and close my door behind me. Crossing my arms, I say, "Yeah, well, I can't really wear a swimsuit today."

He rubs his chin. The faintest hint of satisfaction appears before he asks, "Why is that?"

"Did you really come up here to ask me about my clothing choices?" His lips thin, and his pause grates on my nerves. I'm too vulnerable for his games. "Never mind," I huff as I step around him. I need to put some space between him and me so I can breathe. I can't think straight when I'm smelling him, and every time I look at him, all I see are the eyes that looked at me with complete adoration last night as his mouth explored every inch of my body.

"So, you're mad then?" he says right before I reach the top step.

I turn to him, hand firmly gripping the rail. "Mad?"

"Anger is momentary madness, anger I can fix, anger I can live with but regret..." He pulls in a stuttered breath.

"Am I mad? Yes, but I'm mad because you matter, and I hate feeling like I don't. I told you last night I wouldn't regret you in the morning. That hasn't changed and—"

He's in front of me, backing me against the wall before I can finish. "You matter. You matter more than anything ever has." My heart skips a thousand beats as his words, his touch, the move, all speak directly to my heart. His hand slowly snakes up and around the base of my neck, and he presses his forehead to mine. "I want to kiss you."

"You never have to ask—" His lips smash against mine, and I feel like he's kissing me for the first time all over again. I'm nervous, happy, excited, and dizzy all at once. I melt into his hold as his tongue explores my mouth, and my brain turns to mush. It's utterly pathetic, given how I was mad seconds ago. The faint sound of my bathroom door opening has his lips leaving mine as he pulls me into one of the guest bedrooms.

"You left," he pants, chest heaving.

"What?" I question, my eyes darting between his as I try to keep up.

"When I came back to my room, you were gone."

"I didn't realize you wanted me to stay."

"What gave you the impression there was anywhere else I wanted you to be?"

I step back, putting some needed space between us. "Oh, I don't know. You jumped out of bed like the house was on fire when you heard your ex-wife walking up the steps."

"You pulled the covers over your head to shield yourself," he challenges, pinching the bridge of his nose. His reaction has me questioning my own. "Last night was our first night together, Cameron. We were occupied doing a lot of things that didn't include talking. What did you expect?"

I see now what I didn't in the haste of our rude awakening. We're clearly both emotionally strung out, unsure where the other stands and what's next. I'd like to start with the future first, so I say, "First, you didn't say last."

"I know what I said. It doesn't mean it's what should happen. Cameron, I will never regret last night, but I will regret hurting you."

This time, I'm the one who makes the first move; taking a step toward him, I wrap my arms around his waist. "Then don't."

He growls, and the confliction in the vibration is palpable. "It's not that simple. This morning was a perfect example of that. There are more reasons we don't work, can't work, than that we do, and I don't care to destroy your reputation while you figure that out."

"I disagree. You're older, so what? I could list ten celebrity age gaps just like ours right now."

A small smile splays across his face. "I bet you could." The back of his knuckles rake over my cheek. "But it's not just the age gap, Cameron. It's your father, our family, my career, all of it."

"I thought we went over this last night before you defiled me. My father would want me to be happy. You make me happy. As for your career, I'll gladly sell my shares equally to you and your brothers. We both know I don't need it." I drop my gaze to his chest to find my words. "I'm no match when it comes to Connor. I would never want to come between the two of you. I wouldn't expect that of you, but the Connor I know would have an open heart, just like his father, and I think if he saw that being with me made you happy, he'd want that for you." I risk finding his eyes once again. "What are we living for if not a happy life with the people who make it worth living?" My hand caresses his cheek. "You're one of those people for me."

His eyes soften before his mouth is once again on mine as his hands eagerly glide down my back and grip my ass, squeezing hard before lifting me up and pinning me to the wall. "You're determined to shatter my resolve."

I grind myself against his hardening length. "Does that mean you're saying yes?"

"It means I'm not saying no."

"Everett," the sound of Colton's voice ringing out from the foyer pulls Everett's mouth away from mine as we hear the front door close.

"You've got to be kidding me," he mutters, chest heaving as he tries to calm the adrenaline I know is coursing through his veins, same as me. "I'll be down in just a second," he calls out. His eyes land on mine, and I can see he has a million things he wants to say, but he doesn't have the time. "Can this be ours for now?"

He's not asking me this lightly. He took his time choosing those words because what he's really asking is will I be his secret. I should say no. The rational side of my brain knows I deserve to be loved out loud, but damn if being his dirty little secret doesn't feel good. And because I'm a betting girl, I will make a wager on us. I believe in what we have, and while it might be painful now, I'll love that pain because, eventually, he'll have to trace a line back. All secrets have an expiration date.

A whispered yes falls from my mouth before he takes my lips in his once more and sets me down. "I'll see you downstairs."

CHAPTER 21
EVERETT

"I texted Garrett for drinks to compare notes, and he sent you," I chide as I enter the kitchen and find Colton helping himself to a drink. I can't help but be annoyed. Yesterday, when I invited my brother here for a drink to discuss theories, it was before I let Cameron into my bed. Right now, company is the last thing I want.

"Good to see you too, brother," he mocks as he stirs his vodka and tonic. "The kids were sick, now Garrett is sick. Yet another reason to stay single. No one in my house to pass me their diseases." Pausing to take a drink, he adds, "I'm sure I'm not here to discuss Garrett's health. So what is it you think you know?"

I give him an unimpressed glare as I head toward the refrigerator. He loves to have the upper hand. Being the youngest by over a decade, he's always been super competitive, wanting to top records set by myself and Garrett. This is no different. Some might see it as a character flaw, but I see it as an asset. As important as this conversation is, I'd rather have an empty house.

"Why did Garrett suspect Lauren to begin with?" I ask as I pull out a bottle of water, desperately needing to hydrate after the night I spent with Cameron in my bed. Cognac for breakfast was

238

the last thing I needed, but I had to calm the storm that started raging the second Moira walked into my house unannounced.

"Without knowing whatever it is, you know I'm going to assume the same as you: bad timing. She showed up at the same time Connor's house gets broken into, works at the stadium, which gives her access to you and Cameron, and, to top it off, she's started inserting herself in circles she never belonged to. Why?"

I start rummaging through the fridge for something to put in my stomach when a package of turkey pepperoni catches my attention. My stomach instantly starts to rumble. I hastily pop one into my mouth to quench the hunger pains that have now begun to take root.

"Lauren stopped by unexpectedly a few nights ago. She came with a purpose, which I believe was to deliver Cameron's phone, a detail I didn't find out until the next morning because rather than hand me the phone and take her leave, she wanted to walk down memory lane. Something that seems to be a reoccurring theme every time she's around." I shove another pepperoni into my mouth.

"Hold on, did you say next morning? You let Lauren spend the night?" His eyes widen in disbelief.

"Yes," I answer matter-of-factly. "One, she had too much to drink for me to, in good conscience, allow her to drive home, and two, I was doing my own investigating."

He swirls his drink, seemingly pacified by my response. "How far back did the walk down memory lane go?"

"The better question would be, who are they about." I pause to finish my water.

"Oh hey, Colton," Cameron interrupts with Stormy by her side, now wearing dry clothes. Her eyes briefly flick to mine before landing back on Colton's. "I didn't know you were coming over today. Maybe we should order food since we have a full house."

"I could always eat." He raises his glass toward Stormy. "Who's your friend?"

"Sorry, how rude of me. Stormy, this is Colton, Everett's younger brother." She places her hands on the island. "Stormy is working with me in the team shop for the summer. You might know her aunt, Lauren Rhodes." He raises a brow before taking a long drink of his vodka. His lack of response isn't directed at Cameron. He's in his head, but she doesn't know that. She rolls her lips and reaches to push a strand of hair that isn't there behind her ear. "Well, we're going to head back outside. I'll see what the guys want to order." Her eyes flick to mine disquietly once more before she pulls Stormy out behind her.

"What's going on inside that head of yours?" I ask as soon as the door is closed.

"Two things I'm sure of..." He sets his glass down. "That friendship isn't a coincidence," his eyes lock onto mine. "And... it may not have been true before, but it's true now. You're fucking Salt." I clench my jaw in annoyance. I hate the way he uses the term fucking. I don't know what our future looks like, but she could never be just a fuck. Cameron Salt is anything but disposable. "I don't expect you to argue it. A guilty conscience needs no words." He grips the ledge of the island. "You already know my thoughts, just don't fuck around and hurt her."

My mouth remains shut. He's my brother, and I don't need to give him words. Even if I could, I'm sure saying them out loud would make all of this real, and that's an admission I haven't had a moment to myself to think through.

"Knock, knock. I brought Gioa's Deli," Lauren calls out as the sound of her heels clicking off the hardwood floors draws near.

"Seriously," Colton mutters incredulously as he reclaims his drink.

Lauren rounds the corner with her hands full, and I come to her side to help take the bags off her arms. I may not care to entertain her company, but I'm not rude and am currently very hungry. Plus, with Colton here, I'm sure we'll put our theories to rest by accommodating her antics.

"Perfect timing," I say as I take the paper bag full of salad off her hands. "I'm starving." Setting it down, I gesture toward my brother. "Lauren, you remember Colton, don't you?"

∼

"What's your game here? You're sitting poolside while Lauren is, quote un-quote, inside using the restroom, which we both know means she's inside snooping. Meanwhile, you're out here driving yourself mad watching that biker boy over there flirt with Cameron."

I pull my eyes away from the pool ledge where Cameron has been sitting with Stormy for the past hour and give Colton my undivided attention.

"I'm not worried about whatever Lauren may or may not be up to inside. My office is locked, and if, by chance, she were able to get in, I have an alarm on my phone that would send me an alert. There's nothing of importance left for her prying eyes to find. As far as the rest, I'm still trying to piece together a motive. If our suspicions are correct, why now? Why wait all those years? That's why I'm letting all this play out. Something is missing. We have a time frame, and Jenny Busch's wedding puts Lauren in the same place as Damon. Everyone knows Damon married Amelia because he knocked her up and thought it was the right thing to do. He never told me Kelce wasn't his. He was my best fucking friend, and he never said a word. Which leads me to believe it all comes back to Cameron. The timing of when Damon found out about Kelce not being his blood and Cameron being born is crucial." Or at least I think it is. After talking with Cameron about Kelce and what she believed Amelia's truth was, I couldn't help but hear blackmail.

"Wait a minute. Didn't you discuss this with Cameron after I left the last time I was here? What did she say?" I drop his gaze and finish off my drink in answer. "Are you serious right now? I thought when I gave you the news about Kelce, you talked to her about him, about all of it."

"I did." My eyes find her laughing at something Elijah is saying. Her laugh is everything, and I never want to be a reason for its silence. "She doesn't know. She still believes Kelce is her half brother, and I couldn't..." I close my eyes as the memory of Damon's last words refuse to be ignored.

"Did you find it?" I asked when I saw Damon's name flash across my phone.

"Everett," he pants hard. "Everett, I need you to listen to me."

"D, what's going on? What's wrong?"

"Just listen to me. I fucked up, and now I'm answering for that."

I loosened my tie as I searched the room for my keys. I asked him to swing by my home office on his way to the gala to pick up the plaque we were to give out that night for Outstanding Philanthropic Group.

"D, are you at the house? I'll come to you—"

"You can't fucking come here. There's no time..." More heavy breathing and spitting came through, and I grabbed the back of a chair. I felt it; something wasn't right. "Promise me, promise me you'll take care of my little girl," his voice cracked, and my heart splintered. My best friend wasn't in the kind of trouble we could fight our way out of, but I couldn't just let it happen.

"D, stop. I'm coming—"

"You can't. It will be too late. I'll be at the bottom of the Mississippi before you get to your car. Take care of her..." My knees hit the floor. This can't be real. I'm not listening to my best friend take his last breaths. "Promise me," he spit with heavy breaths.

"I promise... Of course I will." I tried to keep my voice strong for him. I didn't need him to hear my pain.

"I'm sorry, Everett. I'm so sorry, I wasn't..." The connection started to go in and out, and all I could think was that meant his car was sinking further down. "I need you to protect her. I shouldn't have kept this from you, but I couldn't..." He cut out again. I needed to hang up and call for help, but I didn't want to hang up. How could I hang up? My head was a mess. "You can't let her take my girl. You have to keep her..."

"Who, Damon? I don't understand. Who would take her?"

I never got the answer to that question. Those were the last words Damon ever spoke before his car hit the bottom of the river. The accident made the evening news. A semi-truck jackknifed in front of him, and his speed, coupled with the angle of his swerve, was enough to flip his car over the guard rail as they went over a bridge. To this day, I've never told anyone about that call. It has always been my cross to bear. He chose to call me. It was me he spent his last breaths on, and I've never taken that lightly.

"Cole, I couldn't tell her what I don't know. How am I keeping her safe, protecting her, when I don't know from whom or why? The anniversary of the accident is coming up. It didn't feel like the right time."

"I get that, but you must also realize there will never be a right time."

I clench my fists. "I'm aware, but I'd at least like to have answers... closure."

"You said Lauren mentioned Ramsey the night of the wedding. Maybe you should play a round of golf with the new police chief and see what he remembers."

"Already on it. We're having lunch on Wednesday."

The back door opens, and Lauren walks out with a tray of drinks. Maybe she wasn't inside snooping after all. The night she slept over, I didn't catch her poking around either. I got zero sleep that night as I stayed up worrying about Cameron and watching the security cameras to figure out Lauren's angle.

"After I used the restroom, I took the liberty of making everyone a fresh drink." She hands me an orange drink with a lemon peel on top. "Don't worry, I know you like cognac. They're Remy Martin sidecars." After passing one to Colton, she takes her seat in the chair on the other side of me before asking, "So, Colton, is there a lucky lady waiting for you back in Boston?"

"Nope, I've never seen a reason to tie myself to someone else's drama or give them half of what's mine simply because they warm my bed."

"Wow, I can't tell if you're jaded or cynical."

"Maybe a little of both. Being a lawyer, I see firsthand the shitty nature of humanity." She nods in agreement as she sips her drink but doesn't comment. Leaving me to question her take. "How about you? You're older than me and still single."

Leave it to Colton to read my thoughts.

"Hasn't anyone ever told you you're never to comment on a woman's age?"

"Oh, I wasn't... I mean," he tries to back pedal, and she waves her hand.

"I'm just messing with you. Life experiences have a way of hardening us. Sometimes, we're aware; other times, we wake up forty-six, well past our prime. Mr. Right already warmed our bed more than once, and now he's married to someone else."

"See, that's my point though. You spent all those years doing you. The time when most people are focused on finding the one, settling down, and starting a family, you weren't, and that's because there's more than one way to live this thing called life. We don't have to do it a certain way just because that's the way it's always been done. Society has a way of making women feel like they are not real women if they don't get married and bear children. I don't ascribe to that."

She settles into her chair and sips her drink, her eyes forward on the pool. Technically, she has nowhere else to focus her stare, but I can't help but surmise it's more than just a blank stare. It's fixed on a certain person.

"My spinster advice is this: the world has a way of breaking everyone. There are worse fates than having someone by your side who can help pick up the pieces. As for children, if you have a choice in it..." her eyes flick over to mine, "find your person." Her mouth opens like she has more to say, but then she says nothing.

Colton gives a sideways glance. He tried, but if she is indeed who we believe her to be, she wouldn't easily walk into that trap. When I return my focus to the pool, Cameron is gone. That's when I spot her behind the bar. I don't like the way I left things upstairs. She deserves better than what I can give her, but Cole was right when he said I forfeited my ability to walk away. Now I'm left with figuring out how to be what she needs or showing her that I'm not, but the way her eyes woundedly flick up to mine, I physically can't choose the latter. I don't bother excusing myself. I don't need to explain where I'm going or why.

When I reach the swim-up bar from behind, she doesn't acknowledge my presence. "I thought we were on the same page when we parted upstairs." I didn't nearly say enough, but I also didn't have time on my side.

"I wouldn't say we're on the same page, more like different chapters," she mutters as she tosses a can into the trash.

"What would you have me do right now, Cameron? How can I make this better?"

"Kiss me," she says right before she turns to me like it's just that easy. My eyes soften as my body stiffens. She knows I can't do that, not the way she wants anyway.

"Grab me a beer." Her hand finds her hip, and she looks at me like I've lost my mind, asking her to fetch me a beer after she asked for a kiss. "You asked for a kiss, didn't you?" She furrows her brow but drops to a squatting position all the same, to grab me a beer from the fridge beneath the bar, and when she does, I make my move, crouching beside her before pulling her face to mine. "Different chapters, same book..." My eyes drop to her mouth. "It's a start, right?" I watch her lips say yes before I gently take them in mine. Gentle is the last thing I want to be. I want to crush my mouth to hers, feel her body pressed against mine and feel the peacefulness that holding her in my arms brings, but I don't because I know I won't be able to let go. I pull back and run my thumb over her lip. "Are you sore?"

Her face flushes. "Everett..." she draws out my name as she drops her eyes.

"Just answer me," I say as I pull her chin back to center, forcing her to meet my gaze.

"Yes, but it's the good kind. You didn't hurt me."

"Good. When you see me with her, remember you're sore because I spent hours inside the only person I see. It's you or it's no one."

It's an admission of things I'm not ready to face, but it's real and raw. There won't be anyone after her. As much as the thought of celibacy sucks, I know I wouldn't feel anything with anyone else. It would be meaningless. I'd walk away from it feeling worse.

"Stand up, sunshine." My hands grip her thighs, and I place a kiss on the pubic bone before peering up at her. "Help me empty this house."

Everyone stayed much later than expected. Elijah broke up with Annie recently, and after golfing with Kipp a few weeks ago, I know it hasn't been easy on him, especially living in a small town. He didn't just break up with a girl, he broke up with her whole family, but while it may hurt now, I think, in the long run, it will be worth it for both of them. When it's right, when it's love, it doesn't wear off. Seeing him have a good time with the girls had me stilling my hand and letting the night ride, even if it meant I had to watch the biker boy incessantly hit on Cameron. After watching them together in the pool, I understood how hurt she was seeing me sit beside Lauren. I had to grab my chair several times so that I didn't fly out of it and knock him out just for touching her.

Everyone stayed until it was time to go out to the bars. I was going to call them an Uber when Lauren offered to drop them off, which was perfect. I killed two birds with one stone. Since Lauren drove separately, I no longer needed to think of ways to kick her out. I'd like to say I'm freshly showered, with an empty house, and Cameron all to myself; however, that is not the case. Colton stayed. He had too many drinks and apparently gives zero fucks that he's been hogging Cameron's attention ever since everyone else vacated the premises.

Grabbing my phone off the dresser, I sit on my bed and send off a text before I can talk myself out of it.

> Everett: What are you doing?

I click into the security camera app to see where they are while I wait for her reply. When I excused myself to bed, they were sitting in the living room, laughing their asses off about some show I know nothing about.

> Cameron: Lying in bed.

My fingers hover over the keypad. I know precisely what I want to say, but if I open this door, there will be no closing it. Fuck it. I'm already fighting demons that came from the consequences of choices I've made. What's a few more?

> Everett: Want to come to mine?

> Cameron: Is that a serious question?

> Everett: I take sleeping very seriously.

> Cameron: What if I'm not tired?

Christ. I can't tell you the last time I flirted with a woman. The women I've been with since my divorce have been a different breed. The ones who were my age weren't looking for anything more than a good lay, and anything younger than ten years was going to sit on my dick for a shot at landing a wealthy husband. That's not arrogance. It's just the truth. In the end, both parties were using the other. It's that thought that gives me my next line.

> Everett: I could come up with a few ways to help with that.

> Cameron: Colton is downstairs.

After I hit send, I realize the double meaning in that last text. I wasn't going for sexual, but I'm pretty sure that's exactly how it landed. I meant she needed to be quiet while sneaking into my room. The last thing I want is her quiet in my bed. The door to my room slowly opens, and she steps inside, gently closing it behind her. But then, instead of striding across my room and crawling onto my bed as I expected, it's as if the floor grew roots. Cameron Salt is anything but shy. However, you wouldn't know that looking at her now. She's currently the embodiment of the word.

"Is something wrong?" I ask, setting my phone on the nightstand beside my bed. She rises on her toes before pressing her back to the door and rolling her lips. "You had no problem helping yourself to my covers last night." I try to keep it light, not knowing where her head is. She wouldn't have walked down the hall and let herself in if she didn't want to be in here. I didn't force her hand.

"Last night, you weren't watching me walk to your bed," she answers with a shrug before gesturing between us and adding, "This feels different."

"That's because it is." I nod toward the spot next to me, "Come lay with me so we can see how it feels together."

"Okay," she says as she bites back a tiny smile before it spreads, and she steps off the door.

"Cameron." She pauses as though she's done something wrong. "Lock the door this time."

CHAPTER 22

CAMERON

It's been a little over a month since I started sharing Everett's bed at night and waking up in his arms every morning. At home, we're so in sync with each other. We fit together like a custom puzzle, unique, one-of-a-kind, and oh-so-perfect. It's cliché, I know. Everyone who finds their person says it's true, but we fit together because we were made for each other. At least, that's the way I see it. I haven't wanted to rock the boat and talk about the future or what comes next. All I've wanted to do is enjoy every second of pretending this is our new normal. That this is going to be our forever, one where there is no end to these magic moments. Something this beautiful can only be some sort of sorcery. There's no way I'm actually waking up with the man I love naked and wrapped around me like a second skin. No words, just gentle touches, soft smiles, and pure contentment. It's magical, and I'm not ready to return to reality. We'll be forced into a reckoning soon enough. The season will end, and there will be no more shared car rides to work, Connor will come home, and I graduate in a few months. That's why I'm soaking in all the tender, untainted, fleeting moments now, writing them on my heart so it beats with these memories forever. Even if it doesn't work out, I never want to forget what it felt like to be his.

"Why are you staring at me like that?" Everett asks as a nervous smile plays at his lips.

"Just collecting a moment," I answer.

His brow furrows slightly, but his thumb continually strokes over the back of mine as he drives us to work. This is the first time I've seen this side of Everett. For as long as I've known him, he's been all work and no play. Suits morning, noon, and night; quiet and around but not present, hardened. When it's just us, he's none of those things. Holding my hand while he drives has become second nature for him. It's part of his routine as though it's always been there. He puts his key fob in the center console, presses the start button, and then reaches for my hand as he backs out. It's a small gesture that makes my heart flutter whenever he does it.

"Have you put any more thought into starting your own brand?"

His change in subject tells me my words made him feel. He's not ready to own those feelings and face what they mean. I know the age gap makes him skeptical for more than just the face value reasons, like believing my interest is temporary, something I need to get out of my system before I realize we couldn't possibly have anything in common. It's the reminder that I'm his dead best friend's daughter. He's a successful lawyer and a prominent philanthropist who started one of the biggest self-made charity fundraisers to raise awareness, built a support system, and drove funding into the hands of people who can make a difference in the fight against domestic violence and trafficking. Our relationship from the outside looking in sorely contrasts with his image. I get that. However, I don't know that it's his image he cares about. Whatever is besting him feels like a clash of morals and beliefs, and then there's still Connor. If I dare to let myself dream about a real future with Everett, he will always be part of it. He might be the ultimate hurdle. Can he get past seeing me as an honorary sister and transition to stepmom? Can I? Admittedly, that thought sounds off-putting, but if you strip away the titles, all that's left is love. It's why I don't take his change in subject to heart. We're both growing through this in our own way.

"I have. With the inventory management software installed and automatic re-order points set, the place practically runs itself. It's given me extra time between customers to do some market research and determine viability. When I thought about a career in fashion, it was always high-end and couture, but I've worked at baseball fields for the past five years now, and they've grown on me. I considered athleisure. Everyone wears it, but because of that, the market is saturated with options."

"So where does that leave you with your future plans?"

I purse my lips and look out the window. I'm unsure why I'm nervous, maybe because speaking my ideas into the universe gives them wings. It is a manifestation of the highest power, speaking your dreams into existence. "I want to design athletic apparel. After dealing with the uniform mishap this season, I think there's a market for it. And I'm not talking wholesale or retail distribution. I want to be a premium brand known for quality."

He nods. "I like it."

He likes it? That's all he's got for me after I confessed my dreams?

"That's it? You like it... not I think that's a great idea. Hell, I'd even settle for that's a terrible investment as long as you were telling the truth."

He squeezes my hand before bringing it to his lips. "Cameron, that was an honest reaction. If you didn't get the response you hoped for, it's not because you don't have my never-ending support. It's because I was thinking it through. I've already told you the fashion world is not my area of expertise. I'm a lawyer, but I'll admit, since you told me you wanted to go into fashion, I may have read an article or two." An article or two. Everett rarely sleeps, which means he's probably done an entire case study. "On concept alone, I think you have a solid idea that could turn into a lucrative empire."

We pull into the stadium's parking lot, and he releases my

hand. "You really think it's good?" I ask before he has a chance to exit the car. I don't need to find investors; I have my own money, but I also don't want to squander it on half-cocked ideas.

"The dream was put in your heart, Cameron. You're the only one who can nourish, cultivate, and see it through. Dreaming is the easy part. It takes courage to believe in it and bring it to life, but if anyone can make a dream reality, I know it's you." His eyes hold mine, and I know those last words were twofold. He was once only a dream.

I nod and reach for the door handle with a renewed sense of determination, but before I can exit, he grabs my arm. "You know the moments you've been collecting?" It takes me a second to connect what he's referring to, but I nod yes, believing that I do. "I collect them too. Make sure tomorrow morning when I open my eyes, you're right where you were when I closed them."

I can't help but smile, and he releases me. This morning, I woke up at five a.m. with a million concepts that I had to put on paper before I lost them. While I hated leaving his bed, I love knowing he missed me.

I've been in the shop for an hour, opening and getting ready for the game this evening. I don't need to get in as early as I do. I've only been coming in at that time to spend the car rides with Everett. I'm only on the clock an hour before game time. When I offered my assistance to Connor, it was for designing apparel, not working in the team shop. After realizing everything I was doing, he insisted on paying me even though I had told him it wasn't necessary. It's a minimum wage salary. I'm not getting paid extra because of who I am, but he didn't feel right about me being here and taking care of things for free. What he doesn't know is I've been taking that money and putting it back into the shop. That's what friends do. I just wanted this job for my resumè, not the paycheck, and now that I've got things on track here, I'm going to talk to Stormy about taking a step back. I'll still be around, but I really want to get things rolling on my business; plus, things are starting to happen at my property, and I want to be there. It's why I need my computer now. I need to open one of the files Mackenzie sent over last night and review it before approving. I'm about to exit the stadium when I remember the car beeping behind us as we walked inside this morning.

"It's locked." Damn, now I have to run upstairs. At least I wore wedges today.

I've wised up. One day, I wore heels trying to turn Everett's head, and my feet hated me for it. Heels on concrete all day was a certified bad decision. I jog up the steps toward the announcer's booth, where the only two offices are located, and find Everett at his computer. My wedges gave me the element of surprise. I make a mental note, adding cute and stealthy to the list of reasons these shoes are better than heels. I take a second to admire this side of him. It's the side I fell for. I wouldn't say I have a type, I've dated country boys, musicians, and jocks, but there's something to be said about a refined man. Even without a suit, he's poised, meticulous, and astute, not to mention sexy as fuck. He started wearing glasses a few months back, but only when he works on his computer. I swear, every time I see them, my ovaries weep. Great. I just came up here to grab keys, and now my brain is headed straight for the gutter. I rasp my knuckles on the metal door frame, alerting him to my presence as I let myself in. The formidable expression reserved for the world softens when he sees it's me.

Then he's out of his chair. "Is something wrong?"

"No," I say as I press a few buttons on the calculator setting atop his desk. "I need your keys." I haven't made a habit of frequenting his office.

He steps into me and wraps his arms around my waist. "Are you leaving me?"

"To leave you, I'd first need to have you." I slowly raise my eyes to his. "Do I have you?"

He pulls me flush against his front and drops his mouth to my ear. "Wrapped around your finger," he softly answers before trailing open-mouthed kisses up my neck and along my jaw until, finally, his delicious mouth is on mine. Yet another reason not to leave his bed in the morning. His kisses. They're everything. One kiss erases my fear and dissolves time. It's an indescribable feeling of completion, like the coming together of pieces you never knew were missing until suddenly they were there. His hand trails up to my neck, and his kiss grows deeper as a low growl rumbles up through his chest. I fucking love that sound. It's the sound of rapture, and it's intoxicating knowing that I'm the source. His lips hastily leave mine only to drop to my bare shoulder before descending. My head lolls back as his mouth paralyzes me, and I forget why I came up here to begin with. Teeth pinch my nipple through the material of my strapless maxi dress, and I can't help but hiss at the sting of pain. "Shh," he coos before pulling down the front of my dress and sucking my nipple into his mouth.

"Mmm," I moan as warmth spreads through my belly. His fingers slowly bunch in my dress, pulling it up as his lips lock around my other nipple. He sucks hard, and my core clenches, begging for more. Those smooth hands expertly start to knead my bare thigh as they journey closer to the spot I need him the most. He teasingly toys with the hem of my thong. "Ev, please," barely leaves my lips before two digits glide through my folds.

Those soft, plump lips trail back up my chest, and his eyes find mine. "I couldn't say no even if I wanted to. You own me. You've always owned me." I don't get a chance to respond before his mouth covers mine, and his fingers slip inside of me. I couldn't form words even if I wanted to. His tongue dives deeper with a groan as his palm presses into my clit. My pussy starts to clench hard, and his lips pull away from mine. "Fuck..." he hisses. "I want you to come on my fingers, sunshine, and then I want you to do it again on my cock."

The words have barely finished leaving his lips when the sound of heels clicking up the staircase outside of his office has us hurriedly pulling apart. I instantly drop to my knees and duck

under his desk to pull up my dress. When I look up, his eyes
worriedly find mine, and I gesture with my thumb for him to wipe
his lips. My gloss is definitely on them.

"Everett, are you up here?" Moira calls just before she rounds
the corner. Damn. What is with this woman? I swear she's forever
a thorn in my side. They've been separated practically since I
moved in at seventeen. A week after I found Everett watching her
kiss Kipp beside the lake, she started sleeping in another room.
They lived together almost another year before they announced
their divorce. She's constantly inserting herself where she no
longer belongs, and it's infuriating. If this were any other man, I
wouldn't be crawling under the desk, ensuring I'm not discovered.
I'd mark my territory. But he's not. So I push down my pride and
hide.

"Moira." I hear the unease in his voice. "Another surprise visit,"
he adds, taking a seat and slowly scooting in. I'm instantly
perturbed until I see why. He can't stand; doing so would give
away the fact that he's rock-hard. My insides twist at the memory
of him being buried deep inside me when we fell asleep last night.
Fucking Moira.

"I know you've never liked me coming to the office, but since
you took away my house key, this is the only place I knew I'd be
able to find you and not intrude."

The not intruding part is off. She is definitely interfering yet
again, but the part about him taking away her key might be worth
it. That's news to me. It's something that should have been done a
long time ago, but the fact that he did it at all is a step in the right
direction. It's the cutting of yet another tie that bound them.

"What is so important that it couldn't be handled over email or
text?"

She's quiet for long seconds, and I can't be sure since there's
no way of seeing her or him, but if I were a fly on the wall, I'd
imagine their eyes are locked in some kind of stare down. Everett
hasn't placated Moira for some time now. He's been kinder than
she deserves, considering he caught her cheating, and it's obvious

she doesn't like the new Everett. The one that no longer pushes himself aside to serve her. I can't help but wrap my hand around his calf and give it a light squeeze in support.

"We talked to Elijah and Parker about my visits to Texas and Chad Hailsop. They know about the pregnancy."

Moira's pregnant! I never put too much thought into why Connor was an only child, but Everett knew that name when Parker flung his accusations around at the game, which makes me wonder if he's not a fertility doctor. Maybe early on in their marriage, they tried for more children, but it never happened. That has to be why he knows the name.

His chest visibly inflates, and then he says, "How did they take it?"

"I'm not sure. If you ask Kipp, he thinks it went well, but Elijah and Parker have never been my biggest fans. I believe that's why they latched onto you when I married Kipp. It was their form of silent protest. Taking a side, if you will. They saw me as a homewrecker. It didn't matter that their mother was dead." I hear her heels softly pad across the floor. "You can tell me I'm wrong all you want, but the fact that Parker was so quick to assume the worst of me confirms I'm right. They don't trust me with their father's heart."

"Moira, I've never spoken a word about—"

"I know you haven't, Everett." She sighs heavily. "I wasted no time remarrying after our divorce, and everyone who knew us in high school probably assumed I'd been cheating on you our entire marriage."

He draws his foot back and sits a little straighter. "I never did understand your decision to move forward with him so quickly. I don't fault you for it. I've just never been able to wrap my head around why you would move so fast, knowing how everyone assumes the worst. Waiting a year could have lessened the judgment and scrutiny surrounding your relationship. You may not have had to carry the weight of that scarlet letter."

"I'd already waited so long. I don't mean to be cruel in saying that, Everett. You have to know I love you. I'll always love you, but I was in love with him. It was always him. If he could have saved me, he would have. We all knew there was no other option that night when Craig threatened us at the bonfire. It was you and the power of your family or the abuse. We had no choice..." She trails off as her footsteps near the desk. I've heard rumors about this night, but I've never heard anything from the source. Moira and Everett were a power couple for years. From the outside looking in, they had a perfect marriage, and depending on your idea of perfect, maybe they did. If money, success, and status equate to happiness for you, then they were that, but on the inside, their marriage was fruitless. They were roommates, not lovers. Once the news of their divorce started to spread, so did the rumors. This topic is one of them. Everett was forced to marry his best friend's girlfriend. It's the why that's always been hazy, but it all makes sense now. Moira's uncle-in-law, Craig, was a dirty police chief who eventually got caught and spent his last days on this earth behind bars himself. She must have been one of his victims, and since Everett's father was a district attorney back when all of this would have gone down, his name held power. By marrying Moira, he could protect her. "I knew how things would look, but when you have the right person by your side, the rest falls away. At the end of the day, the only person who mattered was the one I was going home to. I couldn't waste any more time."

"And the baby?"

I can't be sure what he's asking, but I hear a faint ache in his tone all the same. Everett can wear indifference like a second skin, but apparently not on this subject.

"I'll be sixteen weeks at the gala. We plan on telling close friends and family then. I just wanted you to know. Last time we talked, Elijah and Parker weren't aware, and seeing as how you are Parker's coach for the season, I thought you should know what's going on at home so you have an idea of what's going on in his head out there." I hear the sound of metal clanging off the top of the desk, and I assume she must have picked up one of the knickknacks on top. "That's all I had to say... well actually, have you talked to Lauren, or better yet, Stormy? What's the story?"

"I have an important email I need to get out for the law firm before practice. I can give you a call on my way home."

"You know what, don't worry about it. I think it's time me and Lauren had a chat," she says as she makes her way to the door. "Lauren Rhodes shows up after twenty-two years and starts working for my son while her niece lies to my ex-husband to get a job. We're long overdue." I hear her stop, one heel sounding against the tile floor. "You'll be at the gala, right? When I brought up the date change, you weren't too happy about it. I'm not ignorant to all the reasons we moved the event to fall. I hope you understand why I had to pull it up."

Quick math, she'd be thirty weeks pregnant if they held it in November, as they have done since my parents' accident. Being older and therefore high-risk, I'm sure she didn't want the additional stress that comes with throwing a charity event that far along in her pregnancy.

"I'll be there, Moira."

"Good. Maybe this year you'll bring a date. Perhaps whoever was warming your bed the last time we spoke."

"It's a possibility." Why do those three little words give me an ocean full of hope? She must nod or smile but since I can't see, I'm unsure. Then he grabs her attention. "Moira?"

"Yes," she answers.

"Lock the door before you leave. I don't need any more interruptions."

"Sure," she says without missing a beat, like he's asked that of her countless times before.

When the door clicks shut, Everett scoots his chair back, and I crawl out.

"Are you okay?" I ask, knowing that the conversation was somewhat heavy.

"I've been better. It's not every day your ex-wife walks into your office while your new girl hides under your desk."

"New girl?" I question because I'm not letting that go, especially after he said maybe in regard to bringing a date to the gala.

His hands swiftly push up the armrests of his chair before he pulls me onto his lap. I fall into him clumsily, the move catching me off guard. Everything with him feels so new. I've never seen him this way with Moira, or anyone, for that matter. His hand pushes a piece of hair out of my face before he says, "Cameron, you know I'm not with anyone else. You're all I want. If it's not you, it's not anyone."

"Everett—"

"Shh," he purrs as his lips find my neck. "I know we need to talk, but right now," his hands find my hips as he rocks his hardening length against my clit, "I'm going to need you to finish what you started."

"We probably shouldn't. We've already been caught once."

"The door is locked." He sucks the skin right below my ear into his mouth as his hands trail up my calves; his fingers tantalizingly leaving a trail of goosebumps in their wake as he pulls my dress up. "Unless there's another reason you don't want me to fuck you, I'm going to pull your thong to the side and bury myself inside of that tight pussy I never want to leave."

I was already turned on from straddling his lap, but those words take it to a new level. Too bad I'm greedy, and I want more. If he wants me, he's going to work for it. I push him back against his chair, and his eyes widen in surprise.

"There is one other reason. I know you don't like to be interrupted while you're in your office. What if office sex becomes my new addiction?"

A coy smile pulls at his lips as his hands squeeze my ass hard. "Then we should probably find out. Penciling in fucking my girl on my desk will definitely be mine." When he calls me *my girl* again, I'm done. His hands slip around to my thighs, where he grabs my dress and commands, "Lift." I do so without pause before he pulls my dress off over my head, leaving me fully

259

exposed in nothing but my white lace thong. His dark eyes hungrily drag down my body before zeroing in on my breasts. "Still wearing my mark." His lips suction around one of my nipples, and he swirls his tongue around the hardened peak before giving it a nip. "Fucking perfect," he growls as he moves to the other.

"Mmm," I groan as he takes their weight in his hands and pushes them together. The way he nips and sucks my breasts is intoxicating. I love the feel of his beard against my skin, knowing it will leave my milky skin deliciously chafed with reminders of where he's been.

Releasing my nipple with a pop, he leaves a trail of open-mouthed kisses up my chest. "Do I need to warm you up again?" His forefinger drags down my stomach, making me clench in anticipation for where it's about to travel. He teasingly plays with the band of my panties before ripping them off, the sting momentarily registering before his digits are running through my wet lips. "So damn wet... fuck," he draws out. "I don't know what I want to do first. Watch you bounce up and down on my dick in this chair or lay you out on this desk and eat that pretty pussy."

His fingers dip inside of me, causing my breath to hitch. I push back down on them and reach for the button on his pants. "I want to ride you," I say as I rock against his fingers and pull him out.

Those dark pools dilate as I pull him out and stroke his silky length. "Take me how you want me. It's yours."

"Mine?" I raise a brow in question.

"Yours," he agrees, his eyes holding mine, confirming the double meaning behind my ask. *He's mine.* I plant my feet on the floor and lift off his fingers before bringing his tip to my entrance. Even his head is thick. I can count on one hand the number of guys I've been with, but Everett is by far the biggest. Every time, it takes me a minute to adjust to his size. I grip his shoulders and slowly start to lower myself down. I get why men enjoy watching their cock disappear. It's hot as fuck watching my body stretch around him. When I look up, his eyes meet mine. "You're so beautiful." His words of praise have me taking another inch. "Do you want to know something?"

I lick my lips. "You know I do."

"This is one of my fantasies."

"I'm one of your fantasies?" I rise up and slowly lower myself back down.

"No, you're a dream come true. It's always been a fantasy to fuck in my office. Never in a million years did I think it would happen with my dream girl." Those words have me bottoming out. We both groan in unison. He is so damn deep. He's had me in a lot of positions, but this one is new. Crushing his lips to mine, he kisses me hard before slapping my ass. "Ride me, sunshine." When I go to push up, the position is too awkward. I can't ride him in the chair. I'm too short. Instead, I pull all the way off and he groans. "What are you doing?"

"I'm too short," I say as I lift my leg to turn around.

"I can lower the chair." I hear the chair's hydraulics as he pulls the lever, immediately accommodating my height.

"You're an ass, man, aren't you?" I ask as I back up to ride him reverse cowgirl style.

"I'm a *you* man," he answers as his hands find my hips. "You're trying to kill me, aren't you?" he questions in jest as I align his cock with my entrance once more and slowly slide down his length. With my hands on the desk, I steady myself and spread my legs so I can watch him disappear inside of me once more. His cock glistens with my juices, and I clench hard at the sight. He might mark me with his teeth, but I know my scent will drive him crazy all day. In this new position, his tip hits my G-spot at a delicious new angle. I bottom out long and slow, letting it drag over the spot before riding him hard. He said this was a fantasy of his. You better believe I'm going to make it the best he's ever had and one he'll want to repeat. I start bouncing hard, and his hands dig into my hips. "Are you trying to make me come before you?" he grits. "Slow down, sunshine." But I can't. I'm already too far gone. His words, the sound of my arousal, all of it.

"I can't. It's too good. I'm coming," I pant as I chase my orgasm over the edge.

I'm suddenly on my back in one swift move as supplies tumble to the floor. Pulling me to the edge, he impales me on his cock as he wraps my legs around his neck. "Fuck," he hisses as my pussy contracts around him. "You're going to give me another one. I'm not done feeling you. I'll never be done." He starts pumping into me hard and fast, my tits bouncing as his balls slap against my pussy. I know he feels the second another orgasm starts to take root because his eyes lock onto mine. "That's it, sunshine, chase it, take what's yours. Milk me." This time when I fly high, he comes with me, a tremor racking his body as he falls on top of me.

We're a pile of sweat and sex as we lay there catching our breath. My hand instinctively curls into the hairs at the base of his neck, tenderly caressing him. I love him so damn much. I know I will never love anyone the way I love him, and I can't tell him. Those three words could ruin everything. His lips gently kiss my shoulder. "I might be yours, but you should know you're mine. I want to take you out tonight. Will you have dinner with me?"

"Out in public... me and you, like a date?"

He pulls back his eyes, finding mine. "Yeah, like a date."

"Okay," I squeak out. Maybe those three little words aren't as far off as they feel.

CHAPTER 23
EVERETT

Things with Cameron feel surreal. I don't understand how it's possible I've lived so long without ever feeling the way I do when I'm with her. If this is how Moira feels with Kipp, I can't fault her for leaving me. Not that I ever did, but I'm unsure how she ever walked away. How do you walk away when you find the person who makes your heart complete? Cameron is my person. I feel it in every fiber of my being. I feared falling for her because of who she is. We aren't supposed to make sense, she's my best friend's daughter and half my age, but nowhere in that fear did I consider my own heart, and maybe that's because I never knew what it was like to be wholeheartedly devoted to someone. If I lose her, I will now lose part of me.

It's why I haven't wanted to talk about things I know are eating her up inside. I haven't wanted to leave this bubble of happiness where everything is right in the world because she's in it and all mine. I know she wants answers. She wants to talk about us... fuck, even saying us does stupid things to my mixed-up heart. I'm so torn between honor, duty, and desire, I can barely think. I've considered that taking her out to dinner tonight is selfish. I've weighed calling it off or canceling for work-related business because I know exactly what kind of step this is. It's one that leads

263

to titles and more than what we've been, all things that scare the shit out of me, but here I am, waiting at the bottom of the staircase, watching her walk down, knowing this soul-deep ache for her will never subside because she is my everything. My world stops and ends with her.

Her cheeks flush my favorite shade of pink when she gets to the bottom and realizes I'm still staring. "How do I look?"

"Like every dream I've ever had come true." I pull her into me and kiss the top of her head, knowing if I do anything more, the emerald-green dress she's wearing will be on the floor. Taking her hand in mine, I lead her out the front door.

"Where are you taking me?"

"Do you realize you've asked me that at least ten times since I invited you to dinner tonight?" I say as I open the car door.

"Yeah, I was just hoping this time you'd actually spill so I'd know if I'm dressed appropriately," she answers sardonically as she takes her seat.

"Not possible. You could be wearing sweats and still be flawless," I answer, closing the door before she can argue the issue any further.

The car ride to the Chophouse was quiet, but Cameron had been uncharacteristically quiet since she left my office this morning, only breaking her silence to try and get answers about where I was taking her for dinner tonight. Because what we shared in my office this morning was fucking perfect, and since she left with rosy cheeks and a smile on her face, I assumed we were good, but as she sips her wine and looks anywhere but at me, I am wondering if it's not something else.

"I want to ask you something," she says, her eyes finally focusing on mine for the first time this evening. Her hand mindlessly sweeps over the velveteen material of her clutch, telling me whatever she's about to ask is something that's been on her mind.

"Okay." I blow out a breath of resolve. I knew this was coming.

I told her we'd talk. I take a long drink of my smoked old fashioned.

"Do you want more kids?"

I'd like to say I'm an expert at controlling my emotions and holding my mask in place, but that question has my eyebrows shooting to my hairline. Out of all the topics I might have guessed were running through her pretty little head, that was not one of them.

"Why do you ask?"

"Because your ex-wife is pregnant, and I could tell it made you feel something earlier. I also knew Chad Hailsop's name wasn't unfamiliar to you when Parker threw it around at the game. I thought maybe it's because the two were somehow connected and you wanted more kids," she finishes quieter than she started, showing her nerves.

Of course she would easily draw those conclusions. Cameron sees the parts of me no one ever has.

"Chad Hailsop was in Garrett's class. They've been good friends for a long time, which is how Moira met him. Chad went to medical school to become a reproduction endocrinologist. He ended up landing a residency in Texas and never left." I take another long drink as I choose my next words. Connor wasn't planned. After he was born, Moira went on the pill. She never expressed an interest in having more kids, and I never pushed the issue. But I'd be remiss if I said seeing her start over and start a new family didn't make me feel something. "As for the rest, hearing your ex-wife is pregnant at forty-five is thought-provoking."

"You realize that last part isn't an answer, right?"

"Not all answers are black and white." I finish my drink as I begin to become flustered. I've laid awake making lists of pros and cons of why we can't work, and this topic is on the con list. I wanted tonight to be something special, but now it's starting to feel like a teachable moment. One where my job is to prove why we don't fit. I can't break her heart and push her away. She'll have to break mine. "I believe my time for having kids has passed. Most people my age stopped having kids ten years ago. What about you? You have an IUD. Is that just birth control until you find the one, or are kids off the table?"

I'm sure she wants kids. This has to be the deal breaker. The moment that proves we aren't soul mates but rather star-crossed lovers.

"People are waiting longer to get married and settle down these days. Your brothers are perfect examples of that. Colton is thirty-two and still single, and Garrett is fifty with an eight-year-old. Life is what you make it; it's okay to color outside the lines. That's how we create our own beautiful masterpieces." She swirls her wine, and her eyebrows furrow slightly before she adds, "I've never put too much thought into having kids. I know some women do. They've either always wanted them or felt called to do it, but I think I could go either way. If the person I was with wanted them, it wouldn't be a hard sell. How could I not want to create a life with the person I love and have a little mini that's half of me and half of them?"

Fucking hell. I should have seen that coming. I keep waiting for us to find something, a hard line that divides us and can't be overlooked, one that tells us to end this before anyone knows it exists. But everything has been too perfect. She's too perfect. Talking about kids right now feels like jumping ten steps ahead, and I don't want to dream about futures that aren't ours to have, so I risk changing the subject. "Do you like the restaurant I chose?"

"I like being with you," she answers before sipping her wine and averting her gaze again. Something is off, and I don't believe it's related to the topic of having children.

"Cameron, if you'd rather go home, we don't have to stay. We can get our food to go."

"Why would we do that?" Her eyes swing back to mine.

The anniversary of her parents' accident is right around the corner, and I've been waiting for the other shoe to drop. That must be what this is now. Her silence is wrapped in thoughts of them. "I wanted to give you something special, but my attempt at it is ill-timed. I was thoughtless not to consider that now is a time of solemnity for you." It is for me too, but I don't mention it. I would never want to take away from her grief or add to it by sharing my own.

"Yes, I like to reflect and be alone around the anniversary of my parents' accident, but that doesn't mean I don't want to replace sad memories with happy ones. When I'm with you, I forget that my heart has cracks. You fill them in."

"Then why does it feel like you're anywhere but here with me?"

"Why did you bring me here tonight?"

"I'm trying, Cameron. Nothing in my life prepared me for this... for you. You mean a lot to me. I've told you that on more than one occasion now. You're changing me. I'm trying to turn the page and get closer to yours. I thought you'd see that."

She nods as though she agrees, but I can tell it's more of an appeasing gesture than a genuine understanding. "You brought me to 801 Chophouse, a steakhouse forty-five minutes outside of town where no one we know would see us."

"I didn't see it that way when I chose this place. It's one of my favorite places to eat in the city. They don't have fine dining like this back home. I thought I was making a memory."

"I don't need any of this. All I need is to be yours in all ways. We're tethered to this story, Everett. It's ours to tell. I know what I want it to say. I've felt what it's like to be yours, and I never want to lose that. Ever. You have me. All of me. All you have to do is want the same."

I reach across the table and take her hand in mine. Her eyes drop to our intertwined fingers. "I want you, Cameron. Probably more than any man has ever wanted a woman. You once asked me what if I was your soulmate. The answer I didn't give you then was souls don't meet by accident."

The way her crystal blue eyes pierce mine is enough to bring kingdoms to their knees. "So where does that leave us, Ev? If we're not an accident, what are we?"

"I don't know..." Fuck, I can't recall a time in my life I've been rendered speechless, but that is exactly what I am now when I need my words more than ever. "If we were storybook, we would have met on the same page, but we both know that's not our story. Of what little I do know, it's this: I wish I could have done everything with you. If I had one prayer, it's that if I can't have you in this life, I will get you in the next. I don't want to lose you, and I don't mean the old you. I mean the one I have now, the one that's mine."

The way her hand lightly squeezes mine and her chest visibly deflates with a stuttered breath tells me my words touched her, but the way her smile doesn't meet her eyes also makes me feel like they weren't enough—they weren't the right ones.

CHAPTER 24
CAMERON

"Hey, wait up," Stormy calls as I walk out to my car to leave for the day.

I haven't had a chance to discuss pulling back on my hours with her. Reece has filled in for us here and there as needed. She had been predominately working in the concessions area, but I talked to her manager on Monday about having her move over to the team shop since I will be in less often during games. The change in hours was sprung on Stormy out of nowhere today, and I have no doubt she wants to talk about it.

"What's going on? How come you didn't tell me you were cutting your hours?"

Technically, I had planned on telling her two days ago, but she called off. Between training Reece on opening and closing procedures, visiting the site of my new lake house, and starting my own business, I've been a little preoccupied.

"We both know I'm not working this job for the money, and Reece has been filling in for us as needed over the past month. She's just going to be picking up more hours than she had." I shrug, knowing my answer wasn't really an answer but uncaring because my mind is elsewhere.

She crosses her arms. "Okay, thanks for the bullshit non-friend response. Now, what is the real reason?"

I pull open the door to my Audi and throw my bag into the back seat. "I'm starting my own business, construction on my house starts next week, and..." I trail off, not wanting to finish the sentence. Since my dinner with Everett a few nights ago, I've felt out of step, and I know why. I put everything out there, but he didn't take it. We're still us but only behind closed doors, and while I'd wait forever for him, I've found myself wanting to wait alone. Being with him has almost hurt as much as being away from him. The thought of losing him and what we have is unbearable. I know what I need and what will help. I need to visit my dad. "I have somewhere I need to be."

"Let me come with you."

"You don't even know where I'm going."

She shoves her hands in her pockets. "I think I could take a pretty good guess. Parker told me what this Saturday is. He said you like to be alone, and maybe that's true, or maybe you've just never had someone to hold your hand who understands the grief of losing a parent."

It's not because I like to be alone during this time that I choose solitude. I choose it so as not to burden anyone else with my grief. I chose it because I deserve it.

"If you want to tag along, that's fine, but I'm not returning tonight. I'm staying at the property."

"That's fine with me. You know I love it out there, and I always keep an extra outfit in my bag. You never know when you might need to get away."

Her comment is somewhat strange, but I leave it. I always have ten outfits in my trunk because my style changes with my mood, and I like to be prepared for surprise outings.

Apparently, she likes to be ready for surprise runaways. That's the Thelma and Louise shit I'm talking about.

I nod toward the door. "Get in. I'm ready to get out of here."

"You ready for some company?" Stormy asks as she joins me beside my father's grave, where night has started to set in. When we got here, the sun was still up.

I've let go of the loss, but the love that remains is the hardest part. There will always be last words we never got to say, a lost ear to bend, and the loss of the only person who could ever really love you unconditionally for eternity. But I hold onto the hope that when I'm here, he's here with me, sitting next to me, listening to me pour out my heart. Every dream, confession, and apology, I lay them at his feet the same way I'd do if he were still here with me. I told my dad everything. His breathing may have ended, but his love never will. There's a scripture that keeps me coming back here., "For dust you are, and to dust you shall return." If we indeed return to the earth as ash, I know his are here. I feel him here, the same way I feel him when I'm at Salt Lake.

Stormy gently nudges my shoulder with hers. "I'm not good with sentimental, and I'm not sure how these conversations should go, so I'm just going to talk. My mother died when I was fifteen. I haven't visited her grave once, but sitting here watching you makes me think maybe I'm missing out on something. You must have really loved your dad."

"I did. He was more than just my dad. He was my best friend."

"And your mom? You haven't moved from this spot at the foot of his grave."

"Life gives us parents. Our hearts make us friends. My mother was only ever a parent, and even that feels like a stretch because parents are supposed to nurture and support their children. I'm not even sure you could say my mother did those things. However, I don't fault her for that. She had us, and I think she did her best. When I think about my mother, I see sacrifice. A woman who got pregnant before she was ready, a woman who forfeited her youth for a baby. I don't know. Every time I think about my mother, I feel like

I'm making excuses for why she wasn't the mom I wanted her to be, and then I feel shitty and selfish. I mean, some children don't have any parents. Who am I to complain that mine wasn't good enough?"

"Hmm... I get that, but maybe she wasn't the woman you thought she should be because she wasn't the person you thought she was."

"I'm not sure I follow," I say as I turn to her in question.

"Forget it. I shouldn't have said that. It was a thought in the moment, one I should have kept to myself."

"Well, you can't take it back now that you said it."

She picks up a twig lying in the grass. "Remember the night we spent at your property, and you told me about your brother Kelce only being your half brother because your parents got married as soon as she found out she was pregnant?"

"Yes," I nod, recalling the day. I'm not sure I used those exact words, but it's the gist.

"Sitting here listening to you talk about your dad with such reverence and love is touching, but hearing the lack of love between you and your mother seems telling. You found out Kelce wasn't your father's blood." She shrugs before snapping her stick in half and adding, "Maybe Amelia Salt isn't your mother. Maybe she got her lie, and he got his."

"Wow," I say before turning to my mother's grave. I can't believe she just inferred that. That's bold coming from someone I barely know. I'm not sure I would divulge those thoughts to someone I've known my whole life, but she did, and now they can't be unheard. My immediate thought is, how could that even work? Lying about a man being the true father of your unborn child is one thing, but how do you hide not being the actual mother? Friends, family, acquaintances, they'd all know if you weren't rocking a baby bump. For Amelia Salt not to have been my mother, literally everyone I know would have to be lying to me, right? They'd have to be in on some big secret, and I don't believe that's true.

"I'm sorry, Cameron. I really am. I didn't mean to hurt you

while you sit in front of your parents' graves, nonetheless. I wouldn't blame you if you want to leave me here and take off."

I stand from my spot and dust off my ass. I've sat with my thoughts long enough for today, and it smells like rain is coming. "I'm not upset. Are we really friends if you have to bite your tongue and watch your mouth?"

"No, but the friend card doesn't give me a free pass to be a thoughtless ass."

"Meh... there's never a good time to be a thoughtless ass. What better company to be an ass with than those that won't judge you for it. Besides, I'm not upset. I can't change the past. Even if Amelia wasn't my mother, I wouldn't trade her for the real one. I'm twenty-two. If I had another mother, she clearly doesn't want me either." I grab my purse off the ground and make sure my phone is inside before saying, "Come on. I don't want to get wet. There's a storm coming."

~

"Is that Everett?"

I tense as I read the message. He's not happy that I turned off my share your location feature. "He wants me to come home."

Home will always be wherever he is, but I need to take a few days for myself. I laid my heart on the line for him, and while I know he cares about me, I don't know if it will make a difference in the long run. He says he's trying, and so am I. I'm trying to give him space to listen to his heart without breaking mine. Loving me shouldn't be hard. It should be as easy as breathing.

"Let me guess, you still haven't told him about this place."

I unwrap the towel on my head and toss my phone on the bed. "Everett knows my father left this property to me, and he knows I come here. I like to camp and throw parties here in the summer. But no, he doesn't know that I have a camper here, or that I'm currently building a house." I pull open two drawers in search of my brush.

"Oh, here," Stormy says as she pulls my brush out of her bag. "I accidentally threw it in my bag the last time we were out here." She tosses the brush at me, and I start combing my hair.

"When the idea to build here came, it was after a shitty misunderstanding between me and him. It sounds lame saying it out loud, but I think I'm scared to talk about this place because the night I chose to start building, I chose me and a future I knew was certain because I was building it. To talk about it with him feels like I'm talking about a future that doesn't include him, and that's one I don't want."

Thunder rumbles in the distance, and Stormy's eyes widen. "How did you know it was going to rain?"

I shrug, tossing my brush onto the bed before grabbing a blanket. "I can smell it, but with the tournament starting tomorrow, I checked the weather for the weekend." The only reason I let Stormy tag along when I cut out early was because I knew she wasn't needed in the store first thing in the morning. Tomorrow I'll have to drop her off for work, but I won't be in. The excavators are coming around ten a.m., and I'm anxious to see the site come to life.

I hear my phone vibrate, and I snatch it off the dresser before walking into the living area to grab a spot on the other end of the couch.

> Everett: How do you expect me to sleep without you?

> Cameron: The same way you have the past forty-six years without me.

> Everett: That's not fair.

It was a low blow. I know it couldn't be helped. I didn't exist for half of them.

> Everett: How can I fix things if you won't come home and talk to me?

I don't say anything. I'm not trying to start an argument. This isn't why I left. I left to visit my dad's grave.

> Everett: I'm asking you to come home, Cameron.

It's just a text, but I feel like I can hear the ache in his heart— or maybe it's just the one inside of me.

"Trouble in paradise?"

I trill my lips to try and let it go, but I can't. "Am I naïve to think that love should be easy?"

"Absolute wrong person to ask, seeing as I've never been in love, but I did come close. I think love looks different for everyone. I think, like with everything, there are peaks and valleys. Falling in love is easy; staying in love is harder but love itself isn't just sweet. It's as bold and exciting as it is tears and devastation. At the end of the day, you trust that person to be all those things, and I think when you endure all those things together and you can still wake up every day unable to picture a life without them by your side, that's love." She grabs a bottle of water from the table behind her. "But take my words with a grain of salt. I haven't lived them." Maybe not, but I don't think she's wrong. Love isn't only flowers and rainbows. Love is raw and untamed. It spreads like a virus without regard for the person or time. The loud crinkling of her water bottle as she squeezes it in her hand draws me from my thoughts before she asks, "Are we good on the love thing?"

I shake my head and clear the fog. "Yeah, I'm sorry. It's been a heavy night."

"I mean, I knew it would be before I got into the car, so there's that, but I'm about to make it heavier. I have a confession. It's kind of a big one."

"Okay," I draw out pensively, unsure where this conversation is headed.

"I lied. I lied about a lot of things," she blurts out before blowing out a huge breath. I can tell that admission alone lifted a weight, but what the hell is she going on about?

"You lied about what exactly?" The whole conversation Everett and Moira had while I was under his desk suddenly comes to mind. I planned on asking him what she was talking about, but then Moira brought up babies, and Everett asked me out to dinner. Those topics took precedence over snooping on whatever drama Moira was having with Lauren. After all, I already knew they were enemies.

"I'm honestly not sure where to start," she says as her fingers nervously pull at the label.

"That many, huh?" I keep it lighthearted.

"Ehhh." Her response, coupled with the uncertainty marring her worried face, tells me they must be anything but light.

"Okay, well, how about we go from small to big, light to heavy, since we just left off on a heavy topic."

"Sure." She rubs her hands on her knees. "Parker and I are sleeping together, and I really like him... like really, really like him."

I can't help the smile that spreads across my face. I love that for them, or at least I think I do. After we get to the heavy, maybe I'll love it less, but so far, these lies are trending in the right direction.

"I'm not sure you can even call that a lie. A white lie, maybe. It's no secret that something was going on between the two of you, and out of anyone, I fully understand not wanting to share something so new with the world until you're sure it's worth sharing."

She gets off the couch and starts pacing the living room as a crack of thunder shakes the ground. "I've lied about pretty much everything since I've been here. Why I'm here, who I am, you name it, I lied." As I think over our conversations, I turn my attention to the threads on the fringe blanket I've been twirling between my fingers. "Lauren Rhodes isn't really my aunt. I assume Everett already told you that."

My brow furrows before my eyes flick up to hers. "Why would Everett tell me that?"

Her pacing comes to a halt. "He didn't tell you that?" My eyebrows raise in question. "Interesting," she trails off before continuing her slow pace. "So he didn't mention Moira, Evan, or any of it?"

"What are you surprised I don't already know about?"

She fidgets with her braid and mumbles, "That's kind of why I missed a few days of work this week. You've been taking fewer hours at work, and my texts go unanswered longer than they used to. I assumed you'd heard something and written me off..." She releases her braid and speaks louder. "Lauren is not my aunt. I was adopted, but that's not really a secret. If anything, it's a mincing of words. She knows we are not related in any way..." She trails off and pauses again. It's clear she's thinking through this revelation about me not knowing something she believes I should, and the fact that Everett knows and didn't tell me feels like a punch to the gut. "I lied about who I am. Lauren believes Evan Graves is my brother, which would make Moira Michaelson my aunt."

That's a super fucking loaded truth bomb, one that makes zero sense. Moira being Evan's aunt is news to me. I should be surprised, but I'm not. I've always seen a side to Moira MacBeth that the world chose to shove under the rug because of who her husband was. The fact that Evan isn't the son of a stranger dropped off on her front porch doesn't faze me. If anything, I'm surprised he's a nephew and not a secret love child, knowing how her heart never belonged to Everett. But never mind that Moira's been keeping secrets, or that Stormy lied about who she is, the better question is: Why that lie?

"That's a strange lie to tell. Why would you choose that lie?"

Her eyes slowly raise to mine. "To get close to you."

Hail starts pinging off the metal roof of my RV, as if her words weren't ominous and creepy enough. I shove down the eerie discomfort and ask, "Why?"

"Rain check?"

"Stormy, it doesn't really work that way. You have me a little creeped out," I admit as I pull my blanket around me, somewhat regretful that I turned my location sharing off on my phone. Since we've met, Stormy has been on the quieter side, but I assumed she was just one of those people who is slow to warm. Now I'm looking back at everything through a different color lens. "Have you been stalking me?" Isn't that what stalkers do? They slowly infiltrate your life and gain access to you through your friends; in this case, Parker.

"It's nothing like that, I promise. I'm going to come clean. I swear it, I just can't. Not yet."

"You realize I'm totally paranoid now. If you sleep here tonight, I will be sleeping with one eye open."

She gently reclaims her spot on the other end of the couch. "I know you have zero reason to trust me after everything I just said, and I feel terrible about that. I told you I had good intentions the last time we were here. It's always my execution that sucks." Her eyes drop to the floor.

"That doesn't really help put me at ease."

"What if I told you Parker trusted me?" Her eyes snap back to mine with a renewed sense of hope.

"Does Parker know your lies?"

"Most of them, yes."

That's actually one truth I believe. I've always felt their relationship was more than she admitted to, and because Parker and I have a history, I know he wouldn't prioritize getting his dick wet if he knew Stormy was out to get me in some way.

"Does he know why you lied?"

"Mostly."

"Are you going to continue being vague as fuck?"

"For now."

Tonight has only proven to be another shining example of why being alone has felt so appealing. Sometimes, the only person who can bring you peace is yourself.

~

Surprisingly, between Stormy's confessions and Everett's texts, I did manage to fall asleep last night. Storms have always had a way of lulling me to sleep. When I woke up this morning, Stormy was gone, but she left a note saying she felt terrible about last night and that Parker had picked her up. I texted Parker this morning, confirming the pickup. I know one of my flaws is that I can be too trusting. After her confessions, I didn't push her for more. I knew she wouldn't give it to me; hell, she said as much when she started divulging everything. Instead, I excused myself and went to my bedroom at the back of the RV. By the time we got home from visiting my father's grave, it was already eleven p.m., and we both had things to do today.

As I laid in bed staring up at the ceiling, I went over every conversation we'd had and got nowhere. I considered that maybe my father had a love child I didn't know about. He and my mother were never affectionate with each other. I wouldn't be surprised to learn that they both had secret lovers on the side. However, nothing pieced together every time I tried to trace a line back to that theory. That left my mind to spin on the details she gave me. I'm not sure if I gave up before or after my eyes closed. All I know is when I woke up, I couldn't find it in me to put any more thought into whatever scheme she might be crafting. I'm not physically threatened by her. The only part that has me messed up is the Everett piece. I hate feeling like someone I trust with my life is keeping something important from me, but it's in that same vein that I question if it's meaningful at all because, if it were, I know he wouldn't be shy about telling me to stay away from Stormy, if not outright forbidding contact with her.

"You must be Cameron." One of the crew pulls me from my latest musing session. The sounds of the excavators downing trees easily covered his footsteps.

"Yes, Cameron Salt. You must be Orion Atsbury."

"The one and only." He crosses his arms and nods toward one of the operators. "I think you know my cousin Nash."

I do a double take and squint at the bulldozer mowing down a tree a few yards away. "Wait, that's Nash in there?"

"Yep, his dad's been trying to get him to take an interest in the family business. He thought putting him with me for the summer might give him a different perspective."

"Has it?" From the few times we've talked, he never once mentioned this type of work. However, when I asked him about school, he mentioned classes at Flight Park in Millstadt. I don't know much about heavy machinery and construction, but aviation feels worlds apart from this.

"For today he has. He was the first one in the truck this morning." I don't miss the implication, intended or not. "Anyway, I came over here to go over the clearing. Everything is pretty straightforward. We should be done clearing the north side this afternoon, but there's a yellowwood I thought you might want to see before we take it out."

"Why's that?"

"Well, yellowwood trees are somewhat rare to these parts, but aside from that, this one has some initials carved in it. It could be nothing, but maybe it is something. If I inherited land, I'd want to check it out. Could be a family carving."

"Show me," I say with a renewed sense of vigor. The wind this finding puts in my sails reassures my divided heart that this is where I'm supposed to be.

CHAPTER 25
EVERETT

It's been two days, two fucking days, since I've seen Cameron, and it's killing me. Wednesday morning, I woke up with her in my arms and kissed her from head to toe until she woke up, as I've done every morning since she started sharing my bed. It's the only way I ever want to wake up, but something felt different that morning, and I hate that I didn't see then what I think I know now. She found her limit, and now she's drawn her line. At dinner, she told me I was her forever. She asked how we moved forward, and I didn't have an answer. I still don't have an answer. All I know is I can't continue with the status quo. It's breaking me.

Thursday was the first day of our tournament, and I missed it because I had to close an important deal with one of our government contractors at the firm. I tried to return to the stadium in time to catch the second game, but it was too late. Before leaving, I went to my office and ran back the security footage in the team shop. Cameron wasn't on it. She didn't come to work yesterday, and she's not here today. The only reason I haven't completely come unhinged is because, while I haven't seen her and I don't know where she is, she has been responding to my texts. It's those texts that were my lifeline tonight as I helped coach the team to a victory that sealed a seat in tomorrow's bracket.

I usually run over plays with Teague and Denver right after games to get a rough picture of how we will stack the lineup for the next game, but right now, my goal is to ensure I get to the team shop before Stormy leaves. I'm sure she knows exactly where Cameron is, and because I know she's been lying and keeping secrets, extracting Cameron's location from her will be easy.

I'm picking up my duffle bag when a voice I'd know anywhere says, "You guys looked good out there tonight."

Dropping my bag, I turn just as Connor walks up behind me. "Con, what are you doing here?" I say, pulling my son in for a hug.

"I came to watch my dad bring home a win for my team."

"How long have you been here?"

"I got here at the bottom of the fifth." He nods back toward the announcer's booth. "I watched from the office. I didn't want to distract you or the team." Leaning up against the fence, he adds. "And watching from up there was a whole different experience. I can't believe this place is mine. It doesn't feel like that long ago I was out there dreaming of making a career out of baseball, and now I'm not only living it, I'm helping other kids do the same."

"It's no secret I wanted to hand over Callahan & Associates to you. I did convince you to get your law degree—

"Convince? You threatened my inheritance."

"Semantics." I grimace at his interpretation. No parent wants to be the evil dictator, but it's not our job to be friends. You hope with age and maturity, a friendship bond is formed, but until then, our job is to support and guide them, give them the tools they need to be good, kind humans that contribute to society, and sometimes that requires us to force our hand. The likelihood of an athlete actually going pro is around two percent. Of course I pushed him to have a fallback by making him attend college. "What I was trying to say is I'm so damn proud of you. You had a dream, and you made it happen. I think this is better than playing in the big leagues. You are living your dream your way."

"Thanks, Dad," he says, adjusting his hat. "Maybe I can assist you in tomorrow's game."

"You're staying? Wait, why are you here to begin with?"

His brow furrows and he nervously looks away. "Tomorrow's the anniversary of Damon's accident. Mackenzie wanted to be here for Cameron." How the fuck did I forget what tomorrow is? I'm not even sure that I forgot, Cameron is a constant reminder of my best friend, but admittedly, this week has been overwhelming in ways my life never has been. I can't lose her. If I lose her, I'll lose me. She owns my heart, and if she walks out of my life, she'll be taking it with her.

"I didn't forget, but I don't know where Cameron is. She hasn't been at the house in a few days."

"You really don't know where she's at?" he asks as he tosses some empty bottles from the dugout into the trash can.

"Does that mean you do?" I attempt to rein in the hope in my tone.

"Well, yeah. I'm surprised you don't. I dropped Mackenzie off with her before I came here." Fuck, the relief I feel knowing she's okay has me feeling like I've just gained five years of my life back. While she had been responding to my texts, I couldn't see her face or hear her voice. My mind started to run away with worst-case scenarios, hostage situations, kidnapping. It's not too far-fetched with everything that's been going on this summer. If I didn't get some kind of proof of life outside of a text today, heads were going to start rolling, secrets be damned. "I thought the two of you were closer than that."

"Closer how?" I question casually. The fact that I haven't had a heart attack yet from the hits my nerves keep taking is promising.

He shakes his head as he tosses a spare ball into the bucket. "Never mind, it's nothing." His eyes meet mine. "I'm heading out there now. Do you want to tag along and check it out, or do you have work?"

"Where is there, and what is there to check out?"

"Come on, you'll see."

~

"This is where she's been staying this week?" I ask as Connor pulls down the road to Damon's property—or should I say Cameron's property?

"Yeah, she's been coming out here daily for the past few weeks. Since Mackenzie's been in Florida, Cameron has been doing the footwork back here on her latest project."

"Project?"

He does a double take, still apparently surprised that I have zero clue what he's talking about. His thumb taps the steering wheel, and he asks, "I'm not trying to change the subject or anything, but do you have any idea why Mom wants to meet with me tomorrow? She said she had something important she wanted to talk about."

"I believe I do. It's probably something you should hear from her, but I'll tell you if you really want to know." I know I told Moira I'd keep her secret, but I won't keep this from him. The secrets I've kept for her have already strained my relationship with him enough.

"I'd like it if you told me." His eyes flick over to mine as he drives slowly down the gravel road through the trees.

"She's pregnant." I watch his eyebrows rise, and he rubs his jaw irritably.

"Are you kidding me? My forty-five-year-old mother is pregnant? Meanwhile, I've been fucking my wife daily for months and nothing."

Not the response I was expecting but I understand. "Well, your mother didn't conceive naturally. She had help, and she's high-risk given her age. Obviously, she wants family to know before she shares it with the world, but I think she's nervous to do even that." A break in the shadowy canopy of the woods draws my eyes away from Connor, and that's when I see all the downed trees in the distance. "What is going on?" I say, trying to piece together what I see as I lean forward in my seat.

"Cameron's building a house, and Mackenzie is designing it."

She's building a house. When did she start building a house? Why hasn't she told me about this? Those are my first questions as a million others begin to flood my mind, the top one being, does this mean she's leaving me? I suddenly want to be anywhere but here. The last place I want to be when she rips my heart out is around people. As we get closer, I see an RV placed at the edge of the woods. This is where she's been staying the past two nights while I laid awake in my bed, a shell of a man without her.

Connor parks the car next to the RV, and it's only when he closes the door and starts walking toward the lake that I realize Cameron and Mackenzie are hanging out on a raft. My mind was too busy taking in this place I didn't know existed and what that might mean. As she walks out of the water, all I can think is she looks like waves on a sunset, the salt of the earth, strong and powerful, a woman who knows exactly who she is and what she wants. She's everything that is light, and I'm the lucky bastard who gets to bask in it, or at least I was a few days ago. At the moment, I'm not sure. I'm the kind of guy her daddy would have told her not to go and fall in love with, but I've turned the page on the old me. I'm not him anymore. I'm whoever she wants me to be as long as it's the man who gets to stand at her side.

She's laughing at something Mackenzie said when her baby blue eyes collide with mine, and my heart skips a beat. Her smile falters, but I don't turn away. If this is the moment she dismantles my heart, I don't want to miss a second of her touching it for the last time.

"You found me," she says, her tone sounding more playful than her face lets on.

"I did." I shove my hands in my pockets when all I really want to do is wrap them around her and pull her into my chest, but I don't because I can't tell if that's what she wants. I have no idea what's going on in her pretty little head. I'm not sure I see disappointment, but I wouldn't say I see excitement either, at least not the kind I used to see when she looked at me.

"Cam, I thought you said you had a grill for hotdogs," Connor calls out from behind us.

Her perfect lips part as she pulls in a deep breath, her eyes briefly searching mine. For what? I wish I knew. Then she's stepping around me. "I never said I had a grill. I said I had a grill thingy."

Her comment makes me smile. My girl doesn't know how to cook. *My girl.* Fuck. As I turn to follow her toward the RV, I see biker boy talking to Mackenzie. What the hell is he doing here? Has he been here with her the whole time?

"Hey, I'm going to run in and grab Connor what he's looking for and I'll be right back out," she says as she enters the RV.

Is this a repeat of the wedding? Is she using Nash to get to me, to make me make a move, or is this her new guy? The guy that fits, the guy that takes her on dates and holds her hand without pause. Fuck that, I'm not going to lose her again. At least not like that. If she's done, I want her to say the words. I need her to say the words. I pick up my pace and follow her inside. The door closes a little harder than I anticipated as I enter, and it startles her as she digs under the sink in the kitchenette.

"How come you didn't tell me about this place?"

She continues her search under the sink, unfazed. "Probably for the same reasons you choose not to tell me things."

"What does that mean? What haven't I told you?"

"Found it," she says, as she pulls out a grill basket, and the towel she wrapped around her waist slips, revealing yet another thong bikini. Fucking hell. She starts toward me with the grill basket, but I don't move from my spot at the door. "Everett," she draws out my name dolefully.

"We need to talk."

"I know that, but now's not the time." She takes a step toward me. "If you'll excuse me, I need to give Connor the grill and see Nash out."

When she takes another step to try to exit, I throw my arm out. The feel of her soft skin against my heated flesh instantly sends a shiver down my spine, and the way her eyes soften when they find mine tells me she's just as affected. Two days have felt like a lifetime. "Has he been sleeping here?"

"No," she answers softly before clearing her throat and looking away. "He's working with his cousin for the summer. Atsbury Construction is one of the contractors Mackenzie hired. He's been out here clearing trees with the crew."

Relief instantly floods my body, and I take the basket out of her hand. "This isn't a grill. It's a grill basket."

She rolls her eyes. "I know it's not a grill. I couldn't think of its name."

"I'll let Nash know you'll be out after you get dressed."

She stubbornly crosses her arms, pushing her perky tits together in the process, as she considers my words. Cameron knows how I feel about her prancing around in swimsuits that are basically underwear. The question is, does she still care?

"Fine," she huffs as she turns on her heel toward the room at the far end.

Still mine. Now, I just need to ensure it stays that way.

"So I guess this house means you plan on sticking around after graduation?" Connor asks as he sips his beer.

"Yeah, I've always felt close to my dad here, and it doesn't hurt that my best friend lives nearby," Cameron says as she clinks glasses with Mackenzie on the other side of the bonfire we're all sitting around.

Before taking a sip, Mackenzie says, "I was thinking maybe we could do something special at the groundbreaking to commemorate Damon. People do stuff like that all the time. Sometimes they'll take something of meaning and put it in the foundation, or we could plant a tree, oh and there's—"

"Speaking of trees, while the crew was clearing, they found a tree down by the lake with carvings." She turns and looks over her shoulder. "It's obviously too dark now, but I'll have to show you guys tomorrow. It must have been from high school or something. It's my dad's initials with his sweetheart's." Her eyes flash up to mine. "Maybe you'll know who she was when you see them." Something about the way her eyes stay locked on mine feels more like accusation than genuine curiosity.

Mackenzie stands up and yawns with a stretch. "Hey, want to help me figure out that sofa bed? I'm an hour ahead of you and have an eight a.m. video call I can't miss."

I hadn't even considered that we would all be sleeping here. I assumed we'd drive back home, but I'm also not mad about staying. Even if I have to sleep on the recliner, it will be better than what I've endured the past two nights. Knowing she's in the same space as me once again, I'm bound to get an hour or two.

Connor is out of his seat before Mackenzie can even take a step. "My dad and I can figure out the bed."

She pats his chest. "We got it. You guys can clean up here so we don't attract bears."

"Bears?" he parrots sardonically.

"Yeah, bears. They're making a comeback in the area, and you have yet to burn the food trash," she says before collecting her drink.

"You forgot to mention we'd be sleeping here," I tell Connor as soon as the girls are inside the RV.

"I can't say I love it when I have a perfectly comfortable bed a few miles away, but Mackenzie is meeting with some of the contractors here tomorrow." He crunches an empty can and tosses it at me. "Come on, old man. Help me clean up. We should try to get some sleep. We got games to win tomorrow."

I've been wide awake for at least two hours. This recliner is ridiculously uncomfortable, and all I can think about is the girl sleeping just feet away from me. All I've wanted to do is talk since we got here. I look back at the curtain dividing her room from the rest of the RV for what feels like the millionth time. She bought a top-of-the-line RV, but it's one of the new open-concept ones, so there's no door, just some thick, farmhouse-style curtain. Fuck it. I'm going back there. Connor's been lightly snoring for the past twenty minutes, and if Cameron's felt an ounce of the ache I have since she left me, I know she's not asleep.

I sneak back to her room and loathe the curtain even more the second my hand feels how flimsy the material is. I hate that this is all that separates us from Connor and Mackenzie, but the second my eyes land on her form, I don't give a fuck. She's worth the risk. I softly pad over to her bed and pull the cover back before sliding in behind her and pulling her flush against my front, uncaring if I wake her. I feel like I might die if I don't. It's taken every ounce of control I could muster all night not to touch her. The anxiety I've felt for countless hours falls away the second her scent hits my nose, and I breathe her in. God, I missed her.

"I didn't think you'd actually come," she whispers softly.

"I probably shouldn't have."

"Why's that?"

"Because there's no door, and now that I'm here, I want more than what I came for."

She presses her ass firmly against my groin. "And what's that?"

"Everything I can't have with Connor and Mackenzie asleep in the other room."

"The only thing stopping you from pulling my shorts to the side is you."

"Is that so?" Her hand snakes behind her and dips inside my shorts. I pull her hair over her shoulder, exposing her soft skin. My lips leave a trail of open-mouthed kisses as my hand slides down her stomach until I reach her sleep shorts, where I toy with the band. "If this is what you want, I won't say no, I'll never tell you no, but I did come back here to talk."

"I want all of your words, and I have a few I'm going to demand, but I only need one right now."

"Ask it." I know what she'll ask me, and I know unequivocally what my answer will be.

"Am I done being your secret?"

"Yes," I answer without hesitation. "You can have me however you want me as long as you promise to keep me." Screw pulling her shorts to the side; instead, my hand slides around to the back and I pull them down. I want to feel the weight of her bare cheeks pressed against my groin as I bury my cock inside of her. "But right now, I'm going to need you to be quiet. I'd rather not have Connor find out about us while I'm buried balls deep inside of my girl." My tip nudges her entrance, and she arches her back deep, where I run it through her lips, unable to hold back the hiss that escapes my mouth when I feel her juices coat my cock. "I fucking love how wet you get for me, sunshine." I nip the shell of her ear before sliding in with one long, deep pump. This position is new to me, and it feels very intimate. While she's been in my bed every night since the first, the way I'm holding her tight against my front as I pump into her in long, slow, teasing strokes is more. With every thrust, I hold her tighter as I pull her down on my cock and dive deeper. I can't get deep enough. I'll never get deep enough until she's mine the way I want her to be, and maybe not even then.

"Ev, stop," she whispers.

I freeze. "Fuck, baby, did I hurt you?" I was so lost in her I drowned out the rest. "Did I grip you too tight?"

"No, shh... it's none of that. You're shaking the bed too much." She kisses the back of my hand. "Let me ride you."

I feel my cock twitch inside her. That's one position we haven't done yet. I've been too greedy, eating her sweet pussy, and tossing her around my bed. "As much as I'd fucking love that, I'm not sure you bouncing up and down on my cock is the solution."

"I'll go slow," she says as she slips her shorts all the way off before pushing me flat on my back, throwing her leg over my hips, and straddling me. My hands glide up her soft thighs as her hand grips my cock, and she lines me up with her entrance. She slides down my shaft, and the sound of her wet pussy taking me in seems like it echoes off the entire trailer. It's so fucking hot, I want nothing more than to slam her down on my cock and hear it over and over, but we can't. Her eyes widen as she leans down, her mouth hovering over mine. "Sorry."

I grab her ass hard, making her stifle a whimper. "Never say sorry when I'm making you feel good. I want to hear that sound every day for as long as I fucking live."

She grinds her clit against my pubic bone. "You're so deep like this." She starts to rock against me, and her pretty mouth pops open as her eyes roll back. "Mmm," she softly moans as I feel my tip rub against her cervix. Knowing what I'm touching and how deep I am has my mind going places it shouldn't.

"Take your shirt off. I want to see you," I say to steer my mind away from the innate desire to do something else.

She continues to rock against me as she pushes up and slowly pulls the baggy T-shirt off over her head. My hand instantly flies to the back of my mouth, and I bite down hard. The room is drenched in moonlight, and she looks like a goddess. Her pale skin practically glowing, perky tits full with the weight of her arousal, and with my cock buried deep inside her. I feel my balls start to pull up tight. She's too perfect.

"Come here," I say. She leans down, and my mouth immediately latches onto one of her nipples, and her pussy clenches me hard. I nip and suck, twirling my tongue around the nipple before repeating the move on the other breast.

"Fuck, sunshine, is this it for you? I am it for you?"

"You've always been it for me. I've just been waiting for you to see it."

My hand grips her neck, and I pull her forehead to mine. "I've always seen it." Her eyes are locked on mine as she rides me harder. Our mouths are inches apart, our breaths ragged as we both teeter on the cusp of coming, neither wanting this moment to end. It's raw and exposed. It's fucking perfect. "Let go, sunshine. Come with me."

Her lips cover mine, and I swallow her moans of ecstasy as I shoot ropes of cum deep inside her as we fall apart.

~

I don't know what time it was when I snuck back into the recliner. Cameron fell asleep on top of me, and the last thing I wanted to do was leave her side. I only want to wake up in her arms for as long as I live, and I plan to do exactly that, but first, I need to tell my son. I'm not sure how it happened, but Connor woke up before me, and somehow, I didn't stir awake. Not even the smell of coffee brewing woke me. Instead, it was my girl, trying to quietly slip into the bathroom without waking anyone. With a cup of coffee in hand, I head outside in search of Connor.

"How long?" he questions the second I'm beside him. "And before you try to lie, save it. I know what sex smells like, and seeing as how I know I didn't get any last night, I know it was you and Cameron."

Well, that's not how I saw this conversation starting, but there are worse ways it could have. "When I came home from Boston."

"Nothing happened before that?"

"Not physically, no. But if I'm being honest, I started looking at her differently years ago."

He nods. "Does she make you happy?"

"More than anything," I stop myself from saying more. I want to tell him everything, but I know that suspecting something and finding out it's true are different pills to swallow. "Are you upset?" I honestly can't tell. It's another reason I was disheartened when he chose to chase his dreams. With a poker face like his, he would have made a damn good lawyer.

"I am, but not for the reasons you think. I like Cameron. I'll admit, she wasn't my favorite person for a while, but that's more on me for making assumptions. She may have been around for years, but her moving in and the timing of yours and Mom's divorce wasn't a good look. I'm not saying anyone else saw it that way, but

I did." He shrugs. "I didn't know how much you always protected Mom, and I think once I found out the truth, I felt even worse about how I acted. I was selfish and didn't know how to rewind. I couldn't take back things I said."

I squeeze his shoulder. "You're my son. There is literally nothing in this world that I wouldn't do for you. You could mess up daily for the rest of your life, and my door would never close."

He turns to me and gives me a hug. It feels like we've finally turned the corner. "Dad, if Cameron makes you happy, I want that for you. You deserve to find happiness. I would never stand in the way of that."

I'm flying high. I got my son, I got my girl, and then the sound of cars coming down the gravel road reminds me I'm standing beside a lake on the site where Cameron plans to build a house— her house. It's about time we had that talk.

CHAPTER 26

CAMERON

"Do you mind if I take my eight a.m. call in your bedroom?" Mackenzie asks as I pour a cup of coffee.

"No, that's not a problem at all," I say as I pour my creamer. "The crew won't be here until nine or nine thirty, and they don't come inside."

The door opens as I put the creamer back in the refrigerator, and before I can turn to see who joined us, strong arms wrap around me from behind.

"Good morning," Everett says as he inhales deeply and gently kisses my neck. I freeze my body, acutely aware that we aren't alone in the room.

"Mackenzie is sitting on the couch," I whisper.

"I'm aware."

I spin around in his arms. "You are?" I question, my eyes darting between his. When I fell asleep last night, he was with me in my bed, but at some point, he returned to the recliner. He said he'd tell Connor, but I didn't expect it to be first thing in the morning, nor did I think those confessions would lead to immediate PDA.

His lips gently peck mine as if holding me flush against his front wasn't statement enough. "I am."

The door opens again. "Oh, come on," Connor pinches the bridge of his nose and turns away. "Mackenzie, I'm leaving for the stadium. Can you come say bye to me outside?"

She closes her laptop. "Coming," she sings as she throws me a big smile.

The second the door closes, Everett's lips are on mine as his hands slide down and grip my ass. A heady moan escapes his throat as he lifts me onto the countertop and pulls back. "Last night, you said I was it for you. I hope that's still true because I don't plan on ever waking up another day without you in my arms."

I wrap my legs around his waist and keep him close. "You told Connor?"

"More or less," he says, his lips trailing my jaw.

"What does that mean, Ev? You either told him or you didn't." I can't help the slight trepidation that seeps into my tone.

"He knew before I could say anything, he could smell you."

I push his chest, my face undoubtedly flushed. "Excuse me?"

"Don't be embarrassed. I love the way you smell."

"Everett," I swat his chest. "Be serious. What did he say?"

"I am." He straightens and runs his hand through his dark hair. "The place smelled like sex, and he said since he didn't get laid last night, he knew it was us. He wasn't mad about it. We had a long overdue conversation, and he wants us to be happy. If being together accomplishes that, he wants that." Everett steps away from the counter and rubs his jaw. "Do I still make you happy?"

"Actually, now that I think about it, you might be getting senile," I say sarcastically before rolling my eyes with a sigh. "Aren't we past this? Why would you ask me that?"

"You're building a house." He gestures to the clearing outside.

"I am," I smile softly. I'm building a house right where I'm supposed to be.

"Are you ready to have that talk, or is Connor your ride? I know the games start early today."

L.A. FERRO

He shakes his head and puts his hands on his hips. "I told him I needed to talk to you. He's going to coach the first game."

I let my lungs deflate the anxious energy I've unknowingly been holding since he wrapped his arms around my waist. This is real. He's ready to talk. I slide off the counter. "I'm building a house. It doesn't mean you're not my home. Maybe you'll consider living here with me if things work out."

His eyes soften before he wraps me in his arms. "There's no if about it. Never doubt that you were always meant to be mine."

"Hold onto those words. You might need them," I say as I push out of his hold and grab my coffee. "Grab a refill. I have a tree I want to show you, and you owe me a story about Lauren and Stormy."

As we walk down to the tree, Everett is quiet. I can't tell if it's a nervous or relieved quiet. He has reason to be both. I will say, even with these unresolved questions lingering between us, it finally feels like we're on the same page, like whatever we're about to talk about is inconsequential because it won't change how we feel about each other, but the discussion needs to happen all the same. If there's one thing Everett Callahan excels at, it's secrets. He'll keep them even when they're not his to keep, but that can't be how our story starts. Love isn't built on secrets and lies. It's built with trust.

"Stormy stayed with me the first night I was here, and she said a lot of things, most of which didn't make sense. I couldn't make heads or tails of it, and honestly, her confessions had me freaked out. For a second, I regretted that I turned off my family sharing."

"Speaking of, I'm going to need you to turn that back on. That's a hard limit for me, Cameron. Not because I don't trust you, but because I need to know where you are to keep me sane. I worry too much, and I can't focus when I don't know where you are." I can't help but smile, knowing how worked up he gets. I've always known I affect him, but hearing him say it is a whole other layer I haven't experienced. I like possessive Everett. "What did Stormy say that made you uncomfortable?"

"She said she lied to me to get close to me. The thunderstorm that rolled through that night didn't help my anxiety, but her next words pissed me off as much as they warded off the stage-ten stalker vibes I was getting. She insinuated that you knew."

He stops. "Knew what exactly?"

"That's what I'd like to know."

"Did I know Stormy was lying? Yes."

My eyes widen as I gesture with my hand for him to continue. "And... is there a reason you never warned me or told me about her lies when you knew we were friends?"

"I did tell you. I warned you to be careful around Stormy because of who her aunt is." He uses air quotes to emphasize the falsity of that title. "I didn't tell you the rest because there wasn't anything to tell you. I still don't know why she lied, but I find it very interesting that she admitted her falsehoods to you."

"Okay... well, just to clear it up and make sure we are on the same page moving forward, I'm going to need you to tell me these types of things when they come up. I'm not Moira. I want a partnership, not a coexistence. I'm the person you tell everything to. If you can trust me with your heart, you should be able to trust me with what's in your head."

He reaches me in two steps and tips my chin up. "I have never once wished you to be anyone other than who you are." His lips gently press into mine before his heavy brow furrows, and his black eyes turn as dark as coal. "Sometimes the things we hold inside have nothing to do with trust and everything to do with pain. If I don't tell you something, it's not because I want to hurt. It's the opposite. I want to protect you."

"Is that what you're doing now?" He looks at me in question. "You gave me something, answered my question and gave me a truth, but didn't give me all of it, did you?" He doesn't say anything, and I don't need him to. His silence is answer enough. Pushing him back, I start down the path to the tree. "That's not going to work for me, Everett."

I hear his footsteps crunching the earth behind me. "I'm not lying to you, Cameron, and I'm not keeping a secret, or at least, I don't see it that way. I should be allowed to process information inside my head alone without fear of persecution from my girlfriend."

"Girlfriend, is it?" I stop when I reach the tree.

"I haven't used that word since I was sixteen, but I'm pretty sure that's where this is supposed to start."

I cross my arms and narrow my eyes. "I'll hold off on accepting the title until after I see how well you answer my next question."

"Cameron," he practically growls my name. "This relationship isn't optional. It's happening."

I don't argue with him on that. I'm bluffing anyway, but he doesn't get to hold all the power in this relationship. "Fine, I'll agree to the title..." I trail off as if that word in reference to me wasn't one hundred percent the highlight of my year. "But last time I checked, I still have my own room, with my own bed, and seeing as how my needs were satiated last night, a couple nights in the doghouse—"

He's on me before I can finish. "If I'm in the doghouse, you'll be there with me, floor, couch, spare bedroom. If I'm there, you'll be there too. You can withhold that sweet pussy all you want, but sleeping arrangements are a hard limit for me." His hand squeezes my cheek hard. "Plus, I guarantee you'd break before me."

"Want to make a bet?" I challenge, his lips inches away from mine.

"No, a gambling man knows to quit when he's ahead. I already stole your heart." He pecks my lips. "Now show me this damn tree so you can go back to liking me."

I nod toward the trunk of the yellowwood we're standing under. "It's cute. You hear about this in old-school love stories all the time. Lovestruck teenagers carving their names into trees, but to find one and know it's your dad who carved it makes it extra special." I watch as he pulls out of my arms and squats at the tree's base, slowly running his fingers over my father's carving. There's no mistaking it's him. His name is clearly notched into the trunk with another.

"Who is Camie?" I ask as he traces the carving. He's quiet before he stands to his full height. "Apparently, someone that meant something to him."

"You were his best friend. You're telling me you don't know who Camie was?" I try to keep my voice even when he's holding back. I know seeing that engraving wasn't easy for him. When Orion showed it to me, it felt like I was getting back a piece of my dad. He's gone, but his hand-carved note remains. He anxiously runs his hand through his hair before looking over the lake. "Everett, he was my dad. When he left this land to me, there was a note saying:

'I'm sure you're wondering why I left you a piece of heavily wooded property with a lake that's barely accessible. The short answer is that I was once happy here, and maybe, if you need it, you'll find happiness here too.'

He was happy here, Everett, and whoever Camie is, she was a part of that happiness. I want to know. If you don't tell me, I'll dig until I figure it out on my own—"

He holds up his hand. "Can you give me a week?"

"I don't understand. Why can't you tell me now?" His silence only allows my mind to run away with the strange things Stormy said the last time she was here. Everett admitted he knew about her lies, and when I asked for the truth now, he countered for more time. My thoughts instantly spiral as I try to connect the dots. My parents married young. It was the summer between his senior of high school and starting college that my dad knocked up my mother, or so he thought. Was Camie the girl before my mom? Stormy was asking questions about Kelce and my parents, and she admitted she wanted to get close to me. Is this why? Is she a love child too? Camie's daughter. "Is Stormy my sister?"

Stormy mentioned she was adopted, and she never knew her dad. She was surprised when I told her Everett hadn't mentioned anything about it. That has to be why he's asking for time. He said himself he didn't understand why she would choose those lies. His eyes soften, and I see it. I know what he meant now when he said he didn't want to hurt me by sharing his thoughts. Sharing something like that is false hope. False hope that there's another piece of him left besides me. False hope for an instant bestie who's also my blood. False hope for a family I thought was gone.

"Give me a week, sunshine. That's all I'm asking for. One week, and I'll tell you everything. I'll lay out every detail, every thought that was ever etched into my mind, every word that ever made an imprint on my heart, and all of it will be yours. I swear it."

"One week," I repeat. "One week or I'll start digging, and you most certainly will be in the doghouse."

He nods with a smile that doesn't reach his eyes before looping his arm around my shoulder and walking us back toward the RV. I try not to linger on his dispirited reaction to my words. I just showed him a piece of Dad, one he didn't know existed, on the day we lost him five years ago. Grief looks different for everyone. It ebbs and flows. Sometimes, the waters are calm like the lake beside us, and other times, they rage like the sea, but today I'm not alone. Together, we share this loss, and together, we'll learn how to swim because I refuse to drown.

CHAPTER 27
EVERETT

"Hey, I'm glad you came, but you probably shouldn't have. How's Cam?" Connor's acutely aware that today is the anniversary of her parents' accident. He was the one that held her in the backseat of the car as we left the charity event the night of the crash.

"She's good," I say. I grab the board to take a look at the lineup. This may be Connor's stadium and his team, but he has yet to be the one coaching it this season. "Have you turned this in yet?"

"No, I was going to have Teague take a look."

I grab the pencil from behind his ear. "McKenna hasn't been hitting for shit this week. We need to sub in a DH and put Dunsmoor behind Reynolds. He's been a beast at cleanup this season," I say as I edit the list before hanging it back up.

"Are you going to trade in that suit and tie and come be a coach permanently or what?"

"No, I'm going to hold out for grandkids that want to take over the firm."

He smirks before nervously adjusting his hat. "Do you want more kids? If things work out for you and Cam, is that on the table?"

"Con, I'm still adjusting to the fact that I'm saying Cameron's

302

name out loud with you like this. Kids are not something I've considered." Other than the times I've come inside her and wished time would have been kinder, that I could have had her years ago.

He nods and pushes his fist into the baseball glove he's fiddling with. "Cam's young, Dad—"

"What is this, Con? Are you having second thoughts about giving me your blessing?" He's had more time to think through everything since we spoke this morning, and there's Moira. His mother is pregnant, and I'm moving on. Connor might be a man with a family of his own, but I'm sure hearing that his parents are starting over with new significant others and creating new families isn't easy. "If this is about me starting over and where you fit, there's no question you're my son. I want you in my life. It's one of the many reasons I was hesitant to tell you about Cameron. I don't want to lose her, but—"

"Don't say it." He holds up his hand. "Don't say you'd sacrifice your happiness for me. I already know you would. You've done it my whole life, and that's my point. Don't hold back. If you're all in, then be all in." He tosses the glove on the bench behind him. "So, besides Evan breaking into my house, Mom's pregnancy announcement, and you dating Cameron, did I miss anything else?"

I can't help but laugh when he sums it up like that. This summer has been a shit show. "Ehh, you left out that the girl who works in the team shop is stalking Cameron, and you hired your mom's archnemesis," I say like it's no big deal as I pat him on the shoulder and step around to hang the bats.

"What the hell? We'll come back to the mom thing. Cameron has a stalker, and you're okay with it?"

"Never said I was okay with it. I'm only allowing it because I believe I know why she's doing it."

"Care to elaborate?"

"Yeah, can you ask Aria to pull some favors over at Red Bud Regional? I need a file." Aria Hayes is married to his best friend, Holden, who went pro years ago, but she still works with patients recovering from eating disorders and makes hospital visits when needed.

He leans against the gate and checks his phone. "Holden's games are in town this week, so that shouldn't be an issue. I know Aria tries to schedule her appointments around his work schedule in the summer."

"I need birth records for June 26th, 2002."

"Christ," he curses as he turns to collect himself. "Balls in," he calls out to the team. "Are you serious?"

I don't say anything as I hold his eyes. He knows I'm not playing around. "Not a word, Connor."

S omething is suddenly throwing Parker off his pitch. He was good in yesterday's game, but tonight, he looks like an entirely different guy. It could be the pressure of tonight's game. He knows there is only one tournament left this summer, and there are at least five scouts here tonight, potentially eight if the three that said they were going to try to squeeze it in actually showed up.

"It's only the third inning. Parker is usually good for six. Has he been like this all summer?" Connor questions.

"No." I rub my jaw and look into the stands. Mackenzie and Cameron showed up in the last inning. Cameron's red hair caught my eye the second she walked out of the tunnel, but it was the jersey she was wearing that pissed me off. For once, it's not Parker's, and I thought maybe it had something to do with that, but then I remembered someone who's not here today. Stormy. I stopped at the team shop on my way in to have a chat with her, but she called off. I was equally as relieved as I was pissed. There are words I need to have with her, but at the same time, if she's not here, I know she's not having any with Cameron either. "I'm going to the mound." I step out of the dugout and signal the umpire for a timeout before I jog out.

"Are you pulling me out?"

"Do you want me to pull you out?"

"No," he answers somewhat dejectedly.

I cross my arms and try to get a read on him. "Your arm is going a little wide, but we both know that's not the problem. Am I really out here because you're hung up on a girl right now?"

"You're one to talk."

"That might be so, but my future isn't on the line right now. Yours is."

"You know it's more than that."

I missed this morning's game to be with Cameron. We talked about a lot of things, one of them being Parker. She told me everything, including how they used each other. She also filled me in on his relationship with Stormy and it being one of the reasons she doesn't believe Stormy's intentions are for harm. Which means there's a good fucking chance Parker knows exactly why Stormy wants to get close to Cameron.

"You know the truth?"

"I believe I do." He spins the ball in hand.

"Then you also know Cameron is mine, which makes her my problem. Get your head in the game, Michaelson, and let me handle my girl." He shakes his head and mutters something under his breath. "I'll buy you a few more minutes. Don't fuck it up. San Diego is in the stands." I know he's had his eye on their feeder team. My words could do two things: make him nervous or strengthen his backbone. I'm betting the latter is true. Parker can be a cocky fucker when he wants to be.

Rather than jog back to the dugout, I make a beeline straight for the stands. Parker needs to get his head on, and apparently, my girl needs a reminder of who she belongs to. When I jump over the wall, my eyes connect with hers, and they don't stray as I take the steps two at a time to where she's sitting in the stands.

"Everett, what are you doing?" she asks nervously as her eyes scan the stands. "You realize the crowd is watching us."

"Take your shirt off," I demand.

"You can't be serious."

"You think I garnered the attention of almost a thousand people for a joke? Take it off," I say, my voice firmer.

She rolls her glossy pink lips as her hands slowly reach for the hem of her shirt. I know she's intentionally drawing this moment out to call my bluff. That's when I speed up the process and meet her hands halfway before assisting her in removing it, leaving her in nothing but a thin white tank top with no bra. I clench my jaw and thin my lips when I see her perfect nipples erect and standing at attention.

"Happy?" She smirks with hands on her hips.

"Not yet." I toss McKenna's jersey to a fan a few rows back before taking off my own, giving her no time to process the move before I pull it over her head. "My girl. My jersey," I say right before the people around us start oohing.

"I can't believe you just did that," she says, attempting to hold back a shy smile.

I quickly peck her lips. "Believe it. I used to dream about you being mine. Now you are." I start back down the stairs. "My dream girl wears my name." I throw her a wink as my heart races faster than my feet back to the dugout. Cameron Salt is my future. I've never been more sure of anything in my life, but I've also never lived in this moment. One where I'm enough and the girl I want wants me back. I saw it on her face. My move was bold, but it was everything, just like her.

"That may not have been the best look. We're here to play ball, not record kiss cam moments," Connor says as I enter the dugout.

I shrug. "It bought Parker time to get his head on, and I made a point. As for the rest, there's nothing donations can't solve."

He shakes his head. "You got it bad."

"I'd rather have it bad than miss something I never had." The entire dugout is staring at me. "Take notes, boys. That's how you get the girl." I clap my hands. "Now, let's play some ball."

CHAPTER 28
CAMERON

This past weekend has been a whirlwind of emotions, from Stormy's confessions, the anniversary of my parents' death, and the status change of my relationship with Everett. I loved him in the dark for so long that loving him in the light doesn't feel real, but it's where we are. After the grand gesture he made at the game on Saturday, garnering the attention of the entire Bulldog stadium, I felt like I was having an out-of-body experience. I was soaring the rest of the day. The day I lost my parents will always be a sorrowful day, one of reflection and remembrance, but the memories don't have to all be bad. Year by year, moment by moment, the bad memories can be replaced with good ones. I no longer have to look back on that day with only sadness. I now have a happy memory to balance out the hurt. I lost people I loved, but I also gained a heart I may never have had. The second I step out of the shower, my phone pings.

> Stormy: Are you busy tonight? I was hoping we could talk.

We keep missing each other. She wasn't at work on Saturday, which sucked. I wanted to catch up with her and see if I could pull more details out of her. Then on Sunday when she was in the shop, I wasn't. I spent the day with Mackenzie talking about the house and doing best friend shit, which included laying poolside and spilling the tea on all the things Everett and me. It figures she'd want to hang out tonight when I am unavailable.

> Cameron: I have the charity gala tonight for the MacBeth Foundation.

There is no way I can miss it, even though Everett has told me a million times that he completely understands if I don't want to attend. After my parent's accident, Everett and Moira moved the event to the fall for obvious reasons, but given Moira's pregnancy, things changed this year. I don't love attending the event so close to the date my life was forever changed, but I also don't want people to tiptoe around me and treat me like I'm fragile. I lost my parents, they didn't. For the rest of the world, life moves forward, but I also don't want to be left behind or excluded for fear that I might break. Plus, tonight is another one of those times where I get to fill my memory jar with happy moments, ones that help replace the bad. Tonight, I'm not just an attendee at the gala. I'm Everett Callahan's date.

> Stormy: Will you be at the stadium tomorrow?

What is tomorrow? I pull up my calendar app. I know tomorrow is Thursday, but I've been juggling a lot between the stadium, my business, and my new house. Things are starting to run together.

> Cameron: Yes, I'll be in around 9 am.

Connor asked me to come in early to brainstorm ideas for surprising Everett at the last game.

> Stormy: I'll bring coffee.

I send a thumbs up to her message and then set my phone

down. I told her nine a.m., but I'll arrive closer to eight a.m. Connor and I should be done before she gets there, and I'll be ready for another cup of coffee. I quickly grab my vitamin C serum and start moisturizing my face. I'm running behind and I need to pull the redness out of my skin after forgetting to wear sunscreen this weekend.

"Why are you getting ready in here?"

"Jeez, you scared the shit out of me," I say, clenching my towel tight as I practically jump out of my skin. When I look up, Everett stands behind me, donning a suit and tie, looking exquisitely dapper and oh-so edible. His dark locks are styled back in a long fade; his beard is neatly trimmed and immaculately sculpted, highlighting his chiseled jaw and those eyes. Fuck, I redirect my focus back to the mirror. We don't have time for what those eyes do to me. I start rubbing in the serum when he approaches me and kisses my shoulder. My skin instantly pebbles under his caress.

"You didn't answer my question," he says as the pad of his thumb gently drags down the side of my arm.

I blink away the fog threatening to settle and try to remember what question he even asked. "All of my makeup is in here." The hand that was skimming my arm wraps around the one I have holding my towel, and in one swift movement, his fingers expertly loosen mine, and my towel drops to the floor.

"I'll move them for you," he says as his lips trail up my neck and big hands cup my heavy breasts.

"It's fine. I don't need to move twice," I stutter out with bated breath. "When I pack all this up, it will be to move into my new house."

"I think you mean our new house." His fingers pinch my nipples, making my pussy clench. "Where you go, I go."

"Everett, I need to get ready. We're going to be late."

"Then we will be late." His eyes find mine in the mirror. "I've already waited long enough to make you mine. The world can wait a little longer to have you." His hands give my breasts one more firm squeeze before they slowly drift down my hips as his lips start trailing open-mouthed kisses down my back. "I'll be quick, I just need a taste." His teeth nip at the curve of my ass. "I want this pussy to come on my face so I can smell you and be reminded of what I have, of what's mine, all night."

His fingers dig into my hips, and I hiss. "Everett, we don't know how to be quick."

"That's a terrible argument if I've ever heard one. Bend over and spread your legs, sunshine." When I hesitate, he slaps my ass. "Now," he orders. I've barely moved into position when his palms grip my cheeks hard, spreading me wide before his tongue runs straight over my puckered hole. I shrink into myself in a way I never have. I'm very body-positive and confident. I've done a lot of things, but no one has ever put their mouth on me there. "Every inch of you tastes like heaven." My mind barely has time to sort through the emotions flooding my body before his tongue spears my pussy deep, and the groan of undiluted ecstasy vibrates through his groan.

"Mmm," I moan with a half whimper as I grip the counter to steady myself. As his tongue and lips alternate between sucking and fucking me, his thumb finds its way to my tight hole. He hasn't tried anything back there yet, and I haven't asked, but I already know I want it. I want everything with him. When he doesn't meet any resistance, he pushes the tip in. "God, yes," I pant as my senses are overwhelmed. There's no way the man I've fantasized about since I was a teenager is on his knees for me right now in a suit and tie with my pussy in his mouth.

"You like this, sunshine?"

"I like everything with you."

His thumb pushes in further at the same time his tongue spears my pussy, and I come without warning.

"So good," he mumbles as he licks me through my orgasm.

"Fuck me, Ev." It comes out as a half plea, half demand. Oral sex is foreplay. I need him to fill me and stretch me to be fully satisfied.

SALT

"I thought we didn't have time for that." He tosses my words back at me. "Maybe if you ask nicely, you'll get what you want."

"Please, Daddy, I want your cock inside of me." He coughs, and his hands fall away as the realization of the words I chose sinks in. "Shit, Everett. I didn't mean it that way. It's your suit and this moment. Me, naked before you in my bathroom. You're fully dressed, looking sexy as hell, exuding power the way you always do when you wear them." I bite my lip. "And I like it when you're rough with me, when you take me the way you want me, when you lose control and don't treat me like I'll break." I try to turn around, but he stops me, and for a second, I believe I ruined the moment.

"Does that turn you on?"

"What?" I ask, searching his face. That's when I see his tongue dip out and moisten his bottom lip. My comment may have caught him off guard, but he doesn't hate it.

"Calling me daddy, does it turn you on?" His eyes meet mine in the mirror as he unbuckles his belt.

There's no way he's not into it. I can tell by the way his eyes are already lidded he's more than fucking turned on. He's borderline feral. "I don't know, Daddy hasn't fucked me yet."

"Cameron, I'm going to give this to you once," he says, his hands gripping my hips as he pulls me back onto his hard length, running it through my slick folds. "I'll always give you what you want, but you tell me if it's too much." I nod, more than ready for him to pound into me. He smacks my ass. "Words, Cameron."

"Yes, I'll tell you if it's too much."

"Good." His tip nudges my entrance, and his eyes lock onto mine in the mirror. "You ready to take Daddy's cock like a good girl?"

I push back on his cock. "As long as you're ready to fuck me like I'm bad."

"Fuck," he hisses. "You're going to pay for that."

"I'm counting on it."

He growls before his fingers dig into my hips, and he pulls back, his eyes dropping to my ass before he slams back in, drawing out a whimper. His eyes flash to mine, and when he's convinced he sees lust and not pain, he repeats the move again. I watch him in the mirror as he bottoms out hard two more times, biting his lip every time he sees his cock covered in my juices. When he catches me watching, he says, "The only thing better than being inside of you is watching you while I'm there. Don't look at me. Look at you." He slams in hard again. "The way those full breasts sway every time I hit that spot deep inside of you." His hands slide up my hips, his fingers lightly trailing up my sides. "The way your skin pebbles beneath my touch." His lips find my shoulder. "And the way you flush from your neck to your cheeks when I'm making you feel good." Those firm hands return to my hips, where he braces himself. "You're fucking beautiful, Cameron Salt. A piece of art worthy of marveling. You better get used to me watching because now that I've seen you, I can never unsee you. You're all I ever want to see." His eyes hold mine for a long moment, ensuring I feel the sentiment before dropping back to my ass. "Now Daddy's going to fuck his girl."

He starts a punishing pace, and I watch on in the mirror. This time, admiring all the parts of me he pointed out, seeing them through a new lens. His lens. My breasts are full, my nipples hard from where they graze the cold granite top, my chest is tinged pink from the sun and my desire. His hands on my hips wreck me every time, especially when they are, as they are now, an anchor for him to push inside me as far as he can go. I can feel my juices dripping, and the way he groans when he loses himself is the stuff I live for. "Fuck, you're choking my cock." His eyes come back to mine, his lids heavy with pure adulation. "Come for me, sunshine."

Damn it, his words shatter me as my orgasm grabs hold of me, and my bones turn to dust. "Shit, baby," he says as his arms wrap around my waist. "Talk to me, Cameron. Are you okay?"

"Mm-hmm," I moan, "So good."

He groans a sigh of relief as he buries his face in the crook of my neck, his lips gently pressing into my sensitive skin as he catches his breath. "So perfect, so beautiful, so mine."

As my heart and my head come back down from the bliss I spiraled into, I say, "Now I need another shower."

His teeth nip my heated flesh. "The last thing you will be doing is taking a shower. The glow on your cheeks and my scent covering your body pair perfectly with the dress I laid out on the bed." He slowly pulls out, and my body instantly misses his warmth at my back—until he spins me in his arms and his lips tenderly kiss mine before he pulls back, his thumb caressing my cheek. "While I loved every second of watching you come undone around me, I'm not your daddy." His chocolate gaze holds mine, his eyes studying every second of what he sees reflected in mine. "I'm your, Ev, and you're my sunshine. That's us, and that's everything to me." I nod as my happiness sets on the perfect curves of his slow smile before his lips press against mine once more. "Get dressed." His hand swats my bare cheek once before he releases me and adds, "Before I change my mind and take you to bed instead."

"Are you okay?" Everett asks as we step up to the bar in the outdoor tent blanketed in Edison bulbs and rustic candelabras with wisteria vines draped whimsically over each fixture. It looks like something straight out of a fairytale. My eyes have been drawn to the décor since we walked in. In the past, Moira has held the event at the Four Seasons in St. Louis, but today, the event is being held outside at the Botanical Gardens in Forest Park. Maybe she is trying to make this different besides moving the date so close to my parents' anniversary.

"I'm fine, Ev, really. Stop worrying about me."

Everett doesn't show his nerves, but I can't help but feel like part of why he keeps asking if I'm okay is a projection. Did he go out of his way to make a show out of claiming me at the stadium?

Yes. But Moira, his brothers, and his colleagues weren't there. A stadium full of strangers is different from a room full of people you've known for years. Besides helping me out of the town car that dropped us off, he hasn't held my hand or made any other gestures that would signal I'm more than I've ever been, aside from the occasional hand on my lower back to steer me through the crowd. I'm not bothered by it, but I've noticed.

"What can I get you?" the bartender asks.

"I'll have a cognac, neat." His hand finds my lower back, and my body soaks in its tenderness as he leans in and asks, "Do you want a glass of Pinot?"

I nod, my nerves easing slightly, knowing that he sees me. I'm not typically a wine drinker. I prefer my drinks spicy or fermented, but when I go out to a nice restaurant or attend events, I usually order wine because I sip it slowly and pace myself rather than going off the rails. "A glass of Pinot will do."

A familiar face starts walking our way. "I didn't know..." My words die off when I realize Everett is talking to the gentleman on the other side of him. His face is not one I am familiar with. He could be from work or someone associated with the charity.

"You clean up nice, Salt," Nash says as he sidles up next to me.

"Thanks, you don't look too shabby yourself. I would have lost money betting on you owning a suit."

He shrugs. "Yeah, well, when your dad is being honored with an Outstanding Philanthropic Award, you suit up." A smirk pulls at his lips before he adds, "I still wore the boots."

I look down at his feet, and sure enough, he's rocking biker boots, scuffs and all. Why is that sexy? "I'm sorry, I didn't realize your father was connected to the MacBeth Foundation."

"I'm not sure that he is. One of the more expensive parts of developing is making the land usable. He had a friend who was gifted land years ago, but he could never do anything with it because of the terrain and the cost of leveling it. After his wife divorced him and left him broke, my dad cleared him a spot on the property his ex-wife didn't want because she deemed it useless, and the rest was history. He started donating his resources when jobs finished early to area men's shelters, and that led to him buying parcels of cheap land, again, cheap because of the developing costs. After making it usable, he'd donate it back to charities that could use it."

"Wow, that's amazing," I say as the bartender slides me my glass. The conversation I had with Orion suddenly hits differently. Why wouldn't Nash want to be part of that? "You must be proud. No interest in taking over the family business?" I ask before sipping my wine.

He shakes his head, and I can tell by the subtle despondence that crosses his face that the topic isn't one he likes to discuss. "Everyone has their why. He has his, and I have mine."

His eyes drag up my body before landing on mine, and a slow smile starts to break across his face. "What?" I question, unable to hold back my own. I find it hard not to smile at anyone who's smiling at me but add in his handsome dimple, and it is impossible.

"What do you say..." He nods toward the dance floor. "Want to take a spin with me? That dress and the way you look tonight deserve to be seen."

"Um..." I slightly turn to Everett and find his conversation has ended, and his eyes are now curiously trained on me. I can't tell if he's waiting for me to make a move or debating making his own. "I..."

CHAPTER 29
EVERETT

It's my own fault another man is standing on the other side of my girl asking her to dance. Admittedly, my public displays of affection have been lacking tonight, but not because she's not one hundred percent mine. It's because I haven't wanted to make a spectacle of myself or overshadow this event with the arm candy that's half my age. Sure, Connor gave me his blessing, but he even said that the way we started didn't look right to him in the beginning. He's my son, and even he had a seed of doubt, and that's all it takes. Cameron hasn't seen the ugly side of rumors, the ones that can villainize you, and I want to protect her from that. It's one of the reasons I've felt out of step since we got here. I haven't wanted the world to pop our bubble with their judgment.

The other reason is one I've only ever admitted to her: fear. Everything about Cameron Salt scares me. She's the one thing I don't want to fuck up. So when Nash Atsbury, a guy her age, asks her to dance, the trepidation I've never been able to shake momentarily casts doubt.

"So what do you say?" Nash nudges Cameron's arm in another attempt to pull her away from me, and it's that thought that has me pushing aside my fear; because the fear of losing her is greater than any other.

"I..." she starts, but I cut her off.

"She's with me," I answer for her.

Nash furrows his brow. "Oh, I'm sorry, Everett. Do you mind if I steal Cameron?"

Fucking hell, I internally cringe at the insinuation that he believes I want him to ask me for permission to spin her around the dance floor. The world will continue to see this until I give them something different. My arm circles her waist and pulls her close. The move catches her off guard, and I feel her body tense from my touch before she relaxes into me.

"No, I mean she's with me. If anyone's taking her out there, it's me."

His eyebrows rise and dart between mine and hers, clearly looking for confirmation that he understood me correctly, before he says, "Oh, my apologies." He raps his knuckles on the bar. "Catch you later, Salt."

"Everett, you didn't need to—"

I spin her around. "Dance with me," I say as I intertwine our fingers. Her eyes lock onto mine, and I know she sees my ask for what it is. I'm ready to tell the world she's my girl in front of all our friends, family, and colleagues. I lead her out to the dance floor when she doesn't argue.

"Ev, you didn't have to do this. I'm happy. I know you care about me."

I clench my jaw, irritated that, with all the truths I've given her, she thinks I simply care.

"Cameron Salt, you make me happier than I ever dreamed possible. No one has ever made me feel the way you do. That's why I'm here with you now. I'm leaving no stone unturned as I collect this moment with you, where no man will ever make the mistake of asking my girl to dance again. Believe it or not, I enjoy being on this side of a jail cell."

She laughs out loud and my heart flutters with the timbre. "You wouldn't. Nash is harmless, and it's not that serious." I tighten my grip around her waist, eliminating any space between us, and she gasps, her eyes flicking around the room where I'm sure we've gained the prying eyes of curious guests, friends, and family.

"Ev, people are definitely looking now."

"Good, that means I'm doing this right."

"People are going to talk."

"Then let's give them something to talk about," I say as I lean my forehead to hers as we dance like no one is watching, eyes locked.

Her tongue slowly moistens her lips before her eyes close, and she says, "I love you, Everett Callahan. I loved you before I had any right to..." She opens her eyes, slowly finding mine once more. I'm not sure what she sees, but it has her suddenly trying to pull away. "I'm sorry."

I capture her hands in mine and place them over my heart. "Slow down, sunshine. You can't tell a man you love him and run away." I pause to pull in a breath of resolve as I let the years I've feared having her like this fall away. I was created to be hers, and that's scary, but now I know my fear was never really fear at all. It was love. Her eyes trail away, and I release her hand to cup her cheek. "Cameron, I need you to hear me. I've never felt love before, at least not the kind shared between lovers. I can't promise I will do it right, but I know there's no one else in the world I want to figure it out with. Never apologize for loving me because I'll never apologize for loving you."

Her bottom lip trembles, and I lean in to kiss away our shared fear of putting our hearts on the line, but before I can cover her perfect mouth with my own, a hand is on my shoulder.

"Everett, I'm sorry to interrupt, but I think it's better to interrupt this moment than another. I need you to come with me," my brother Garrett says before adding, "Oh hey, Cam. I'll bring him back in a minute."

"One second, there's no way I'm walking away from the first girl I ever said I love you to without a kiss." I quickly press my mouth to hers. I may have spent half of my life married to another woman, but she wasn't the woman I chose because of love, I chose her to save her, and she chose me for protection. We've spoken of love, and if you ask me if I loved Moira, I'd say yes, she is the mother of my son, and we are friends, but never did we share the words I love you, not in the way I just said them now. "I'll be back," I say, before following after my brother.

"Someone better be dying. Otherwise, I might consider killing you as a justifiable cause for pulling me away from that moment."

"Lauren just showed up."

Connor joins us as we head out of the tent and into the gardens. "Did you get the records?"

"Yes, but, Dad, it doesn't add up. She had a baby girl... She didn't leave with one."

I stop in my tracks. "You're sure?" I'm rarely wrong. I was certain I knew precisely who Lauren Rhodes was and why she was back.

"He's sure," Lauren says, stepping around a hedge wall. "It's why I left town."

"Your story didn't end because you left that hospital empty-handed. We both know you walked out of it with secrets. It's why you're here now, prying, getting close, and asking about the past."

"Did I have secrets? Yes, but I'm not the bad guy here. I left with a broken heart, devastated and forever changed." Her voice cracks with the same hurt written all over her face.

But I don't believe her. I'd hoped to have the DNA evidence to prove what I still feel in my gut is true; however, it doesn't change the other two damning pieces of evidence. The first being Damon's dying words as his car sank to the bottom of the river, "You can't let HER take my girl." My conversation with my late friend has replayed on a loop in my mind since the day he died. Never forgotten. I just never knew who he meant by her. After I saw the initials carved into the tree, more pieces started falling into place, and that's when another lost memory resurfaced. The same month Cameron was born, he sold his family's estate in the Central West End. It was worth millions. We assumed it was to cover the cost of moving cross country and having a baby while attending a prestigious law school, but after everything that has come to light over the last few days, I did some digging, knowing right where to look now that I had a name, and I found it. Damon paid Lauren one million dollars. The question is, for what? Damon didn't trust her, which means I don't either.

"You're going to have to excuse me if I don't buy whatever sob story you're trying to sell. I know you had a relationship with Damon Salt. I saw the carving in the yellowwood tree, and if that's not enough, I know he paid you one million dollars, and the second that money hit your account, you left town. I don't for one second believe those two events are unrelated."

"What is it you believe Damon gave me one million dollars for exactly?" she says, with a renewed sense of moxie, before adding, "Because when I left town with one million dollars, it was to start over and never discuss the affair I had with a man I loved."

Are you kidding me right now? She's trying to say she loved him? I pinch the bridge of my nose. "You loved him?" I saw the tree. I know Camie is her, Lauren Camden Rhodes. It was what her friends called her back in school. We were not friends; therefore, it's not a name I've ever used. But things still aren't adding up. How could I not know they were a thing? "Explain it to me, Lauren, because the way I remember it, you and Damon never crossed paths aside from the night we were all at the Busch wedding."

She looks at something on her phone before shoving it in the back pocket of her jeans. "You have one part of that statement right. Damon and I weren't a thing. He hated me just like the rest of you, but one night during the summer before college, we were both drunk at the same party, and that dislike turned into hate sex." She shrugs and takes a seat on the ledge of the fountain. "After that night, we kept meeting up secretly at this lake in the middle of nowhere, knowing we wouldn't be caught. Believe it or not, I didn't like you guys either."

Garret holds up his hand. "You said the summer before college. Damon met Amelia that summer."

Lauren releases a heavy sigh. "I was getting there. It started out as hate fucking. Neither of us was in it for anything more. We were by no means monogamous." She shakes her head from side to side. "At least, not when it started. By the end, we wanted to be. That's why you found those initials in the yellowwood tree. The night he carved that into the tree, we talked about only dating each other and telling our friends, but literally the next day, I saw him and he told me it was over. That he had messed up in a big way, and he couldn't take it back."

"Amelia turned up pregnant," Garrett interjects as he rubs his chin, deep in thought.

"Bingo," she confirms. "Damon was a good man. When he found out she was pregnant, he did right by marrying her. We didn't sneak around behind her back. I had no interest in being the other woman. But fast forward four years to the summer of the Busch wedding, add in lots of alcohol, old feelings that never died, and a wife with a debt to settle..." She trails off before standing up. "We hooked up again, but unlike before, we didn't walk away unscathed."

She starts walking down one of the garden trails, and we follow. "What debt did Amelia have to settle?" I ask. I believe I know exactly what score she was settling for, but I want to hear it all the same.

"His son had a serious reaction to a mix of medicines he was taking after getting sick and became severely anemic. The quick solution was a blood transfusion. Of course, Damon was first to volunteer, and that's when he found out Kelce wasn't his. However, it was how he found out that had him ready to divorce Amelia. He didn't find out via blood test that Kelce wasn't his. Amelia told him point blank he wasn't his father. She had known all along. By the wedding, he wasn't thinking straight, and Amelia was in his ear, telling him to take his pass. She knew he and I had a thing before she turned up pregnant, and she was hoping he'd bite, and he did."

"She set him up, and then she fucking blackmailed him," Connor chimes in. "How could he have been so dumb?"

Lauren shakes her head. "That's one way to look at it, but the other was a man who was conflicted. Kelce may not have been his blood, but for the first few years of Kelce's life, Damon didn't know that. Finding out Kelce wasn't his blood didn't turn off his feelings for the kid he believed was his."

"Okay, that's his story. What's yours? Why did you screw a married man?" I ask curtly. Lauren has done a great job trying to paint Damon in a different light, but what about her? She's not innocent in all of this. She still screwed a married man.

"The list is endless." She holds her fingers up. "Young, dumb, naïve, drunk," she ticks them off one by one. "I foolishly thought maybe he would leave her, maybe we could get our shot, the one she stole. I don't know. It was a long time ago. I made bad choices, and so did he. In the end, we both paid dearly for them."

Garrett is quiet, and I can tell he's assessing her words, tearing them apart the same way I am. The difference is that he's not as close to the facts as I am. He's able to take a more neutral approach. If we were in court, I'd have no choice but to recuse myself. I can't be impartial. Like now, I can't find it within me to feel sorry for her. She walked away, and for money, nonetheless.

"What was the money for?" Garrett asks.

"Before I was discharged from the hospital, money was transferred into my account, and a process server showed up to my room with an NDA to stay quiet about the affair and the subsequent pregnancy that resulted."

I scoff. "So you took the money and gave up your parental rights, and now, what? You want her back? It doesn't work that way. You don't just get to come back."

Her hand clenches in her shirt as her forehead pinches. "That's what you think happened? You think I took money and gave up my baby?"

"It's not what I think happened. It's what did happen," I say flatly.

"I wanted my baby girl. That baby was my everything, Everett. I loved her so damn much. I couldn't wait to hold her in my arms and give her the world, but I never got the chance..." Her voice cracks as a tear runs down her cheek. "I had a traumatic birth, and after my daughter was born, she was rushed to the NICU before I even got a chance to hold her. Three hours later, the nurses brought me a cold, lifeless little girl who didn't make it, and my world was forever changed. I was so fucking broken. I had to grieve the loss of my little girl alone because the father was a married man who had no idea she existed. The next day, when that man showed up in my room and the money was placed in my account, I wanted to scream. I wanted to burn the entire hospital to the ground. I couldn't believe Damon knew. I never said a word about the pregnancy to him. He didn't leave Amelia, and I never asked him to, but I thought he cared about me enough to show some kind of sympathy. Something more than a check and an NDA. I would have rather had a phone call, a card, anything would have been better in that moment than a check, but the longer I sat there with my pain and hate, the more I saw that money as a chance to start over. That money saved my life. It allowed me to get away from this place because there was no way I could have stayed here without her. Everywhere I turned were memories of feeling her kick inside of me, places I planned on taking her, and love I'd never get to have. So I left."

"You're lying," I spit as I start pacing. She has to be. That's fucking sick. There's no way Damon would do what she's insinuating.

"She's not lying," Stormy says, walking up the path with Cameron and Mackenzie in tow.

Cameron's eyes connect with mine, and she's immediately at my side, wrapping her arm around mine. "What's going on?" I close my eyes, wishing this were unfolding differently. The last time I spoke with Cameron about this, I asked for time, but that's once again being stolen from me. I don't have a smoking gun, but what I do have is damning.

"Remember when I said I lied?" Stormy asks Cameron, to which she nods. "Well, she was my reason. Lauren Rhodes is your biological mother."

"What?" Cameron gasps with a laugh. "You can't be serious." Her eyes flick around the group, and reality settles quickly as she sees the sober expressions on everyone's faces. Her hands tighten around my bicep before her eyes lock onto mine. "Did you know?"

"Cameron, it's not that simple," I try, unsure where to begin.

She unwraps herself as her hand rises to cover her mouth. "You did. You knew, and you never told me."

I shake my head. "It's not what you think." I run my fingers angrily through my hair. This is such a fucking mess. Did I know Amelia wasn't her mother? Yes. Did I know her mother was Lauren Rhodes? No. I'm just as stunned as she is. The story Lauren has spun has shaken me to my core and turned everything I thought I knew about my best friend on its head. He's not here to defend himself, but the evidence against him is strong. My eyes rise to hers, and I see nothing but hurt. Hurt that breaks me. "I didn't know," I say so softly I'm unsure it's audible because I know it's too little, too late. I knew enough, even if it wasn't this.

She turns to Connor and Garrett. "You guys too?"

"Cameron, none of this was black and white," Garrett tries.

"That's an excuse, and you know it."

"We don't have DNA evidence. We have stories. Her words against your father's." Connor steps in. "Cam, you have to remember. You lived with your parents on the East Coast until you were eight years old—"

I raise my hand for him to stop. I know where he's going, and I can't stomach it. I hate feeling like I've aided my best friend in covering a lie, but I also can't stand by and watch his character get ripped apart with speculation instead of evidence. What Connor's implying isn't improbable. They didn't live here when Amelia would have been pregnant with Cameron. None of us saw her with or without a child. When Damon broke the news, it was with a picture of Cameron that read, "Surprise, we've been keeping a secret." He forgot to add it was a really fucking big secret.

That's when Stormy reaches into the bag she's carrying and pulls out a book. I know it is Damon's because it's from his collection—the same collection I keep in my office. I've stared at that spine countless times. "I have his words."

"Give me that." I demand, reaching her in two steps and snatching it out of her hand before she can react. Not only does she have something that belongs to me, she had to have stolen it from an office I always keep locked. "How did you even get this?"

"How I got it isn't as important as the truth it holds."

Before I can respond, Cameron takes the book out of my hands. "If anyone gets the book, it's me. He was my father, and this is my life. If these words belong to anyone, it's me."

I drop my head, place my hands on my hips, and step back. I've failed her again. "You're right. I don't even know what I'm protecting you from anymore. Not that I ever did." I slowly bring my eyes back up to hers. "You know everything I do now. I guess you have everything you're looking for right there," I say as I nod toward the book in her hands. "You can make your own choices."

I take another step away, giving her space. I've spent years defending something untenable, and what's more, that's not even the whole of it. I've been trying to uphold an oath, a promise I made to my dying friend, one whose death was my fault. I have no business being here.

"Why does it feel like you're leaving?"

I tell her she's more. I believe she's more, yet here I am, failing her. I've been so blinded by everything she makes me feel that I'm holding her back. History feels like it's repeating itself right before my eyes. I'm standing in a cornfield at seventeen, determined to save the girl. All this time, I saw Lauren's push to get close to me as something else. I missed signs that were always there. For years, I've been her protector: duty instead of love. She's no longer a fragile obligation. She's the woman I want at my side and one who can handle the truth.

"Because I am. You're a grown woman. You have things to figure out, and I can't be what you need. All this time, I only wanted to guard your heart, but all I was doing was poisoning it."

"That's not true. I'm upset. I'm hurt. I'm not poisoned. We'll figure this out together. You just said yourself you didn't know—"

"But didn't I?" I throw my arms wide. "I knew enough, Cameron."

"You said you loved me, Everett. Was any of that true?"

"I meant every damn word. I love you so damn much. It's because I love you that I'm letting you go..." My eyes flick over to Lauren's. "So you can make room to love someone else. All I've done is turn that heart of gold into heartbreak."

"It's my heart, Everett. I get to decide how I want it, and I'd rather have broken pieces that include you than a whole one that doesn't."

Her words slowly dig out what remains of my own. I fucking hate knowing that I'm hurting her. If I were her, I'd hate me. I turn on my heel before she can argue anymore. Her hate is deserved. I'm not walking away because I want to. I'm walking away because she won't, and while she may want me, she deserves so much better than me.

"Ev, please don't do this," I hear her say, but my feet don't stop. I hoped our story would end with me being her destiny, but the sound of my footsteps as I walk away sounds like the deafening silence of me being part of her history. Good.

"Dad, this is messed up. You shouldn't be walking away right now. She needs you," Connor says, following me out of the gardens.

"You think I want to walk away from her? Connor, I love her with everything that I am. You're my son, but she's the other half of my soul."

"Then why are we walking away? We're her family."

"That's why I'm walking away. We're not her everything anymore, Con. I don't have the DNA tests, but I already know what it will say, Lauren Camden Rhodes is Cameron's mom." As

SALT

if I needed another slap in the face. Damon named his daughter Cameron, no doubt an eponym for Lauren. The signs seem so utterly obvious now, which makes this all the more harsh. I should have realized sooner. Maybe if I had, I wouldn't be walking away now. Perhaps then I could have had the time to find my words, to tell her differently, or maybe it was always meant to be this way.

"You're supposed to be there for her when she's hurting."

"Not on this, Con. This is different. Her pain needs to be her strength." I run my hands through my hair, pulling hard as I do. I can't save the girl. I did that once and lost myself and the girl. This time, the girl has to save herself. When I reach the valet with Garrett and Connor hot on my heels, I look to Connor and say, "You guys are more than welcome to stay. I'm not asking you to take a side."

"The car is here," Garrett says as he opens the door. "I'll let Moira know you had to leave."

"Thanks," I say as I climb in.

Leaning in, Garrett says, "This isn't the cornfield, you're not seventeen, and that girl back there doesn't need you, she wants you. There's a difference, brother."

He shuts the door and hits the roof, signaling the driver to take off before I can respond. As the driver pulls out of the park, all I can think is I may have just made one of the biggest mistakes of my life.

327

CHAPTER 30
CAMERON

Watching Everett walk away, I try not to let it hurt. He just told me he loved me, and I know those words weren't flippant. They weren't said out of obligation because I said it first. They were felt in his soul, and I would know because we share the same one. The man walking away from me now hasn't healed. He's hurting too, and part of loving someone is trusting them with that pain. I can't fault him for not knowing what to do with the emotions he's fighting now. Before he walked away inside the gala, he said, "There's no way I'm walking away from the first girl I ever said I love you to without a kiss." I loved him yesterday, I love him today, and I'll love him tomorrow, and right now, I'll love what I know exists between us, *for us*.

"Hey," Mackenzie says as her hand finds my shoulder. "Let's tackle one broken piece at a time and see if we can't put some hearts back together."

I pull my father's book tight to my chest. She stayed. She didn't walk off with Connor and Garrett as they followed after Everett, and it means the world to me to have her by my side. I nod and turn around only to find Lauren staring at me with the same contemplative curiosity she always has, but where I used to see conniving, someone trying to get close to me to steal my man, I now see it for what it potentially always was: curious unbelief.

"When did you figure it out?" I ask blankly.

"She found the book hidden in my room. I had planned to talk to you about it tomorrow—"

Lauren raises her hand, and Stormy shrinks back.

"The day I stopped in the team shop and brought the two of you lunch, Stormy mentioned your birthday, and then you told me your father was Damon Salt. That was the first time in twenty-two years I ever had any reason to doubt that you weren't in the grave I left you in. My eyes immediately saw someone else standing before me. I was convinced I was going mad and seeing ghosts. It's why I excused myself. There was no way the thoughts running through my head were real. It had to be a coincidence. Amelia must have been pregnant at the same time I was, and I didn't know. That's what I told myself anyway..." She pulls her phone from her back pocket. "Can I show you something?" she asks as she takes a cautious step toward me.

"Sure," I say, as my lungs expel breath I hadn't realized I was holding.

She clicks open her phone and shows me a picture of a woman holding a baby in front of a statue of Mother Mary. The picture is faded and worn, but the auburn hair, porcelain skin, and blue eyes are unmistakable. "Who is she?"

"That's my mother holding me."

"I don't understand..." Obviously, I follow her suggestion that the woman in the photo is my grandmother. "How? Or better yet, why?" I turn to Stormy. "When you said you had been lying to get close to me, and then I thought back to our conversations about my brother, I thought you were going to come out and reveal you were my sister. Not this."

Stormy shoves her hands into the front pockets of her overalls. "In hindsight, I see how you could think that. My bad. If it makes you feel any better, I lied to Lauren too. She followed me here blindly, unaware of the morsel of information Sage Graves shared with me."

"Maybe not blindly. It was time for me to face the past I had run from. It was time to find closure. I just never expected that closure to be my daughter alive and well." Thunder rumbling off in the distance catches all of our attention as a few sprinkles fall.

"How about we take this inside? Our table is empty now that the men have left," Mackenzie says as she gestures toward the tent.

"We're not really dressed for a gala," Lauren states plainly.

"It's fine. We'll find a table in the corner," I say as a big gust of wind picks up.

We've just found a table in the back when Mackenzie leaves us to grab some drinks, and I notice Garrett and Connor at the bar. My heart beats out of tune as I discreetly look around the room to see if Everett stayed too.

"He's not here," Lauren says, noting my wandering eye.

"How can you be so sure?"

She mindlessly starts fidgeting with the twine wrapped around the silverware on the plate before saying, "He loved your dad, and hearing his ugly truths wasn't an easy pill for him to swallow. It doesn't help that he blames himself for the accident."

"Wait a minute. How do you know that?" Her comment has my palms instantly sweaty. How does she know that and I don't? What reason would Everett have to blame himself?

"Well, he didn't use those words exactly, but it was easy enough to infer. The night you and Stormy went camping, I took your phone back to Everett's..." She rests her elbows on the table. "Spoiler alert. I was digging. I was trying to find anything that could corroborate the speculation that had existed since the moment I found out your birthday and who your father was." Her guessing the password to my phone, which was my father's birthday, makes a lot more sense now. "Anyway, part of my snooping included asking many questions about the past. I was trying to put together timelines, such as when Damon moved to the East Coast, when you guys came back, and what, if anything,

Everett knew, and that's when the accident came up. He was pouring a drink when he mentioned that, the night of the gala, Damon was late because he swung by Everett's house to pick up an award he had left in his office. He paused mid-pour, and without words, I knew why. He had just told me something he didn't mean to share."

How could I not know this? That little nugget of information changes things. It wasn't just our age gap or the fact that I'm his best friend's daughter that stood in the way. It's his penitence. He can't find it within himself to be happy with me because, in his mind, he's not deserving.

"I grabbed a bottle," Mackenzie says, returning to the table. "It was easier to grab a bottle of wine than four glasses." I notice the way Connor quickly glances in our direction to check on his wife. When he catches me looking, he gives me a small smile that feels sad, but I push it away. I have words for his father, but right now, I need answers.

"Stormy, how did you get this book?"

The one time she was at the house with me, I walked her in and out. She didn't have an opportunity to roam the house freely. I look at the spine, and this is indeed one of the books that has sat on Everett's shelf since my father passed. When we cleaned my father's place, Everett asked if he could have his collection. He said he liked having a piece of my father that he knew he enjoyed. My father loved collecting first-edition books of classics. I don't recall seeing him read them, but he enjoyed collecting them. We had a small library at my childhood home because of it. Most of the collection was put into storage except for the few that Everett took to display in his office.

She grabs the bottle of wine and pours herself a glass. "I suppose I owe both of you a story. Sage Graves adopted me. She wasn't my biological mom." Her eyes connect with Lauren's. "A detail I hadn't realized Lauren already knew but went along with all the same. Pain knows pain, and she believed my lies reflected that. What Lauren didn't know was Sage told me something that stuck with me before she died. Sage never liked to discuss why she left Waterloo. I only ever knew she had a son who she said she left with family, but one day after one of her group sessions—"

"What kind of group sessions?" I cut her off as I take the glass of wine Mackenzie slides in front of me.

"I'll answer that," Lauren says. "Sage and I met through a support group for mothers who had lost children. While Evan may have been alive and well, Sage wasn't a complete monster. She loved him, but it hurt too much to stay. She struggled with the guilt of abandoning him and also grappled with her own pain from the circumstances surrounding his conception. It was a vicious cycle of depression that she seemed to never win."

Stormy takes a drink of her wine and starts again. "After one of their group sessions, I asked her why she bonded with Lauren. Sage didn't have friends, and she and Lauren didn't seem to have anything in common. At least, not the way I saw it. That's when she said, 'We both left a piece of our heart in the same small town. The only difference is the piece I left behind is sick, poisoned at its core and can't be saved, but hers is beautiful and has the power to make her whole again.'"

Lauren sets down her glass. "I don't understand. If she knew Cameron was mine, why wouldn't she have told me?"

Stormy shifts to sit cross-legged on the chair. "I don't know if she meant those words literally. Sage could have been saying it metaphorically, knowing that you needed closure. The closure you'd never get if you didn't come back and put your demons to rest, but..." She holds up her finger and lets out a sigh. "Regardless of how she meant it, literally or metaphorically, it always weighed heavy on my heart because I've been missing a part of me my whole life, from not knowing my dad. I thought if there was even a small chance you were real, it was worth pursuing, especially knowing how much the absence of you impacted Lauren. I knew my time with Lauren was limited. The tiny house situation wasn't a lie. I did buy one, and this summer was our last hurrah together, so I knew I needed to act sooner than later if I was ever going to get a shot at discovering the truth. I honestly had no idea what I was looking for. I knew Sage's name, and an easy search gave me Evan's. The rest, I was winging it."

Waiters delivering entrées to the table have her pausing. The savory smells of chicken and candied green beans have my stomach rumbling. I didn't realize how famished I was until the aromas hit my senses. I set my glass of wine down and grab a fork.

"Okay, you had a name, but how did you know the lies to tell without a story?" Mackenzie asks.

"The world has a funny way of working things out sometimes. A week after we moved into our apartment, I walked down to Main Street and ran into a group of guys who asked if I wanted to tag along to a party. I said no until I was checking out at the convenience store, and another guy with a cart loaded full of beer asked me the same question, but he said, 'My name's Evan, and you look like you're ready to go to your next party.' Needless to say, I said yes. My thought was, even if he wasn't the same Evan I was looking for, if this many people were going to the same party, there was a good chance I might run into him."

"You were at the divorce party he threw the night Everett got back in town," I say, almost spitting out my chicken. "So that day you came over to hang out with me wasn't your first time there?"

"Nope, but it was my first time in the pool house," she adds before snatching up one of the rolls off the table.

"And the book?" Lauren waves her hand in prompt for her to continue.

"Right, I didn't get the book until I ran into Evan a few days later, when you came home and caught us in the living room. I ran into him again at that same convenience store, but he was a different person this time. He looked defeated, and of course, I had a vested interest because, by that time, I knew he was indeed Sage Grave's son, so I invited him up. He had no qualms about telling me how he fucked up." She nods toward Lauren. "You were there for some of his story time, but you missed the parts about how he needed a place to stay. When you went into the kitchen to grab a drink, I told him to follow my lead, thinking maybe you'd buy my lie and let him stay so I could get more information. That's how I walked myself into that lie. As for the book, it was in Evan's bag that day. I ransacked it when he went to the bathroom, and I snuck it under a couch pillow when I noticed it was a journal within a book. When I took it, I assumed it was his. I had no idea what I grabbed belonged to your father, so it took me some time to piece together what and who I was reading about." She takes a big bite out of her roll before saying, "Oh." Reaching into her back pocket, she pulls out an envelope. "I probably should have pulled this out when Everett was still here, but you guys were having a moment, and I'm not sure what difference this would have made." She slides it across the table. "I didn't accidentally throw your brush in my bag. I stole it. Those are the DNA results."

The envelope sits between Lauren and me, and we stare at it. Do I want to open it? Yes. But at the same time, I already know what it will say. The question is, how do I feel about that?

"What do you want from me?" I ask softly as I look up from the envelope.

She nervously rubs her thighs. "I can't go back in time and make up for the years I lost, and I don't expect you to call me mom. I'm not trying to be a replacement for the mother you lost, but I'd like to try and be your friend." She picks up her glass and takes a drink. I don't bother filling in the silence with comments about how the mother I did have wasn't really one at all because she's right. We can't change the past, and those comments will only give her more reason to abhor my father. Dead or not, I don't want to feel divided. "I know we missed out on so many firsts, but there's also a lot of firsts still to be had. Graduation, marriage... babies. I'd like to be there for them if you let me."

"I think I'd like that, but let's try the friends thing first." I pick up the envelope and try to lighten the heavy by adding, "I thought you were trying to steal my man all summer so..."

She laughs. "I had a feeling you thought that, but it couldn't be helped. I'd be lying if I said I didn't shamelessly try to flirt a few times, but only because of you. I wouldn't have pursued it; believe it or not, Everett Callahan isn't my type."

"Oh yeah, then what is? In this town, Everett Callahan is every woman's type," Mackenzie chimes in just as a loud crack of thunder shakes the ground.

Lauren's lips quirk to the side as she fights back a smile. "The apple must not fall too far from the tree. Cameron likes them older, but I've embraced my cougar era. I prefer inexperience. I enjoy teaching them exactly how I like it."

We all smile wickedly just as Moira's voice echoes across the room. "We're going to need everyone to evacuate to the main building." She barely gets the words out before the tornado sirens blare loudly and chaos ensues as a massive gust of wind blows through the right side of the tent and the entire structure starts to fall.

"Get under the table," Lauren yells, but I'm not quick enough, and searing pain shoots through my head before everything goes black.

CHAPTER 31
EVERETT

It only took five minutes after my driver pulled away from the park for me to fully embrace the error I had made in walking away. I thought I was making the right decision. I thought the pain I felt every time I put one foot in front of the other, leaving her behind, was my own selfish heart battling what it wanted versus what was best. Even my brother's words as I left the parking lot weren't enough for my stubborn ass to move. My mind still hadn't caught up with my heart. That didn't happen until I was driving over the Mississippi to a destination unknown. When I left the gala, it was to go home, but as the miles that separated us grew, so did my fault. There was no home for me to go to if she was not there. She is my home.

Once my mind was made up and I was going back for my girl, I couldn't turn around quick enough. The nearest exit to turn around once you cross over the river into Illinois is five miles, and in the time it took us to change course, the storm that had been brewing was in full force. Rain was pelting the car in sheets, and the driver had no choice but to pull over, unable to see the road in front of him. Now I'm stuck hopelessly on the side of the highway, refreshing my phone every five seconds thinking maybe this time it will load the weather radar so I can see when the eye of the storm will be past us.

"Fucking useless." I pound my fist into the leather seat beside me as I throw my head back against the seat rest. The service right now is shit. My phone won't load past twenty percent. It's why I'm surprised when it vibrates in my hand. Holding my phone up, I see it's a call from an unknown number with a St. Louis area code.

"Everett Callahan," I answer hastily, hoping the call doesn't drop.

"Mr. Callahan, this is Renee at Barnes Jewish. We have you down as the emergency contact for Cameron Salt. There's been an accident, and..." There's silence. I pull the phone away from my ear and see the call says it's still connected.

"Hello. Can you hear me?" I demand as I rake my hand through my hair and my stomach churns. I lean forward and grip the seat back in front of me. "Start driving," I say to my chauffeur.

"She's resting now," comes through as her words trail off again.

"You've got to be fucking kidding me," I mutter to myself. "Can you hear me?" I yell loudly into the phone as if that will strengthen the connection.

"We didn't know about the baby before she was sedated and..."

"The baby! What baby?" I screech before I throw open the back door, giving zero fucks about getting drenched as I walk to the driver's side door, pull it open, and say, "Get out. I'm fucking driving."

The driver's eyes widen. "This is my car."

"Do I look like I give a fuck? Get out," I grind out forcefully.

My hand darts out to pull him out, done with wasting any more seconds when he throws his hands up. "Okay, okay, I'll get in the back."

He climbs out, and I cut the call. I have the name of the hospital. I'll figure out the rest. Going to my contacts, I pull up Connor's number. He was there, maybe he's with her. The call takes forever to connect, and once it finally does, it goes straight to voicemail. "Damn it."

Why the fuck did I leave? How could I be so dumb? I'll never forgive myself if something happens to her or the baby. Baby... I clench my jaw. How is that even possible? She told me she had an IUD. As I pull onto the highway, the rain still hasn't let up. It's nearly zero visibility. I go slow because it's the only option, but slow is better than not at all. There's no way in hell I'm going to sit stranded on the side of the highway knowing my girl is in the hospital with a broken heart, one that's in pieces because of me, while carrying our baby nonetheless. Our baby.

I let that sink in as I try to decipher how it happened. Did she lie to me about having an IUD? It's possible. I know Cameron had a crush on me for years, but what she didn't realize was that the feelings weren't completely one-sided. She could have lied in hopes of trapping me. It's a fucked-up thought, but maybe the better one is, do I care? Did I see myself having more kids this late in life? No, but I want everything with her, including the baby. Her words from dinner echo through my mind, "How could I not want something that's a piece of me and the person I love?"

"Fuck." I need to get to the hospital. I hit my hand on the steering wheel, pissed that I put myself in this position to begin with. If I hadn't left, I wouldn't have been in this position. There's no way she would have gotten hurt. I would have sacrificed myself a hundred times over to ensure it.

An hour later, I'm finally pulling up outside the emergency room. I exit the car without a parting word, unworried about settling up. He has my information, and whatever he saw on my face when I insisted on driving kept him silent the entire way here. I rush to the reception desk.

"Excuse me," I try to grab the brunette's attention.

"I'll be with you in a moment, sir. There's a line in front of you."

That's when I look around and notice the full lobby and nurses walking around with boards assessing injuries and assigning numbers. "I'm here to see a patient that's already been checked in. I'm not here for an injury."

She holds up her hand and answers a call on her hospital phone. Fuck this. I can't stand here and wait. I've been doing that for the past hour, and I'm seconds away from causing a scene of my own. That's when a nurse swiping her card to go back to the rooms catches my eye. I make a quick decision to slip in behind her.

"Sir, you can't go back there," I hear one of the nurses behind the desk call out, but it's too late. The door closes, and I take off down the hall without knowing where I'm going.

A doctor stops me when he sees what's going on. "Hey, you have to be checked in."

"I know, but I need to get to my girl, and it's packed out there."

He nods. "Who are you looking for?"

"Cameron Salt, she was brought in earlier."

He pulls his phone out of his pocket and calls someone using the speakerphone. "Sara, can you tell me what room Cameron Salt is in?" His eyes slowly trail up and down my disgraceful appearance. My suit is wet, and I'm sure my face is marred with stress, but I couldn't care less, especially when I believe it's his pity that's earning me his cooperation now.

"Dr. Montgomery, Ms. Salt has been moved to the fifth floor. She's in room 510."

"Dr. Montgomery... Are you Aria's brother?"

His eyes narrow on mine. "Everett Callahan?"

"Yeah," I answer. I've only met him once, and that was years ago at Holden and Aria's wedding reception.

"There's an elevator at the end of this corridor. Take it up to the fifth floor. When you get off, go right. Her room will be about halfway down the hallway. I'll have a nurse bring you a visitor's pass."

"Thanks," I say, grasping his shoulder before jogging toward the elevators.

When I finally get off the elevator and reach her door, I take a second to compose myself. I have no idea what I'm walking into, and the last thing I need to do is run in panicked and make things worse. I blow out a breath and turn the knob. The steady sound of an EKG machine beeping greets me as I pull back the curtain and see her lying in bed. My fists clench at my sides as my heart pounds heavily in my chest. If she doesn't hate me when she wakes, I'll hate me enough for the both of us. I approach the bed cautiously as though moving wrong could break her. She looks peaceful as she is, and I want her to have that. I don't want her to feel any pain, and waking will undoubtedly cause it. If not physically, then emotionally. I fucked up. My hand gently pushes a few strands of her auburn locks off her face before I let my knuckles drag with a feather-like weight down her side until I reach her delicate hand.

"I'm so sorry, sunshine," I say as I gently lace my fingers through the tops of hers. Why is it that we hurt the people we care about most? Some will say it's because we care too much, that the relationship is worth fighting for, and others will tell you it's because hurt people, hurt people, but I think it's both. I've been hurting for so long. Living with guilt and grief has left me bleeding out on the people I care about, and now I'm paying the ultimate price for it.

My free hand instinctively reaches for her stomach, and my thumb gently strokes over it. "I told you I'd mess up. I warned you that I didn't know what I was doing when it came to love. I just didn't know I'd fuck it up before I got the chance to live it with you." I drop my head to the bed and pray to a God I haven't spoken to in far too long, hoping he answers. "God, if you give me this, I won't mess it up. I'll be whatever she needs me to be. You created her for a purpose, and I think it was to save me." Her fingers twitch, and I instantly raise my head to look at her. Her eyelids flutter like she's trying to open them, but they remain shut. "Wake up, Cameron. Wake up so I can spend the rest of my life making up for this moment." Her hand squeezes mine, and I know she can hear me. "I love you, sunshine. I'm not going anywhere. I swear it..." I trail off, not wanting to push her if she's not ready. I watch as the fluttering behind her eyelids subsides, and I pull up a chair before reclaiming her hand. I'm just settling into my new position when my phone pings. I reach into my coat and pull it out.

Garrett: Where are you?

I'm not texting. Not on this. I immediately hit call.

"Everett, where are you? You need to get to the hospital."

"I'm here. What the hell happened? Are you okay?"

"I'm good. That's why I stayed back. Everything was fine. It was just supposed to be rain, and the tent was event-grade. It had fucking steal-beams. There would have been no issue handling rain. Tornadoes are another story." St. Louis is in tornado alley, and summer storms can turn ugly quick. "Moira had just announced the need to evacuate to the main building when the sirens went off, and a huge gust of wind took out the right side of the tent. I ducked behind the bar with a few other guests. Ten people were taken to the hospital, including Cameron, Moira, Kipp, and Mackenzie."

"Christ!" I pinch the bridge of my nose. I need to find my son.

"I'm covering our asses and documenting everything, making sure none of this comes back on us."

"Moira hired an event planning team. I'll send the contracts over. I was copied on them."

"Ev," Cameron's voice is small and groggy.

"I'll call you back. Cameron's waking up," I say as I cut the call.

"I'm here, baby." I bring her fingers to my lips and kiss each one. "Are you in pain? Do you need me to get a doctor?"

"My head hurts," she groans as she turns her head slightly toward me. "And my neck is stiff."

"I'll see if we can get you some medicine."

Her hand squeezes mine before I can move. "Don't go... please."

"Cameron, I swear to God I'm not going to leave you. Let me

make it better. I'm just going to get you some medicine." The thought of medicine and the fact that maybe she's in pain because they can't give her any more has me closing my eyes. Her free hand slowly starts to move across the bed. "What do you need? Let me get it."

"The remote thingy. We can press the call button for a nurse."

I reach across the bed, careful not to put weight on her body, and press the button. "I'm so sorry, Cameron. I never should have left. I already plan on spending the rest of my life making it up to you, but..." I draw off my hand, finding her stomach.

"You called," a nurse interrupts, walking into the room.

"Yes, she just woke up and said her head hurts and her neck is stiff."

The nurse swipes her badge and pulls open her notes on the computer. "That's typical from the injuries she sustained."

As she clicks through a few different screens, Cameron asks, "Can I take something to help manage the pain?"

"Isn't Tylenol an acceptable pain medication for women expecting?" I ask, ensuring there's no further fuckups. I'll sue for negligence if there are.

"Everett—"

"I know about the baby, Cameron. I'll never forgive myself if something happens because I wasn't there to protect you." My hand reaches for her stomach. "Both of you."

Her hand covers mine before she squeezes it, drawing my eyes to hers. "What baby? Who told you I was pregnant?"

"Our baby. When the doctor called, he said they didn't know you were pregnant before they sedated you and—"

"She wasn't sedated," the nurse interjects, walking to the bed and checking her wristband. "Ms. Salt has a concussion. She's been out since she was brought in, but the fact that she knows who you are is a good sign."

Her eyes return to mine. "Everett, I'm not pregnant. I told you I have an IUD."

SALT

"I'm going to get you some Tylenol and let the doctor know you are awake."

I squeeze my eyes closed and try to piece together how I messed this up. When I received the call, the woman mentioned Cameron by name and said there had been an accident. That's when the connection got bad, and words were lost.

"You thought I was pregnant? Does that mean you thought I lied too?"

"Cameron, that's not important—"

"It is important, Everett. I would never lie to you, especially about that."

"Sunshine, I didn't care if you did. That was the first thought that crossed my mind when I got the call." I run my hand through her hair. "I wanted the baby. I wanted to have that baby with you. You are the forever I don't deserve, the reason I lose sleep, and the reason my heart beats. Your light defeats my darkness, and I'll spend every day fixing what I've broken if you'll let me. You are my reason, Cameron Salt."

"I love you, Ev." I bend down, and my hands cradle her face as I press my forehead to hers, my lips skimming over the tops of hers when she adds, "No more hiding, Ev. If this is it and I'm what you want, I need you to trust me with all your pieces, even the sharp ones."

"Maybe I don't want to cut you?"

"And maybe I want the scar that trusting me with your heart leaves on mine." My lips skim over the tops of hers as a burst of emotions I've never felt tear through my heart. It's a kaleidoscope of bliss, a treasure from the divine. I press my mouth onto hers more firmly, scared to give her more. Her hand fists in my shirt, and she speaks against my lips. "Kiss me like I'm your forever, Everett. I won't break." Her tongue seeks entrance that I instantly grant. Her sweet mouth on mine makes me feel like magic is real; it sweeps me off my feet, and for the seconds I'm wrapped up in her, I'm high above the world in a place where only she and I exist.

I release her mouth, knowing the nurse will be back with her meds, and if I keep kissing her like that, I won't be able to stop. I peck her lips softly as I pull away.

"You really thought I was pregnant?"

"I did. I might be a little disappointed knowing you're not." I pull away, a little nervous to say the words on the tip of my tongue, but she asked me to give her all my pieces, so I do. "What if I asked you to have that IUD removed while you're here?"

Her eyes search mine, and her face is impassive. "Everett, I hit my head hard, and I'm not sure I'm following what you're suggesting. Are you saying you want to have a baby with me?"

"Yes..." I let out on bated breath, unbelieving that I'm having this moment.

"I could go for an Everly."

"Everly?" My brow furrows, and she smiles.

"Yes, Everly. That's the name of the little girl you'll give me."

I smile bigger than I ever have. "I can't promise it will be a girl."

"Well, we'll have to keep trying until we get one."

"Oh, I can get behind the trying part." I bend down to reclaim her mouth once more.

Her smile matches my own as lips press against mine, but before I get a chance to take more, her hand is on my chest, pushing me back. "As much as I love talking about forever and babies, you're skipping ahead about ten steps. Someone once said he didn't want me falling pregnant out of wedlock on his watch—"

"Cameron, I thought it went without saying, but since you need the words, I'll give them to you. I want you to be my wife, the mother of my children, the bearer of my soul."

"Good. Let's start with the promise you made to me a week ago when you asked for time. You told me then that you'd give me everything, and until you do that, we can't move forward. I need something real. I need more than just your dreams. I need the real reason you walked away from me tonight—the one that tears you up inside, the one that scares you."

Fuck, she would ask this of me now, but I suppose I knew it

was coming, and she's right. It's the only way forward. I can't give her all of me if I'm still choosing to hide parts of me. Releasing her hand, I leave her side of the bed and walk toward the window.

"The last time I jumped in and saved a girl, I married her. If you ask Moira, she'll tell you it was the only option. I would have agreed back then, but now that I'm older, I know there's always more than one option. We just tend to choose the ones with the path of least resistance. I didn't want to stand in the way of you choosing a relationship with Lauren. I felt betrayed by my best friend. I've spent the past five years on a crusade to protect an oath I gave him upon his death, one I gave without knowledge of what I was protecting. The inferences Lauren was making were untenable..." I run my fingers through my beard, buying myself precious seconds where she is still mine. All my words about being her forever, keeping her, giving her babies, and making her my wife could be for nothing when I give her my next truth. "Damon was late to the gala the night of his accident because of me." I drop my head as my lungs deflate from the heaviness that keeping that detail to myself held. "I forgot the award to be given that night in my home office. I asked if he could pick it up since I was already at the event. It's my fault he was on the highway when that semi jackknifed. I'm the reason he's gone."

"I wish you would have told me sooner so that I could have loved you through the pain you're going through because it's my pain too." I turn to her. "Dad was still in town because I forgot my overnight bag at the house. I was supposed to leave the gala with Waverley's daughter that night to go camping for the weekend."

My chest tightens with her admission. I would have given her my truth years ago if I knew I could have spared her a second of carrying the burden of guilt I know she's had haunting her every day. I know because it's the same one that claws at the recesses of my mind daily, stealing moments of joy, reminding me that I'm here and he isn't.

"Cameron, it wasn't your fault," I say, reclaiming my spot beside her bed. "You have to know that."

Her eyes drop to where my fingers instinctively wrap around hers. "If it's not my fault, then it's not yours either. If you had asked me at the beginning of summer, I would have said accidents don't happen. They are caused, but I no longer see it that way. Maybe it's coldhearted, but now I think accidents happen for a reason. We don't always see the reason right away, but they're always there. I wouldn't have the things I have now if he were still here holding onto his secrets."

"Oh, I'm sorry. I didn't know you were here. Am I interrupting? I can come back," Lauren says, popping around the curtain.

Lauren's intrusion reminds me there are other people here I need to see, even if I don't want to leave Cameron. As foreign as the thought feels, I'm glad she's here. I was so worried about getting to Cameron and making sure she was okay that I hadn't put too much thought into how she got here or that she was alone when I arrived, though I should have. Cameron wasn't alone when I left her. I don't doubt that Lauren is the reason she's here now.

"No, it's fine. You can stay," Cameron answers before her hand squeezes mine. "Is Moira here? That must have been who the nurse was referring to when they called. I bet she still has you listed as her emergency contact too. People don't think about that stuff when they're healthy."

That has to be what happened. For those few short seconds that felt like they stretched into eternity while the call went silent, the nurse must have started talking about Moira. As much as I don't want to leave Cameron, I must check in with her and Kipp to ensure everything is okay. We may be divorced, but I would never wish her harm. "I'll be back. I need to find Connor too. His phone went straight to voicemail when I tried to call him earlier, but Garrett said they were here."

"I just ran into them downstairs. Mackenzie was getting her ankle wrapped. She's okay. It's just a sprain," Lauren offers from the chair she claimed on the other side of the hospital bed.

Thank god for small miracles. Connor would be beside himself if something happened to Mackenzie. "Okay." I lean down and kiss Cameron's forehead. "I'll be back. I love you."

"I love you too, Ev," she says as I leave her side, and my heart fucking soars. She still loves me, and that's the beginning and the end of everything. As long as I have that, nothing else matters.

CHAPTER 32
CAMERON

L ips trailing down my bare stomach as the blanket shifts, exposing my nipples to the cool air, have me stirring awake right before a tongue licks me straight up my center. "Mmm," I moan as Everett's strong arms wrap around my thighs and pull me closer.

"Good morning, sunshine," he says right before his tongue slips inside of me, melting me at my core. It's been two weeks since the accident and two weeks of him worshipping my body and waiting on me hand and foot. Waking me up like this is one of his favorite love languages. Everett loves physical touch, and living in my RV has only turned touching me into an obsession. One I'm more than okay with. The day I was discharged, I told him I didn't want to go back to his place. I wanted to come here, to my RV, on my property, because the place I was building here felt like home. It felt like ours, and we've been here every day since.

"Ev, you don't have to do this every morning." I'm not complaining, but I feel a little guilty for how this has become my new normal. Upon being discharged, I was given strict instructions to take it easy. When we got home, we laid in bed for hours, talking about everything, and it was during those talks that I divulged my favorite sex is morning sex. I like starting my day with a smile on my face. I love waking up with him wrapped around me and going through my day feeling where he had been. It's a reminder that all of this is real and he's mine.

"Turns out your favorite way to wake up is mine too, but since you mentioned it..." His big hands trail up my thighs, and my stomach tightens. My body feels like clay in a potter's hands, yielding to his every touch, until suddenly they're digging into my sides, and I squeal as he flips us over.

"Everett, what are you doing?" I ask as I brace myself on my forearms. Blowing the hair out of my face, I look down and find his midnight eyes peering up at me from between my thighs.

"You said I don't have to do all the work every morning and you're right." He slaps my right cheek hard. "Ride my face, baby girl."

"Ev, that's not what I meant..."

My argument dies the second I feel his tongue run up my center, and I instinctively grind against it. Both hands grip my ass as his groan reverberates through my body. My hands move to the headboard for better positioning. I'm not fat, but I'm also not a twig. I don't want to smother him. I slowly rock against him as he alternates between running the tip of his tongue down my center and sucking me into his mouth.

"Stop teasing me, sunshine, and sit this pretty pussy on my face."

"Ev, this is hot as fuck," I say, peering down at him between my legs as he deliciously continues to nip and suck. "But I'd rather not suffocate you, and that's a very real possibility since I've never done this."

I'm no stranger to oral but sitting on someone's face is a first. I'm young, and most guys my age are orgasm chasers. They play around down there, never doing it quite right, until getting impatient and going straight for sex, which doesn't always end with you being fully satisfied.

"I couldn't think of a better way to die."

"Everett, I'm serious."

"So am I. This is happening. Especially now that I know I'm your first. Release the headboard and sit up." I wordlessly follow his instructions. Hovering above him, his hand skims up my stomach before cupping my breast and pinching my nipple. The move instantly has me clenching. "The only way I can fill you and give you what you want is if you lower yourself. You can ride my face willingly, or I can tie you up and make you submit. That roof hatch has caught my eye a few times now." My eyes drift to the ceiling and the pull bar on the hatch. I bite my lip hard as images of being tied up flick through my mind. Great, now that's exactly what I want. "Christ, baby. I should have known my girl would want that. We're not doing that today, but if you're a good girl and give this to me now, I'll give you something else."

I roll my lips. I really want to know what something else is. "Fine, but if you ever want me to get on this ride again, you better make it one I'll never forget."

He bites my inner thigh, and I gasp. "Challenge fucking accepted. Now put this pussy in my mouth."

Fuck. I love it when he talks dirty to me. This is the unhinged side of the man behind the suit. The one that comes out to play when he wants to fuck. He's been gentle with me since the accident, nothing but vanilla sex, too scared to risk anything more; but I know he craves more, especially now that he knows I like it rough. I lean on my palms rather than reaching for the headboard, knowing the angle will spread me wider and I'll feel him deeper.

"Fuck yeah," he hisses before he dives in, and I know I'm in for it. Every time I tell Everett something sexual is a first for me, he gets feral. He's definitely going to go hard.

His tongue spears me as his pinky slips to my tight hole, and I try to relax. I can't help but clench a little when the tip slides in, but the second his teeth nip my bundle of nerves and my thoughts are diverted, he's all the way in. "Yes," I moan as I grind down hard, and he pushes back on my thrust. I'm so turned on. My hand reaches back further, and I grab his hard length. "Mmm, I want this Ev." I stroke him from root to tip, and he groans before sucking my clit into his mouth, and I detonate. His tongue laps up my juices as I rock out the aftershocks of my orgasm. Strong arms grip my hips before he places a kiss on each inner thigh and pulls away. I let myself fall forward, completely spent until I hear the drawer on his side of the dresser open. "What's that?" I watch as he pulls out a little box.

He removes the lid but doesn't show me. "Ass up," he commands as he smacks my cheek.

I pull my knees up and do as I'm told, knowing I want whatever he gives me, but I still ask, "Are you going to tell me what was in the box?"

"You'll find out soon enough," he says as cool metal glides between my cheeks. He runs it through my wet lips, teasing my entrance with its tip before dragging it back up to my puckered hole. "You like it when I play here..." He lets the words hang between us, then, slowly adding pressure, he adds, "Are you ready for more?"

"You got me a plug?" I question nervously. Do I like it when he plays there? Hell yes, but his fingers are a lot smaller than a plug.

"You didn't answer the question, Cameron."

He used my name. That means he's serious about this and I need to answer. "Yes, I want more. I want more with you." It's honest. I trust him. I know he wouldn't do anything to hurt me.

"Good answer, sunshine." I feel the metal slide back down to my pussy where he teases my entrance before pushing it inside of my pussy. "See how big it is..." He pumps it inside of me a few times. "You can take it." Just as I'm relaxing into the sensation of having the plug inside of me, he pulls it out and drags it back toward my tight hole. "Relax, sunshine," he says as he slowly inserts the plug. My body instantly tries to push it out until two fingers slide inside of my pussy, and the sensation steals my focus away from the intrusion. "That's it, baby, you're so fucking sexy. I wish you could see how you look with this ass in the air for me." His words of praise, coupled with his fingers and the plug, have me on the brink of coming again. I'm just cresting the hill when he removes his fingers. I groan my displeasure, and he slaps my ass. "Get dressed. I'm going to make breakfast."

"What?" I question, flipping onto my back when I hear the band of his boxer briefs snap around his waist. "Shit," I hiss when I feel the plug is still inside of me. "You left it in!"

"You said you like morning sex because you enjoy feeling where I've been. Well, today, you get to feel where I will be tonight." Why do I find his cockiness sexy as fuck? As he struts out of the bedroom in nothing but his black boxer briefs, I admire his tight ass and defined back. A back that I had really hoped to dig my nails into before work. "Do you want eggs for breakfast?"

"You don't have to make me breakfast. I can grab a granola bar, and you can come back to bed."

"Not going to happen," he calls out before asking, "Toast or English muffin?"

"Why am I complaining?" I mutter to myself before saying, "Toast, please."

I'm stretching like a Cheshire Cat, getting used to the sensation of being full without him being inside of me, when he says, "I'm going to stop by the house and grab some more clothes. Do you want me to pick up anything while I'm there?"

"If you can wait until tomorrow, I'll go with you."

He peeks around the corner. "Are you sure?"

I pull a blanket around me and climb out of bed to meet him. "Yes, I'm sure. I said I'd like to stay here from now on, but it didn't mean I never wanted to go back. Staying there doesn't bother me. I just prefer to stay here." I watch the muscles in his back flex as he whips the eggs, and I add, "I know it's cramped here. We can stay at your house on the weekends if we want. Living in an RV isn't ideal, but when I pulled the trigger on all of this, I didn't exactly see it playing out this way..." I trail off, looking down at the table. The last thing I ever expected was for Everett to come live with me in it.

He abandons the bowl and turns around. "Baby, I'd live with you in a cardboard box. I just don't prefer it," he tosses my words back at me before finishing his task. "Believe it or not, I actually like it here. I built that house for Moira. She used to clip things out of magazines that she liked and paste them into a journal. Once I made enough money, I brought her clippings to life. I never needed anything that big. I'll admit the closet thing is a small issue." I can't help but laugh. I might be the one getting a degree in fashion, but Everett likes to dress nicely. His shoe collection rivals my own, and don't even get me started on his suits. "What?" He glances back with a crooked smile.

"I'll see if we can't change the floor plans to accommodate a bigger walk-in closet."

"I may have already spoken with Mackenzie about that."

"What do you mean you already spoke to Mackenzie about a bigger closet?" I question, somewhat taken aback.

"Well, I needed an office, and the house you were building only had one, so while I was reviewing the plans to add another office, I made a few slight changes."

"Everett," I stand out of my chair, and I'm reminded of the plug that's still inside of me, but it doesn't lessen my annoyance. I'm peeved that he took those liberties without me.

"Are you mad?" He turns, his brow furrowed in disbelief.

"Yeah, a little. Not because I don't want you living here but because you didn't include me."

His eyes close, and I know he understands. We aren't married. It's technically my name on all the loans and paperwork. The only reason he was able to pull weight and make changes is because the designer is his daughter-in-law and my best friend. He knows this is my project, something I've been working on every day. We might be talking about forever, and he may have plans to propose, but we aren't even there yet, and he's cutting me out.

"Cameron, I'm sorry. I didn't even think of it like that. I'm used to getting things done. Mackenzie was in the office at the stadium with Connor and had the floor plans pulled up. I make calls like that every day on the fly for work. I'm not used to having a partner that wants to do everything with me." He crosses the trailer and pulls me into his arms. "I'm going to mess up. I messed up. Please forgive me."

I know his words are true. I witnessed the marriage he had with Moira. It was cohabitation. They collaborated on the charity and Connor, but with everything else, they had their roles. She stayed in her lane, and he stayed in his.

"I forgive you," I say as I hold him around the waist. "But why do we need two offices? You just said you liked how this trailer is small. I'm not building another mini-mansion."

"I assumed you'd want your own office for designing, and since I plan on working from home more often, I needed a separate space where I could have meetings and—"

"You're going to work from home?" I pull back and look into his eyes. Technically, Everett has always worked from home, but it was after he had already put in a ten-hour day at the office. It's not like he worked in his home office all day.

"I want to be here with you. I no longer want to live to work." His eyebrows rise. "Technically, I don't need to work. I could step away, but I don't know who I am without the law firm. It's part of my identity, one I'm not ready to give up, but I do want to take a step back. I want to be present in this life I'm building with you." His lips press against my forehead. "The universe always has a plan, and for me, it was you. I love you, Cameron Salt." He smacks my ass, causing heat to spark low in my belly as I clench around the plug. The wicked grin cresting across his mouth tells me he knew that would happen. He bites his juicy bottom lip before adding, "Now get ready. It's the last day, and I don't want to be late."

I smile as I watch him walk back toward the eggs and take a second to collect a moment, the first one in this new reality where we fall into step doing the mundane tasks of cooking breakfast, getting ready for work, and loving each other out loud without reservation.

When he realizes I haven't moved, he looks over his shoulder. "What are you doing? Why are you just standing there?"

"Just admiring the man I love," I say as I make my way toward the bedroom, only to pause when I get to the hallway. "Don't forget the ketchup."

∼

"You're here," Stormy says, somewhat shocked when she sees me behind the counter in the team shop.

"I am. I'm not working today. I'll be out there watching the game. Reece is working."

"Yeah, I know. I'm working the first half of the game with her," she says before hopping onto the counter to sit. "Are we still surprising Everett with a party at Connor's after the game?"

"Yes," I say as I press print on the report I was working on. I wanted to see what items sold the best this season to identify trends. Did they sell because they were cheaper? Were there sales that helped push the product, etc.? The data will help me in my new venture and aid me in getting Connor set up for next season. "Did Parker mention if Moira and Kipp were still coming to the party tonight?"

After Everett knew I was okay, he searched for Moira, knowing she was hurt when the tent collapsed. Kipp was knocked unconscious when he pushed Moira out of the way of a falling beam. She tripped on the dress she was wearing and took a hit to the head, but it didn't render her unconscious. However, when she sat up, she found Kipp lying beside her, out cold. He didn't clear the beam, and his right leg was caught beneath it.

Apparently, she had a severe panic attack, her mind immediately believing he was dead. She couldn't form sentences because she was in complete hysterics, nor could she walk. The paramedic on the scene was young and gave her morphine, believing she was in shock from pain. That's the part Everett heard when the nurse called. She's doing fine, and the baby is safe. The doctors said the amount she received wasn't enough to cause any long-term effects, but she was already taking it easy before all of that happened. Now, between her high-risk pregnancy and Kipp's injury, they don't leave the house.

"They are both going to try and make it. With Parker and I moving to the West Coast at the end of the month, they want to soak up all the family time. However, I know she let Evan move in two days ago. So, depending on how that's going, they could be a no-show."

"Really? They let Evan move in?"

Everett told me his story and the truth about who his father is. I was shocked to learn all that and felt bad for him. We don't get to choose our parents. I was trying to convince Everett to let him stay at his house since we were living in the RV, but then he told me why Evan had my dad's book. Apparently, he was planning to use it to blackmail Everett if he didn't help him. Everett's done nothing but show him kindness even when it was the last thing he deserved. That move sealed his fate. Evan had already crossed lines with Connor, but Everett continued to give him grace. This time, he went too far. So now he's at Moira's.

"I understand why she's helping him. He's her nephew, but he's old enough to know better, and unfortunately, from what I've seen and the things Parker has shared with me, I think he's one of those people who will never get it until he's forced to. Handouts are only helping him remain the same because he takes them for granted, believing they will always be there. I think the only kind of love that can help him is tough love, but..." She raises her hands. "Not my circus."

I grab my papers off the printer and shove them in my bag. I agree with everything Stormy has said, but she doesn't know the root of Evan's problems, and it's not my place to share, so I change the subject. "I still can't believe Parker got an offer, and not just for a feeder team. He's going to be playing for San Diego," I squeal in excitement.

"Yeah, we're going to stay with his cousin who lives there until my tiny house is ready. We've already found some great parks we want to stay at."

One of the things I love most about Parker is that he's a simple man. He's signing a contract next week that would more than allow him to afford a number of nice houses, but he doesn't want them. He wants to live the nomad lifestyle with Stormy. My only hope is that celebrity doesn't change him.

"Well, you know you always have a place to park here."

"I'll probably be taking you up on that when we come home for Christmas."

A hand pounding on the doorframe steals our attention. "It's go time! Operation create-a-distraction-for-Everett has commenced," Mackenzie says before adding, "Come on, come on, let's go."

I snatch my bag off the counter as Stormy slides off. "Wait, I thought you already gave Connor everything he needed to hand out to the team for the game."

She jiggles a bag at me. "No, they just delivered."

"How much time do we need?" I say as I follow Mackenzie down the breezeway.

"I don't know... twenty, thirty minutes. I guess it depends on if they're dressed yet." I roll my lips as I think of a plan. "Is that going to be a problem?"

I smile big. "Nope. Just make sure Connor has no reason to come upstairs for that time." I shoot off a quick text.

> Cameron: Can you meet me in the office?

> Everett: I'm with the team.

> Cameron: I know. I wouldn't ask if it wasn't important.

I know he'll come, but to ensure it sooner than later. I hit below the belt.

> Cameron: Never mind, I just saw Nash. I'll get him to help me.

> Everett: I'd rather not go to jail today, Cameron.

Everett: I'm on my way.

"Shit, he's on his way. Go," I say as I take off toward the office.

~

H e must have lied when he said he was on his way because, while I may have run up the stairs, it shouldn't take him this long to get to the office from the locker room. I consider sending him another text, but I left my phone across the room, and I'm already in position. I have no doubt that if I walk over to grab it off the table by the window, he'll walk through that door, and I don't want him to see any view other than the one I currently have set up. It's fucking hot, and he'll be in the doghouse, no questions asked, if he leaves me hanging as he did this morning.

The door opens, and he curses, "Fucking hell," before I hear the door slam shut and the lock turn. Got him. "Cameron, what the hell? What if someone else walked in and saw this?" I'm currently bent over his desk wearing nothing but blue heels, his Bulldogs jersey, and the plug he put in my ass this morning.

I don't break character. "But no one else did walk in. You did."

His hands skim up my cheeks. "You were going to let Nash help you with this?" he questions as he presses his fully clothed, hardening length against my ass. The sensation renders me speechless. Having this plug inside of me all morning has left me thoroughly aroused. I'm so worked up that I'm certain I could come from his dirty talk alone. He runs a thick digit through my slick core when I don't respond. "Answer me, sunshine."

"Ev, we both know there's no one else. I can't wait until tonight—"

His finger dips inside of me, and I'm instantly done talking. I need him. I need him to make me come. "I don't have time for this. I want to take my time with you and this," he says, twisting the plug, "takes time. The game starts in an hour." I can hear the ache in his voice. "And I'm not prepared to take you this way. I don't have—"

"This," I say, flipping the lid on a bottle of lube.

He presses into me again with a groan. "You're seriously trying to kill me. Wearing my fucking jersey nonetheless."

"Please, Ev," I beg as I push my ass into his groin.

"Cameron..." His hands glide over my hips.

"If you say no, I'll be forced to take care of myself on top of your desk."

I hear his belt loosen. "The fuck you will. You're mine. Your pleasure belongs to me." Without warning, his tip is at my entrance, and he shoves in hard. We both moan as his cock twitches deep. Weeks of vanilla don't compare to this angle. My thighs pressed into his desk, his weight at my back, his length fully seated, hitting the spot only he ever has. After he collects himself, he slams in hard again, pulling back teasingly slow. "My god, you're so fucking sexy." He twists the plug and pumps in hard. "Knowing I'm hitting that spot does things to me, sunshine. Do you feel it?"

"I feel you, Ev, and I want it." My hand reaches back to his thigh, where I squeeze. "I want this with you." I had my IUD taken out. The doctor suggested we abstain from sex for a week to avoid getting pregnant. Everett was gentle with me, only giving me oral sex for two days, scared I'd be sore from the procedure even though I told him I wasn't before he decided he couldn't take it anymore. I didn't make it easy on him either, wearing sexy lingerie to bed every night to taunt him, in hopes of getting him to cave. The vanilla sex we've been having since the accident is everything, but this angle puts him deep. He feels my cervix, and I know he wants to coat it. "You won't hurt me. I'm good, Ev. I promise."

His hands grip my hips, and he pumps me long and slow. "You want me to put a baby inside of you?"

"I'm already going to love you for the rest of my life. I'll love all the pieces of you."

His hands glide up my back before his lips kiss my shoulder. "You are the most beautiful gift I never saw coming. I want everything with you, Cameron Salt. But I'm selfish. I want you all to myself a little longer." He thrusts into me one more time before saying, "Hand me the lube, sunshine." He's still buried deep when he slowly pulls the plug out, and his index finger rims my tight hole. "You sure you still want me here?" When I subtly nod my agreement, he slips out and brings his tip to the place no man has ever been. I can't help but tense from the sensation. His hands glide up my sides under his jersey, and he cups my breasts. Bringing his lips to my ear, he whispers, "Relax, if it's too much, we stop. You're in control here." Those words were the right ones. I instantly relax into his touch. His fingers pinch my nipples before he releases my breasts, letting them fall back to the smooth surface of the desk. I hear the click of the lubricant lid before I feel oil drip between my cheeks. His thick tip drags between my cheeks, spreading the oil and coating his cock before coming back to my entrance. "This ass you've teased me with for years is mine." He dips inside of my pussy, and I instantly clench around him, my body begging for release. "So greedy," he growls, pushing in deep.

"Mmm," I moan as my hands grip the edge of the desk.

"Say it, sunshine. Say it's mine."

When I hesitate, he pulls out and slaps my pussy, and fuck if I don't need more. "It's yours, Ev."

"Only mine," he states as if I need a reminder after I teased him earlier. I instinctively tense up when he spreads my cheeks and slowly starts to push in. "Reach back and play with this pretty pussy." Snaking my hand between my thighs, I start rubbing slow circles over my bundle of nerves, and as I do, I feel myself relax, and what felt like an intrusion starts to feel pleasantly full. "You're doing so good, baby. So fucking good."

"More, Ev," I beg, desperate to have him like this. "You don't have to go slow. You won't hurt me." I know he's been scared to lose himself because of the hit I took to my head, but I want him to. I need him to.

"Fuck, sunshine. Do you know how hot it is listening to you beg for my cock?" I feel him fully seat himself, his thighs butting against mine before he says, "My god, don't move." He drapes himself over my back and kisses my neck, his breath heavy as he composes himself. "So, damn perfect." His short, ragged breaths against my neck make my skin pebble, and my nipples tighten with need. The hand he has on my breast notices, and he tweaks the hardened peak before saying, "I love how your body responds to me." He nips my ear before slowly retreating, running his hands down my waist, and digging his fingers into my hips just the way I like. "My god, I wish you could see how perfect you look wearing my jersey with my dick disappearing inside this tight ass." He slowly starts to increase his pace, his words loosening me.

I'm high off the way he's losing himself and how I'm the one that's making him feel good. I already know having sex in his office was a first for him, so I'm certain this is, too. His grunts and low moans of ecstasy as he slowly thrusts into me have me on edge. I move my fingers from my clit to my entrance and insert two.

"Oh god," I moan, not expecting it to be so good.

My words spur him on, and he picks up the pace. "That's it. Pump your pussy, baby."

His words have me pushing back on him. I love the unhinged side of him. The side that let's go and trusts me with his heart. I love knowing that I own his pleasure as much as he owns mine. "You want more?"

"Yes, Ev. I want everything." I hear him let out a groan.

"Fuck, I'm going to come." Slowing his thrusts, he reaches around and removes my hand to replace it with his own before saying, "Come with me." His groans and pants already had me on edge, but his words send me over. He feels the second my orgasm hits and holds in deep, finding his own release before falling on top of me. With ragged breaths, he says, "I love you, Cameron Salt. I love you with everything that I am."

"What if we don't win? I didn't even think about that."

"Don't say that," Mackenzie and I say in unison as Stormy threatens to jinx the game with her bad juju. The Bulldogs are taking their last at-bat for the season. We have a man on second and one on third, with two outs. If we don't show up now, that's the game since the Sharks are ahead by one.

"The one thing about this year's team is they perform well under pressure. They all want to go out with a win," I say as I drink my beer and try to calm my nerves. The first batter comes up, and it's Deke. We'd hoped to have a solid lead when Connor and I planned this all out, but maybe a little fun is what they need to swing for the fences this inning and bring home a win, so I call out, "Show 'em those socks, Deke."

Everett's standing at the top of the dugout, his jersey stretching over his biceps and clinging to his back in all the right places, but his fit physique is no match for those molten eyes that turn toward me with an assessing glare, narrowing as he scans my body from head to toe before tracking back to Deke at the plate, raising his pants and sporting socks with pictures of Everett running. Deke's move triggers our players on second and third to do the same. Each pair of socks has different images of Everett working out.

All season, he trained with the team. Harder if you ask me, considering he always started his routine before they arrived. In the beginning, it was to earn their respect and prove he wasn't just a fill-in who wasn't invested in seeing to it that the team had a good season. Game after game, the team saw his dedication, and what started out as respect morphed into something deeper, a reverence, a level of admiration for giving it his all when others may not have. Tongue in cheek, he drops his head, but his smile can't be hidden. From here, I can see it pulling at the corners of his perfect mouth. Connor clasps his shoulders as the guys in the dugout pull up their socks and smack his back.

My eyes are so keenly zeroed in on Everett and watching him have his moment that I miss the pitch, but I don't miss the sound of the bat connecting with the ball as Deke slams one into right field. The right fielder dives to catch the ball and misses it by a foot, and the stadium goes crazy as we close out the season with a nail-biting win.

Mackenzie and Stormy jump up and down and hug as I make a beeline for the field with one target. My man.

When I reach the field, the guys are still huddled around him, chanting, whooping, and hollering, but that doesn't stop him from feeling me. His midnight eyes connect with mine, he starts pushing through the team, and I take off running. He catches me in his arms and twirls me around.

"I like what you're wearing," he breathes against my neck.

I pull back, slap his hat, and say, "Your girl, your jersey." He gives me the biggest boyish smile and I know without a doubt my words, coupled with my grand gesture of running out to him on the field, made his heart swim. "Nothing like closing out the season with a win, two major league contracts, and three farm team drafts. Tell me, Coach, did the season go as planned? Did you know your team would be number one?"

"This season was nothing I could have planned for because I never saw it coming. It was nothing I wanted and somehow everything I needed."

"Is that so?" I wrap my hands around his neck. "You doubted your ability to read a game you love, manage personalities, and change lives? Game part aside, it's what you do as a lawyer too."

He sets me down. "Maybe I'm not saying it correctly. All season, my goal was to change them, help them grow into their full potential, show them their weaknesses so that they could harness their strength. That was planned. It's the incidentals I didn't see coming, that I could never have planned for..." His thumb brushes over my cheek. "Ones like you. You were the absolute last thing I wanted. I hated myself for wanting you, and fuck if you weren't dead set on making my life hell, but hell is exactly what I needed. I had to walk through its fire and test my strength, only then would I know if I was worthy of standing at your side. All season I thought I was changing them, but it was the summer that changed me."

My hand covers the one he has rested on my face. "Change is good, Ev. I liked the old you, but I'm madly in love with the one that's standing before me now."

He leans down and pulls me tight against his front. "I'm glad." He kisses my forehead. "I would much rather be in love with you than the idea of you," he says against my mouth before his lips run away with mine, and the lines that separate where he stops and I begin dissolve, blurring us into a perfect forever.

CHAPTER 33

EVERETT

6 MONTHS LATER

"Shit," I hiss when I burn myself on the pan. I never fucking burn myself cooking. I suck the sting out of my forefinger before reclaiming the wooden spoon to scrape the bottom of the pan. I know why it happened, I'm nervous as hell. Tonight is a big night. Cameron graduated this afternoon, and rather than go out, she wanted to stay in. It threw a wrench in the plans I had until she insisted on cooking dinner. That's when I made her a deal. If we were going to stay in rather than going out and celebrating her achievements because, to be fair, there are more than one, I would at least be the one cooking the meal.

She didn't easily relent, which I didn't understand. But that's how I ended up cooking alone in the kitchen while she whips up a dessert downstairs. Apparently, cooking for me tonight was a big deal because she had a new recipe she learned. So we met in the middle and agreed I would cook dinner, and she would make dessert. I'm unsure why we can't share the kitchen upstairs, but I digress.

Cameron is excited about getting into the house early. We weren't supposed to be in the house until February, but with her approval and extra money thrown at the contractors, she allowed me to flex my pull and expedite the construction phase. Last week, we moved out of the RV and into our new home on Salt Lake. Interior work still needs to be completed. The built-ins in my office still need to be installed and trimmed out, and the two spare bedrooms on the first floor need lighting fixtures and crown molding. Cameron's been working closely with Mackenzie on that side of the house since her office is in that wing also. But décor and finishing touches aside, we are in, and I think that's partly why she is downstairs now. She's eager to use everything and start collecting moments.

"Ev, is dinner almost ready?" she calls up from the basement.

"It will be ready in ten minutes, but you're welcome to join me now. I have a margarita waiting for you."

"I'll be up in five minutes," she answers before I hear her footsteps pad back down the steps.

She built a ranch-style, and the square footage compared to my last house is a downgrade. My house was ten thousand square feet. The one she built here is a little over four thousand. The size doesn't bother me. People live happily in less, but when it came to the basement, I convinced her to put in a bar with a full kitchen. It's just the two of us for now, but it won't stay that way forever. She went off birth control months ago, and while we're not trying to get pregnant, we're also not preventing it either. I know she'll want that space for entertaining, and I could see Cameron using that space as a casita of sorts for Lauren if and when we do have children.

The two of them have become inseparable. It wasn't immediate, and I was somewhat to blame for that. It took me a little while to warm up to Lauren, but it couldn't be helped. We already had a tumultuous past before I found out she was the woman Damon had been warning me about with his dying breath, but after reading his journal, I was able to piece together what happened, and I think the truth was worse than the lie. Damon did love Lauren, and it was that love that ultimately destroyed everything.

Damon couldn't stop thinking about Lauren after the night they shared at the Busch wedding. He stalked her from a distance, all the while trying to figure out how to outsmart Amelia, who had ensured she had evidence of the infidelity so that she could take half of everything if he divorced her. Damon was determined to make sure she didn't get away with it, especially since it was she who trapped him from the beginning, knowing all along that Kelce wasn't his. During that time of digging up evidence against her, he learned Lauren was pregnant. He knew without a doubt it was his. Her due date aligned with the time they hooked up. He waited for months for her to call. In the journal, he shared his innermost thoughts about how he battled, believing she was scared to tell him because he was married and choosing to stay with Amelia versus intentionally hiding it until she could use Cameron's DNA to extort him. Neither was necessarily good.

That was the crux of his pain. He thought Lauren saw his heart, but when the pregnancy carried on month after month in secret, he lost his faith in what they shared, ultimately believing her to be an opportunist just like Amelia. It's why he stole Cameron. His journal never mentioned how he pulled off his feat in getting her out of the hospital, nor did it discuss what happened once he brought her home. Cameron and I think maybe there's another journal waiting to be found in the collection she has in storage, but at the end of the day, to her, it didn't matter. She couldn't change the past. She could only move forward, but his why brought her some comfort. His truths weren't easy to consume. I know they broke me as much as they healed me.

"What are you making me?" she says as I finish putting away the unused ingredients.

"Your favorite."

She gives me a coy smile as she approaches the island to peer into the pan. "Marry Me Chicken?"

"Yes." My hands instantly wrap around her waist as I pull her flush against my front and kiss her neck. "I'm so proud of you, sunshine."

"You said that a time or two today." Her hand reaches up to run her fingers through my hair. I squeeze her tighter, loving the way she feels in my arms. She was meant for me to hold, meant to be mine. We fit together perfectly. "Ev, if you keep kissing my neck like that, we'll likely burn the dinner."

"Wouldn't be the first time," I say as my hand squeezes her breast and I slowly lose myself in her.

She lets me nip and suck until she feels me start to stiffen against her back. "Ev, there's time for that later. I'm actually hungry, plus, I'm excited to share my dessert. It's edible. I swear."

I groan and reluctantly release her, swatting her ass. "Go back to your side of the island so I can finish this dinner." The direction my head was going would have derailed my plans for the evening anyway.

"Seriously, we did that on the way to my graduation. You're insatiable."

"It couldn't be helped, that cap and gown was equivalent to a schoolgirl outfit..." I pause to take a drink of my cognac before adding, "And you're one to talk. I may have initiated backseat sex, but I didn't hear you saying no."

She rolls her eyes as she absentmindedly runs her fingers over the condensation on the margarita I made her, which doesn't help the situation in my pants. It only makes me want to tread across the island and correct her, knowing how much she likes it when I'm rough, but I don't because I know I want something else more: her.

"If you want to eat your dinner, you better keep your insolence in check before I bend you over this counter—" The doorbell rings, and I set down the wooden spoon.

"I'll get it, you're cooking." She's exiting the kitchen before I can refute. I turn around and stir the dinner, knowing exactly who's at the front door. My palms get sweaty, and I take a drink of my cognac, but it does nothing to settle my nerves or help me figure out my next move. I am not this guy. Of all the things I am good at, things I'm known for, sureness is one of them. Confidence has always been second nature for me; you plant your feet and stand firm. But that's only true if you're standing on the ground, and I am not. Cameron Salt is a tidal wave, wild and untamable. Her love carried me out to sea; it's depth enough to make even the ocean envious. "It's not my birthday."

"I'm sorry," I say as I turn from the stove and find her placing the two dozen roses I bought onto the island.

"You only get me roses on my birthday." She inhales their sweet scent before pushing them into the center for display.

"I didn't know you only liked getting them on your birthday. I assumed you loved them year-round since you walk around smelling like one."

Her lips curl up into a half smile. "Roses aren't my favorite flower. I'm not sure I have a favorite... If I did, I think it would be a sunflower; even on rainy days, they're still sunflowers." She runs her index finger along the granite. "I smell like roses because of you."

"Because of me?"

"Yes, the first year we moved here from Boston, Dad threw a big party to try and lessen the blow of moving across the country, changing schools, and making new friends. I wouldn't call the birthday a success by any means. He basically invited all his friends, including you, and you brought me roses. Everyone else brought gifts befitting an eight-year-old, but you brought me roses." She shrugs. "It stuck with me, kind of like the man. You bought me roses for every birthday since, and if roses made you think of me, I was going to ensure I smelled like one too. If you looked at a rose or smelled its decadent scent, I wanted you to think of me."

And here I thought all these years she was partial to roses because they matched her red hair. I reclaim my cognac. "You've been thinking about me since you were eight years old?"

"Yes, but not like that. My not-so-innocent thoughts didn't

start until high school. I already noticed you, but it was then that my stomach would twist into knots every time I knew I might see you, and I'd get nervous about picking my outfits because I wanted you to see me differently. I don't think I need to explain further the lengths I went to ensure you looked my way," she says with a sly smile.

The summer she moved into my house, I remember coming in the house fuming after I went outside to grab a drink from the pool bar and found her lounging on her stomach beside the pool, wearing one of her infamous thong bikinis. I was slamming cabinets in the kitchen when I laid into Moira about how inappropriate it was. My then-wife had to talk me off the ledge, explaining that it's not as unusual as I was making it to be; while her bathing suits weren't typical Midwest swimwear, they were completely acceptable choices elsewhere. I hated them then, but I love to hate them now. Only because she looks sexy as hell wearing one, and what's on display is now all mine and only mine. Mine... it's that last thought that has me stumbling into an important segue.

"Cameron, I have something—"

An alarm on her phone goes off. "Hold that thought. I'll be right back," she says before taking off toward the stairs.

The ring in my pocket feels like it might burn a hole through the material every second I don't ask the question that's been on the tip of my tongue for weeks. I've known since the first time I made her this damn dinner that this is what I wanted. Hell, I knew before that. I just didn't allow myself to dream things I believed could never be. Now that it's here, everything feels surreal, like I've been living in some alternate reality and reaching for the stars has the potential to tear everything away. If I ask this of her, there's a good chance I'll wake up, and all of this will have been a dream.

I've gone over the words I'd give her when I asked her for forever a thousand times, but now that I'm in this moment, I can't remember any of them, and getting down on one knee feels insincere. That's what everyone does. Running my hands through my hair, I look around the kitchen and think quick, pulling open cabinets to try and find something. What, I'm not sure, maybe a prop that says I put thought into this when my words threaten to fail me. That's when the chaffing dishes Lauren brought over for the party tomorrow catch my eye.

"Perfect." I grab two plates, hurriedly place the ring on one, and cover it before she comes back upstairs. Then I hastily return to the stove and make her a plate of chicken on the other. I'll serve her the ring and then the chicken. I'm just placing the covered chicken next to the dish concealing her ring when she returns. "Just in time. Dinner is ready."

Her eyes flash to the covered plates before they latch onto mine, and for a second, it feels like she sees everything. Those crystal blue eyes already see straight through to my soul. Right now, they feel like they can see exactly what's beneath this chaffing lid too. Her tongue darts out and moistens her lip, and I see her nerves. *She doesn't know. She can't know.* Fucking relax, I remind myself. That's when her thumb anxiously tapping the lid on her own dish catches my attention. It's the dessert that has her rattled.

"Sunshine, are you seriously that nervous about me trying your dessert?" I tease in an attempt to settle my own nerves. Her brow furrows before her eyebrows rise. She may have been looking at me, but she wasn't seeing me. Her thoughts were a million miles away. "What's wrong?"

"Nothing is wrong." She shakes her head. "I just spaced out for a second, that's all. I've had a lot on my mind between work, school, and the house. At least the school part is off my plate."

"Have a drink." I grab the margarita I made and place it in front of her. "Relax. We're in the house. There's no rush to get anything done, and if there is, let me handle it. Isn't that what we're supposed to do? Share the load. I don't expect you to run your own business and come home and manage the house too."

"I don't want to hire people to cook my dinner and clean my

house. My parents did that, and I don't want anything that resembles it. I enjoy cooking meals with you, and maybe one day I'll tire of doing your laundry, but not right now. For now, I enjoy it. I like taking care of you, putting your things away in a way I know brings you joy..." Her eyes leave mine. "I don't need some housecleaner making you happy when she organizes your tie drawer."

I can't help but bark out a laugh. "Are you serious? You sound jealous, and that's the last thing you should ever be." When she doesn't spare me a glance, I know that she is. Cameron is not this girl. She oozes confidence. I would have expected this before we officially became a couple, but not now. I should have given her this ring sooner. Perhaps that's where this insecurity is coming from. Asking her to have my babies but not putting a rock on her hand is backward. I know this, but I continue to try and do what I believe is best instead of what I feel in my heart. Allowing her to graduate with her surname, giving our relationship time to marinate and flourish without a title that she couldn't easily walk away from felt like what should be done. It doesn't mean it's what I wanted, but old habits die hard. I'm still determined to protect her at the expense of my heart, and that will never change, but it would appear, once again, in my pursuit to safeguard her heart, I've inadvertently wounded it.

"I'm not..." She fiddles with the handle on the lid covering her dessert, giving herself away. "I'm just hungry." She waves her hand and starts toward the dishes, intent on plating her own, making me awkwardly careen in front of her. "Ev, what are you doing?"

"Sit, I want to serve you, is all."

She crosses her arms. "Seriously?"

"Humor me." I smile.

"Fine." She sighs as she pulls out a stool at the island, and I slide the plate with the ring in front of her. "This better be good. Last time you made this recipe, you used different tomatoes, and it wasn't as good..." Her words die off as she pulls off the lid, revealing a pear-shaped engagement ring set inside a blue velveteen box. She sets down the lid, and her hands cup her mouth. "Ev, really? Is this happening?"

I'm instantly at her side, spinning the stool so that her eyes are on mine. "It's happening. I feel like I've waited a lifetime for this moment..." I trail off, my nerves getting the best of me because, while I may have been married before, I never proposed to Moira. Giving her my last name was the only option. It had to be done, so we did it. I didn't choose her, not in the way I'm choosing Cameron now. "I wasted a lot of time pushing you away because I didn't understand love. I thought it looked different. You and I on paper don't make sense. You're my best friend's daughter. I'm old enough to be your father—"

"Everett." She sighs, dropping her head.

I lift her chin. "Let me finish... You were off-limits, a dream I thought I had no business dreaming, but that was because I didn't see it for what it was. It was always love, Cameron. Our love isn't a storybook, but that is because no love has the same beginning or end. It overcomes obstacles and fights when you have no fight left. Love isn't always easy. It's work, but it holds on and endures. Our love won't always be perfect. I've messed up, and I know I'll mess up again, but my heart belongs to you. I am yours, Cameron Salt. I just need to know if you'll take my heart and let me love you forever."

Her baby blues are filled with unshed tears before she rapidly blinks and they spill down her pretty face. "Yes, Everett Callahan, I'll take your heart. I've never wanted anything more."

My lips crash to hers, and the world around us dissolves. I'm no longer walking through this life alone. I'm no longer the guy in the corner watching my heart live a beautiful life without me. I'm her guy, and she's my girl. The sound of her stomach rumbling has me releasing her perfect mouth.

"I'm sorry. I was selfish. I should have fed you first."

"Proposing to me is not selfish." She slaps my chest. "But you could speed it along, put this perfect ring on my finger, and make it official."

I smile big and bite my lip as I reach for the ring. "If you don't like it, we can pick out something else—"

"Nope. You picked this one for me, and it's the one I want."

I hold her delicate hand and place the ring at the tip of her finger. "I can't wait for the day I get to call you my wife and make you mine forever."

She lets out a stuttered breath once it's wrapped around its home. "Good, because you're kind of stuck with me, ring or—"

"Dad," Connor calls out. "Where are you?"

Cameron's eyes widen as we hear the front door close.

"We're in the kitchen," I shout back before kissing Cameron's hand. "I'm sorry. I didn't know they were stopping by."

"It's fine." She smiles. "We can share our news."

Connor rounds the corner, his hand wrapped tightly around Mackenzie's. "It smells good in here. What are you cooking?"

Before I can respond, Cameron holds her hand up and squeals, "Marry Me Chicken!"

"Shut up," Mackenzie rushes to her side to check out her ring, and I smile from ear to ear. My heart explodes because she's so happy she can't contain her excitement to tell the world that she's mine.

Connor comes to my side and gives me a pound hug. "Congratulations, Dad." He releases me and turns to Cameron. "Let me see that." He grabs her hand and examines the ring before saying, "I will never call you mom. Let's just get that straight now." His eyebrows shoot up, and he drops her hand. "Too fucking weird."

"Connor," Mackenzie scolds, punching his shoulder.

"I'm happy for you guys. Really, I am." He holds out both his hands. "But come on, you realize it's a little weird for me, right?"

"Yeah, calling me mom would make it weird, so don't be weird," Cameron tosses back.

"We should probably talk about wedding dates," Mackenzie chimes in as Connor walks to the stove and picks up a plate, helping himself to dinner.

"I mean, it just happened. Aren't most engagements a year?"

I swallow my cognac before I choke on it. "A year? Cameron, I'm not waiting that long to give you my last name."

Connor smacks my shoulder. "Yeah, Cam. Dad's clock is ticking. He doesn't have that much time left."

"Connor—" I start.

"No, a year would be good. I shouldn't have any problems fitting into a bridesmaid dress by then," Mackenzie says.

Cameron drops her fork. "Are you serious?" Her eyes dart from Mackenzie to Connor, and it takes me all of that time to understand what Mackenzie is insinuating.

"You're pregnant?" Mackenzie nods as her eyes start to well with tears.

"No, don't cry," Cameron says, vacating her stool to hug her. "Why are you crying?"

"I can't help it. Hormones are a bitch, and I'm just so happy. You're getting married, and I'm having a baby." She hugs her tighter and rocks side to side excitedly. "We came straight here as soon as we took the test."

"To clarify, we took three tests, not one," Connor adds before taking a bite of chicken.

I squeeze Connor's shoulders. I know he's been trying to get her pregnant for almost a year now. "Congratulations! We both clearly have a lot to celebrate, and since Connor has already helped himself to dinner, you guys should stay. Cameron made dessert."

Cameron releases Mackenzie and waves her hand. "No, I didn't." She quickly grabs her covered tray. "It didn't turn out." I furrow my brow and watch as she hastily walks the tray across the kitchen. Her eyes flash to mine briefly before dropping back to the pan in her hands. She's lying. That dessert is perfectly edible, and she knows it. I watch as she pulls open the oven and shoves it in. "But we have ice cream." She clasps her hands together.

"Mackenzie, do you want me to make you a plate?"

"Yes, please. Marry Me Chicken smells delicious."

"That's because it is. Dad made it."

Cameron ignores Connor's antics rather than snapping back like usual; something has rattled her. I stand behind her at the stove as she dishes Mackenzie's plate. "Why aren't we sharing the dessert you worked so hard on?"

"I told you, it didn't turn out."

My hand finds her hip. "And we both know that's a lie."

"Everett, please leave it alone," she pleads.

"Okay," I relent, hearing the desperation in her tone. "Will you tell me later?"

"There will be no hiding it soon enough," she says before stepping out of my reach, leaving me to process her words while I stare blankly at a pan of chicken. Tonight, there are two things I am certain of: my love, something I never had before, and Cameron Salt will be my wife. The rest is all joy. As I slowly turn back around and watch my future wife serve dinner to our family, the chatter and laughter fade away as I collect a moment, soaking in a life I never believed I'd have.

She was my secret, the kind that haunted my dreams and ran away with my sanity. Sometimes the secrets we keep are bad, but sometimes they are the very ones worth guarding and protecting at all costs. We were forbidden, every stolen moment a priceless memory shared between secret lovers. Our love was a tangled web of two lost souls dancing on the edge of temptation, teetering between right and wrong. She was off-limits, but her love was just like the girl, a wildfire burning without borders. The love we found in the dark had the power to burn bright and outshine the shadows where it used to hide.

"Ev, are you going to join us?" Cameron says, extending her arm for me to come sit beside her at the island. Without thought, my feet carry me to her side, where I'll stand until the end of time.

She leans back into my chest from her seated position on her stool, her hand reaching back to lace our fingers together, a move that knots my stomach still. Feeling her need to be close to me stops me in my tracks every time. My heart always knew what it wanted because the heart wants what it wants regardless of consequence; love doesn't require reason or logic, it just is. But it only could have been her love, the forbidden kind was the only love that was strong enough to conquer my mind, for it is the best love of all. It battles the rules, triumphing over reason and transcending time, and proving that love really does conquer all.

As Mackenzie and Connor talk giddily about things to come in hushed tones, she asks, "What were you thinking about?"

"Our future," I say.

Her hand tightens around mine, and I feel her breath catch in her chest, confirming the fleeting thought I had beside the stove is likely true. God, I love her so much it hurts.

"Is it beautiful?"

Our love looks different because we are different. We aren't storybook. We were better than that. We are more than I could have ever imagined. There wasn't a trail of heartbreak that led to her. For that to be true, I would have had to have loved before her, and it's only because of her that I know what love is. I didn't keep my faith like I was supposed to, but I didn't know what I didn't have. However, it didn't stop me from praying for the things I have now. I prayed, if not in this life, then the next. I prayed for someone to love me like she does, and the Gods answered. She's perfect.

"It's more than beautiful. It's the salt of the earth."

THE END

BONUS EPILOGUE

Did the story end too soon? Are you wondering what Cameron's surprise was? Did she and Everett make it down the aisle, and what about Connor and Makenzie? Do they have a boy or a girl? And is there another Callahan with a story to tell?
Find out in the Bonus Epilogue.
Thank you for reading!

Link to Download: https://dl.bookfunnel.com/i42xytdbrp

ALSO BY L.A. FERRO

Coming this Fall: Colton's Story

Hating the Book Boyfriend

Tropes: Best Friend's Sister, All Grown Up, Snowed In, One Bed, Holiday Romance.

DIG: A Second Chance Romance

Trope list: Sports Romance, College Romance, Dark Secrets, Emotional Scars, Second Chance, Redemption.

Fade Into You

Trope list: Arranged Marriage, Sports Romance, Small Town, Single Dad, Mistaken Identity, Unrequited Love

Rewriting Grey: Romantic Thriller

Trope List: Reclusive Author, Siblings Ex, Forced Proximity, Secret Identity, Small Town.

The Delicate Vows Duet - A Billionaire Romance

Trope list: Billionaire Romance, Off-limits, Age-gap, Secret Virgin, Different Worlds, He Falls First.

Wicked Beautiful Lies: A Taboo Romance

Trope list: Taboo/forbidden, Mistaken Identity, Enemies to Lovers, Dark Secrets.

Sweet Venom: A Why Choose Romance

Trope List: Taboo, Enemies to Lovers, Friends to Lovers, Dark Secrets, Different Worlds, Unrequited Love.

ACKNOWLEDGMENTS

To the woman who will forever be mentioned in every book I write, **TL Swan.** Were it not for her selfless decision to share her trade secrets with the world and inspire writers with a dream to put pen to paper, this journey would never have begun.

To my Beta Team: Lakshmi, Mindy, Thorunn, and Brittany, I've said it before, but it bears repeating. You guys are invaluable. Reading my words is one thing, but reading them via a Google Doc, one that wasn't spaced correctly, is another. It's not easy to share your heart and ask someone to poke it, too, but I know it's in good hands with you guys at my back. Thank you so damn much for being amazing and helping me put the shining touches on my work. I appreciate you guys so much!

To my author besties: I can't write a book without mentioning you guys. Jade, AK, and Carolina, you guys are the best. Our daily conversations, big or small, whether I have anything to add or not, are a lifeline. They reassure me I'm not alone on this journey. Thank you for making it better. I can't wait to bring the Book Boyfriend Builders to life with you guys.

To my ARC Team: I will forever shout your praises. This team of readers, most of whom have been with me from the start, has so much faith in me. Their support knows no end, and for that, I am eternally grateful. The confidence this team has in my ability to tell a story helps push me forward on the days when my words don't come easy and my faith stumbles. Thank you for always lifting me up and sharing your love with me. Your support means everything!

Shoutouts to my team: Aliyah Smith, Allison Thommen, Alyssa Hoffman, Amanda G, Angie, Ashlyn Romero, B. Tilley, Becky Jaegle, Blair W, Bookaholic Shaima, Brittany Fraser, Brittany Vitu, Carla Dionne, Catherine Boudreaux, Christina Rybka, Cierra, Court Anne, Dania Diaz, Dawn Vinot, Dawn Wilson, Deborah Dow, Diana Moreno, Doni Smith, Eliza Callaghan, Elizabeth Satala, Emily Cherry, Erin Rougeau, Gabbie Canteras, Gabrielle Hurt, Graviti "Jewels" Hess, Hayley, Heather Douglas, Honey-Marie Lashley, Janeeta, Janelle Sequin, Jayde Skillington, Jen Slotter, Jenn Trocine, Jennie Cathcart, Jennifer Borner, Jenny Fiordaliso, Jessica Michalski, Kailey D, Kamara Burkett, Kamron Rainey, Kari C., Kass Baker, Kassandra Marie Lopez, Kat Parkins, Kat Schumacher, Kate Schaeffer, Kayla Price, Kaylen Trejo, Kelani, Kimberly Weber, Kimmy, Kristin Graves, Leah Edwards, Lisa Conant, Lisa Gray, Layla Towers, Maizie Love, Meagan, Melanie Sweeney, Merrit Townsend, Mindy Menotti, Molly Ryan, Nancy Pasquale, NaToshya Reed, Nicole Kincaid, Nicole Scarborough, Nikki Johnson, Nikki Schuermann, Olivia Pace, Olivia Rose, Patricia Medina, Raeann Wolfley, Rebecca Shingledecker, Regina Nagy, Rhonda Ziglar, Roisin, Sarah Lyndsey, Sherrece Tanner, Stefanie McLain, Stephanie DeWaide, Tabatha Slagle, Taylor Nobles, Taylor Sims, Teri Salgado, Terry Wilson, Tianna Delgado, Tiffany Webb, Victoria Shelton, Victoria Wyatt, Wendy Kairschner.

Thank you, everyone!

ABOUT THE AUTHOR

L.A. Ferro has had a love for storytelling her entire life. For as long as she can remember, she put herself to sleep, plotting stories in her head. That thirst for a good tale led her to books, where she became an avid reader.

The unapologetically dramatic characters, steamy scenes, and happily ever afters found inside the pages of romance novels irrevocably transformed her. The world of romance ran away with her heart, and she knew her passion for love would be her craft.

When she's not trailing after one of her three crazy kids, she loves to construct messy 'happily ever afters' that take her readers on a journey full of angst, lust, and obsession with page-turning enchantment.

Made in the USA
Middletown, DE
08 June 2025

76708784R00216